"I RUE THE DAY I FIRST MET YOU . . ."

"I swear you are naught but a bedeviling little witch."

Chandra was pulled closer to him. Then his head descended slowly. Not again, she thought, her heart hammering wildly. "No!" she cried, twisting against his hold. "King James will punish you for this."

"Punish me?" Aleck whispered just above her enticing mouth. " 'Tis you who have mocked, not only me, but our king. James will not begrudge me this. Because I am English, you despise my touch. Were I Scot, would it still be the same? Whose kisses would you prefer?"

"Neither," she blurted, knowing far and away it would be Aleck's. But she'd die before she'd admit it.

"You speak falsely, little one. Open to me," he rasped; then he drew back slightly to look into her eyes. Mutiny evinced itself in her gaze. "Damn your stubborn Highland pride." He caught hold of her hair, and with a quick yank, her head fell back. Insanity, he thought, just before his eager mouth swooped, covering hers fully. . . .

Books by Charlene Cross

A Heart So Innocent
Masque of Enchantment
Deeper than Roses
Lord of Legend

Published by POCKET BOOKS

Charlene Cross

Lord of Legend

POCKET BOOKS

New York   London   Toronto   Sydney   Tokyo   Singapore

This book is a work of fiction. Names, characters, places, and incidents are either products of the author's imagination or are used fictitiously. Any resemblance to actual events or locales or persons, living or dead, is entirely coincidental.

An *Original* Publication of POCKET BOOKS

 POCKET BOOKS, a division of Simon & Schuster Inc.
1230 Avenue of the Americas, New York, NY 10020

Copyright © 1993 by Charlene Cross

ISBN: 0-671-73825-9

First Pocket Books printing August 1993

10 9 8 7 6 5 4 3 2 1

POCKET and colophon are registered trademarks of Simon & Schuster Inc.

Cover art by Donald Case

Printed in the U.S.A.

For my father-in-law and mother-in-law,
Cecil and Wanda—
Because of you, my life is complete.
Thank you for the gift of your son.
My love always.

In loving memory of Cecil Cross
April 7, 1992

Forever in our hearts.

Lord of Legend

Chapter

1

Montbourne Castle, Northern England
June 1610

Quick strides carried the Earl of Montbourne's chief
steward along the castle's freshly scrubbed corridors.
Several centuries old, the huge stone fortress had been
kept in good repair, and Felix Marlowe took great pride
in his family's contribution over the course of years
toward its conservancy.

His swift feet never missing a beat, Marlowe surveyed
the familiar surroundings; a wistful feeling overtook
him. In less than a year's time, the old stronghold would
be shuttered and abandoned for a more modern structure, palatial in nature. The new stone edifice, being
erected on the hillside opposite the castle, boasted upward of a hundred rooms, but Marlowe was not particularly impressed. To his eyes, the rising monstrosity was a
blot on the lush landscape. Truth be known, had James of
Scotland not succeeded to the throne of England upon
Elizabeth's death, allaying any further fears of war with
the Scots, the ugly thing would not have been set under
construction.

But the chief steward would never voice his thoughts
openly. For generations, the Marlowes had served with

quiet dignity, watching as the Hawkes of Montbourne gained in rank and distinction. First a barony, Montbourne was now an earldom. Presently, it was rumored, James planned to bestow a dukedom upon the sixth and current Earl of Montbourne. Only moments before, a messenger, accompanied by fifty men, had arrived with a missive from the king, and Marlowe wondered if the weighty packet he carried confirmed the rumor as truth.

Quickening his gait, the man rounded a corner. A dozen more steps and he stopped before the door securing his lordship's chambers. Knuckles poised, ready to strike, the steward heard the muffled sounds of feminine laughter, followed by a deep, masculine growl. Both were drowned out as the ropes supporting the feather mattress creaked loudly, straining against the wooden side rails of the huge canopied bed.

At the sound, Marlowe flushed from his Adam's apple to the tops of his ears. Although the earl had left strict instructions he was not to be disturbed, the steward decided that the king's missive took precedence. With a hard swallow, he squared his shoulders and straightened his doublet. In rapid succession, his fist struck the wood; his voice rose: "Lord Montbourne . . . sir!"

A curse exploded from Alexander Hawke's lips. The emerald-encrusted gold medallion jingled on its heavy chain as he jerked away from the lush body beneath him. "The castle had best be burning, Marlowe, or I'll have your head for this disruption!"

"Th-there is no fire, milord," the steward replied through the wood. "But 'tis of equal urgency. The king's messenger has just delivered a letter. He waits below for a reply."

While he viewed the tempting brunette stretched out beside him, a teasing smile lighting her hazel eyes, the young earl shrugged, then reached for the sheet at his feet. With a snap of his wrist, white linen billowed upward to float down over the couple, concealing their nudity.

Seeing his mistress was modestly covered, Aleck stashed a plump down-filled pillow behind him. "Enter," he ordered, drawing his long, hard body into a sitting position. He leaned back against the headboard, the Montbourne crest carved into its polished oak surface. Sky blue eyes beset by thick black lashes watched as the door creaked open; the steward's uncertain face peered around its edge. "Enter, I said."

Marlowe shoved the panel wide. As his booted feet scraped across the stones, their hasty tread was intermittently lost in the assortment of handwoven carpets dotting the chamber's expansive width of floor. Such appointments were rare in most castles, but not at Montbourne, for its master hated the feel of cold stone against his bare feet.

Reaching his master's side, Marlowe passed the packet into the earl's hands. "Shall I await your reply?" he asked.

A distinct tightness had sounded in the steward's voice causing Aleck to observe the man. Marlowe's fingers fidgeted with the lace-edged ruff encircling his thin neck. A violent red hue stained his face, and anyone except Aleck would have thought the man was choking. Unable to look at his master, Marlowe had attached his gaze to the ceiling, examining it with great interest. Positive the man suffered from acute embarrassment, the earl smiled.

A man of high morals, Marlowe obviously felt a great deal of discomfort when faced with his master's lusty habits. The man had never voiced his opinions, yet Aleck knew his steward wished he would marry again, and soon. But to Aleck, that was out of the question.

Betrothed during childhood, he'd married his intended—a girl he neither knew nor loved—at the age of nineteen, only to discover that his pale, virginal bride was frigid. Every time he had approached her, she'd immediately sustained an attack of the vapors. No words could gentle her, and after listening to her hysterical cries for close to an hour on each occasion, he would at last cease his attempts to soothe her. Quietly he had slipped from her chamber, swearing he'd come to her again, for he'd been determined to bed her. But their physical union never came to pass. She'd come to him a virgin and had left him a virgin. Alas, the jittery Elinor had died less than four months after their nuptials. Since she'd not been ill, Aleck imagined she had succumbed to her own fright.

Having endured one such disastrous marriage, short as it had been, Aleck was content to remain a widower. Over the ensuing six years, he'd had his share of mistresses to entertain him, Felicia Emory being his latest. When the time came to sire an heir, then, and only then, would he take a new bride, but she would be of *his* choosing. High-spirited, willing to please him in every way, she'd be one whose desires matched his own. Aleck chuckled to himself; as passionate as he was, he suspected they might never leave his bed. Truly, should he ever find such a woman, he might be persuaded to try the state of wedlock once more. Until then, he would have none of it.

The soft body next to him shifted against his side; Felicia's hand crept across his chest to move low over his taut belly. Aleck swallowed the breath that had nearly hissed through his teeth. "Wait in the hall, Marlowe," the earl commanded. He noticed the man still inspected the ceiling. "I'll call you when I have drafted a reply."

After the door had closed, Felicia sat up. The cover fell to her hips. Her voluptuous breasts pressed against Aleck's back as she rested her head on his shoulder and fingered the parchment in his hand. "Are you not interested in what James has to say?" she asked, her throaty voice drifting into his ears. Certain their sovereign had bestowed the much-talked-about dukedom on her lover, Felicia felt her heart swell with excitement. A long fingernail broke through the wax seal. "Read it, darling. Hurry."

Aleck also believed the letter stated he was now a duke, but he wondered at what price. James, along with his wife, Anne of Denmark, was infamous for being a spendthrift. He was equally notorious for presenting titles of nobility, at first knighthoods, then baronetcies, but the honor was not bestowed out of the goodness of the king's heart. The title's recipient had to pay a hefty sum for the distinction—and if he refused to accept the honor, James fined him, the figure being far higher than the original cost of the title. In order to fill his empty coffers, James, at the prompting of Lord Salisbury, had devised this ingenious plan. His sovereign was no fool, Aleck decided. No doubt a provision was attached to his dukedom. His skepticism rising, he pondered again whether he could afford James's price.

"Well?" Felicia prompted impatiently.

Slowly the packet was unfolded in Aleck's hands. Another sealed document lay within. He set the second one aside, his blue eyes scanning the contents of the first. With a jerk, he sat straight up; Felicia's head hit the wood behind her. A volatile curse escaped through Aleck's lips, followed by another.

Her hand rubbing the lump growing on her scalp, Felicia peered over at the missive. "What is it? What's happened?"

Hard eyes turned on her. Spying the flame of wrath in their depths, Felicia swallowed a frightened gasp. She knew Aleck possessed a temper, had beheld the effects of his ire once, perhaps twice. Fortunately, his fury had not been turned on her. But never before had she seen him this angry. Unknowingly she moved away from him. "D-did James deny your appointment?" she asked, eyeing him carefully.

"No," he said through clenched teeth. "He gives it to me, but at a stiff cost."

"Surely, Aleck, of all those in England, *you* can afford his fee." Absently she fingered the heavy gold chain resting against his chest. "Your wealth exceeds nearly all others."

"It is not my gold he wants, Felicia."

Astounded, Felicia stared at him. "If not money, then what has he requested of you?"

"There is no request. It's a royal command. If I refuse, I'll most likely find myself ensconced in the Tower, possibly in the same cell that was occupied by your late husband."

"Harry? Surely you could never anger James the way Harry did. After all, you are one of his favorites at court."

Aleck shot her an inquisitive look. "Favorites? Do you equate me with the likes of Hay, Herbert, and Carr?" he asked, naming the more renowned of their king's male companions.

Felicia's light laughter rang forth. "It was not meant as it sounded, darling. I know, as does everyone else—including James—that you are interested only in the fairer sex. I meant that he values you as a friend. Because he does, he'd never send you to the Tower."

Glancing at the letter, Aleck did not respond, and Felicia rambled on. "James simply placed Harry there to teach him a lesson. It was to be for only a month. Had Harry not been so deep in his cups and made such a bawdy remark about Carr, he'd still be alive today. No one thought he'd take a chill and die so quickly, least of all James. No, Aleck, he would never risk losing you. Your friendship means too much to him."

"Does it?" he asked.

"Yes, it does."

"Well, it's about to be tested."

"In what way?" Receiving no response, Felicia found she'd grown weary of his secrecy. "Aleck," she demanded, "tell me what it is that he wants you to do."

"Our heedful sovereign has made me guardian of a Highland lass, one Chandra Morgan. She is the heiress of Lochlaigh, its lands and barony—*Lady* Lochlaigh, if she can be deemed such—and is chieftain of her clan, The Morgan of Morgan. James fears some sort of insurrection is about to take place and has ordered me to the north of Scotland, where I am to make certain she is married off to a man who has sworn fealty to our sovereign and the Crown. I'm not to return to England until it is done."

"Is that all?" she asked, surprised by the vehemence of his anger.

"Is that all!" Aleck sprang from the bed to stride naked about the room. "Damnation, Felicia!" he shouted, his hand raking through the thickness of his black hair. "James knows I cannot abide the Scots, especially those in the northernmost climes. They're all heathens—a filthy, ill-bred lot who run unclothed through the wood and over the hills." Felicia's laughter spun him around. "What is the source of your merriment?"

Pinpointed by Aleck's frigid glare, Felicia tried to swallow her giggles, but they continued to bubble forth.

"Do not mock me, Felicia," he warned, stopping at the bed's edge. "Why do you laugh?"

"You speak of unclothed heathens, while you yourself prance about the room without so much as a stitch to hide behind. As for mocking you, perhaps it is not I but James who is laughing the loudest."

"What, pray tell, is the source of *his* merriment?"

"Did you not hear yourself just now, maligning the Scots? When at court, you are equally vocal, though, fortunately for you, in a far more diplomatic manner. James knows you are loyal to him, that you would lay down your life for him. He also knows you oppose a united Britain. But remember, Aleck, his birthplace is Scotland and he was king there long before he was made ruler of England. Maybe he is sending you to the Highlands for a dual purpose."

"Which is?"

"As his loyal subject, you are to quell the insurrection you mentioned. He knows that if anyone can prevent the clans from rising again, it is you."

"And?"

"Which would you prefer by way of punishment? The Tower or chasing off to the wilds of Scotland?"

Aleck dropped his taut backside onto the mattress. "So, he means to teach me a lesson, does he? Perhaps I shall turn the tables on him."

"What do you mean?"

"He can keep his dukedom. I am more than satisfied being an earl. And I can easily survive a month in the Tower. I'm not a weakling like Harry was."

Felicia's thoughts spun wildly. She certainly didn't want Aleck to be thrown into the Tower, but even less did she want him to give up his dukedom. To be a duchess meant more to her than anything. She hadn't flirted and teased, used every contrivance she could think of in order to find her way into his bed, simply because she thought he might be an exceptional lover. That he was, and discovering such became an added bonus, but Felicia's main desire was not for the man himself, but for the power he exercised at court. He was already one of James's favorites, and as a duke, he would be even more revered. Felicia hoped to share in that honor by becoming his wife.

Unfortunately, her schemes to trap him had been constantly thwarted. She couldn't use the excuse of being with child to extract a proposal, for Aleck was far too careful. He never came to her without protection. Not until today.

Tutored by an exuberant Frenchman who had found his way to court less than a fortnight ago, Felicia had applied what she'd learned to Aleck. His desires raging out of control, her erotic overtures driving him nearly insane, he had forgotten to sheathe himself. According to her calculations, today was the day, the time for her to conceive. That was why she had arrived this very morn from London. Had not that pompous steward come banging on the door, pulling them apart before they were completely together, she was certain Aleck's seed would already have found its mark.

"Aleck," she said pensively. "Would it not be wiser to do as James has requested?" He opened his mouth to protest, but she waved him off. "Listen to me, please. There has been talk that the plague might hit London again."

"There is always talk of the plague hitting London. It has yet to come—at least, during the last several years."

"True, but if it does, and if you are in the Tower, you will not survive. I could not bear to lose you." Her agile fingers trailed coaxingly over his shoulder. "Especially when it is mere stubbornness that keeps you from doing what James wants. Go to Scotland, marry the girl to the first man who swears fealty to our king, then ride back to England as fast as is humanly possible. I'll be here awaiting your return."

Aleck's brow furrowed. Mayhap Felicia was right. The thought of breathing fresh air, even if it wafted over the likes of Scotland, seemed far more appealing than the stagnant dankness inside the Tower. Besides, how long could it possibly take to marry the twit off? A day? A week? Certain that the entire expedition could be completed inside of a month, Aleck came to a decision. But it had not been Felicia's words that prompted him to make his choice. For some strange reason, he'd suddenly felt compelled to see his mission through, and it had nothing to do with James or a dukedom.

He turned a quick smile on Felicia. "Will you await me in this very bed?"

"I await you now." She lay back on the feather mattress. The sheet slid away, exposing her nudity. "Come," she cajoled, arms opening to him. "I'll give you a taste of what you will be missing."

Aleck regarded Felicia's ripe, womanly body and her enticing pose. "Tempting, but I fear our union will have to wait."

"Why?" Felicia asked in a near screech as she sat up again. "What is so pressing that we cannot enjoy this next hour together?"

"According to the letter, fifty of our king's finest men stand ready in the courtyard. We are to strike out immediately. It is by James's orders." He placed a light kiss on her lips, then rose from the bed. "When I return, Felicia—less than a month from now, I hope—I shall be eager to find you as you were a moment ago, ready and waiting. We can enjoy an entire summer together, if you like. Right now, I must see to other matters."

Felicia watched while Aleck searched through the hanging cupboard, selecting his clothing and laying items across a chest, then she fell back onto the bed. Thwarted again, she thought, her frustration growing. But all was not lost. Aleck would soon be a duke. And shortly after his return, a little less than a month hence, she would be his duchess. Again, according to her quick calculations, the time would be right for her to conceive. He'd not escape her.

She viewed his handsomely proportioned form with admiration. Already she yearned to have him beside her, his passion flaring out of control. But she was willing to wait. Long ago, Felicia had learned that to place demands on Aleck Hawke, sixth Earl of Montbourne, meant an inevitable end to their relationship. He was not a man to be ordered about, not even by his king. Knowing as much, Felicia decided that her lover desired a dukedom more than he'd let on. Why else would he dash off to a place he could not abide? *Unless* . . .

"How old is your new ward?" Felicia asked. "Thirteen, fourteen?"

"Seventeen." Aleck's head popped through the top of his loose, flowing shirt and he tucked its tails into the waistband of his tight-fitting doeskin breeches, then tugged at the legs to straighten them. "Why do you ask?"

Felicia scrutinized her lover momentarily. A leather jerkin slipped over his head; muscular arms covered in white linen punched through the side openings. He smoothed the leather over his flat belly, then banded a wide leather belt around his narrow waist. "I was just wondering," she stated.

"Do I detect jealousy, Felicia?" Aleck commented, dropping onto the arm of a sturdy chair. In four swift moves his stockings and thigh-high leather boots were in place. He stood and moved toward the bed. "Do not worry about my fidelity to you," he said, retrieving the two letters, tucking them into his waistband. "You are the fairest of all my mistresses, and I have not yet tired of you. As for the Lady Lochlaigh, she is most likely big-boned, toothless—a fright to behold! Let's hope she has some redeeming qualities or I'll never find her a mate."

Have not yet tired of you. The words rolled through Felicia's head. Would he? she wondered, vexed by the thought. "I shall pray for your swift return," she said, a tempting smile crossing her face. She stretched sinuously, hoping to seduce him. She wanted him to stay, at least a bit longer. "I shall miss you. I already ache to hold you."

Aleck watched the serpentine movement of her body. While doing so, he remembered that in the moments prior to Marlowe's pounding on the door, he hadn't protected himself. Had his steward not interrupted them, his mistress might now be with child. "It will make our reunion all the sweeter," he said, his suspicions growing. She'd driven him nearly insane with her expert lips and teasing tongue, a first for Felicia. Where had she learned to excite a man so? And from whom? "Farewell, Felicia." Offering a wave, he strode to the door.

"What? Not even a kiss?"

"You'll receive one on my return," he said over his shoulder. "Be waiting, just as you are."

Peeved because she couldn't entice him, couldn't even elicit his kiss, Felicia did something she'd promised herself she'd never do. She issued a threat. "Should I get bored, Aleck, I might return to London. After all, there are others who seek my attention, Whitfield being one," she said, knowing there were years of animosity between the two.

Placing his hand on the latch, Aleck cast a hard look on his mistress. "You are a free woman, Felicia. You may do as you wish. If you desire another man—Whitfield included—then go to him. I'll not stop you. But be aware, should you decide to leave, you will never return. The decision is yours."

Not giving Felicia the chance to respond, he was out the door. While he and Marlowe made their way down the corridor toward the stairs, Aleck gave the man instructions. "Pack the clothes I've laid out. You know what else I'll need. But before you enter the chamber, knock. Otherwise, you might be wearing a brass urn for a hat. The Lady Emory says she wishes to stay. She has my permission to do so, but she is to be moved into another apartment while I am gone. However, should she leave here for any reason other than illness or death, then attempt to return, she is to be barred from entering Montbourne." He saw his steward's startled look. "Do not trouble yourself over the woman. Just keep the gates closed to her."

"I'll do my best, sir."

"I know you will, Marlowe. Now, tell the king's messenger that I'll be leaving shortly to fulfill my duty. I go to see about extra provisions."

At dusk, Aleck, with fifty of James's men at his back, left the gates of Montbourne Castle. In less than an hour, the entire company had crossed the border into Scotland. As his large steed galloped beneath him, torches held high by nearby bearers to light the narrow road ahead, Aleck was amazed by his own haste. Strangely compelled to drive himself and the king's men late into the night, edging ever closer to the northern climes, he thought not about his mistress but about the Lady Lochlaigh instead. Was she beast or beauty? In a few days, he would discover the truth.

Chapter

2

Wings outstretched, a hawk soared high above the Morgan stronghold. Sitting atop a fallen log, Chandra Morgan viewed the magnificent hunter as it searched relentlessly. The great wings folded, and Chandra tensed. Her deep blue eyes watched as the large bird swooped, its target an unsuspecting sparrow that had flown into the hawk's path. Entranced by the drama in the sky, she prayed that the small bird would somehow escape.

Talons poised, the hunter took aim, only to miss its mark as the sparrow flitted first up, then down. The hawk pursued its quarry, the sparrow's wings fluttering wildly in its desperate attempt to escape. A stand of trees loomed mere yards away. Exhausted by its harrowing flight, the tiny bird plunged toward the protection of the leaves.

"She made it, Devin!" Chandra cried in jubilation as the great hunter swept the treetops, then winged toward the clouds once more. Thwarted, the hawk made its way north, quickly fading from view. "The ladybird escaped him." Devin Morgan's laughter met her ears. Three years older than herself, Devin, her third cousin once removed, had been Chandra's constant companion since childhood. "You make light of me," she accused.

"'Tis hard to tell from here if the wee creature was male or female, but yes, *it* escaped." His brown eyes studied the beauty beside him. "You think of the legend. Why?"

"I don't know," she said with a shrug. "Watching the hawk brought it to mind. 'Tis supposed to be a bad omen when the winged hunter flies above the castle."

"Were that true, ill fortune would befall us most every day of the week. 'Tis only a myth, Chandra. The legend has no substance." The pine boughs whipped furiously as a cold wind swept through the meager stretch of forest where he and Chandra sat; she shivered violently. "Cold?" he asked.

Chandra decided the reaction had been induced not by the abrupt chill nipping the air, but by the sudden foreboding that had filled her. Were she to voice such a thing to Devin, she knew he would laugh, then say that the premonition was caused by talk of the legend, and that she was too superstitious by far. In turn, she'd have to agree. She *was* too superstitious by far. Although she tried, she was unable to quell the mysterious feeling.

Not sharing her thoughts with Devin, Chandra drew her plaid atop her head. The excess cloth settled around her shoulders, and she scanned the sky anew. Dark clouds fomented in the not too far distance. Deciding that she was being childish and silly, she quickly attributed her apprehension to the approaching storm. "The rains will soon betide us again. We'd best go back or we'll be drenched through and through."

Noting that she was still plagued by misgivings, caused by thoughts of the old Morgan legend, Devin bounded to his feet. "Aye, we should go back." He extended a hand toward Chandra. "'Twould not do if The Morgan of Morgan appeared in front of her clansmen soaked and looking like a drowned kitten," he teased, trying to

lighten her mood. "A chieftain must be fierce, strong."
His fists beat against his slim chest. "At least, she should
seem such, even if she's not. Besides, caught in the frigid
rains, you might take a chill. These harsh climes are not
favorable to the health of a genteel lady such as yourself."

"You mock me, Devin," she said, playfully swatting
his outstretched hand. As she pulled a strand of lustrous
red hair away from her face, tucking it under the plaid,
her bare feet hit the cool earth. "If you did not amuse me
so, I, as your chieftain, would have you cast from the
clan—banished forever. *But,* since you have the ability
to make me laugh, I shall keep you at my side." Her smile
faded as melancholy overtook her. "It is not often I am
given to merriment. Not lately."

Devin beheld the despondent look on Chandra's exceptional face. Tears shimmered in her eyes, which she
tried to hide. His cousin thought of her beloved father, he
knew. Since Colan Morgan's untimely death, Chandra's
natural exuberance had faded nearly into extinction.
Faced with her grief, plus the added responsibilities of
being chieftain to the clan Morgan, she had fallen into
a depressed state. She desired to be a good leader, hoping to live up to her late sire's faith in her, but Devin
knew she was unsure of herself. Likewise, her uncle's
constant interference did little to reaffirm Chandra's
position, and he wished the man would keep his advice
to himself.

As he saw it, Cedric—no actual relation to Devin—
was a power-hungry man who wasn't to be trusted. But
he'd kept his thoughts to himself, for Chandra respected
her kinsman, even sought Cedric's counsel. Why, Devin
didn't know. But to speak adversely of the man meant
raising Chandra's ire, and Devin didn't wish to feel the
effects of her quick temper, nor the lash of her sharp
tongue. He'd be flayed to ribbons!

He looked at Chandra more closely. Always mindful of
her moods—for Devin loved her more than as the

brotherly figure she thought him to be—he realized he must do something to lift her sagging spirits, lest she slip further into the depths of her gloom.

"Ho!" he cried, mischief dancing in his eyes. "A court jester—is that what I am to you?" He gathered three sturdy sticks from the ground. "Shall I juggle for you, then?" The dried foot-long limbs flew into the air in a haphazard fashion. Watching the missiles descend from aloft, Devin ducked, wrapping his arms protectively around his head just before they bounced off his linen-covered back. "What next?" he asked, spying a renewed sparkle in Chandra's gaze. "I know. I'll tumble for milady." Not wanting to embarrass Chandra or himself, he pulled the tail of his knee-length plaid upward between his legs to tuck the extra material against the folds belted at his slim waist. "Ready?" he asked, rubbing his hands together.

Suppressing her laughter, Chandra watched while Devin clumsily sprang hand to foot around the small clearing. Seeing his direction, she blinked. "Devin! Watch out for the—" Too late! He disappeared over the edge of a small ravine. She took off at a full run. Stopping where her cousin had vanished, she peered down the slope. "Devin?"

"You could have warned me sooner," he snarled, pulling himself from the midst of a squat shrub. Gaining his feet, he looked at his bare legs to note a wealth of ugly scratches. "I'll be scarred for life. And not even one wee chortle from milady. My efforts were wasted."

Chandra's crystal laughter rose into the air. "You are a fool, Devin," she said, her mirth subsiding. Her cousin's bare feet trod the soft ground, moving up the side of the shallow chasm, and she extended a hand, helping him over the crest. "But a wonderful and caring fool."

Devin drew a ragged breath into his burning lungs, basking in the brilliance of her perfect smile. Another breath crept into his chest, but it was not enough. A spasm struck. Covering his mouth, he coughed fitfully, turning away from Chandra to lean against a nearby tree. His fingers clenched the rough bark until finally the seizure had passed.

"Why do you exert yourself so?" Chandra asked, her tone admonishing. In truth, she was angry not at Devin, but at herself. She should never have allowed him to frolic about when he'd risen from his bed only a fortnight ago, a good stone lighter in weight than what he had been. Looking at him now, she thought he might be lighter still. "You know you are not completely well." The cold wind beat through the pines again. She scanned the heavens to see that the heavy, gray clouds were nearly upon them, and her gentle hands fell from his back where they had tried to soothe him. "Come, we must make the hall before the rains hit."

Devin pulled himself upright to look down on his cousin. Concern lit her face, yet the worry he saw there was not for herself, but for him. A quick smile curled his lips. "This cough is naught but a nuisance," he said, drawing a full, cleansing breath. "I'm well and stout. To prove it, I'll race you to the castle gates."

Devin sped off toward the centuries-old stone fortress, sitting atop the opposite hill. Damn him! Chandra thought. He would kill himself yet.

Pulling her skirt up between her legs as Devin had done with his plaid, she tucked it in at her waist. The loose ends of her own plaid were thrown over her shoulder to trail down her back. Her skilled feet flew over the ground as she took off after him through the short span of forest, to descend the barren hillside as it sloped away from the trees.

A quarter of the way down, she overtook him, then slowed her pace. "I'll race you, but only to those rocks," she said, pointing toward the outcrop at the bottom of the hill.

"Done," Devin rasped. "But only if you run like the

wind. You hold back, Chandra. 'Tis not fair that you purposely lose."

To punctuate his statement, Devin pushed himself all the harder, leaving her a stride or two behind. More certain than ever that he *would* kill himself, Chandra decided to end the race. They were mere yards from the rocks, and with the speed and grace of a red deer, she loped past him. "You've lost," she called over her shoulder when she'd reached their goal. "Give up the cause."

Devin stumbled to a halt. Clutching the pitted limestone, he gulped in volumes of air, trying to catch his breath. Chandra's concern grew. Her mind commanded her feet to stop, but their momentum carried her beyond the jutting rocks, down a steep embankment, and out onto the flat plain.

The loud neigh of a horse filled her ears; Chandra spun round to see its great, black hooves pummeling the air scant inches above her. A virulent curse shot upward as its rider tried to regain control with a harsh tug of the reins. Eyes rolling, the frightened beast obeyed the command; its forelegs struck the ground less than a yard from her.

Over the stallion's bobbing head, blue eyes immediately crucified blue. "Wench," the man gritted through his teeth, "do you have so little regard for your life that you dash aimlessly about these miserable hills with no thought to your safety? You could have been trampled!"

Sassenach! Chandra's mind screamed in Gaelic. Her gaze fired past the Englishman who'd spoken to view the legion behind him. *Mother of God! Invaders have descended upon us!* What was she to do?

"Answer me, wench!" the leader's voice boomed. "Or are you a simpleton? If so, that would explain your indifference to your existence." He appraised her wealth of lustrous red hair, now freed of its plaid covering, then surveyed her perfect features. Finally, his eyes raked her womanly form to linger with masculine interest on the shapely curves of her bare legs. "Though I don't know how anything can survive in this scarred and dreary land."

Several snickers rose up from the men behind him; his own lips cracked into a wide, even grin. The devil, he was, Chandra thought, though unable to deny his attractiveness.

Swathed in leather, he was broad of shoulder and lean of hip. And very tall. Or so she imagined. Atop his noble head, thick black hair shone like ebony, even in the gloominess of the day. His chiseled features, including the dimples set in each cheek, appeared to have been sculpted by the hands of a master. He was possibly even more handsome than the evil Lucifer himself.

Chandra was tempted to cross herself, but wisely she held back. Fear him she did, but she'd not show her alarm. Then, as she stared at the man who had maligned her and her homeland, the wind whipped around them all. The first few drops of rain pelted the earth.

It was Chandra's turn to smile as she watched the man shiver. Cursing, he fixed his helm on his head and pulled his heavy cloak around him.

"I am no simpleton," she responded, her voice low and even, her shoulders squared. "Being a Morgan, I run these hills at will, as do all the clan Morgan. 'Tis you, Sassenach, who have little regard for your own life, and the lives of those who follow you. Unless you leave here, and leave here quickly, you will remain forever in this 'scarred and dreary land.' Be gone, or the scavengers will soon be picking your bones clean."

A dark brow arched as Aleck looked down at the young woman who'd threatened his life, and the lives of his men. What harm she alone could cause any of them, he was unable to say, but he felt certain it was minor at best. Intrigued by her courage, false as it was, captured by her beauty, its quality unmatched, he thought that if he must remain in this hellish land for very long, he would gladly spar with a high-spirited lass such as her. *Only her,* he corrected silently, knowing he'd happily take her to his bed.

His interested gaze tracked along her smooth legs once more, and he imagined their satiny length wrapped around his waist, her slender hips undulating beneath his own. In this dismal clime, he would welcome a soft, willing body beside him, keeping him warm the night through. In truth, though she was obviously of peasant stock, the ripe young creature standing only a few feet away fascinated him greatly. As for the woman he'd left behind, what was kept secret from Felicia would in no way upset her.

He leaned an arm across the pommel of his saddle. "I'm sorry, lass, but the scavengers will have to find another offering to dine on, for neither I nor my men will become their banquet. Nor can I leave these lands. Not until I've finished with the king's business. Tell me, is the Lady Lochlaigh in the castle proper?"

"What do you want with her?" Chandra asked, eyeing him suspiciously.

"'Tis the king's business, as I've said. The Lady Lochlaigh must learn of it first. But after I've informed her of my mission, I'd very much like to renew our own acquaintance. What is your name, lass?"

Knowing chuckles rumbled forth from the men nearest him; Chandra stiffened. English swine! she silently deemed them all, glaring her hatred. "Morgan," she snapped finally.

Aleck's lips twitched. "Morgan Morgan—an interesting name, but not very creative."

"But it is hers," Devin said as he stepped into view. Slowly he made his way down the small incline to stand beside his cousin. "'Tis mine as well. What is yours, Sassenach?"

Their gazes locked, masculine eyes momentarily assessing one another. Then the newcomer placed a protective arm around the young beauty's shoulders. To Aleck, the gesture proclaimed that the two were wedded, or at least betrothed. Inexplicably, his disappointment soared. He viewed the smaller man again. His challenging look dared Aleck to trespass. Aleck knew he could easily defeat him, stealing the lass away, but other matters were far more pressing.

"Forgive my bad manners," he said with a slight bow of his head. "I'm the king's servant, the Earl of Montbourne. These good gentlemen are the king's men. Now, if you will excuse us, we ride to the castle to see the Lady Lochlaigh."

"But she will not see you!" Chandra exclaimed.

"Then we shall wait in the hall and feast on her food until she grants an audience. Good day to you."

Chandra surveyed the procession of men as they slowly trailed past Devin and herself. At a command from the one who called himself Montbourne, the line of mounts uniformly struck a quick cadence up the barren hillside. The abrupt change of pace, she realized, served to display their fearlessness. Audacious they might be, but they were also fools, for Chandra was certain her uncle watched the whole from the battlement. One false move and they would all be dead. "We'd best get to the castle," she heard Devin say.

"Aye," she responded, not taking her eyes from the man who had pronounced himself James's emissary. The sporadic drops of rain grew in number. "Come, there is work to do."

A steady rain had begun to fall by the time Chandra and Devin slipped inside the secret passageway, its entry hidden behind a pile of boulders. The corridor exited into the cellars of the north tower, its spiral stone staircase carrying them up through the castle's outer wall. "Take yourself to your quarters and change into some dry clothing," Chandra ordered, dodging the stores of grain and supplies warehoused there while moving toward the door that led to the inner ward.

"What do you plan to do about the Sassenach and those who ride with him?" Devin asked.

"I go to find Cedric. Surely he will have the answer."

"If he has not already killed them," Devin interjected. "Take care, Chandra. Do not let him persuade you to act in haste."

"I won't," she said, noting his cautioning look. Although she often sought her uncle's counsel, she did not always heed Cedric's advice, despite what Devin assumed. What her cousin deemed a lack of confidence was actually her need to be prudent in all that she did. If she ever lost her temper with Devin, it was because she was weary of being caught between her cousin and her uncle, the two standing in constant opposition to the other, and not because she favored Cedric, as Devin thought. Knowing all too well how her uncle felt about the English, she would weigh his words carefully. Only then would she act. "Just pray I am not too late."

Her plaid safeguarding her head from the rain, she lifted her skirt, now untucked from her waistband, and scurried out the heavy wooden door at the tower's base into the inner ward. Reaching the stone steps leading to the battlement, she ran them to the top, then walked swiftly to where her uncle stood. Red-faced, he shouted at the English rabble who waited not far from the gate. Keeping herself from the view of those below, she listened to the exchange.

"The Lady Lochlaigh does not wish to see you," Cedric stated hotly. "Take your English hides back across the border while you still have the chance."

"It amazes me, sir," Aleck called upward, "that you would know what is in the Lady Lochlaigh's mind when you have not left the spot where you stand since I rode up this hill. I am here on the king's calling to deliver a letter from James to The Morgan of that ilk. Only she may see it first. Therefore, I suggest you find your chieftain and tell her I have urgent business with her."

"If it is so urgent, mayhap you will consider entering the castle alone. I would be most happy to carry the missive to my chieftain personally."

Aleck assessed the man who appeared to be no more than four or five years older than himself. Should Aleck enter the Morgan stronghold alone, he was positive he'd never leave the place alive. In his mind's eye, he saw James's letter riding high on a silver platter, alongside Aleck's head. His short burst of laughter rose through the heavy mists. "It is not *that* urgent," he said, a cool smile on his lips. "If I enter, so do my men. Now, find your lady and give her my message. I will not leave these heathen lands until I see her."

"Damn your English eyes!" Cedric shouted, sounding even more incensed. "I said begone with you!" James's emissary remained fixed, as did his men. Cedric slipped his claymore from the scabbard resting along the length of his back. The blade rose high and a band of archers rushed to the battlement. Bows and arrows ready, they awaited the command to let their deadly missiles fly. "Prepare to die!" Cedric bellowed.

Chandra's eyes widened. She wanted the Englishman and his soldiers away from her lands, but she did not want them dead. If Montbourne was truly James's emissary and the clan Morgan murdered him, then woe unto them all. Much like the clan Gregor, who, by James's orders, had been stripped of its lands, homes burned, its name declared extinct—all because of its disobedience to the Crown; she feared the Morgans would suffer a similar fate. That she could not allow. Not after her father had sworn fealty to their king.

"Uncle!" she cried softly, not wanting her voice to carry below. "Cease these hostilities."

Cedric turned her way. Beneath his harsh frown, his dark eyes examined her; then he waved off his men.

Striding across the wet stones, he faced her. "Niece, they trespass and refuse to leave. There is only one way to deal with them. They'll all be buried by nightfall."

"The one at the fore says he was sent by James. If so, Uncle, we risk severe punishment should we kill him. We could not defend ourselves against the avenging army that would be sure to follow him. I do not wish to see my clansmen slaughtered, all because of one man."

"'Tis more like fifty!"

"One or fifty, it does not matter. They were sent by James."

Cedric's jaw clenched. "Then what is it you want me to do?"

Seeing his anger, Chandra knew he thirsted for blood, for he hated the English, hated James, but she would not allow her uncle's abhorrence to destroy them all. "Tell him that you go in search of the Lady Lochlaigh and will request an audience. Let him sit in the rain until dusk, then allow the whole into the castle. Feed them cakes and gruel. Give them no wine, only water. When the time is right, I will make my appearance as the Lady Lochlaigh."

"If that is your wish, so be it, but our own men will be armed and ready. Should even one Englishman make a false move, they'll all be slain."

"Arm the men, but temper yourself, Uncle. I do not want bloodshed, if it can be avoided. Those are my orders."

"And I will attest that she gave them," Devin said from behind her.

Over Chandra's head, the men's gazes collided with animosity; then Cedric strode to the wall. Following Chandra's instructions, he informed the Englishman that the Lady Lochlaigh would be sought out, an audience requested. However, until a response came from her lips, the one-and-fifty men were to remain outside the castle gates.

"Your hospitality is unmatched," Aleck called up to

his adversary, a distinctive edge to his voice. He blinked the water droplets from his eyes. "Cannot you at least offer us shelter from these cold rains?"

"If you do not desire to wait, England is that way," Cedric snapped, pointing to the south. "Otherwise, keep your positions." His orders fulfilled, Chandra's uncle turned away from the wall. Motioning the archers from their posts, he again strode toward his niece. "The sentries will keep an eye on the swine," he said, his lip curling. "It may come to pass, Niece, that you'll regret we did not finish them off while we had the chance. By your own resolve, you have put us all in jeopardy. Will you not reconsider?"

"No, Uncle. I stand by my decision."

"Then whatever follows lies solely upon your shoulders," he said, loud enough for those nearest them to hear. Obviously, he wanted his clansmen to know he stood in opposition to her. "To make certain none of us comes to a quick end, I go to order the men ready."

Chandra watched her uncle descend the stone steps. As she fretted over her decision to admit the men into the castle, her teeth worried her bottom lip. Cedric was displeased with her, she knew. But, under the circumstances, she'd had no other choice. She'd not spur James's ire.

"Do not let his words upset you." Devin's gentle hands settled on her shoulders. "More than two hundred people, Morgans all, reside inside these walls. The Sassenach has only one-quarter that many with him outside. There is no cause for alarm."

"Except that they will eventually be inside with the rest of us. That, Devin, is what worries me. Should Cedric react too swiftly to anything this Montbourne says or does, I fear a great slaughter will result."

Her cousin frowned. "Aye," he said. "Knowing your uncle, the English will all be dead."

"So will we," Chandra stated, again thinking of James.

"It might be best that I remind Cedric—the others, also—to contain his anger."

Her foot hit the first step, and Devin followed. "What of the Sassenach?" he asked. "If he's kept waiting, isn't his own anger bound to grow?"

"I'm certain of it, Devin. Especially since he has such an exceptional opinion of the Highlands. A stint in the elements will undoubtedly make him even more desirous of his beloved England. Good fortune may have it that when we finally open the gates, he will already have departed."

"But he might not."

"That is a chance I shall take."

At dusk, the rustic gates leading into Lochlaigh Castle slowly creaked open. Having sat for hours in the cold rain, looking at naught but the gray stone fortress or the equally colorless landscape surrounding him, Aleck watched as a squat little man slipped from inside the ancient stronghold. Bare legs bowed beneath his stout trunk, his hips and thighs draped in what Aleck assumed was the Morgan plaid—a weave of green, yellow, and red—the man dodged the puddles that lay like miniature lakes on the soggy ground, striding toward the waiting troop.

"The Morgan apologizes for the delay and bids ye welcome now," he said, stopping before Aleck. "A meal awaits ye and yer men in the hall."

Now. The word exploded inside Aleck's head, and he gritted his teeth. Contempt shone in his eyes as he stared down at the man, for he could barely control his temper. His clothes were sodden, while rivulets of moisture trickled down his back; he was chilled to the bone. His already low opinion of the Highlanders had deteriorated even further. Crude, moss-headed provincials, he thought in irritation, deciding each one needed to be taught the meaning of civility.

Taking hold of his emotions, for he refused to behave as discourteously as did the clan Morgan, Aleck smiled politely. "Thank you, my good man. Please, if you would, lead the way."

The stout little Scotsman spun on his heel and signaled to the guards at the gatehouse. The scarred panels swung wide. Following the man as he again dodged the puddles, Aleck and the troop of fifty soon passed under the portcullis, into the upper bailey. As the line of men advanced through another set of gates into the lower bailey, Aleck was aware that no fewer than a hundred sets of eyes watched the procession. Their owners stood along the battlements and on the stone stairs leading to the former's heights, as well as around the perimeter of the yard itself. Heavily armed, each man kept to his post, his hand positioned on his weapon. The entire scene boded ill for Aleck and his men.

The riders halted near the stables. Remaining vigilant, Aleck and the others cautiously dismounted, then twenty-five warriors followed him to the entrance of the hall, the rest staying behind to attend the horses. When he'd passed through the aged doors, Aleck noted that the place stood strangely empty, but he imagined that he and his men were being closely watched, just as they were outside. His gaze swept the hall anew, observing that it was clean. The appointments, however, could at best be described as paltry.

Along the drab stone walls ranged long trestle tables, not a length of damask covering their exposed tops. Wooden benches sat beside them, their rough boards looking dangerously harsh. Briefly Aleck thought of the hoard of bare-legged men who occupied this place, their plaids the only protection they wore. A quiet chuckle escaped him. Undoubtedly their legs and rumps were scarred from the trove of splinters that greeted them each time they sat down to eat.

The tableware was no better than the furnishings.

Instead of pewter or silver, the trestles were set with stained wooden bowls and cracked wooden spoons, not a morsel of food to be seen. Like his men, Aleck was tired, wet, and hungry, yet it did not surprise him to see there was no provender awaiting them. Where bad manners were shown in one area, they were bound to extend to another, and Aleck's conceptions about the Scots were quickly reaffirmed: They were and always would be an uncouth lot.

"Take yerself a place at one of the tables," said the man who'd escorted them into the castle. "Yer food will be here shortly."

"What of the Lady Lochlaigh?" Aleck asked. "Will I see her shortly?"

"Ain't got no idea. She's seein' to matters concernin' the clan. When she's through, I suppose she'll send for ye. Go, take yerself a seat." The man strode off without waiting for a response.

Gritting his teeth, the Earl of Montbourne motioned his men to the benches. At the same time, the outer doors to the hall swung open. Shaking the rain from their heads, the rest of the troop tracked across the stone floor, joining their companions. However, one made his way toward Aleck.

"The horses have been rubbed down, watered, and fed," Sir John Farrell told him once he'd reached Montbourne's side. His dark brown eyes scanned the tabletops. "'Twould be nice if I could say the same of us."

Aleck looked at the knight. Approaching the age of thirty, he was one of James's most trusted soldiers. "My thoughts exactly," Aleck agreed. Then he asked, "What think you of this situation?"

Farrell glanced around the empty hall. "It makes me nervous. The fellow at the battlement seemed extremely desirous of spilling our English blood. I would not be surprised if, while we ate, he and the others fell on this place and assailed us all."

"I feel the same, Sir John," Aleck acknowledged. "Tell your men to keep alert, for we might soon have to fight our way out. Otherwise, this dismal hole might become our tomb."

"They will be ready for whatever is to come," Sir John promised, "and so will I."

"Well enough." With impatient hands, Aleck untied the knotted strings that secured his cloak. "Let us hope they allow us enough time to fill our bellies and renew our strength." He viewed the back of the hall. "This interminable waiting is testing my forbearance. Are we expected to prepare the food ourselves?"

Across the length of the hall, Chandra Morgan peered around the edge of the stone curtain that separated the large room from the entrance to the kitchens. Eyes centered on the one called Montbourne, she saw that he briefly looked her way.

"I wonder what they are close in conversation about," Devin commented from behind her, watching the two Englishmen over her shoulder. "'Twould be interesting to know."

"Aye, it would," Chandra said, a slight frown creeping across her brow. Then she smiled. "However, it shouldn't be too hard to find out." She turned to Devin. "Is the food ready?"

"Aye. The kettles have been standing on the back tables for nearly an hour. The gruel has grown cold and lumpy, and has the consistency of paste."

"Good." Chandra peeked around the stones once more to see the sodden cloak swing from the Englishman's shoulders; he tossed it onto an unset table. Water dripped from its hem onto the floor. He slipped his helm from his head and tossed it atop the cloak, then raked his fingers through his long, damp hair. "They deserve no better—the arrogant lot."

Just over an hour ago, while the king's men waited

outside in the cold rain, the clan Morgan had feasted in the warmth of this very hall. Trenchers of meat had lined the tables, along with bowls of peas and turnips. Brown breads and cheeses had passed from hand to hand, as had offerings of dried fruits. Wine and ale had flowed freely, but not too much was imbibed.

After the whole had eaten their fill, the hall had been cleared, the tables stripped of their damask covers and scrubbed clean; old benches had been exchanged for the new. Not a trace remained of the fine appointments or sumptuous fare, except perhaps a faint lingering scent of roasted meat.

"Tell the women to bring the kettles and cakes. 'Tis time we serve our guests."

"We?" Devin inquired. "Surely you do not intend to minister to the Sassenach yourself?"

"I do."

"Make certain, Chandra, that by doing so, you are not placing yourself in danger."

"Since he knows not who I am, I foresee no danger. He and his men are tired and hungry, and so might be less cautious with their tongues. Perhaps I can discover why he is here." She looked to the opposite end of the curtain, where her uncle stood in the shadows, four dozen men filling the narrow passageways behind him. "Besides, Cedric ogles him as a hawk would a rabbit. The English-man is no fool. He knows he's being watched. There will be no trouble—not just now."

Devin studied his cousin for a long moment. The Englishman, he'd noticed, had shown a masculine inter-est in her. Obviously the man believed her a common wench who, with a little persuasion, could be used for his own pleasure. Should Cedric become aware of this, the English rogue would soon find himself castrated. "A word of caution, cousin," he said close to her ear. "The Sassenach looks upon you with lust, so when near him, make certain he does not touch you. Your uncle will not abide such intimacy. Beware, or the hall will suffer a bloodbath the likes of which no Morgan has ever seen."

Lust? The word bounced through Chandra's mind. Staring after Devin as he strode to the kitchens to instruct the women to bring forth the kettles and cakes, she considered her cousin's statement.

Certainly she'd noticed the spark of masculine interest in the Englishman's eyes when they'd first met, but she'd thought it no more than a reflection of his own male vanity. His words about renewing their acquaintance had been said seductively, the insinuation not lost on anyone, yet she was certain they had been meant to entertain his men, thereby calling attention to himself.

Chandra's gaze again focused on the Sassenach; she studied him closely. Handsome he was. Pompous, too. In truth, she thought, he was much like the cock that strutted in the yard beyond the doors of the hall. Puffing himself up, the arrogant fowl would crow loudly. On that cue, the wisest of the hens scurried to the opposite ends of the bailey, for instinctively they knew what was to come, while the more doltish of the brood suffered the consequences. Chandra knew enough to keep herself far away from the Englishman, swaggering rooster that he was. Devin had nothing to fear.

When the women had gathered at her side, Chandra gave careful instructions that they were to remain attentive to all that was said. "Report whatever you hear to me," she said. "Remember, I will serve the tall one with the black hair and blue eyes." Taking hold of a kettle and a ladle, she stepped from behind the stone curtain, the other women trailing after her.

Aleck looked up to see the line of females headed his way, the beauty he'd nearly trampled at their fore. "Finally," he said to Sir John, closely watching the lass who'd again captured his interest. Viewing the red flame of her hair, he wondered if her passion was as fiery. Then he examined her perfect features; her pouting lips looked temptingly delicious, and he contemplated how they might taste were they to find their way beneath his own. His attention dropped to her shapely body, and he noted that she moved with a natural grace unmatched by any Englishwoman he knew. Wild and untamed, she was much like the country of her birth, and Aleck decided he'd very much enjoy mastering her. But the lass was undoubtedly spoken for, and he'd not chance incurring the wrath of these heathen Scots, for it meant certain death, not only for him but for his men as well.

From the corner of his eye, he saw Sir John move toward the table; Aleck followed. Seated, his back to the wall, he awaited his fare. A moment later, to his surprise and delight, the red-haired lass stepped behind him. His thick-lashed eyes crinkling at the corners, Aleck offered her a smile, one that he knew sent most women into an immediate swoon. Unbelievably, she seemed to be immune. She stared at him unresponsively; slowly his smile faded. The ladle dipped into the kettle, then withdrew. A large clump of cold gruel fell into his bowl. Viewing the unappetizing gob, Aleck grimaced. "What is *this?*"

"Oats," she said while another woman set a platter on the table directly in front of him. "And those are bannocks, or oatmeal cakes."

Aleck could not help wondering if the grain was the only subsistence on which the Morgans lived. He doubted it, for the scent of roasted meat still clung to the air inside the voluminous hall, and he suspected that the oats, in their adapted forms, had been prepared especially for the clan Morgan's uninvited guests. His gaze traveled to the large plate in front of him, the contents of which looked very much like round, flat rocks, then back to his bowl. After a moment, he turned to Sir John, who'd just received his own share.

The knight shrugged, retrieved the wooden spoon beside his bowl, and poked at the mound of cooked oats.

Fastidiously he tried to pry a small section from the gummy whole, but it would not budge. Losing his patience, he jabbed at the mass while twisting his spoon. A piece broke free to fly over Sir John's and Aleck's shoulders. Turning, they eyed the pasty glob that had plastered itself to the stones.

"If it thus adheres to the wall, I shudder to think what it will do to one's stomach and intestines," Sir John said, a frown wrinkling his brow.

"I think I shall forgo discovering the effects in either case." Aleck's suspicions rose, and a frown crept across his own brow. "'Tis only an observation—and certainly one would not think it possible—but the stuff seems to match the color of the mortar, does it not?"

Sir John grunted in agreement; both men shoved their bowls aside, then appraised the cakes. "Do we attempt to eat one?" the knight asked. "Or do you think this, too, is part of the castle's fabric?"

Aleck retrieved a bannock from the platter. It crumbled in his hand. "Other than being as old as the place itself, I think this might be the safer of the two."

Behind him, Chandra bit her lip to keep from laughing aloud. She watched as the Sassenach sniffed the cake, then took a bite. He chewed the overcooked fare—so ordered by Chandra—for a long while. "Wine!" she heard him croak after he'd attempted twice to swallow.

She stepped to the table. "Water is all we have, milord." The clear liquid poured into the squat cup by his hand. "I hope it is acceptable."

Aleck stared at the two-eared vessel. Damnation! he thought, wiping the tasteless food—its consistency much like that of raw flour—from his mouth by way of his tongue. Were there no comforts at all in this place? "Am I expected to drink from a bowl as would a cat?" Aleck questioned, becoming even more annoyed. "Do you not have a decent cup on the premises?"

"That is a cup. A *Scottish* cup. It is called a quaich.

Were you not so ignorant and untraveled, you would know as much."

"Ignorant? Untraveled?" he repeated, his voice low, his temper flaring. "Ignorant, I am not. Dull-witted, I am. But only because I had not the good sense to follow my own mind. Against my better judgment, I agreed to come to this miserable land and have suffered for it ever since. As for being untraveled, I can assure you no one in his right mind would ever set foot in this dismal clime, unless it was ordered by his king."

"Why did James send you?" Chandra asked, hoping his mounting anger would cause him to spew forth the reason.

"That is for the Lady Lochlaigh to know, if she ever shows her face."

"She is engaged with matters concerning the clan."

"So I've been told. But it seems to me that when the king's emissary arrives, carrying a message from the Lady Lochlaigh's sovereign that is to be delivered to her immediately, all else becomes unimportant. Apparently, you Scots think differently. But that is not surprising, for it is obvious the Morgans lack proper breeding. None of you know what the word *decorum* means."

A red hue blazed up Chandra's ivory skin to settle on her sculptured cheekbones, sparks of anger flaring to life inside her. "P-proper breeding?" she sputtered, desperately trying to calm her fury. Were she to lose control, she knew her uncle and the others would be on the Englishman in a breath's time. "By whose definition do we Morgans lack what you call proper breeding?"

"By my own," Aleck responded tersely. "Your clansmen have displayed extremely poor manners, not only to me and my men, but also to our king. By dealing with us unfavorably, you have done the same to James. I suspect, however, that this shoddy behavior is an inbred trait that has perpetuated itself over the centuries." Aleck heard the young beauty sputter anew; he waved her off. "It is widely known that the different clans cannot even show civility to their own neighbors. They war with one another constantly. The only time they band together is when a foreign invader encroaches on the Highlands as a whole. The intruder routed, the clans immediately go back to fighting among themselves as though they had nothing better to do."

"I assume, when you use the terms *foreign invader* and *intruder,* you naturally refer to the English," Chandra interrupted.

Her statement was accurate, but it did not deter Aleck. He was too incensed. "That is as it may be, but the fact remains: Such conduct is uncivilized, barbarous. Your countrymen are as wild as the savage land in which they live. Therefore, one cannot expect even a shred of courtesy from any of you. Tell me, lass, would you not agree that the ill-treatment afforded us this day is none other than the result of shoddy behavior?"

Chandra took issue with several points, but could not deny much of what the man had said. Until recently, the clans, more often than not, had warred with each other. A few still did. But the clan Morgan, under her father's guidance, had been at peace with its neighbors for nearly a decade. It was the English who stirred the Morgans' blood, rejuvenated their hatred—specifically her uncle's —for the clansmen resented their southern neighbor's desire for control.

Over the centuries, much violence had passed between the two nations, the stories of those happenings living even unto this day. The Scots would not soon forget how the English had invaded their lands, killed their kings, beheaded their discarded queen. It was only fair justice that a Scottish king now ruled both north and south, but James was not without flaw, for he'd ingratiated himself with the English, hoping to gain the crown on Elizabeth's death. He'd made little protest when his mother was to die under the axe. Most would agree that Mary had dictated her own fate, her treacherous actions—for one of which she was branded a whore and a traitor—culminating in her inevitable death; but in the Highlands, where family allegiance meant all, James's sort of behavior was considered disloyal. Because of this—along with the fact that he desired to unite Scotland and England—James was not revered. Hence the ill-treatment of his emissary.

By the same token, this haughty Sassenach had brought much of his woes on himself. He spoke of shoddy behavior, accusing the clan Morgan of such, when in fact he had exhibited the very same. Had he not maligned her homeland, called her a simpleton, and insinuated that he wanted to bed her, drawing knowing chortles from his men, practically all in one breath? If anyone had displayed a lack of proper breeding, it had been he, first and foremost. What had followed was merely payment in kind.

"I take it that you are not fond of my homeland," she said at last, again quelling her ire.

"Fond of your—" Aleck cut himself off. "I will tell you this, and know it is true. I loathe this place and one will not fault me when one considers why. I have been made to sit in a cold rain for hours, then when bid welcome, I am fed a pasty porridge and overcooked cakes not even the hogs could stomach. My eyes have seen naught but braky browns and gloomy grays since coming to the north of Scotland—Lochlaigh Castle, in particular. I'd give anything to be served a decent meal, to soak in a hot bath, and to have the lush greens of England surround me once more, for that is the only place I will ever find such comforts."

Clamping her teeth together, Chandra studied the pompous Englishman. So, he desired the "lush greens" of his beloved England, did he? If wishes were but reality, she'd gladly dispatch him there in the blink of an eye. An idea struck her. "To be surrounded by English green, that is what you desire?" Chandra inquired.

"Yes," Aleck snapped. "That is what I desire!"

"Mayhap, milord, you will soon receive your wish."

Chandra started to turn away, but a warm hand caught her wrist, long fingers encircling it completely. A sudden clatter sounded at the back of the hall; her attention shot to the stone curtain, where her uncle now stood in full view, his hand on his sword, several men pressing close behind him. She caught Cedric's eye and gave a quick shake of her head. From across the distance, Cedric's hard gaze bored into her. Her jaw set, Chandra returned his challenging look. Strong wills momentarily clashed, their owners refusing to back down. Then Cedric's eyes dropped, and he retreated behind the wall.

On an inaudible sigh, Chandra turned back to the Englishman. He seemed not to have noticed the commotion. Whether he knew it or not, good fortune had shone on him. But it might not do so again.

Aleck had not missed the disturbance, though he pretended otherwise. Just as he'd suspected, the hall was filled with well-armed men, concealed in the shadows. When he'd captured the young beauty's slender wrist, the whole had dashed nearly into full sight. Luckily, they'd withdrawn—but not before he'd recognized their leader as the man who'd tried to bait Aleck and his men into engaging themselves against the clan. It was quite likely he was a close relative of hers; hence, on spying Aleck's too-familiar touch, the man's quick temper had erupted. Understandable, for it was apparent that he hated the English. But why had the others charged forth, and in such haste?

Those questions bothered Aleck. But after a moment's thought, he decided they were also close relatives— undoubtedly a result of inbreeding among the tightly knit group. That would certainly explain their urgency.

Marking that she heeded him fully, Aleck released her arm. "My greatest wish, lass, is to meet with the Lady Lochlaigh. Would you see if that might be arranged with your chieftain?"

"I will inquire, but I cannot promise she will see you tonight. However, I am certain she will order clean accommodations and a hot bath for milord when she learns of your desires. The food, unfortunately, is all that we can offer."

A tantalizing smile crept across the Englishman's extraordinary features, while his sky blue eyes shone with a seductive twinkle; Chandra's breath caught in her throat.

"Thank you, lass," Aleck said, observing her reaction. "By seeing to all my needs, you could service me well."

The words were fraught with insinuation. Or so Chandra thought. The arrogant ass! she fumed. Why, she'd sooner die than play the mare as he acted the part of the rutting stallion. Were he not careful, he'd soon find himself gelded. Masking her anger, Chandra offered him a captivating smile of her own, then noticed that the Englishman's eyes had turned a deeper blue. "My pleasure, milord," she whispered throatily, the words nearly choking her.

Unknowingly, Chandra rested her hand on the small knife lashed at her waist, but the movement was not lost on Aleck. No sooner had his own words left his mouth than their dual meaning had hit him. Intuitively, he knew what she was thinking. "You can release your weapon, lass. I did not mean what you imagined." *Liar!* The word shot through his head, for in truth he would not object to bedding her at all. "I apologize for my choice of words. I beg your forgiveness."

"All is forgiven," she fibbed, another smile crossing her lips. Then she turned on her heel and headed toward the curtain. As Chandra strode the length of the hall, she felt the Englishman's gaze on her. Strangely, her heart skipped a little, and she commanded it to behave. Rounding the corner, she motioned to Devin. "I need your help. The Sassenach wants a hot bath. I believe we shall oblige him."

In a half hour's time, a large wooden tub, steam rising above its rim, stood in the middle of a sparsely furnished room situated on Castle Lochlaigh's upper level.

Viewing his cousin as she slipped the stopper from a large bottle, Devin grinned. "Chandra, you are truly wicked," he said, a chuckle rumbling from inside his slim chest.

"Tsk, tsk, Devin. The Sassenach said he desired to be surrounded by the color that most reminded him of his beloved England. I'm simply trying to fulfill part of his wish."

Chandra tipped the bottle; green dye, used to color the wool thread for the Morgan plaid, flowed generously into the depths of the tub. Then, their merry laughter rising into the air, the two cousins quit the room.

Chapter

3

Aleck stretched out fully in the steaming tub of water; a contented sigh escaped his lips as the chill slowly left his bones. Having bade Sir John to see to the comfort of the men before rejoining Aleck for a much-needed discussion about the impasse in which they'd found themselves, he'd been shown to his quarters by the squat little man who'd earlier escorted him into the castle. As the door to his austere-looking room had opened, he was greeted by the sight of his bath. Delight rippled through him, and he'd silently thanked the flame-haired lass for having interceded with her chieftain on his behalf. Perhaps the clan Morgan was not as uncivilized as he'd initially deemed them.

Grabbing a crude bar of soap placed atop a length of toweling, the whole resting next to the doffed medallion on a low stool beside the tub, Aleck lathered himself from head to toe. He sank beneath the water, rinsing the suds from his hair. Coming up from the tub's depths, he caught hold of a pitcher of warm, clear water and dumped it over his head, rinsing himself anew. Then he leaned back and relaxed. When the water had grown tepid, he stepped from his bath and began drying himself off. A firm knock sounded on the door, then he heard Sir John's voice. Retrieving the medallion, Aleck draped the chain around his neck. "Enter," he said, wrapping the long sheet of wool around his lean hips.

Sir John stepped into the room and closed the door. Viewing Aleck in the dim candlelight, the knight frowned. "Are you feeling well?" he asked.

Aleck stared at the man. "I feel fine. Why do you ask?"

"You look a bit green. I thought those cakes might have turned your stomach."

Frowning, Aleck stepped to the candle that sat on a low table beside the bed. He turned his arms and hands beneath the light; then, stripping the toweling aside, he lifted his leg. There was a distinct green tinge to his skin. A curse rolled off his tongue as he strode to the tub. The pitcher dipped into the water, then Aleck poured its contents back into the tub: green. "'Tis the color of grass," he said.

"More like an 'English green,' wouldn't you say?" Sir John remarked.

The two men stared at each other, then Aleck cursed again. "Why, the little vixen. . . . I should have caught on that she seemed a bit too eager to grant my wishes. Instead, like a doltish adolescent, I found myself bewitched by her beauty. The minx shall pay a heavy price for this. No woman makes a mockery of me."

"You have no proof the lass did this to you," Sir John said in the girl's defense.

"Who else heard my words? Naught except us three. It could be no one but her."

"She was going to speak with the Lady Lochlaigh, was she not? If she revealed your unflattering comments about the clan Morgan, along with your stated aversion to this clime, the Lady Lochlaigh may have ordered the dye put into your bath. Someone else might have done the deed." Aleck cast the knight a disagreeing look, and

Sir John shook his head. "Remember, Montbourne, you are here on the king's business. 'Twould not do to embarrass James. Nor would it be wise to get yourself killed. Let your temper cool. The dye will soon wear off. Death, however, is everlasting."

"You are right," Aleck said after a bit, thinking that when he met the girl again, she would soon wish she'd bitten her tongue. Appraising himself, he decided that he resembled a brine-soaked cucumber. Green flesh, however, was far better than rotted flesh, an undeniable result of the grave. "After I've had a good night's rest, I'm certain I'll see the humor of it."

Seeing the humor of it *now,* Sir John guffawed. "Even if it was the lass who did this to you," he said when he had quieted, "you must admit you deserved it. You were not very polite to her. You caused much offense by defaming her birthplace, maligning her clan, and then, of all things, using the word *service.* What had you expected? Rose petals in your bath?"

"I did not mean it as it was construed," Aleck insisted. "The term slipped from my lips before I realized how it had sounded. I apologized, did I not?"

"Yes, but the expression in your eyes said something else entirely. A word of advice, Montbourne—until you've learned to exhibit more favorable manners yourself, you'd best be highly attentive. Otherwise, I imagine you will be made to look the fool again."

"Perhaps once, Sir John, but never twice," Aleck promised, arrogantly certain he'd not be tricked again. "I will be on my guard at all times." He again wrapped the length of wool snugly around his hips, tucking in the loose end at his slim waist. "Before we retire for the night, we need to discuss this situation. I plan to draft a letter to James, telling him we have arrived but that the Lady Lochlaigh has refused to see us. I am also requesting that more men be sent north. I feel very uncomfortable with the meager force we have at present."

"I agree, but if James dispatches more soldiers into Morgan territory, it might create further animosity. Do you think it wise to risk doing so?"

"I think it would be unwise to risk not having them here. I have an ill feeling about this place. The clan's hatred of the English seems to flow from the very walls that surround us. I have no idea what the Lady Lochlaigh thinks of us, but I do know her father had sworn fealty to James prior to his death. She might favor us, but I do not trust the others, especially the one who stood at the battlement. Had those arrows flown, I shudder to think of the casualties. In truth, I am surprised we are not already resting in our graves. Something or someone must have stopped him, for he was bent on killing us all. No, Sir John, it would be far safer if James sent us another contingent of men. As for creating further animosity, they can remain away from the castle and stay hidden in the wood."

"Do you think no one will see them and report that they are there?"

"I'm sure they will not go unnoticed, but by the same token, with the Morgans being alerted that another troop of James's men sits just beyond the hillside, the more antagonistic parties of the clan might think twice before harming any of us. Knowing such security exists will allow me to rest easier."

"Undoubtedly you are right," the knight said. "I will dispatch a courier, along with several guards, to London on the morrow. Within a fortnight, our reinforcements should be camped only a short distance away."

A fist rapped against the door; both men looked toward the panel. "Enter," Aleck called; Sir John's hand settled on the hilt of his sword. When the door swung open, Aleck recognized the young man standing in the archway as the same he'd met on the path leading to the castle. Two other men were close behind him.

"Has milord finished bathing?" Devin asked, trying to

keep a straight face, his eyes dancing with merriment. "If so, we have come to empty the water and store the tub."

Aleck didn't miss the mirthful twinkle in the younger man's brown eyes. It confirmed what he had already known: The flame-haired lass was the trickster who'd tainted his bath. "Yes, I am finished," he said, waving the three men through the door. He watched as the trio, their shoulders shaking with repressed laughter, carted bucket after bucket to the open window, dumping the green water over its sill. Their task finished, they tipped the tub on its side and rolled it through the doorway. "Incidentally," Aleck said, catching the young man's attention, "please tell the comely lass with the red hair—Morgan Morgan, I believe she called herself—that I am grateful to her for having seen to my needs. Someday I hope to repay her in kind."

The impish light quickly faded from Devin's eyes. "To be certain, I will, sir." Intent on warning Chandra, he shut the door behind him.

"You're right, Montbourne," Sir John said, having also recognized Devin. "It is undoubtedly the lass who colored your skin. When you finally encounter the Lady Lochlaigh, your deliberations should go well, then, for there won't be any ill feelings to spoil your first meeting."

"I doubt it, Sir John," Aleck returned. "The initial meeting might go very well indeed, but once she learns why I am here, I'm certain she will fast scorn me."

"Why would she scorn you?"

Apparently Sir John knew nothing of the contents of James's missive to Aleck. "Because I have been appointed the Lady Lochlaigh's guardian. I am to find her a husband quickly—one who has sworn fealty to James. I cannot imagine that a young woman who is chieftain to an entire clan, answering to no one but herself, will be very receptive to discovering she has an overlord whose commands she must now obey. Make ready for a rebellion, Sir John, for when the Lady Lochlaigh and I do meet, that is precisely what will happen—a full-scale revolt!"

A heavy frown settled on the knight's brow. "I wish you good fortune, Montbourne. The task you have at hand is not an easy one. Be assured that my men and I will stand behind you. With luck, the revolt will be naught but a small one." Sir John strode to the door; Aleck followed. "The hour grows late. I will see you on the morrow."

The knight closed the panel, and Aleck secured its bolt, then he sauntered over to the rope-strung bed, a lumpy mattress resting atop it. He jerked back the covers, his eyes searching carefully for any crawly things that might have found their way beneath them. Spotting nothing out of the ordinary, he cast the toweling aside and sat naked on the bed. His unsheathed sword was placed on the floor beside him, an arm's reach away. Snuffing out the candle, he lay back, hands cupped beneath his head, and stared through the murkiness at the rough stone ceiling.

So, he thought, the spitfire felt he needed to be chastened for his rudeness. He had not been chivalrous, true. But then, the clan Morgan had not shown him any generosity either. The minx, he decided, would soon receive her due. Her punishment wouldn't be severe, for he refused to be harsh with her. She intrigued him, excited him, tempted him. Confident he could gain his reparation, stealing a kiss or two along the way, Aleck grinned into the darkness. The little vixen was in for a huge surprise. The despised Sassenach was going to make her life miserable. Exquisitely so.

Far down the hall, in a nicely appointed room, Chandra lay on her own bed, rolling with laughter. The crystal sound filled Devin's ears, but her cousin stood stern-faced. "Chandra, I tell you he knows who did the deed. He plans to repay you in kind."

"Oh, pooh, Devin!" she said, sitting up. "You worry

46

too much." She hopped from the huge canopied bed. "What could the Sassenach possibly do to me? Before he got within two strides of me, his head would roll across the floor."

"You are not always in Cedric's or my sight. There may be a time when he finds you alone. Then what will you do?"

"I'll scream. That should chase him off."

"One of these days, Chandra, you will not be so confident. Mark my words. You'd best carry a dirk with you."

"I do not want the Sassenach harmed, Devin. James would not let such a thing go unanswered. Besides, Montbourne has paid for his transgressions. Green as he is, he will look the fool in front of his men. Tomorrow the Lady Lochlaigh will serve her visitors a fine feast. They will be treated as though they were royalty. Now, if only I could discover why he has come." The women servers had previously reported to Chandra that Montbourne's men were untalkative. No help there. "Did Angus have the opportunity to search through his things before they were taken to his room?"

"He had no opportunity at all. The earl carried his possessions with him." Devin watched while Chandra stamped her small foot in frustration. "Why don't you just present yourself? The charade over, you'll learn why he's here."

Turning away, Chandra slowly walked across the room. "I have a strange feeling that when I do, I'll lose my freedom of choice."

"What do you mean?" Devin asked, coming up behind her. "You are The Morgan and the Lady Lochlaigh. No one can strip you of your power, except our king."

"That's what I am afraid of," she said, facing him. "Montbourne was sent by James. Maybe our king thinks I'm incapable of overseeing the clan . . . that I cannot control the factions who oppose the Crown."

"Besides Cedric, and the few who follow him, there is no faction. None of us is particularly enamored of James, but your clansmen revere you, Chandra, as they did your father. This feeling you have is naught but the effects of the dreary weather."

"You may be right, Devin, but I'm not certain it is the weather. Remember when we were up in the wood, watching the hawk?"

"Aye, and you were reminded of the ancient Morgan legend, all that superstitious babble about it being a bad omen when the hawk circles above the castle. 'Tis naught but blether, Chandra."

"Nonsense it might be, but at nearly the same time, a strong foreboding overcame me. The hawk's foretokening had to mean something, for moments later, when we ran down the hill, there was Montbourne."

"You think he is part of the legend—the 'winged hunter'? And I suppose you are 'the ladybird,' the wee creature that he is to carry away in his sharp talons."

"No, I do not. But I fear he has the power to alter my existence as I now know it. The change will come once he discovers who I am. I'll not reveal myself to him, not just yet. First, I hope to uncover why he is here."

"If that is what you desire, you know I will help you." His hands settled on Chandra's soft shoulders and his light kiss fell on her cheek. "The day has been long and I grow weary. A good night's rest will renew us both. Mayhap things won't seem so bleak for you on the morrow."

Caught up in her own worries, Chandra had forgotten about her cousin's weakened condition. She gazed fully at Devin. Set in a chalky face, his doe brown eyes were ringed by dark circles. Short breaths rattled in his lungs. He wobbled on his feet, much like a newborn colt. "I have kept you far too long," she said, trying to mask her concern, for he appeared close to collapsing from fatigue. Devin was still ill, but were she to point out that fact, she knew he'd try to persuade her otherwise. Undoubtedly he would perform another stunt, hoping to convince her he was stout and strong, which was certain to result in a strength-robbing fit of coughing. Devin could not afford such an attack on his already frail body. "I too am tired," she said, feigning a yawn. She rose on tiptoes to place a kiss on his pale cheek, then smiled. "As you say, a good night's rest will renew us both."

"Aye, I shall see you on the morrow," Devin responded, moving toward the door. Chandra followed. "Secure it well," he said, opening the panel. "Despite his cool outward manner, I'm certain the Englishman possesses a hot temper. While he lies abed thinking about the rude welcome we Morgans have given him—especially the aftereffects of his much-desired bath—his anger might erupt. I'd not put it past him to come searching for the trickster who turned him green."

"English green," Chandra corrected, an impish twinkle shining in her eyes. She noted Devin's raised eyebrow. "I'll bolt the door and sleep with a sharp knife under my pillow. I promise."

"Better it were a claymore," Devin said, waving his good night.

Locked in her chamber, Chandra continued to pace the floor, the ancient Morgan legend spinning through her head: *Ladybird, ladybird, flee, else the winged hunter transform your destiny. Ladybird, ladybird, fly, sweep to the heavens ever so high. Sharp talons aimed at a tender young breast; quick, quick, lest he carry you afar to an alien nest.*

Chandra's feet came to a sudden halt. Silently she chided herself for having worked herself into such an agitated state. The legend was naught but a silly tale holding little truth, a story meant to entertain the children—blether, as Devin had said. Yet Chandra could not shake the strange feeling that had overcome her in the glade.

Gazing at her wide bed, she concluded the troubling sensation had possessed her because she was worn and weary, both physically and mentally. So much had happened in such a very short time—her father's sudden, unexplained death, Devin's upsetting illness, her uncle's constant interference in her overseeing the clan, the Sassenach's unwelcome arrival. Especially the latter! She must discover the Englishman's mission, and quickly. Given Cedric's disposition, Chandra knew she could not chance a wrong decision, otherwise disaster would result. Yes, a good night's sleep should restore her wits and stamina, thereby quelling the mysterious foreboding.

Thrusting any thoughts of the legend from her mind, Chandra disrobed, then marched to the basin, where she bathed herself and cleaned her teeth. Garbed in a light woolen shift, she slipped beneath the covers of her bed. As she leaned toward the candle, intending to snuff its flame, she caught sight of her sheathed knife resting on top of the chest opposite her bed. Remembering her promise to Devin, she hopped to her feet to retrieve the weapon, then settled under the blankets anew.

In a quick breath, darkness fell upon her secured chamber. Punching her pillow, her knife hidden beneath its plump mass, Chandra stared through the shadows at the door, silently daring the arrogant Englishman to attempt entry. It would be the last time he encroached on a Morgan's turf. That she vowed!

Sunlight shone through the open window, the low-lying clouds having dispersed. Standing under the warm glow, Aleck stared at his hands, turning them over and over. As green as grass, he thought, his anger fermenting anew. When he'd awakened, nearly as weary as when he'd taken to his small bed, he'd hoped the memories of the previous night were nothing more than a bad dream. Unfortunately they were not. Cursing, he thrust his fingers through his hair, then wondered if it, too, was tinted green.

A knock sounded on the door, and Aleck strode to the panel, unlocking it. On the other side stood Sir John. The man's gaze traversed Aleck's face, then dropped to his hands, the only other parts of Aleck's well-muscled body not concealed by his clothes.

"I had hoped it was not as bad as we first thought." Sir John shook his head and sighed. "Were the sun not shining, it might not be as noticeable. Maybe we should pray for the rain to return."

"Have you any more glad tidings to share?" Aleck asked discontentedly.

Sir John chuckled. "Just that the messenger is on his way to London, as you requested, and that a feast awaits us below. I came to see if you were desirous of breaking the fast."

"A feast?" the earl inquired. He stepped to the table and retrieved the packet James had sent him, tucking it into his waistband beneath his jerkin. Smoothing the leather over the parchment, he belted on his sword, then headed for the door. "Are you certain it is not poisoned?"

"So far the men have felt no ill effects," Sir John responded as Aleck shut the wooden panel behind them. "Of course, we could wait and watch, but I think it is a peace offering. The Lady Lochlaigh probably is feeling some remorse over her clan's ill treatment of us—you, in particular. If so, I'm certain the food is safe."

"We'll see," Aleck grumbled, leading the way to the stairs. As he and Sir John descended the stone steps, the rich aroma of roasted meats filled Aleck's nostrils. His stomach rumbled, protesting its empty state; saliva flowed into his mouth, the small glands at his jawline burning. Then as he rounded the corner, his attention fell on the hall, its many tables laden with a delicious assortment of provender. Each offering appeared to have been prepared to perfection. "This day, should I die," Aleck said, heading for his seat, his eyes searching the corners of the room for the beauty who'd served him the night before, "I shall do so in a state of repletion."

Sir John laughed aloud. "I also," he rejoined, positioning himself on the bench next to Aleck. He skewered a plump partridge with his knife, then bit into the basted bird, its skin golden brown and tender. "'Tis delicious, Montbourne. Satisfy your hunger."

While the two men ate heartily of the roasted game, warm brown breads, aged cheeses, and dried fruits, washing it all down with several helpings of fresh goat's milk, Aleck's ears were periodically attacked by the muffled laughter of the servers who refilled the platters nearest him. Clenching his jaw, he ignored the annoying giggles. Other than an initial few gasps and open-mouthed gapes, his own men remained silent, their gazes wisely affixed to their plates. When he'd eaten his fill, Aleck again searched the hall, but the flame-haired vixen was nowhere in sight.

"Why is it, Sir John," he commented more than questioned, having recognized most all of the Morgan clan from the night before, "that the guilty one always vanishes."

"Undoubtedly it is a matter of survival."

"Aye," Aleck agreed, trying to quell his temper, for a loud guffaw had shot from behind the stone barrier at the hall's rear. "Fortunately for her, she had the sense to disappear. That wan-looking fellow along with her."

The pair to whom Aleck referred stood mere inches beyond the barrier, waiting for Cedric's mirth to settle. Having just come from his quarters, he had not seen the Sassenach since the previous night. At his glancing around the stone divider, Cedric's raucous laughter had surged forth, full and loud. With her lips pressed into a tight line, Chandra stared at him. "Be still, Uncle," she whispered harshly, "lest you irritate him to the point where he'll refuse the Lady Lochlaigh's request to meet with her at last."

"But he is green," Cedric pronounced after he'd quieted.

"Aye, he is. But what matters to me now is that you have understood my instructions."

"I do. But why, Niece, is the Sassenach to meet you outside the castle gates?"

"Because it is my wish that he does," she replied, having told Cedric no more than that he was to extend the invitation to the Englishman and inform him that the Lady Lochlaigh would meet him several miles away from the Morgan stronghold on a deserted moor.

"What if he refuses your invitation?" he asked. "Suspecting a trap, he might not wish to leave the security of these walls. What, Niece, shall I tell him then?"

"Security? He is not stupid, Uncle. He knows he can be attacked here as well. But if he questions why we are to meet away from the castle, tell him . . ." Chandra paused, trying to think of a plausible explanation that would entice the Englishman from inside the fortress. "Tell him the Lady Lochlaigh is engaged in clan business outside the castle. On its completion, she will be traveling north to attend the wedding of a close friend, and will be gone for nearly a month. He is to meet her on the moor, for it will be his only opportunity to do so, unless he wishes to await her return."

"Why the deception?" Cedric asked.

"I have my reasons," she said, refusing to elaborate. "Just do as I say." Appearing as though he wanted to argue the point, Cedric hesitated, but to Chandra's relief, he moved from behind the screen, heading toward the Sassenach.

Chandra turned to see her cousin inspecting her. "Do not chastise me, Devin. I know you think me foolish, but I'll not come forth as the Lady Lochlaigh until I know why James has sent him."

"And you believe that in his anger, he will blurt out the truth?"

"Yes."

"Chandra, have you considered that your plan might very well have the reverse effect?"

"How so?" she asked, confident it would not. "His arranged mishap should do naught but make him a laughingstock."

"You said you feared the consequences should anything happen to him at Cedric's hands. Yet you yourself are tempting fate. What if he breaks his neck?"

Chandra frowned. Was she tempting fate? No, she decided, refusing to believe it. "He's an excellent horseman, and the ground is soft from the rain. Naught will happen to him," she said, positive the only injury suffered by the arrogant Englishman would be to his pride. "Hush, Devin. I'll hear no more of it. We will do as I've planned." Sighing heavily, her cousin seemed resigned, so she peered around the barrier's edge. Cedric addressed the Sassenach from across the table. When his words were finished, the younger man first looked to his companion, then with a barked command waved his men away from the benches. "They are headed toward the door," she said, swinging around, her long braid snapping like a whip. "Come, let's make our way out the back to the stables."

As Aleck and the knight headed toward the doors at the front of the hall, Sir John whispered, "I do not like this."

"Nor do I," Aleck concurred, his eyes examining Cedric's back.

"The whole thing reeks of deception."

"Agreed, but if we are to do battle with these heathens, I'd much rather do it out in the open. Should our skills fail us, we can at least attempt an escape. Locked inside these walls, we have nowhere to go. Tell the men to keep alert for an attack."

Word was quickly passed to the others as they followed the Earl of Montbourne out into the sunlight, Sir John having positioned himself by the door. When the last of the men had exited from the hall, the knight sought Aleck's side. "They know to be on their guard," he told him.

Aleck responded with a nod, then watched as his saddled mount was led by a young lad from the stables. The stallion seemed skittish, prancing nervously, jerking at the reins. Aleck wondered at his strange behavior, then decided that the steed had undoubtedly caught scent of a mare. A firm hand would be needed to settle him.

Sidestepping puddles of water, Aleck took the reins from the lad and issued a sharp command; the stallion calmed his edgy movements, but his frequent snorts told Aleck he was still agitated. Then, while the other horses were guided from the stables, Aleck assessed the Morgan men who were to accompany the group, hoping to gauge their moods. They seemed at ease, unconcerned about the upcoming journey out onto the moor. Maybe they actually intended to meet the Lady Lochlaigh as he had been informed.

Aleck released his breath, and the tension that had strained the muscles along his neck and shoulders freed itself. Turning to survey his own men, he glimpsed a flash of fiery red hair. Immediately he pinpointed the beauty whose plaited tresses had captured his attention. She stood a half dozen yards from him, her sickly companion at her side.

The two appeared to be engaged in a serious discussion, for her exceptional features were fraught with concern, a slight frown etching her brow. As the young man listened, his jaw set, his expression one of exasperation, her soft lips moved in rapid speech, her low voice drifting away on the light wind that flowed through the yard.

Briefly Aleck wondered again how that sweet mouth

would taste beneath his own. Were he not about to set off to meet the yet unseen Lady Lochlaigh, and were the girl's relatives not around—especially the latter—he'd span the few feet separating them, take the beauty in his arms, and kiss her senseless, satisfying his curiosity as he did so. Like her clansmen, she despised the English. Yet once his lips claimed hers, he was arrogantly certain, her revulsion would fast turn to desire. Discovering it had, she'd suffer the punishment she rightly deserved. Green his skin might be, but as a lover, he certainly was not. Aleck smiled to himself, positive that, through the mastery of his kiss, the girl would melt at his feet.

Unfortunately, there was no time to carry out the tempting scenario that spun through his head, for he would soon be riding out the castle gates. However, no harm came from utilizing his imagination; decidedly he'd be safe in his fantasies. So, as the rest of his men received their mounts, he thought of several other ways to chasten her, each one more wicked than the last. Chuckling to himself, Aleck continued to study the imp who had made him look the fool, only to wonder what she was saying.

"I fear more for the horse than the man himself," Chandra said to Devin. "The beast already suffers. The thistle—it wasn't overly large, was it? It won't wound him too badly, will it?"

"A fine time to show your concern, cousin. Especially after the thing has already been placed under the saddle." Devin spied her look of remorse. "'Twill be no worse than a bee sting. 'Twould be better if you were to save some of that fear for yourself."

Not absorbing the last of his words, Chandra bit her bottom lip. Silently she chastised herself for the cruelty the poor stallion was suffering and would yet suffer. She was irritated with the Englishman, not his steed. Damn him! Why had he come here?

An odd feeling overcame Chandra. She was being

watched. Her head turned and her eyes met those of sky
blue. The Sassenach's assessing gaze raked over her
suggestively; his lips broke into a knowing smile. As he
lazily continued to view her, Chandra felt strangely
warm. Then conversely she shivered.

He was undeniably attractive, she thought. Extremely
masculine, too. But he was English—arrogant and brash.
For that reason alone, she desired his attention as much
as she would a bout of the plague. Her narrowed eyes ran
over his face. In the sunlight, he resembled a clump of
moss. Unable to contain herself, Chandra fell into the
giggles.

Aleck gritted his teeth, then called out: "We shall see
who has the last laugh." He turned and placed his foot in
the stirrup, pulling himself astride his horse. Snared by
his ire—the girl dared to snicker in his face!—Aleck
paid little heed to the stallion's nervous snort. But when
Aleck's backside hit the saddle, the beast expelled an
angry neigh; the stallion's hindquarters jerked, then he
bucked violently. Once, twice, Aleck's bottom met the
leather seat, then he flew through the air. With a whoosh,
he landed flat on his back in the mud.

First there was silence, then uproarious laughter exploded in his ears. Above the bellowing guffaws, which
stung his pride and piqued his anger further, Aleck heard
Chandra's mirthful cries. Like a crystal bell, they tinkled
merrily in his ears. Springing to his feet, he sloshed
through the mire toward the galling sound. Shortly
he stood before the vixen who'd duped him a second
time.

As she tried to suppress her glee, Chandra's dancing
eyes were met by those of blue ice. Unwisely, she ignored
the warning written in their frigid depths. Viewing his
mud-spattered face, she stood her ground, her giggles
still bubbling forth.

Like a taut wire, Aleck's restrained fury snapped. His
fingers banded her arms, and he jerked her fully against

him. "Witch," he hissed, "I am tempted to thrash you until you beg for mercy." Then one hand slowly moved toward her throat. "On second thought, I should break your sweet little neck and be done with your bedeviling tricks."

The sound of cold steel sliced through the air a hundred times over; Aleck tensed. Certain the multitude of claymores were all aimed at his back, he searched the flame-haired beauty's eyes. Morgan pride glistened in them, daring him to follow through with his threats. Behind him, the whole clan stood ready to slay him for having boldly challenged this one woman who was not too far from being a girl. But why?

The murky veil of confusion that had clouded his brain was quickly stripped aside. A sudden dawning took its place. *"You,* I presume, are the elusive Lady Lochlaigh."

Chapter

4

"You presume correctly," Chandra said curtly. "Unhand me or you shall presume no more."

A reckless smile crossed Aleck's lips. "I think not, milady. Were I to release you, you might slip from my sight, and *that* I cannot risk. You and I have some important matters to discuss."

"You arrogant lout," she snapped. "Have you not enough sense to know that, were I to give the word, in a twinkling you would be dead?"

"I do," he stated, "but I also perceive that you have enough sense to know that were I to die, James, along with his full army, would lay waste to Castle Lochlaigh. The clan Morgan would quickly fall into extinction. If that is what you desire, give the word. If not, tell the whole to lower their weapons and sheathe their swords."

For a long moment, their gazes clashed. A war of wills ensued. Finally, knowing she had no other choice, Chandra shifted her attention to Cedric. The man's sword was held mere inches from Aleck's spine, ready to plunge. "There will be no fighting," she said, then noted her uncle's hesitation. "Lower your weapons," she called for all to hear. Discontented rumblings were heard throughout the yard, but each sword soon slipped into its scabbard, including Cedric's. "Peace shall prevail this day, Sassenach. But only because I willed it," Chandra said, her jaw set mutinously. "Now, take your hands off me and tell me why our king has sent you."

Aleck released her. "Directly," he said, "but first I need to scrape some of this muck from my person. Then I will join you in the hall."

"Would milord be desirous of another bath?" she asked, her head tilting haughtily.

"No." His terse reply came over his shoulder as he strode toward his mount. Checking beneath the saddle, he pulled the thistle free to observe that the barbs were stained with blood. "I have endured enough of the Lady Lochlaigh's benevolent hospitality." He tossed the thing aside. "And so has my steed."

Chandra watched the stallion being led back into the stables by the Englishman's own hand, remorsefulness welling inside her. The feeling, however, was for the horse, not for the man. The beast had suffered needlessly, for her scheme had unraveled like a worn piece of Morgan plaid. He was aware of her identity, and she could no longer evade him. For all her childish maneuvers, she'd gained nothing, except perhaps the pleasure of watching him fall from his horse into the mud, taking another blow to his lordly pride. But the answer she sought remained a mystery to her still.

Her shoulders sagging, she headed toward the doors of the great hall. Devin and Cedric followed her. Inside, she turned to her uncle. "When the Sassenach enters, show him to my antechamber. I'll await him there." She took hold of Devin's hand, pulling him toward the stairs.

"What will you do now?" her cousin asked as they climbed the ancient steps.

"There is not much I can do, except wait. Soon I shall learn the truth."

His clean leather-clad hip perched on the corner of a table, Aleck watched as the Lady Lochlaigh tore through the wax seal and read the missive sent by their king. Her hands began to tremble, then her gaze shot to his face. By the set of her jaw, Aleck could tell she gritted her teeth.

"'Twas not my doing but our king's," he said in response to the accusation written on her face. "In truth, I wish he had chosen someone else."

"Chosen?" Cedric asked, coming away from the door where he'd positioned himself. Sir John moved closer to Aleck. "Chosen for what?"

"Aye," Devin seconded, taking a step nearer to Chandra, where over her shoulder he tried to read the contents of the letter. "What has James done?"

Chandra's eyes remained locked with Aleck's as she folded the parchment in half. "James, in his far-reaching wisdom, has decreed that the Earl of Montbourne—this *Sassenach!*—is now my guardian."

"Guardian!" The word exploded in unison from both Cedric's and Devin's lips.

"She needs no guardian," Devin insisted, moving even closer to his cousin's side. "She is The Morgan of Morgan, chieftain of the clan. She leads all of us. She needs no overseer. No one is allowed to dictate what she can and cannot do."

"Aye," Cedric chimed in, "especially when he's not a Scot."

"Wrong," Aleck said, shoving to his feet, his gaze swinging away from Chandra's. "There is one who has the right, and he is by birth a Scot. Since he has decreed that I am her guardian, it is so. By his writ, which gives me full power, *I* shall dictate what she can and cannot do. To question my authority means you question James's authority and the authority of the Crown. Only a fool would do so."

Cedric's eyes sparked fire. His hand reached for his sword's hilt.

"Uncle, temper yourself," Chandra commanded. "There will be no bloodshed, I tell you. Until you are able to control your anger, I ask that you retire to your quarters." She noticed how her uncle's lips, already drawn into a tight line, compressed further. He seemed unwilling to honor her request. "Go with him, Devin," she ordered. "I wish to speak with Lord Montbourne privately."

"But—"

"No mischief will befall me, cousin." Her gaze shifted back to the Sassenach. "James would not find pleasure in hearing that my new guardian has harmed the one he's been sent to protect. There is no cause for worry, is there, milord?" she asked of Aleck.

He smiled. "None, milady. None at all."

The door to the antechamber opened and a reluctant Cedric and Devin walked into the hallway. Montbourne nodded for Sir John to follow the pair. The panel closed with a sound thud.

"You didn't share the rest of James's letter with your clansmen," Aleck said. He again settled his hip on the table's corner, folding his arms across his broad chest. "Is that why you wanted to speak with me privately?"

"It is," Chandra snapped. "If you think I will allow you to select a husband for me, you are mistaken. When it is time for me to marry—which it is not—I shall take unto myself a man of my own choosing. James won't have any say in it, and neither will you."

"Oh, but I will, milady."

"Will not!"

Aleck gazed at her impudent mouth, its lower lip thrust forward, and the desire to claim it with his own leapt through him anew. He'd punish her with his kisses until she was whimpering with want. Or until she bit him. The last thought made deep laughter rumble in Aleck's chest while merriment twinkled in his eyes, for he knew she'd do it. He noticed that his ward stared at him. Undoubtedly she thought he'd gone mad. "You're tempting fate," he said, then his lips spread into a devastating grin; a dimple marked each cheek. The Lady Lochlaigh seemed mesmerized; a sudden flush rose on her cheeks. "By contradicting your guardian," he continued, growing more confident in his male prowess, "you're certain to lose any leniency he might have showed you."

Once fascinated by his smile, Chandra quickly came to her senses. "Leniency?" she cried. "I doubt *you* would show any leniency to me or to any Morgan."

"I might, if I were granted the courtesy I deserve and given the regard due me as your guardian."

"Courtesy? Regard? You ask much after what you've done!"

"What *I've* done?" he returned, shooting to his feet, his need to taste her lips momentarily forgotten. "I may have given offense by speaking my mind about this desolate clime, the dreary weather, the unappetizing food— which somehow had miraculously improved a hundredfold this very morn—and the ill-mannered lot who inhabit this drafty old keep, but in doing so, I merely voiced the truth. If anyone has been offended, it is I."

"Truth? Ha! Before you came here, your perceptions of us were already formed."

"Perhaps—to an extent. But those perceptions were based on what other Englishmen were made to suffer by you Scots, especially the Highlanders. Their stories are numerous. Now I have my own tale to tell."

Chandra knew what he would say, but wanted to know if he dared to embellish the truth. "What is your tale?"

"It is this: On my arrival, I stated fully that I had been

sent by James to see the Lady Lochlaigh. Am I invited inside? No. Instead I am greeted by the threat of arrows descending upon me and my men. Wondrously, they did not fall, yet I am made to sit in the soaking rain until dusk, waiting for approval to enter. When I am finally bade do so, I am fed an inedible paste and dry cakes, the latter washed down with water. Of course, as an *honored* guest, I am shown to a pauper's room, where I am dyed green in my bath and forced to spend my night's repose on a lumpy bed. My horse was cruelly injured, and I made to wallow in the mud as would a lowly swine. Who has given the greatest offense, Lady Lochlaigh? You or I?"

Guiltily Chandra stared at her feet. "They did not fall because I ordered it so," she said after a moment.

Aleck's brow knit in confusion. "What?"

"The arrows—I ordered them placed back into their quivers."

"An act of courtesy? Forgive me, I shall strike the aforesaid threat from my list." Aleck waited, but Chandra gave no response. "A word of advice. I am usually not a very tolerant man. In fact, my forbearance has been imposed on quite enough. I did not ask to be sent here. Nor do I wish to stay. As I see it, the faster I find you a suitable husband, the quicker I can return to England. Therefore, I suggest you call together all the eligible men who are loyal to James so that I may conduct the necessary interviews and have you wedded by month's end."

"Month's end? I'll not marry any man, suitable or otherwise," she stated defiantly. "Especially not one chosen by you."

"Oh, but you will," Aleck repeated, his eyes again focused on her lips. "But first, I am most curious." With the fluid movement of a big cat, he lazily walked toward her; Chandra stood fast, refusing to back away. He stopped mere inches from her. "There's something I have wanted to know since the moment I first saw you, Morgan Morgan."

"Chandra," she snapped, but didn't know why.

"Yes, that is the Lady Lochlaigh's real name, isn't it?"

"What is it you need know?" she asked, dismissing his question.

"Simply this." His hand caught hold of her plaited hair to quickly coil the braid around his wrist. Her head fell back, her lips opening in protest, and his mouth descended, covering hers fully. The kiss was hard, hot, wet, and over when it had barely begun.

He released her braid, and Chandra stumbled away from him; the back of her hand scrubbed furiously against her mouth. "Don't *ever* touch me again."

"Each time you decide to provoke me or to disobey, you may expect more of the same. A fair punishment is it not? Especially when you cannot abide being near me."

She glared at him. "Arrogant Sassenach!"

"I'll forgive you that one, but next time I may not," he said over his shoulder as he strode toward the door. "Know also that I too have a name." He turned and shot her a wicked smile. "It's Aleck. Or more formally, it's Alexander Hawke—with an *e*—the sixth Earl of Montbourne."

As Aleck opened the door, his surname echoed through Chandra's head. *Hawke! Hawke! HAWKE!* On the last reverberation, she nearly crumpled to the floor. The winged hunter in the old refrain and this man Hawke, they were one and the same. Was the legend about to be realized? Impossible, she thought, wanting desperately to deny that it might be true. She watched as the panel closed behind him. "Swine!" she yelled loudly, only to hear his low laughter seep into the room through the aged wooden barrier.

Not long after her guardian had left her, Chandra paced the floor of her bedchamber. With her hands clasped tightly in front of her, knuckles gleaming white from the pressure, she tried to fight down the anxiety swirling through her. His surname was merely a coincidence, she told herself. A quirk of fate. But that was the problem. Like the winged hunter in the legend, this Hawke possessed the power to change her destiny. Unlike the ladybird, however, Chandra had no place to flee. Her agitation grew, for she resented the control he had over her. Her jaw set, she continued her monotonous trek, expending her anger as she did so.

Arrogant beast! her mind screamed with fury. He would not dictate what she could or could not do. Nor would he choose a husband for her. She'd go to her grave before she'd allow any man to have say over her. James's edict be damned! But what was she to do?

From the chair where he sat, Devin had watched Chandra's measured tread for the past quarter hour. Her impending marriage was no secret to anyone, for the couple's heated words had shot through the door like cannon fire. None of the three waiting in the corridor knew what had transpired during the moment of silence, but by Chandra's reaction, Devin had his suspicions. Finally he could take no more of her pacing. "Cousin, you are wearing out the carpet—your feet as well."

"It is *my* carpet and they are *my* feet," she snapped without thought. "I shall ruin them if I wish."

"Whatever you say, but you are exhausting yourself needlessly."

Chandra came to a standstill. "Needlessly? I am about to be married off to some stranger who will be chosen for me by that odious Sassenach who calls himself my guardian. I'm not exhausting myself for naught. In order to think, I must pace. I'll not rest until I've found a solution."

"The solution is here in James's letter. Or at least, I believe it is."

"Where?" She strode toward Devin and took the letter

from his hand. Reading it anew, she frowned. "I see nothing by way of a solution. It says the same as it did: I am to be married. And Montbourne, as my guardian, is the one who will select my husband."

"As I read it, there are two requirements set forth by James that the prospective bridegroom must satisfy and Montbourne must make certain are fully met prior to any marriage being arranged. One is that the man has sworn fealty to our king; the other is that he is loyal to the Crown."

"There are dozens upon dozens who fit those requirements. How do you see a solution in that?"

"There are equally as many, if not more, who *don't* fit those requirements. Montbourne wants you married off by month's end, whereupon he can make a swift return to England; therefore, he instructed you to call together all eligible men so he can arrange the appropriate interviews in order to find you a suitable husband, correct?"

"Aye, that is what he said."

"What if you called together only those men you know are not altogether in conformity with James's way of thinking? It wasn't so long ago that our cunning king enacted his sly hoax at Mull."

Chandra remembered that unsettling time. Irritated that his Highland subjects flouted the rule of the Crown, James had sent a great army north. A conference was called in the Castle of Aros. With the promise of hearing a sermon, a number of clan chieftains—including her father—had been invited aboard ship, quickly arrested, then imprisoned all over England, until one by one they had sworn fealty. James's action had been highly unfair —at least where her father was concerned. Colan Morgan truly had desired peace and had demonstrated such by remaining in harmony with his neighbors for nearly a decade.

"Why do you mention Mull?"

"Although many of the clans' leaders have acquiesced,

there remain scores and scores of Highlanders who have refused to resign themselves completely to the rule of the Crown. They suffer in silence, ready to revolt. For centuries, the clans have striven for the right to rule themselves—not that they have accomplished much with their continual wars, except to weaken their numbers."

"Aye," Chandra agreed. "Too many young men have lost their lives, and for naught."

"It is the way of the Highlander. Headstrong Scotsmen all. Each believes he's right and will go to his grave trying to prove it."

"Aye," she repeated, knowing she was nearly as headstrong as the rest of her countrymen. "But I see no solution here," she said, her free hand striking the letter. "My father swore fealty to James, and I cannot break the pledge he made. It would bring ruin to us all."

"The solution is there, but it is only temporary. It will merely delay the inevitable." He noted her questioning look. "Montbourne must interview each man who asks for your hand, correct?"

"Aye."

"He desires to return to England, does he not?"

"Aye."

"What if your guardian, through all his interviews, cannot find a suitable mate, one who is loyal to James and the Crown?"

Chandra was beginning to see his point. "I imagine he will become quite frustrated. The longer he is made to stay in Scotland, the more annoyed he'll become. Thwarted, desiring to return to his beloved England, he'll soon abandon his search. Given his temperament, he should be gone from here by month's end—possibly sooner. I'll still be unattached and without a guardian, too." Her crystal laughter bubbled forth. "Oh, Devin, do you really think it will work?"

"Aye, if we plan wisely. With Montbourne out of the

way, you can then find yourself a husband, one whom you can love." Chandra frowned down at him. "If you don't marry," he said, "James will simply send someone else to take Montbourne's place. We are only delaying the inevitable. You will have to wed, and soon."

Chandra sighed heavily. "You are right, I suppose. But I refuse to think of that now. Come," she said, urging Devin from the chair, "we need to make a list of those whom we are assured will fail the test."

Having gathered quills, ink, and paper, Chandra and Devin sat opposite each other at the writing table in her room. Nearly an hour later, they had compiled approximately two hundred names. The prospective bridegrooms ranged from those who despised the Crown's authority outright to those who wavered in their loyalty depending on the time of day. "Do you think these will be enough?" she asked, scanning the list once more.

"I would hope so," Devin responded, stretching his cramped fingers. "Remember, we still must write the letters inviting them all to Lochlaigh Castle."

"I wish we knew twice this many," she said, the tip of the quill's feather brushing the edge of her lower lip. "'Twould be nice if the line wended out the castle gates and down the lane. At the prospect of interviewing such a staggering number, Montbourne might reconsider his duty and flee back to England in haste."

"'Twould be nice, but let's keep to the list we have at present. Once the word is out, there will probably be others who show themselves."

"But what if they are truly loyal to James?"

"I'll question each one myself, long before Montbourne ever sets eyes on any of them. If they don't pass my test, they will be sent on their way."

"Devin, you are truly the finest cousin I could possibly have," Chandra said, gathering his hand from the table to kiss his knuckles. "What would I ever do without you?"

He smiled weakly. His strength was waning day by day; his coughing seizures had grown more worrisome. Blood now showed in his sputum. He feared it would not be long before Chandra learned the answer to her question. "You would find another champion, cousin. One who cares for you nearly as much as I."

Startled by his response, Chandra searched the angles of his pale face. Tears stung her eyes when she realized how very ill he was, yet she refused to acknowledge what it meant. "Never," she whispered, squeezing his hand. "You are not only part of my family, but my best and dearest friend. No one could ever replace you. No one." Before her tears welled and fell, she quickly changed the subject. "Are you certain the Sassenach won't suspect our deception?"

"I hope not," he said, releasing Chandra's hand with a gentle caress. "The truly subversive ones are a mere handful. The majority of the others have some sort of petty grievance against the Crown or against James himself. The remaining few are simply inept. The first sign of a confrontation, they'd flee over the first hill. Whether any of them likes James or not, remember, they are all Scots and Montbourne is English. One by one, they are certain to insult the man. Considering his disposition, he's bound to dismiss them all. The choice, of course, is his."

"That's my greatest fear. This has to work."

Over the next half hour, the pair duplicated the list onto another sheet of parchment, then drafted a letter. Both documents were sent to the Earl of Montbourne with a note requesting his approval. Within ten minutes, his written reply was returned to Chandra's door by the same messenger. The letter had been approved, but the list was to be cut in half. A suitable bridegroom, he had decided, could readily be found among the smaller group.

"We should not have sent the list," she said, once her guardian's response had been read.

"Not to worry. Eventually all the names will be utilized. It simply gives us more time to write the remaining letters."

"Then we had best get started, for he wants the first of the men to arrive by next week."

During the following day and a half, Devin and Chandra had written the nearly one hundred letters inviting her suitors to Lochlaigh Castle. Fortunately they were not disturbed by her guardian or by her uncle. In fact, they saw neither man, which might have been due to their having taken their meals in Chandra's room.

At present, as Chandra stood by the open gate, watching the final courier ride out across Morgan lands, the last ten invitations tucked securely into his leather pouch, she felt her nerves grow taut. "What now?" she asked Devin, who was close at her side.

"We wait to see if there is any response. In the meantime, we should see to the needs of the Lady Lochlaigh's most honored guest."

"You expect me to show *him* civility?"

"'Twould not do any harm. Were you to demonstrate some courtesy toward him, charm him with your wit and intelligence, when he's faced with interviewing the glum lot we've invited he may take pity on you. The plan is for him to become even more discriminating in his selection than he'd originally intended to be. Not only would he consider James and the Crown, but he'd consider your desires as well. 'Tis worth a try."

"But we already know he'll not find a loyal one in the bunch."

"True, but mind you, in his eagerness to return to his precious England, he might pick the one who comes closest to James's mark. We want to prevent that from happening. Therefore, he must be made to see that none of these men are well suited to the *endearing* Lady Lochlaigh. Although unaware of his motives, he'll dismiss them all."

Leniency. The word spun through her head. Her guardian had suggested the same himself. Much as it pained her to show him the least bit of kindness, it seemed she had no other alternative. She'd try anything, so long as it kept him from choosing her a mate. "I'll attempt it, Devin. But I refuse to be too amicable. Knowing my feelings for him, he would quickly perceive it for what it is—another trick."

Having gained the castle's upper floor, Chandra set a course for her guardian's room. Winded from the climb, Devin followed at a slower pace.

Standing before the portal to his austere quarters, she squared her slender shoulders; her fist rose and struck the wood. Footsteps were heard coming toward the door, then the panel opened. "The letters have been sent," she told Aleck, her chin high. His height intimidated her, but she withheld any sign that it did. "The last courier left only minutes ago."

"Thank you for informing me." He marked that she stood rigidly, hands clasped at her waist, fingers stained with ink. "I know I had said I wanted the first of your suitors to arrive by next week, but I had not expected such swift compliance, especially from the one who insisted she would not be made to wed." He glanced at Devin, who was passing behind Chandra. Briefly he noted that the man wobbled on his feet and his breath wheezed in his chest. Devin withdrew from his sight, and Aleck's attention again centered itself on his ward. "Have you suddenly changed your mind?"

"Never!" she snapped, forgetting her need for courtesy. "You ordered it done, and so it is."

"I'm gladdened by the news," he said, crossing his arms over his solid chest, his muscular shoulder leaning against the door's casing. Only moments ago, he'd watched from his window as his ward and her cousin made their way across the yard. Heads together, they seemed to be devising a plan. Studying her, he cocked his head. "But why is it I feel you've grown a bit too eager to see this thing through?"

Chandra noticed the wry smile on his face. "Eager?" she questioned, wondering if he'd somehow discovered their deception. "You are mistaken, Lord Montbourne," she said after surveying him closely, deciding he was by nature suspicious. "If there appears to be any eagerness on my part, it is because I have other matters that concern me. They pertain to my position as head of the clan. With the letters written and sent on their way, I am now free to attend to them. If you will excuse me, I—"

From the corner of her eye, she saw her cousin collapse against the wall just outside his chamber door down the hallway. He fought to get inside his room, then nearly fell through the opening when the panel was freed, to disappear from sight. The sound of violent coughing fired into the corridor.

"Devin?" she cried, and ran toward his chamber.

The frightened tone of her voice set Aleck into action; he sprinted after her. By the time the two reached Devin's door, silence met their ears. Through the opening, Aleck caught sight of Devin who was leaning over a small table, a basin atop it. His face was colored a dark red, verging on purple; it was obvious that he was unable to breathe.

Brushing past Chandra, who stood frozen in the doorway, Aleck quickly strode toward her cousin. His fist hit the younger man's back—once, twice. With the last blow, the copious amount of mucus that had clogged Devin's throat expelled itself. Hearing the air rush into the younger man's lungs, Aleck frowned. There was blood in the basin, and he grasped how ill Chandra's cousin really was.

"Devin?" Chandra questioned, her feet now carrying her toward him.

"Keep her from me," Devin pleaded with Aleck on a rasp, his face turned from the Englishman. "Do not let her see." Then he tried to push himself from the table, intent on making it to his bed, but his strength failed him.

Cognizant of the man's weakened state, knowing his ward was almost beside them, Aleck lifted Devin in his arms. Turning around, he stood between Chandra and the basin, blocking her view. He nodded toward the bed. "Throw back the covers," he said. She rushed to do his bidding, and Aleck carried Devin's slight weight across the room. "You have my gratitude, Sassenach," Aleck heard Devin say as he lowered him onto the mattress.

Aleck straightened, and his gaze connected briefly with Devin's. An acceptance of his fate was written in the depths of the younger man's eyes. Any spark of concern was meant for Chandra. Then Aleck fathomed how very much Devin loved her, not just as a close relative, but also as a man.

Pity welled inside him, as did another emotion, though he could not put a name to it. Watching the gentle care being given the man—Chandra propping pillows behind his head, her hand softly stroking his damp brow—Aleck understood how strong their relationship truly was. Never having formed such a tight bond with anyone himself—at least, not since childhood—Aleck thought what he felt was a twinge of envy, but without the usual spite or malice. Then again, the odd sensation might have been caused by the knowledge that Devin would soon succumb. Death, he decided, was such a waste.

As he regarded his ward's perfect profile, her flaming hair loose and tumbling down around her slim shoulders, caressing the length of her back, he knew her grief would be great, and his heart ached. A vital need to protect her surged through him; the strength of the emotion stunned him. Turning away, he moved toward the small table, a bewildered frown marring his brow. Not finding a place to dispose of the bloody mucus, which attested to the seriousness of Devin's illness, he draped a cloth over the basin.

Aleck eased back around to survey Chandra again. She was no fool, he thought, wondering why he'd taken such measures to hide the evidence. By the way she had run toward her cousin's room, by the look on her face when they had entered, by the way she fawned over him now, Aleck knew she was aware that it was far worse than her cousin had let on. He sympathized with her, but none of this really concerned him. By month's end, he would be gone, his ward wedded, his duty fulfilled. So why did he suddenly feel as though he were about to suffer a heavy loss of his own?

Growing angry over the mix of emotions teeming inside him, Aleck stalked to the foot of the bed. "Should I summon someone to assist you?" Her eyes met his, and Aleck was momentarily entranced. "If not," he said, forcing himself to look away, "I shall return to my quarters."

"I will care for him, alone." He nodded and headed toward the door; Chandra followed, stopping him as he stepped into the corridor. "Thank you for acting so swiftly. You saved his life," she said, gazing at him with a new expression in her eyes. "I am forever indebted to you."

Aleck's nerves had grown taut. Something was happening to him, something he didn't understand. Nor did he desire that it continue. "Don't be," he snarled, jolting Chandra's sensibilities. He looked at the slender hand resting on his arm; it quickly fell away. "You should find another to care for him. That is why you have servants."

Chandra bristled. "I do not think of my clansmen as servants. They are my family. As such, we care for each other."

"'Tis your choice," he said, then walked to his room.

Chandra stared after him. A moment ago she thought she'd seen something in his eyes that bespoke a certain tenderness, a concern and caring. Obviously she'd been mistaken. The Sassenach's door thumped closed, and she spun on her heel, marching toward the table and the pitcher of water sitting by the basin.

"Chandra, don't bother."

She heard Devin's weak voice just as she cast aside the covering that hid the basin, intending to pour water over a face cloth she'd retrieved. The sight that met her startled and frightened her. She turned toward the bed. "He tried to hide this from me—why?"

"He did so at my request."

"Oh, Devin, why did you not confide in me?"

"I did not wish to worry you. 'Tis bad, Chandra," he rasped. "I know not what it is. I forever fear having you near me. If it is contagious, you might be struck by it also. Henceforth, you must keep yourself away from me." His head rolled on the pillow and he faced the wall. "Go, leave me now—I must rest."

"Rest you shall, but I'll not leave you."

Wetting the cloth in the pitcher, she moved toward the bed, where she gently bathed his face, then pulled the bedcovers over him. Afterward, she sat in a chair not far away. His ragged breathing had eased somewhat.

"Remember, Chandra, treat the Sassenach with courtesy," Devin said, a weak smile crossing his face. "Despite his sullen moods, I suspect he is not as disagreeable as you think."

"He's more so."

"We have formed a strategy. Follow it through. 'Tis for your own good."

Devin fell silent; soon he slept. While Chandra kept

vigil over him, she reviewed her cousin's words. The pair *had* formed a strategy. For it to work, she had to play the perfect hostess. The thought of treating him with the least form of civility sickened her, for it was obviously something he could not easily reciprocate, but she knew she had no choice. She would do anything to dissuade the arrogant rogue from fulfilling his duty, even it meant killing him with kindness.

"It appears, Montbourne, that you've gained in status," Sir John said, looking around Aleck's new quarters. Having just finished their evening meal, the two men had sought out the earl's gloomy little room for a short discussion, only to be met by the bowlegged Angus, who led them down the hall. "Perhaps things will improve for you altogether, since the clan Morgan seems more receptive to your being here."

Aleck was in a surly mood. Though he knew why, he denied it. His eyes traced the same path as the knight's. The chamber was far larger than the one in which he'd originally been installed, its appointments more acceptable, but it was not anywhere near as large as his own room at Montbourne nor did it contain the finer amenities to which he was accustomed.

"'Twill do, but it is not home. At least the bed is larger and softer. I won't have to cling to the thing as I did the past several nights, fearing I'd meet the floor." He removed his sword, placing it across the table, then saw that his possessions had also been moved. "As for the Morgans, they desire me here no more now than they did earlier. It is their chieftain who has instructed them to be more civil, and I believe I know why." He noted the knight's raised eyebrow and waved his hand in a wide arc. "All this is a bribe—the room, the sumptuous food and good wine of which we just partook, the friendly service we were given. She's hoping for clemency when I select a husband for her. She probably hopes I won't choose one at all. She's wrong, though. Take note, friend, when the marriage vows have been said, we'll undoubtedly be fleeing here with arrows raining down on our heads—if not sooner."

"Then you believe her motive is concern for her own welfare and not because she feels guilty over how she has treated you, or possibly that she is compensating you for saving her cousin." Sir John caught Aleck's surprised look. "I overheard one of her clansmen telling several others about your heroic act."

"Heroic? 'Twas more like a reflexive response. I did nothing out of the ordinary. Compensation? I doubt it. Guilt? Unlikely. She is Scot and I English—it would go against her nature to feel remorse over what I have suffered."

"And her cousin?"

"She could have saved him herself. I simply reached him first. No, I am certain it is the thought of her own welfare that motivates her. Had I not mentioned that courtesy and regard could gain her my leniency, I might have taken it for genuine remorse. Even compensation, as you've suggested. But I did mention such—hence you see the marked changes. I do not blame her, considering her fix, but it will do her little good, for my allegiance belongs to James." Her schemes would not work, Aleck vowed in silence, his mood growing even more sullen. "She *will* be married," he continued with strong determination. Purposely he kept the memory of his ward's lovely face far from his thoughts, knowing if he envisioned it, he'd surely relent. "Whether her husband is young or old, fat or thin, tall or short, I care not, just so long as he meets the criteria that have been set forth."

"I hope you do not tell her that, else we might be eating dry cakes and drinking naught but water again."

Aleck chuckled wickedly. "I'm not that foolish. No, I intend to enjoy all the attentions bestowed upon me, as will you and your men, Sir John. However, no matter how great the pleasures given us, none of us should become too passive. I do not trust these Morgans, especially the girl's uncle. He is overly eager for a fight."

"Aye, he is."

"While I entertain the Lady Lochlaigh, making certain she doesn't take flight, I ask that you keep a close eye on this Cedric fellow. I do not wish to be slain in my bed."

"Nor I," the knight said, watching as Aleck pulled a folded piece of paper from inside his jerkin. "He will be watched. Count on it."

"Good."

"In her note to you"—Sir John nodded toward the paper—"did your ward explain your change in quarters?"

Aleck looked around the room again. It appealed to him more than before, but it was still not home. *England.* Why had he left it? "No, but I assume she meant it as a surprise." His eyes returned to Sir John. "She said only that she still attended her cousin. She begged my forgiveness for not joining us at the evening meal, but said she could not in good conscience leave him. On the morrow, if he is recovered, she has asked that I ride with her to see the extent of the Morgan lands."

"Will you go?"

"I hazard too much should I not go," Aleck answered. "What good will it do to find a bridegroom if there is no longer a bride? As I said, I plan to keep the Lady Lochlaigh entertained."

"Then, if you think she feels no remorse, do your entertaining well armed. She might be small, but I have a feeling she is quick. You'll find little enjoyment with a knife in your gullet."

"I shall keep that in mind."

Sir John soon left, and Aleck took himself to bed, his mood darker than before.

He thought he'd dismissed the strange emotions that had roiled through him earlier in the day, while watching his ward attend her cousin. Their force both surprised and confused him. Adamantly he wanted to deny their true import—he felt something for her, and it was not based on mere lust. How convenient it would be to attribute the whole episode to his having ingested something that had disagreed with him, thus the unaccountable pressure near his heart becoming a mystery no more. But he could not do that.

Damnation! The girl means nothing to me.

The insistent words shot through his head as he thrashed about his new bed while trying to find some comfort. Settling finally, he lay there, staring at the ceiling. With great effort, he at last gained the control he desired, convincing himself that he held only a passing interest in her.

Shortly, his thoughts turned to Sir John's words of warning. To Aleck, having seen the couple's heads together, it was apparent that the Lady Lochlaigh and her cousin schemed against him. After the way he had dealt with her, he could not blame her for seeking out a plan, hoping to foil him while making him look the fool once more. In her mind, he deserved no less.

Remembering the last few moments of their heated discussion in her antechamber, Aleck cringed. She had deemed him arrogant, and that he'd been. His male curiosity piqued, he'd taken undue advantage of her, excusing his actions by telling himself she'd merited such punishment. In truth, it had had the reverse effect. Briefly he relived his response to the kiss, but just as quickly locked all memory of it away.

Directing his thoughts to the present, he conceded he'd erred in his treatment of her. She was not some peasant girl whom he could tease and try to bed; she was his ward. He was responsible for her. Admittedly, her beauty still tempted him, but he knew he had to restrain his masculine urges. Otherwise he would incur James's wrath.

Aleck did not relish having his head separated from his body. Nor did he wish to have a knife stuck in his gullet—a serious possibility. Again he heard Sir John's words of warning. Despite the shift in his circumstances, the courtesy now being shown him, naught had actually changed between the Lady Lochlaigh and himself. She still despised him. Entertain her, he would. But he would do it with great caution.

Chandra quietly closed the door to Devin's room, relieved that he still slept peacefully. As she made her way to her own bedchamber, recollections of the last few hours seized her; she began to tremble. On entering his room, her feet had been rooted to the floor, her mind a blank on how to aid Devin. Had her guardian not reacted as he had—brushing past her to strike Devin's back— Devin would surely have died. His condition was far worse than she'd originally thought. Or was it simply that she'd refused to see the truth? She could not lose Devin. He must not die!

The door to her room opened, and she nearly fell inside. Irrepressible tears flowed down her cheeks as she stumbled toward her bed. Too much had happened of late, too much to worry over. Her father's sudden death, whereupon she'd had little time to grieve; her duties as clan chieftain and all that entailed; Devin's illness and the possibility that he, too, might die—the weight of it all was more than she could bear.

Then there was the Sassenach!

Ladybird, ladybird, flee, else the winged hunter transform your destiny. The ancient refrain rolled through her mind unbidden. No! The legend was false, she silently insisted. Or was it?

Overwhelmed by the strain on her emotions, Chandra wanted nothing more than to lash out at someone. "Damn him!" she shouted to the walls, cursing Aleck, cursing the fact that he'd invaded her home. Yet deep inside, she was thankful he had, for Devin still lived. Nevertheless, she resented owing him such gratitude, he being the source of her latest worry; she denounced vehemently, "Damn him to hell!"

Given Cedric's disposition, *that* could very well be the Sassenach's next destination.

Chapter
5

Nerves drawn taut as a harp's strings, Chandra waited in the yard for her saddled mare to be led from the stables, Montbourne's stallion alongside it. Her teeth punished her lower lip as she repeatedly reminded herself to be polite to her guardian, else her plan would come to ruin. Positive that their outing would end in failure, she prayed he'd send his regrets. Wrestling a wild boar might prove a far easier task than adopting a civil attitude toward the man. To treat him with anything but contempt when she despised him so was hypocrisy.

"You are a fool, Niece, to ride with the Sassenach alone," Cedric said, at her side once more to argue his point. "He cannot be trusted, I tell you. How do you know James's letter is not a forgery or that this Montbourne is who he says? He could be an English mercenary, intent on stealing you away in order to hold you for ransom. By ignoring my warnings, you are giving him license to do precisely that."

Weary of her uncle's constant haranguing, his words of doom having attacked her ears off and on for the past quarter hour, Chandra turned on him. "I tell you, naught will happen. We are to ride alone. Were he intending to steal me away, as you imply, do you think he'd leave his men inside these walls? What would be his purpose?"

"He would leave them behind in order that they could strike us down."

Chandra laughed openly. "Ridiculous, Uncle. They are outnumbered several times over. They could not win were they to fight. Besides, we have no wealth to speak of. What would he hope to gain?" Cedric's mouth flew open, but Chandra quickly cut him off. "No, Uncle, what you suggest is ludicrous. You are inventing trouble where none exists. James's letter is genuine. His insignia was affixed in the wax seal, which remained unbroken until I opened it. I am the one who invited the Sassenach to ride with me, not the other way around. Should he decide to accept, you can be assured he knows the consequences were he to do me harm. Our king would not condone such an act."

"Just the same, I do not trust him."

Chandra concurred with her uncle's statement, but to say so aloud would merely give rise to another round of bickering, something she'd rather forgo. Her decision was already made, and even though she would have preferred to have several of her clansmen beside her for security's sake, she knew Montbourne would have none of it, not unless an equal number of his own men were allowed to join them. The mix would not do, for her concentration would be centered on the group surrounding them. Absorbed in keeping peace, she'd accomplish little. Like it or not, she needed to be alone with the man. Somehow, she had to gain his sympathy. Given his arrogance, she belatedly wondered if he possessed such an emotion at all.

From the corner of her eye, she saw the man of her thoughts exiting the hall, the knight beside him. "Argue with me no more, Uncle, for it is decided. We ride alone. But if it gives you any ease, know that within my boot, I carry a dirk. Should the Sassenach come too close, I shall not hesitate to use it."

His gaze trained on Chandra and her uncle, Aleck noted the dour look on Cedric's face. "There appears to be a disagreement between them," he commented to Sir John. "Something tells me the dispute stems from the fact that his niece and I are to ride unattended."

The knight chuckled. "Given your notoriety with the opposite sex, I cannot say I fully question the man's hesitancy on allowing you such freedom. Dare I ask if the girl is at risk?"

Aleck came to an abrupt halt, as did the knight, whereupon the earl cast a harsh eye on his companion. For some reason, he'd taken offense at the man's question. His reputation was well known: A monk, Aleck definitely was not. But neither was he a connoisseur of innocent young women. "We are not at court, Sir John, where males and females frolic openly, their lewd behavior going unchecked. We are at Lochlaigh Castle," he said, his tone annoyed. "I know my affairs are reputed to amount to upward of several score—an exaggeration fueled by the gossips. Because of it, I have been termed 'a womanizer.' But know this: Summed together, my mistresses have numbered not more than a dozen, and that includes the one who led me into manhood when I was five-and-ten. I am most selective, Sir John, and I can assure you my interests do not lend themselves to unseasoned virgins." Not after what he'd suffered by way of his late wife! "The Lady Lochlaigh is quite safe with me. Damnation, man, she's my ward, not my paramour!"

"I ask your pardon, sir," Sir John stated. "I meant no offense. My words, although spoken carelessly, leapt to mind simply because, by her uncle's expression, I'd say he trusts you not."

Aleck viewed Cedric anew. "Aye," he agreed, "the man is not at all pleased by the arrangement. Make certain when the Lady Lochlaigh and I have left the castle that he does not follow."

"Be assured he won't," Sir John promised.

Noting that the knight seemed suddenly withdrawn, Aleck felt contrite over the fierceness of his attack. Normally he accepted any good-natured teasing that came his way, laughing at himself as loudly as did the others, especially when the jest had to do with his masculine prowess. But for some strange reason, he'd not tolerate any challenge about his intentions toward the Lady Lochlaigh. Whatever its cause, it could not be denied: Aleck had become most protective of his ward.

As the two men approached them, Chandra heard Cedric say: "They conspire, I tell you."

She closed her eyes and drew a cleansing breath. On its release, some of her mounting anger flowed from her. "'Tis naught but your imagination. Now, make yourself busy and see to the mounts." With a piercing look, her uncle stalked off toward the stable doors.

"Good morn, milady," Aleck greeted her, coming up behind Chandra. "Are you ready for our ride?"

Startled, for her attention was riveted to her uncle, Chandra spun round. Captured by his striking blue eyes, she could do naught but stare. Compelling, they were, and as she gazed up at him, she thought she might do anything he asked—anything. Her mind distracted by Cedric's ravings, she'd had little time to fortify her senses, hence her womanly interest grew. A wide smile spread across his bronzed face, his unblemished skin now radiating a pinkish hue instead of the sickly green she'd grown accustomed to.

Blinking, Chandra knew she must answer. "'Twill be but a moment," she said, her voice sounding oddly breathless. "As soon as the mounts are ready, we'll be on our way."

"Excellent," Aleck responded, seeming not to notice her reaction. "I am eager to see what awaits us. Perhaps our outing will convince me there is some worth to be found in this otherwise barren wilderness. Based on what I've seen so far, I'm at a loss as to why you Scots protect it as fiercely as you do."

Chandra quickly regained her wits. The man wore his superiority as a pauper would a gold-threaded cloak— the strutting peacock! She wondered if anyone had instructed him on even the most rudimentary manners. Eyeing him closely, she decided that someone had undoubtedly tried, but considering the student, the hapless teacher had been destined to fail. Miserably, at that. Silently dubbing him a buffoon, yet not forgetting why she'd asked him to ride with her, she smiled most civilly. "Since you English think there is no worth to be found in the Highlands, I also am at a loss as to why you continually invade the site. Apparently there is something of value here, else you'd forever remain on your side of the border."

Aleck studied her momentarily, only to find he was unable to fault her logic. His deep laughter rumbled forth. "A truce, milady. The day is far too lovely to ruin it with talk of the political intrigues of kings long dead. We will resolve nothing should we attempt it. Although our two countries have warred continually, let there at least be peace between us."

"Yes, the day is far too lovely." Her smile widened, for she knew she'd bested him. "Since we both recognize its worth and wish to enjoy it, I shall accept the truce."

"Then a truce it is." He glanced around him. "Your cousin, has he recovered?"

"He is feeling far better, but I have ordered him to rest," she said, feeling certain Devin was watching from his window. "Again, I thank you for your timely intervention."

"I was glad to be of service. And I thank you for your own intervention," he said.

Her gaze ran over his damp hair. The color of a raven's

wing, the thick tresses shone like polished ebony in the sunlight. "Then milord's bath was satisfactory?"

"'Twas far more enjoyable than the first," he said, reviewing the experience.

At first light, a knock had sounded on his door, and Aleck opened it to see Angus standing on the other side. As the man ambled into the room, two crocks tucked under his meaty arms, three of his clansmen rolled the large tub through the doorway. Seeing Aleck's frown, the squat man stated: "My chief has instructed that I brings ye this stuff." He'd thrust the crocks into Aleck's arms. "This one here"—pointing to the one under Aleck's right arm—"ye're to use first. Rub it all over ye, even yer hair. 'Twill burn, but it won't scar ye none. After ye've bathed yerself, put this other stuff on ye." He'd jabbed the crock under Aleck's left arm. "'Twill stop the itch. Don't forget the second, or ye'll prickle all over."

"What sort of mischief is your chief up to now?" Aleck had asked, his suspicions rising.

"Ain't no mischief to it," the man had snapped, scowling. "'Tis supposed to turn ye back to yer natural color. But if ye enjoys lookin' like a clump o' moss, I'll simply tell her ye refused her charitable offering. It were me, I'd have left ye as ye are."

The two men had briefly tussled over the crocks, Aleck winning out. "Assist me with my back," he'd ordered the man, but without result. "Please?"

"Ye'd better take off yer whigmaleerie." Aleck's brow had arched. "That ornament round yer neck," Angus had said, nodding at the medallion. "Else it might turn on ye." Uncertainty had flickered in Aleck's eyes. Nevertheless, he'd complied. He'd whipped the chain over his head, then laid it aside. A cold glob of oily paste had hit his skin, and the squat man quickly rubbed it over his back. "Ye can do the rest," he'd said, standing aside.

As Aleck lathered a generous portion of the pasty

substance over his face, hair, neck, and arms, then down his chest to his belly, the whole began to tingle, then burn. His backside, legs, and feet were quickly covered. Straightening, Aleck had grown hesitant. Staring at his private parts, he'd closed his eyes and gritted his teeth. The deed was swiftly done. By the time the contents of the last bucket had flowed into the tub, his skin was on fire. He'd nearly dived into the water.

After scrubbing himself from head to toe with soap, he'd stood, rinsing himself with several fresh buckets of water. Once dried, he'd spread the contents of the second crock all over his body. The balm had cooled his skin immediately.

"See," Angus had said, after helping again with Aleck's back, "weren't no mischief to it. Yer soft as a babe and nearly as pink as its wee behind."

Aleck could readily have disputed the man's statement about there being "no mischief to it," but as he thought back on it, the suffering he'd endured was well worth the results. "It was most kind of you to take pity on me," he said to Chandra, smiling. "By way of your charity, I'll no longer blend into the trees."

Chandra's tinkling laughter filled the air; the sound of it left Aleck feeling oddly affected. "Had you acted in a gentlemanly fashion in the first place," she said, wishing he'd take pity on her in kind, "you would have suffered none of what you did."

Staring down into his ward's upturned face, her extraordinary eyes smiling at him, Aleck experienced a strange stirring deep inside him. Beautiful and innocent, he thought, desirous of threading his fingers through her lustrous hair, its freed length hanging to her waist. Of its own accord, his hand rose. *Take hold of yourself, you fool!*

Swiftly the wayward urge was checked. To cover his error, Aleck whipped his arm in front of him, posturing a bow. "I promise I shall remain on my best behavior." The vow was made to her, but meant for him. Then from the corner of his eye, he saw that her uncle had exited the stables. "Our mounts are arriving."

When Chandra was seated on her mare, Cedric strode to where Aleck's stallion stood. "Make certain no harm comes to her, Sassenach," he said, glaring up at Aleck, "or you'll suffer in the aftermath."

Aleck spied the hatred in the man's eyes. "She'll be kept safe, I assure you." Resting his arm on the saddle's pommel, he leaned toward the man. "Just make certain," he growled in a low voice, so only Cedric could hear, "that you have not contrived against us as we ride this day, or you, Highlander, will suffer far more than I."

Straightening, Aleck jerked a nod at Sir John, silently reminding the knight to keep an eye on the quarrelsome Scot; then he and his ward rode out through the castle gates.

High on a brae overlooking a small loch, Chandra reined her mare to a halt. She and her guardian had been riding the perimeters of Morgan territory for more than an hour. Most of that time had been spent in silence, the pair speaking only when they'd stopped for Chandra to point out a particular place of interest, explaining its historical significance. Occasionally she directed Montbourne's attention to the awe-inspiring beauty of the wild and rugged land that he'd said he abhorred, hoping to change his mind. As she studied his handsome profile, his stallion standing shoulder to shoulder with her mare, she wondered if he had.

"Do you still think there is nothing in these northern climes that captures the eye and exalts the soul? Can you not feel the majesty of it?" she asked, her hand sweeping wide above the loch. "Or do you just see an ordinary pool of water, insignificant and dull?"

Aleck could not deny that the view was breathtaking. Like glittering diamonds, rays of sunlight danced atop the deep blue water. A warm wind swept through the pines below, rustling their boughs. Fresh, sweet air lifted from the loch to travel up the hillside and into his lungs. He felt invigorated. "I'll admit," he said, turning to Chandra, noting that her eyes were as blue as the water, "this place gives one a feeling of reverence. Its beauty is unsurpassed." A smile lit Chandra's face. Entranced by her loveliness, Aleck stood corrected: She was even more magnificent than the view. Mentally shaking himself, he forced himself to examine the loch again. "Shall we take a closer look?"

"Aye," his ward responded, patting the mare's neck. "The horses are in need of water. 'Tis as good a place as any."

Aleck glanced at the trees standing alongside Chandra and himself; he spied a quick movement. A tousle-haired lad, his years no more than two-and-ten, ran through the wood barefoot, dressed only in a saffron shirt. A dead rabbit dangled from his hand. "You have a poacher," he said, turning his stallion, ready to give chase. "Shall I catch him?"

"No. 'Tis Owen." She spied her guardian's questioning look. "Owen—at least, that is what I call him—is mute. He lives in the wood alone."

"Is he a Morgan?" Aleck asked.

"I don't think so. He appeared one day, shortly after my father's death. He shuns people, and very seldom is seen. Whether he is a Morgan or not, he is welcome here. I've given orders that no one is to harm him."

Chandra had tried to make friends with the boy, standing face to face with him twice. But he would not respond to her urgings to come live with her at the castle. So, to make certain he was cared for, she left him food, along with various supplies. Someday Owen might answer her overtures of friendship; that was her greatest hope.

"You are generous to a fault," Aleck commented. "Not everyone would be so kind."

"Owen is special," she said. "Shall we see the loch?"

"Aye," he answered, the boy quickly forgotten.

Leading the way, Chandra directed her mount down the steep incline. Watching her, Aleck felt his admiration grow. Intelligent, cheery, witty, and charming, in many ways she was far older than her years. Yet inside dwelled an impish little girl. To that he could attest!

Unlike the sophisticated Felicia, who was artful, manipulative, and exploitive, his naive young ward, on the whole, remained unspoiled, guileless, and unpretentious. However, by nature of her sex, he knew she was capable of using her feminine wiles, hoping to maneuver him as expertly as she did her horse, to attain what she wanted most. After all, she was a woman.

This outing, he deduced, was meant to foster his compassion and earn his sympathy. Having acquired such, when it came time to select a bridegroom, she could count on his being charitable while making his choice. So far, her plan was working. In good conscience, he refused to encumber her with just anyone. The man clearly needed to be one of exceptional quality, willing to place Chandra's interests before his own. Pray that he was able to find such a man, Aleck thought. And with haste. For despite his changed opinion about the land of the Scots, its rugged beauty undeniable, he still longed for his beloved England and all that was familiar. He wanted nothing more than to return home.

The mounts finally reached level ground and were allowed full rein. In a quick gallop, the horses headed toward the shoreline, stopping at the water's edge. Aleck slid from his saddle, his boots striking the stones that littered the area. Reaching up, his long fingers spanned Chandra's small waist. "Brace yourself," he said.

As he swung her around, her doeskin-clad feet settling on the ground, he found her weight was slight. Soft yet firm, the Lady Lochlaigh did not lend herself to simple idleness, allowing others to wait on her as did the women at court. From all that he'd seen or heard about his ward over these past several days, he knew she was one to work diligently beside her clansmen. No task was too monumental or too paltry for her. Staring down into her upturned face, his gaze traced the line of her jaw; Aleck attributed her tenacious spirit to unadulterated stubbornness. She was Scot through and through.

Thinking of her faceless bridegroom, Aleck pitied the man, whoever he was. No male could ever best her. Should he try, whether by broom or by sword, he'd go down to immediate defeat. He imagined the newly wedded pair meshed in battle, the man's face inexplicably having become a replica of his own; a smile claimed Aleck's lips.

"Your mind has conjured waggish thoughts, I see," she said, her hands falling away from his shoulders where they'd rested. Their hard, corded strength was not lost on her. "Am I the source of your mirth?"

While the horses were allowed to drink, Aleck and Chandra strolled along the loch's edge. Crystalline water lapped gently against the shoreline. " 'Twould be best if I declined to answer," he said, fighting back his grin.

"Then you do laugh at me," she accused, but without malice.

"Not you, milady. 'Twas thoughts of your bridegroom that made me smile."

Her mood grew uneasy; she studied him closely. "By the look on your face, I'd say you've cast me as a shrew. Undoubtedly you are laughing because you believe the man will suffer."

At mention of the word *bridegroom,* Aleck noticed that the bright sparkle in her wondrous eyes had quickly grown dim. The thought of being forced to wed troubled her greatly. "The term never crossed my mind," he avowed softly. "Stubborn, yes, but never a shrew. If I laugh, it is because I doubt there is a man on your list who can tame you, not that he should try. In mind and in spirit, you are a strong woman, Chandra Morgan, and you need a man equally as strong, so that he might enrich your life. Were he any less, he'd destroy you, slowly and surely. Do you think I'll find such a man for you?"

Chandra felt a weight lift from her. The Englishman seemed most sympathetic, his concern for her welfare nearly equal to her own. Devin would be delighted to learn that at least one part of their plan had worked. As for the rest, she knew her guardian would not find a decent bridegroom in the lot. "I cannot say," she fibbed, feeling a bit guilty. She knew not why the lie bothered her, especially when it was her future that was threatened, but it did. "I suppose we shall have to wait and see."

"I suppose we shall," he said, a gentle smile on his lips. His easy stride slowed to a halt. So did Chandra's. "Know this, milady. I plan to take pity on you. Instead of choosing the first man who meets James's criteria, I shall be most selective. I cannot ignore my king's requirements, but I assure you, your bridegroom will be someone whom you can abide, perhaps even learn to love. With luck, he'll be every bit the man I proposed he should be." A captivating smile lighted Chandra's whole face; Aleck's breath caught in his chest. For some reason, his ward played havoc with his emotions, something no woman had ever done before. Angered that he'd lost his composure again, he sought to destroy her pleasure. "I see you are gladdened that your scheme has worked."

Chandra sobered. "Scheme?" she asked warily, heeding his wry expression, wondering how much he knew. "I—I do not know what you mean."

Aleck noted that her eyes refused to hold his. "You evade the truth."

"Are you accusing me of dealing with you falsely?"

"You have schemed, both you and your cousin. You've had your heads together from the moment of my arrival, and more notably since you read James's letter. I am not so much the fool as to believe your sudden change in attitude is not fueled by selfish need. If such a transformation had not promised to benefit you, I doubt it would have come about. You would still be thinking of ways to cause me embarrassment. My question is: Since I have vowed to be selective when choosing a husband for you, will you again treat me with the same discourtesy and insolence as before?"

Chandra had promised herself that she'd remain polite, but his words managed to fuel her anger. "You deserved what you got," she stated, caring little if her whole plan came to ruin. "You were arrogant and brash."

"And you were impolite and unfeeling."

"You provoked it," she defended herself. "On the way to the castle, did you not sit high upon your horse and look down on me in a superior fashion? Did you not belittle and tease me as though I were some slattern whom you could easily bed at a toss of a coin? You might think to excuse yourself because you did not know my identity at the time, but no woman, whether peasant or queen, should be treated in such a patronizing manner by any man. That, milord, is why you were made to sit in the rain."

Trapped by her impeaching stare, Aleck appreciated the truth of her words. Having lately spent most of his time at court, he'd grown nearly as satyric as his peers. His manners and morals were lacking, he knew. He'd intended to reverse his ways, unhappy with what he'd become. That's why he'd gone back to Montbourne and the north of England. Perhaps the time had come for him to enact that change.

His face reflected his guilt. It was his turn to look away. "I beg your forgiveness for my repulsive behavior," he said, inspecting the toes of his boots. A moment later he recaptured her gaze. "My actions toward you were vile, base. As you have said, no woman deserves to be treated in such a lewd manner, whatever her circumstances."

"You have not treated the rest of my people much better."

"No, I have not," he admitted. "I must confess, by way of the stories I had heard about the Highlanders, I had anticipated the clan Morgan as being a savage lot, ill-bred and with few morals." He fell silent, knowing on that point he should be the last to judge others. "I even pictured the whole of you running naked through these hills," he continued. " 'Twas ill-conceived of me to draw such conclusions based solely on the tales spread by my countrymen. That in no way excuses my actions, but I want you to know: I had no desire to come here. It was ordered of me, and because of that, my mood had grown exceedingly ugly. As I rode north, my belligerence escalated with each passing mile. Hence my reprehensible conduct all around. The arrogant and brash boor whom you first met is not in reality the true me."

"Who are you, then?" she asked, again following the water's edge.

Aleck strolled alongside her. "An Englishman of noble birth who is usually quite amicable, yet wishes he'd not been summoned to duty by his king."

"You take great pride in your heritage. I suppose, because of it, you think you are a man without flaw?"

Aleck chuckled. "Being English does not make me perfect. You have already witnessed a few of my more disagreeable traits."

"Are there others?" she asked incredulously, stopping in her tracks.

Her wide-eyed stare drew a quick smile from Aleck as he came to a standstill beside her. "Yes, there is one other. My temper, when aroused, is highly volatile. Its thrust is something no one would wish to bear."

"Much like a tempest," she commented.

"Far worse," he conceded.

"I shall heed your warning," she said, and then

thought of the list. Pray, she implored silently, should he ever learn what she and Devin had devised, that he could see the humor of it. In no way did she wish to feel the force of his fury. Even if he were to unearth their deception and the truth provoked his anger, she felt certain no harm would come to her. Like a cocoon spun tightly around a newly forming butterfly, her clansmen would gather close to her, offering their protection. Knowing she had nothing to fear, Chandra relaxed; briefly she looked out over the water.

"Your concepts about us were not entirely wrong," she said, hoping to ease the tension between them and form a new rapport. "In battle, sometimes the men strip from their plaids and *léines.*" The word seemed to confuse him. "Their saffron shirts, as you call them," she explained. "Less encumbered, they can fight more freely. So, you see, you were not entirely wrong. Highlanders do run naked through these hills. 'Tis a fierce sight to behold."

Envisioning his countrymen encountering such a spectacle, the look on their bewildered faces quickly turning to one of alarm, Aleck could not help laughing aloud. Seeing his ward's quick frown, he waved her off. "'Tis not your Highland warriors whom I laugh about, but my English brethren. I know now why they have maligned the Scots as they have."

"Why?"

"The English fight by strict rules, facing their opponents head-on—in gentlemanly fashion, as it were. As to why anyone would term it such, I have not an inkling. War is a vicious slaughter—uncivil, abhorrent, and repugnant. There is nothing gentle about it."

"I agree," Chandra said. "But what does that have to do with maligning the Highland Scots?"

"Cannot you imagine the reaction of these alleged English gentlemen, who are avowed to conform to a high standard of correctness no matter the circumstance, as they confronted your naked kinsmen in the heat of battle?"

"I suppose many ran from the field."

"Precisely. Hence in their embarrassment over their failure to remain at their posts, they have termed your people savage, barbaric. I admit that I have said the same. My words, however, came not from personal experience, but hearsay. It was wrong of me to repeat them without first searching out the truth."

"Yes, it was. I suppose in some instances we are much the same. I had never met a Sas—an Englishman before," she corrected, "but I, too, have maligned your kinsmen, simply by virtue of what I've been told."

Aleck's eyebrow rose in query. "Would you care to share any of your epithets?"

"I think not," she said, observing her feet as she walked on. "I am a lady of the peerage and chieftain to my clan. It would not be proper to repeat such inelegant words aloud."

Her guardian's deep laughter filled the air. "But I suppose you still intend to use them under your breath, correct?"

"Perhaps," she said, peering up at him. "But only when provoked." Aleck's laughter subsided, and they walked in silence for a moment. "You should be made aware that the Scots are usually a generous lot, friendly and caring," she said. "But considering the history between our two nations, we are naturally suspicious." She stopped and looked up at him, Aleck drawing up beside her. "I wish to keep peace between us. As chieftain, my clan will follow my directives. But you should know there are those who do not agree with me."

"Your uncle," he stated, and saw her nod. "His hatred of the English is apparent. I doubt you will ever change his mind."

"He is of the old thought that the Highland clans should be allowed to practice self-rule. He bristles at the least mention of James or the Crown. That is why he has reacted the way he has to your being here—that, and because you are English."

"What was your father's position on this?" he asked with true interest. Already aware of some of the clan Morgan's history by way of James's letter, Aleck wished to hear his ward's own account. With luck, it might give him some insight as to what he faced, both from her and from the militant Cedric. "Did he think the same as your uncle?"

"A long time ago, when he was younger, he felt much the same. But his thoughts slowly changed over the years. He became weary of the warring, the destruction, but most of all of the loss of human life. As you know, if the Highlanders were not fighting the English, they were fighting against their king, and when they tired of that they fought each other. My father had grown impatient with the continuous slaughter. He desired peace. When the clan chiefs were taken at Mull, he was among those imprisoned. After nearly a year, he was also among the first released, having sworn fealty to our king. Had James been aware of my father's feelings—that he wanted nothing more than to put an end to the unrest—my father might have been released on his capture. On his return, all seemed to be remedied, the majority of the clan elders supporting his stand. Then, barely six months later, he d-died."

Aleck heard the catch in her voice, saw the sheen of tears in her eyes. That she still grieved for her sire was most apparent. Oddly, his heart ached for her. His hand captured her arm, and as his long fingers pressed gently, he said: "I am saddened that you have suffered such a loss. My parents, first one, then the other, have also passed from this life. I shall always miss them, but the great sorrow I first felt is not as weighty as it once was. Time will eventually ease the heaviness in your heart, fond memories taking its place. Know it is so."

"Then you no longer have any family?" she asked.

The look in Aleck's eyes grew distant; then he appeared to return to the present. "None to speak of," he replied. "I was an only child. I am alone." The wind skimmed across the loch; Chandra's hair whipped across her face. Reaching out to smooth the strands away from her eyes, Aleck smiled tenderly at her. "Do not fret, little one. Joy will one day fill your heart again. I promise."

As she settled the errant tresses behind her shoulder once more, his hand fell away. Their gazes held for an indefinite length of time, and Chandra could not help but feel an irrefutable comradeship with this man. His caring manner at first surprised her; then, realizing his concern was genuine, she felt comforted. By blood, they were meant to oppose one another, but by virtue of their mutual loss, they were now closely linked. Few could understand such a bond, not unless they were similar souls, as most certainly were Chandra and Aleck. "From experience, I know what you say is true. Yet it seems far worse this time than it did the first."

"Then your mother is also deceased?" he asked, certain of it, for he would surely have met the woman if she lived.

"Aye," Chandra whispered. "She died when I was four. I do not remember her very well, except that she was soft-voiced and that her hair was the same as mine. Her laughter is what I remember most, always light and gay. My father said I was the exact image of her. 'Twas so long ago, I do not recall her face. She died in childbirth —my brother was stillborn."

"Naturally, you became quite close to your father," he stated.

"Aye. Quite close."

"His death—had he been in poor health?" he asked,

thinking that if she talked about her father, it might allay some of her grief.

"No. He was very stout and hale. That is why I cannot accept that he is gone. He'd never been ill a day in his life. Not until his last." She stared out over the loch, remembering the day as though it were yesterday. "He'd finished his midday meal and the two of us climbed the steps leading to his chamber. Near the top, he grew light-headed and clutched the wall for fear he'd fall. Several clansmen helped me get him to his bed, where he complained of a dry mouth and burning stomach. His thirst was intense. It would not be quenched. Then he became violently ill and cursed the meat he'd eaten. 'Twas not long after that his talk began to ramble. He suffered delusions, insisting that my mother was in the room, telling her he'd soon be joining her. In his last lucid moment, he called for the elders and named me as his successor. An hour later, he fell into a deep sleep. By midnight, he was gone."

A frown wrinkled Aleck's brow. "Did anyone else become ill?"

Chandra's attention swung toward Aleck. "Several, but not nearly as ill as my father. They all survived."

"Was your uncle among them?"

"Yes, but the poisoning did not affect him as badly as the rest. Why do you ask?"

Poisoning was right, Aleck thought, but it did not come from a tainted piece of meat that had been hung overly long. Belladonna, he decided, knowing the symptoms. In England, deadly nightshade, as it was termed, grew in forests, meadows, and wastelands, having once been cultivated in gardens. Children had died from eating as few as three berries; men and women had been poisoned by ingesting rabbits or birds that had fed on the same. It was possible that the game had been contaminated by such, but why had Chandra's father died when everyone else had recovered? "I was merely curious," he said, keeping his suspicions to himself. "Were you expecting to be named his successor? Does the title not usually go to a male?"

"Our laws of selection are based on tanistry. There were no male heirs." She saw he was confused. "If you are thinking of Devin or Cedric, I should explain. We are not all closely related and simply use the name Morgan to avoid confusion. Devin is my third cousin once removed, and my uncle is my father's brother only by half. They did not share the same great-grandfather, grandfather, or the same father. Shortly after my grandfather died, my grandmother remarried. Cedric is a product of that marriage—there was nearly twenty years' difference between Cedric and my father—and he holds no claim to the title because he's not in the line of direct male descendants. Each of my ancestors, from my great-great-grandfather down to my father, had one heir. All were sons, except for me. Through Tanistry, any male who is of the strength, age, and character, and who shares the same great-grandfather who was at one time chief, could bid for the title. In this case, no one can claim such a right, except me."

Aleck chuckled. "But you are obviously not male."

Under his masculine appraisal, Chandra felt the heat rush to her cheeks. Nervously she looked away. "No, I am not. Had my brother lived, he would have had the only true claim, but by age he would have been too young. Besides, none of that matters. By right, the chief can designate his own successor, which is what my father did. The clan elders accepted me as chief, as did James." Her gaze regained his. "But our king, it appears, is having second thoughts. He now wishes to saddle me with a husband. Does he think I am too weak to keep the pledge my father made?"

"Did all your clansmen support your appointment as chief?"

"There was some argument as to whether or not a

woman could do the task of a man, but the protests were few."

"But those few might cause the greatest trouble," Aleck countered. "Maybe our king believes—and wisely, I might add—that if The Morgan of Morgan has a strong and loyal man by her side, no one will try to usurp her authority. Hence, your father's pledge is certain to be kept."

Chandra's ire rose. "'Tis male vanity that speaks here. You men are all the same. You fancy a female as being naught but a simpleminded fool, who can do little else but sew her embroidery, tend her garden, and fuss over her hair and clothing. You seek to protect us, believing we are weaklings who swoon at the least little thing. 'Tis a farce, I say."

"By what I've seen at court, I must disagree." Somewhat, he thought, allowing that many of the intrigues played out there were perpetrated by women. They were not all as frail as the masculine gender would like to believe. "Besides," he finished, needing to convince her she needed a husband, "it is a given fact: The gentler sex can in no way compete with a man."

"Perhaps, by raw strength alone, they cannot. But a woman's intelligence is equal to a man's, if not well above it."

"I concede there are many intelligent women, but it is their emotions that make them weak. By their nature alone, they are unable do the job that is meant for a man."

"Have you so readily forgotten your virgin queen?" Chandra asked, feeling her ire rise. "By means of Elizabeth's rule, England has become a power unto itself. Never, in the sum of its history, has your country been held in such awe. 'Twas all because of a woman, too. And I wager that England will not see such reverence again— at least, not until another woman rules."

Aleck considered whether or not he should acquaint

his ward with the fact that over the years, Elizabeth had always sought counsel from a man. Not wishing to continue their argument, he withheld the information. He'd allow her to think what she would. However, there was one thing he wanted to know. "Why is it, little one, your anger has suddenly been cast upon me? I have told you that I do not take any pleasure in being your guardian. The role was commanded of me. I was given little choice."

"Were you given any choice at all?" she asked.

" 'Twas this or the Tower."

"And what is your reward?"

"A dukedom, should I succeed."

Chandra's eyes sparked blue fire. "So," she accused, "despite what you've said, you did have a choice after all."

"I would not call going to the Tower much of an option."

"But you do get a reward, correct?"

" 'Twas stated I would."

Throwing up her hands, Chandra stomped off toward the horses. Stunned, Aleck looked after her, then quickly strode in her direction.

"What is your point?" he asked, catching her arm.

She spun toward him. "My point is, I have been given no choice at all. No reward awaits me. Regardless of her title, regardless of her circumstance, unless she is queen, a woman is always at the mercy of a man. She is treated as though she were chattel—a possession, a slave. She's told what to do and when to do it. Her own desires are of no concern. Simply because James thinks I am weak, I'll be forced to wed. He has not come here himself to see if his fears are well-founded. No, it is because I am a woman that he assumes it is so—that the clan Morgan is in turmoil."

"Our king's fears *are* well-founded," Aleck insisted, thinking of Cedric and those who followed him. "Else he would not have sent me. All you have to do is look around you to see maliciousness spawning within the midst of the clan. Alone, you will not be able to quell its growth. Whether by cunning or by force, only a man has the power to stop it."

Incensed that he thought her powerless, that he believed her clansmen would turn on her as would a rabid hound, Chandra attempted to twist free of his hold. "Loose me," she hissed when his grip remained fast.

"First, you'll hear me out." Her sharp nails dug into his flesh; clenching his jaw, Aleck felt his own anger burgeon. He propelled her toward the horses. Stubborn wench! he silently pronounced, for she refused to believe anything he said. More than ever, he did not wish to become embroiled in the clan Morgan's intrigues. Her husband could expose the treachery and stem the revolt. He was going back to England. "Let me repeat: Our king's fears are well-founded. But that is of little importance. When James has issued an order, whether it be to a man or to a woman, one had better comply, or risk finding oneself without a head. I am in no way eager to go to the block, and I'd hope neither are you."

They reached their mounts, and Aleck tossed the mare's reins to his ward. Anger smoldered inside Chandra, but wisely she kept silent. She'd known this day would end in disaster, and it had. After they were astride the horses, her guardian studied her long and hard.

"By our king's behest, I have a function to perform," he said, "and so do you. I have promised to find you a good husband, and that I will. But be assured, Chandra Morgan, by month's end you shall be wedded. You'll not escape your fate. Is that understood?"

Her jaw clamped tightly, her gaze raked over his face. Then, with a rebellious toss of her head, she spurred the mare into a gallop, heading toward the base of the hill and the narrow path leading up it. Hooves beat a quick tattoo as the refrain of the old legend whirled through her mind:

Ladybird, ladybird, flee, else the winged hunter transform your destiny. Ladybird, ladybird, fly, sweep to the heavens ever so high . . .

Were she simply a bird, she thought, indignant tears blinding her eyes, she'd fly far, far away, where it was safe.

Blinking hard, Chandra guided the mare upward to the top of the brae, then again pushed her mount into a gallop, aiming them toward home. She cared little if the Sassenach was left way behind or got lost altogether. The man understood nothing about her or what she needed —his pity be damned! Her sights set on the distant castle, she heard the powerful tread of her guardian's stallion coming up behind her. Horse and rider edged ever closer, and she urged her mare to go faster, wanting only to be free of him.

All at once, her gaze shot to the sky. There, high above the Morgan stronghold, soared the hawk. Round and round it circled, searching relentlessly.

You'll not escape your fate.

Chapter
6

From where Aleck sat at the head table in the great hall, he viewed the multitude of male guests who had begun invading Lochlaigh Castle nearly a week ago. The number had expanded to at least three dozen beyond those on his ward's list, which, thank goodness, he'd cut by half. As he stared at the group, Aleck wondered if there was even one among them who would satisfy James's requirements. So far, of the nearly fivescore interviewed, all had failed.

Sighing, he knew he should get on with his task, but after each interrogation it took more and more effort. By the end of the first day, he'd already grown weary of listening to these Highland cocks crow about their alleged merits—none of which could be substantiated, in Aleck's view. Yet each had insisted he was the best man possible and should be chosen as the Lady Lochlaigh's lifelong mate. Not one seemed worthy of his ward, being either too weak or too domineering, too closefisted or too much the spendthrift, too gruff in manners or too foppish. To Aleck, in one way or the other, they were all flawed. And not one, it had soon become apparent, was loyal to James. Multiplying the continuous line of applicants by six long, tedious days, Aleck understood why he was in such a sullen mood.

A list of names had been drawn from the new arrivals at Lochlaigh Castle. As Aleck studied it, he saw he had reached number one hundred of the one hundred forty who were bidding for Chandra's hand in marriage. Another full day of this and he was certain to go insane. "Sir John, please escort the next man forward."

While he waited, Aleck's fingers unknowingly drummed the table. He watched as the knight approached a large man with russet hair. Separating himself from the milling crowd, the man followed Sir John to the fore of the room; Aleck scrutinized him carefully. From beneath his belted plaid protruded thickset legs covered by red fur pelts. On closer inspection, Aleck discerned it was the man's own hair. The thick, wiry stuff even sprouted from the caps of his knees.

Distantly he envisioned his ward's shapely limbs entwined with the ones that marched toward him, and the quill in his hand immediately marked an X next to the man's name. Realizing what he'd done, Aleck scratched it out, reminding himself that he needed to be objective. Then the man was facing him.

"Gavin MacElroy of the Clan Elroy," the man introduced himself, sitting in the chair opposite Aleck. The newcomer leaned forward, propping his arm on the table. "'Twould be best for both of us were we to get on with it. This waiting has near driven me mad."

Aleck opened his mouth, intending to present himself and start the questioning, but the man rambled on. His jaw sprang closed, and he stared at MacElroy's features, specifically the large wart that grew at the corner of his nose. The unsightly growth annoyed Aleck; his hand clamped around the quill, nearly snapping it in two, as he forced it away from the parchment, lest he mark it anew.

"I knew her father," Aleck heard him say. "He was a good man, but he'd grown weak in the end. The girl needs a strong hand to guide both her and the clan Morgan. This hand"—he thrust his meaty fist before Aleck's face—"is the one that shall do it. It wields a sword with the force of ten men. No one shall invade this place and live. Aye, with me as her protector, she'll see her clan's power again become what it once was."

"You speak of power and protection, MacElroy," Aleck said. "Do you plan to use your sword solely in the name of our king?"

MacElroy's eyebrows shot up. "James? Pah! He coveted the English throne, and to get it, he played a sly game, slavering to those bastards from the south. He deserted his country and his people. He's a weakling who fancies pretty young men. Peculiar, he is, no man at all. I owe him nothing. No true Highlander does."

Unlike many of the others, this man did not hedge his words. He cared little if what he said gave insult. The man had failed the test within a few short sentences, but Aleck found himself quite interested in MacElroy's views. "You are forthright in your opinions, sir. Most candid, indeed. Tell me, have you always felt this way about James?"

"'Tis well known that I have. His laws and the laws of the Crown are useless to us Highlanders. The ways of the clans are as old as time itself. To survive, we must live by our own law. We will fight to the death to keep what is ours."

A decided insurrectionist, Aleck thought, surveying him for a long moment. "Are there many who believe the same as you?"

"Aye—to one degree or another, nearly everyone in this room. The few who are left bend with the wind, much like a young tree—first this way, then that. They have not the stomach to take a stand." He leaned back in his chair. "Aye, with me as her husband, the Lady Lochlaigh will keep her lands safe. Maybe even claim more."

To one degree or another, Aleck silently repeated, his suspicions rising. His attention turned to the woman who had just entered the room. Her long, flame-red hair flowed down her back, swinging gently against the curve of her slender hips. The Morgan plaid was draped over one linen-covered shoulder and belted at her tiny waist, its tails clinging to her soft blue woolen skirt. Doeskin boots covered her small feet. "And the Lady Lochlaigh, what do you have planned for her?" Aleck asked, still staring at Chandra.

"Why, I'd keep her with child, naturally. We shall have many sons—warriors all—to carry on the fight. One day, the eldest will be named chief." MacElroy leaned forward again. "The girl is quite bonny. A tempting little thing. 'Twould be highly enjoyable to lie with her on the long, frosty nights through the winter ahead. Once we're wedded, I'll bed her within the hour." He chuckled. "No sense in delaying my pleasure. Who knows? My seed might meet its mark. A son could result from our first joining."

Under the pressure of Aleck's hand, the quill suddenly disintegrated into several pieces. The thing still clutched firmly in his grip, he met MacElroy's eyes. "You have enlightened me on many things, sir. For that, I thank you. You may take your leave. When I have come to a decision, the whole of you will be informed."

With a quick nod, the Highlander got up and strode toward the group that now surrounded the Lady Lochlaigh. Greeting her suitors, for it was the first she'd seen of them this day, she smiled brightly, offering each one her hand. Aleck studied her intently.

"It does not go well, does it?" Sir John said near the earl's ear.

"No, it does not." Taking hold of what was left of the

quill, he plunged the stubby tip into the ink, then struck MacElroy's name from the parchment altogether. Chandra's laughter erupted into the air; Aleck's eyes were drawn to her again. "For one who insists that she'll not be made to wed, her spirits seem extremely gay. Especially when she's in the midst of those who have offered for her." He studied her more closely. "Sir John, tell the Lady Lochlaigh that I wish to speak to her in private. I shall await her in her antechamber."

With that, Aleck rose from the table. He headed toward the stairs, his hard strides crushing the herbal grasses strewing the stone floor; a sweet fragrance wafted into the air. His nostrils were flared, but the Earl of Montbourne did not notice the normally soothing scent. He was far too busy trying to control his temper.

"What do you think he wants?" Devin asked, trailing Chandra up the stairs.

"Maybe he's grown weary of his interviews and wishes to inform me that he is leaving for England while it is still daylight."

"Do you truly believe that?"

"I can only pray it is so." They had reached the door of her antechamber, and Chandra turned to her cousin. So gentle a spirit, she thought, looking into his doe brown eyes. Without knowing why, she rose on tiptoes and kissed his cheek; then her hand caressed the area where her lips had settled. "Wait for me here," she whispered. "He has ordered me to come alone."

Devin captured her hand as it started to fall from his cheek. He lightly kissed her palm. "I hope, Chandra, that your lord of legend will be forever kind to you," he said, then smiled softly.

A small frown creased her brow. Lord of legend. She had never thought of him as such, but she supposed the term was correct. "Why do you say 'forever'?"

"As in the old myth, you seem to believe he has the

power to change the course of your destiny. If so, your future is in his hands. I hope that whatever happens, all your tomorrows will be happy ones." Gently he squeezed her hand. "Now, go. Don't be afraid of this winged hunter. For all his fierceness, he might actually be a dove."

Chandra smiled up at Devin, then turned and faced the door. Smoothing her hand over the length of Morgan plaid resting against her skirt, she squared her shoulders. With a twist of her wrist, the latch was released; she entered the room.

"Close it," Aleck said coldly, nodding toward the door. Startled by his tone his ward merely stared at him. "I said close it."

While the heavy panel swung to, the latch clicking into place, Chandra assessed her guardian. His taut backside leaned against the sturdy oak table. His muscular legs were outstretched, his feet crossed at the ankles. Arms folded over his jerkin-covered chest, he did not move. Knowing his mood was grim, she kept her position by the door. "Y-you asked to see me?"

"Come hither," he commanded.

His voice was much like the thick frost that covered the Highland moors in winter; Chandra hesitated. Trouble brewed, she was certain. Then, as she eyed him, a determination rose inside her. She'd not show this man any fear. Slowly she walked toward him.

"Closer," Aleck ordered when she stopped several yards away. "Stand at my feet."

Defiantly she tilted her chin. "I am near enough. Say what it is you have to say."

"Come closer, I said. Or has the Lady Lochlaigh suddenly become a coward?"

"Safety dictates that I stay here," she said, noting the small tic pulsating along his clamped jaw.

Hard eyes bored into her. "Safety dictates that you obey me. Do as I've commanded."

Chandra refused to move. "'Twould be better for us both if I do not."

A cold smile crossed his lips. "I take it that you fear me. Is there a reason you should?"

"N-no," she lied, suddenly certain he'd discovered the truth about the list.

"Then obey me and come hither."

A myriad of thoughts raced through Chandra's mind. She was far closer to him than she was to the door. In two strides he could be upon her. Devin stood outside in the hall. Alerted by her scream, her cousin would most likely rush to her aid. But he was no match for the Sassenach, especially in his weakened condition. Devin knew that, too. Should he sound the alarm, calling out for Cedric, a bloodbath was certain to follow. Neither she nor the Sassenach could risk such an event, their king's ire falling on them both, were they to survive. Yet, in the end, the clan Morgan was bound to suffer the worst of it. For by James's own hand, the Sassenach had been appointed her guardian, and she was expected to obey him. There was no way around it. She must comply.

Slowly Chandra moved to the spot that he'd indicated. The spark of defiance flickered in her eyes. "I obey you only to avoid trouble."

His stare was frigid. "I'm afraid it is too late for that." He watched for a reaction; her chin tipped higher, nothing more. Stubborn, she was. And foolish, Aleck decided. For despite his calm appearance, his temper was simmering. "You know why I've sent for you, don't you?"

Chandra felt her knees quiver. Why didn't she just confess the truth and take her punishment, whatever it was? "I have not the ability to know what is in your mind," she said evenly, evading his question as best she could.

"Oh, but I believe you do."

The thought of his anger descending on her frightened

her. But deep inside, something else frightened her even more. Something she'd refused to think about from the moment it had occurred. Memories of this very room spun through her head. She'd been alone with him then, too. Pray it did not happen again, she pleaded silently, wishing she were anywhere but here. "You speak in riddles," she said, surprised by the steadiness of her voice. She turned aside, needing to be away from him. "I have no time to play such silly games."

Aleck's feet hit the floor; catching her shoulders, he spun her around. Stunned, she gazed up at his face, then at his lips. A curious emotion quaked through her. Distantly she recognized that the feeling lay somewhere between wonderment and dread.

"'Tis no game I play, Chandra. It is you who are the riddle. After I promised to keep your needs in mind, it amazes me that you would again play me false. But no more, milady. I'll not play the fool another time. Tell me, what punishment shall I give you?" Her head shook slightly. To Aleck, it appeared as though she were denying any wrongdoing. A sardonic smile touched his lips. "Perhaps I should give you to the one who constantly scratches his head as though a nest of vermin have taken up residence in his hair—MacGarron, isn't it? Or maybe you'll better enjoy that malcontent MacElroy—the one with the hairy legs and the wart by his nose. He's very forthright. I was enlightened by much of what he had to say. Did you know he intends to keep you with child, much as though you were a brood mare? He purposes also to bed you within an hour of your nuptials. Said he didn't want to delay his pleasure. Maybe I'll stay just long enough to see if it is done."

At the thought of MacElroy's touch, Chandra felt nauseated. She could never tolerate the man—not now, not in the past. Certainly not in the future! Commanding her stomach to behave, she gathered her strength and glared up at her guardian. "James will not allow such a marriage. Not to MacElroy—not to any of them. Not one of them measures . . ."

"Measures up? That's why you invited them to Lochlaigh Castle, isn't it? You knew they'd not pass the test." Chandra tried to break free of his hold, but Aleck refused to release her. Propelled by fear, she aimed a kick at his shin. Cursing, he jerked her fully against him. The touch of her body sent a prurient energy sparking inside him; it flamed through him as she continued struggling. "By fighting me, you do naught but fuel my anger," he grated, knowing she fueled his passion as well. Desperately he tried to quell his heated lust. "Be still or you'll be caught in its tempest," he ordered, wondering to which emotion he actually referred.

The strange energy had sparked inside Chandra also. Uncertain of its meaning or what might result, she quieted. "Release me . . . please."

As her forlorn words flowed into his ears, his gaze remained affixed to her supple mouth. Her full lower lip teased him, taunted him. Closing his eyes, he drew what he thought was a steadying breath, then relaxed his grip and opened them again. So tempting, he thought, viewing her lips again. Reflexively his fingers crushed her shoulders. "I rue the day I met you, Morgan Morgan. I swear you are naught but a bedeviling little witch."

Chandra felt herself being pulled closer to him. Her hands pressed against his firm, flat stomach, frantically trying to keep him away. The heat from his hard body radiated up her arms. Then his head descended slowly, pliant lips parted and moist. Not again, she thought, her heart hammering wildly. "No!" she cried, twisting against his hold. He seemed not to hear her. "James will punish you for this."

"Punish me?" Aleck whispered just above her enticing mouth. "'Tis you who have mocked not only me, but our king. James will not begrudge me this. Because I am English, you despise my touch. Were I a Scot, would it still be the same? Whose kisses would you prefer, my sweet enchantress? MacElroy's or mine?"

"Neither," she blurted, knowing far and away it would be her guardian's. But she'd die rather than admit it.

One hand moved from her shoulder to clasp her jaw. "You speak falsely, little one," he accused, his hot, clean breath fanning her face, "just as you always do. Were you a child, I'd sprinkle bitter herbs on your tongue. But you are a woman, and there is another way to still your lies." His thumb lightly caressed the curve of her lips. "Believe me, it is sweeter by far."

"No!" Chandra cried again. The word was but an agonized groan. "Do not do this."

"Far sweeter," Aleck insisted, before his lips trapped hers. Chandra stood frozen, her mouth held in a rigid line, but Aleck was not deterred. Hot and moist, the tip of his tongue played along the softness of her lower lip, his thumb pressing lightly on her chin. "Open to me," he rasped; then he drew back slightly to look into her eyes. Mutiny evinced itself in her gaze. "Damn your stubborn Highland pride." He caught hold of her hair, and with a quick yank, her head fell back. He pulled harder, and her lips parted on a gasp; Aleck saw his chance. Insanity, he thought, just as his eager mouth swooped, covering hers fully.

The tempest was upon her, and as his experienced lips foraged hers—first hard and angry, then soft and teasing —Chandra felt herself buffeted by the force of his masculinity. Her whole body quaked under his mastery, expert that he was. His tongue broke the barrier of her lips, lightly thrusting and withdrawing, and she felt her head spin crazily. Fingers curling into the smooth leather covering his taut belly, she clung to him, fearing she might be swept away. But to where? she wondered distantly.

Frightened by the surge of emotions rioting through

her, all of them new, she fought to regain her senses. His intimacy was not an act of tenderness or love, but was meant as punishment for her disobedience. By way of his kiss, he chastised her for tricking him again. She was hot inside and out. She burned as though she'd been set afire. He'd called her a bedeviling witch, and she pictured a stake, a young woman lashed to it, flames licking up around her. Suddenly Chandra was certain he had the power to destroy her. A small whimper escaped her throat, flowing into his mouth.

The tiny sound registered somewhere in Aleck's brain. His lips sluiced across the soft curve of her cheek, stopping to play at her ear, as his hand slid the length of her spine. "You suffer no more than I," he whispered, his hand finding the enticing roundness of her firm bottom. Fingers splayed, he urged her to him. "This is my agony, little one. And there's only one way to ease the pain. Too bad you cannot have a lover before you wed. 'Twould be nice for you to enjoy what is shared between a man and a woman, at least once. I could show you what ecstasy really is, and you could give me the remedy I seek."

Stunned by his words, then immediately enraged, Chandra sputtered up at him, "You—you—"

Aleck grinned. One finger fell across her lips, silencing her. "Although it will be wasted on MacElroy, you must go to your husband a virgin," he said, then watched as her eyes widened. "Of course, there are other ways for us to gain our pleasures, and the man will be none the wiser." His hand moved. Fingertips stroked the nape of her neck, his thumb brushing along the line of her jaw. "What say you, little one? Shall we seek the forbidden?"

Staring up at him, Chandra realized that he mocked her, baited her, while laughing at her silently. "English bastard," she said through her teeth. "You speak with the serpent's tongue. Just because I am woman does not mean I'm as naive as was Eve."

Aleck arched an eyebrow. "First it is lies, now it is profanity," he said. "I see you have yet to learn your lesson. Alas, another kiss it will be."

"No!" Chandra shrieked. The word had barely left her mouth when the door crashed to the wall; Aleck's attention snapped toward the sound and he tensed.

There in the opening stood Devin and Cedric, a dozen men at their backs. "Lowland bastard," Cedric denounced, his eyes flinty and cold. "Do you mean to ruin her before she is wedded?"

Aleck knew the situation boded ill. His one hand held her face, the other pressed against the curve of her womanly hips, while his ward's virginal body touched his fully. Insanity, he thought again, knowing that the real madness was about to begin. And he had brought it on himself. "She is still pure," he said, hoping to allay Cedric's temper. "Naught has happened here of great consequence. That is the truth."

A vehement curse rolled from the man's lips as the sound of steel ripping against steel pierced the air. His claymore drawn, Cedric growled, "Make ready to die, Sassenach."

Grabbing Chandra's arm, Aleck swung her around as he stepped free of the table, then shoved her behind him. "Get back," he ordered as he freed his own sword from its sheathe, its point aiming at the tip of the claymore, ready to deflect its charge. "Keep out of the way." Then to her uncle he said, "You fight needlessly, Highlander. Your niece is untouched."

"Not from what I saw, Sassenach."

"Stop it," Chandra ordered, rushing forward, intending to step between the pair. At the same moment, Devin leapt between the already shifting swords, fearing for Chandra's life. As though time barely moved, she watched in horror as her guardian's blade impaled her cousin. *"Devin!"* she screamed, the life seeming to drain from her own body.

His name resounded through the small room, and Devin reached out to Chandra. "Cousin?" He staggered, a look of disbelief on his face. It quickly changed to one of sorrow, then one of resignation. "Don't fret, Chandra. 'Tis easier this way," he stated, his hand groping for hers.

Chandra barely caught it when his eyes rolled back. Devin fell away from the blade and crumpled to the floor. "Mother of God, no!" she cried, dropping to her knees beside him. Her shaking fingers smoothed the side of his face. So cherubic, she thought, noting how the lines of strain caused by his illness slowly faded away. In a twinkling, she remembered every moment they'd shared together, every tender smile he'd bestowed on her, every gentle touch of his hand, including his last. "Why, Devin? Why?" she questioned on a sob.

Aleck stood frozen. Intent on deflecting the oncoming blade, he'd reacted from instinct, to save his own life. But Chandra's cousin had bounded into his sword's path, and he could not stop the blade's thrust. Seeing his ward kneeling a yard from his feet, eyeing the blood-soaked tunic of her cousin, Aleck looked to Cedric. His own death was imminent, Aleck knew. So were his men's. In a trice, he grabbed hold of Chandra, jerking her up in front of him. The edge of his sword pressed just below her breasts as he held her against his body. "Back away," he ordered, "or your chieftain will suffer a similar fate." Aleck saw that Cedric stood fast, and the pressure of the blade increased. Cold steel cut through Chandra's tunic. Aleck heard her gasp. "Back away," he repeated, his voice glacial. "Let us pass."

"He means to kill her," Angus said from behind Cedric, having heard Aleck's words. "Clear the hall. Let the Sassenach pass." A hand clamped onto Cedric's shoulder. "Do ye want yer niece dead?" Cedric did not answer. "If ye remain stubborn, know ye will not live to see her buried," the man warned. "Step away and let them pass."

Aleck watched as Chandra's uncle backed out into the corridor. "Don't cause me any trouble, little one," he said near Chandra's ear. "No harm will come to you if you do as I say. Now, walk ahead."

Still in shock, Chandra had not taken her eyes from her cousin's lifeless form. Her throat was paralyzed, as were her limbs. Other than the gasp that had fled her lips, she remained dazed. *Not Devin!* her mind screamed over and over. The arm clamped at her waist lifted her and urged her forward. Wide-eyed, she stared at her cousin. Then Aleck and she broke into the hall; she blinked. "Loose me," she commanded, struggling against his hold, but her strength was outmatched. "Let me go. I'll not leave him."

"Don't fight me, Chandra," Aleck ordered, his sword still close beneath her breasts. "My men and I leave Lochlaigh Castle, and you shall be our protection, for you are our sole means of escape." She refused to move, so Aleck hoisted her fully in one arm. "Get from the hall!" he shouted at the men who blocked his path. "Get down those steps or your mistress will die."

The contingent fled to the stairs, all except Cedric. A dozen yards away, he slowly backed toward the steps, watching for a chance to skewer Aleck. "You'll pay for your treachery, Sassenach," he said, waving the claymore in front of him.

Undaunted, Aleck pushed onward, Chandra held tightly against him. "And you, Highlander, will suffer for your own. The clan Morgan will not forgive you should their leader sustain any harm. Continue to disobey me and soon the carrion eaters will be picking at your bones."

Cedric's foot met the steps; slowly he backed down them. "Steady on your feet, Sassenach," he baited when Aleck came to the stairs. "One slip, and it is your bones that will be picked clean."

Aleck pressed his back to the stones for support as he

started to edge down the steps. Her uncle's words must have registered somewhere in Chandra's fogged mind, for she tried to twist free of his hold. His shoulder bit into the wall, attempting to keep them from falling. Her heels kicked his shins, and with a curse, Aleck pulled her harder against him. Lightning fast, the sword came up mere inches from her neck. "Don't make me injure that lily white throat of yours," he gritted between his teeth. "'Twould be a shame to mar it."

Chandra stared at the shiny blade, Devin's blood smearing it. Overwhelmed by the sight, she went limp. To Aleck, she was far easier to carry when she held herself rigid. Shifting her weight against his hip, he swung the tip of his sword toward Cedric. "Get down those steps—now."

The dozen men who'd preceded Cedric down the steps backed around the corner, coming into full view of all who stood below in the hall; a shout went up. Aleck recognized the voice as Sir John's. Swords rang from their scabbards; then came the sound of running feet, and as Aleck turned the corner himself, still threatening Cedric with the sword's point, he saw the knight and his men clustered at the bottom of the stairs. Some faced him, others faced away, poised and ready for an attack from all sides.

Sir John waved his sword. "Move your Scottish hides off those steps," he ordered to the dozen men who now met him head-on. They scrambled from the stairs. "Set your weapons on that table." Using his sword, he pointed to the one he meant. Metal clanked loudly in the hall as the dozen claymores fell onto the wood. "You too, Highlander," he said to Cedric, then smiled as the surly Cedric tromped down the last four steps and marched to the table, his claymore falling atop the others. "It seems we have a small problem," the knight remarked to Aleck, who was again shifting the load in his arm.

"Aye," Aleck said, his feet finally meeting the level,

grass-strewn floor. Gratitude showed in his eyes, for the knight had assessed the situation and acted swiftly. "We are bound for England, Sir John. Herd the lot of them outside so that they can make ready our mounts."

So, he planned to run, Chandra thought, listening to the exchange, her body held rigid once more. It was useless to fight, and she refused to lose another of her clan to him. James would take care of the bastard, and she prayed his head would roll. "You can release me now," she said, her hands pushing against his arm.

"Not yet, little one. Not until we are free of the gates."

Fearing their chieftain would be injured or killed, all Morgans who stood in the hall relinquished their weapons as ordered. Her suitors did likewise. Then they all paraded out the doors toward the stables. Under guard, the mounts were saddled, meager provisions for each man placed across the pommels in leather bags. When Aleck's steed was brought out and led to his side, his grip tightened around Chandra's waist. His sword still unsheathed, he stepped into the stirrup. The muscles in his leg knotted, then stretched as they bore both his and Chandra's weight, lifting them into the saddle. Chandra's bottom hit the leather, where she was held fast in front of him. Taking hold of the reins, he again pressed the edge of the blade to her middle. "For safety's sake," he muttered. Once all his men were astride their mounts, he called out, "Open the gates."

Slowly the portcullis in the lower bailey drew upward, as did the one in the upper bailey. Passing through the first gate, Aleck eyed the walls as he led his men from the heart of the castle. A bevy of Morgans stood watch, but no one moved. All, it appeared, were unarmed. The group had passed through the second gate, and the mounts were urged into a full gallop, heading south toward England.

Halfway down the hill, they heard a Highland war cry above them. At the eerie sound, Aleck drew his steed to a halt and looked back. The clan Morgan bled through the castle gates, giving chase. Like a rushing river, they streamed down the hill, some with weapons in hand. "Damn," Aleck said, looking at the knight. "'Twas too easy, wasn't it?"

"Aye," Sir John said, a worried frown creasing his brow. "We'd best be moving."

Chandra's wild laughter pealed into the air, and Aleck wondered if she'd gone mad. Pulling her hard against him, he spurred the stallion into a full gallop. To the foot of the hill they rode, then up another, the clan Morgan after them. Arrows flew by the fleeing group, fortunately missing their marks, and Aleck thought the pursuing band would never grow tired. Eyes centered straight ahead on the rugged terrain, he refused to turn round to see if any of them ran naked.

The cries continued down the second hill and up the next. As Aleck and his troop crested its peak, his gaze leapt to the brae across the way; the tension drained from his body. One hundred of James's finest soldiers rode his way. Crashing hooves cut into the mossy soil as the smaller group aimed itself toward the larger. Down, then up again, and the winded mounts finally broke past the friendly line.

Pulling the stallion to a quick halt, Aleck turned to look back the way they'd come. On the opposite hillside, the clan Morgan stood, their war cries erupting into the air. The sound sent a chill down his spine. They were safe, he reassured himself silently. The madness was over.

"Free me," Chandra said, trying to slip from the saddle. "You have escaped."

Aleck's blue eyes settled on her. "I think not, milady. We are not yet away from Scotland. I fear you go to England with us."

Sharp talons aimed at a tender young breast, quick, quick, lest he carry you afar to an alien nest.

The legend! It had come true. All of it. On a defeated moan, her head fell back against Aleck's shoulder; she stared into the distance.

"Chandra?" When she did not answer, concern knitted Aleck's brow. "Little one." He smoothed her tumbled hair from her face. Still she did not respond. He closed his eyes and drew a jagged breath. "Forgive me," he whispered, but he was uncertain if she heard. Cradling her close to him, he nudged his steed forward. "Let us be on our way," he said to Sir John.

"What about the girl?" the knight asked.

"She goes with us."

Aleck turned his horse toward the south. The knight and James's men followed.

Steadily, the group pressed onward. The sun sank low in the sky, then fell beyond the horizon. Night was upon them, but Aleck continued toward his homeland. His thoughts on his ward and her cousin, he cursed himself, berated himself, lashed himself mentally, until his soul was torn to ribbons. In his anger, he'd sought to punish the sweet beauty in his arms. He'd accomplished that— in fact, he'd probably destroyed her. Himself as well.

Momentarily he gazed down at Chandra. Remembering the tortured look on her face as Devin groped for her hand, only to fall away from the blade that had sliced into him, his life slipping from him on a whisper of time, Aleck felt the light ache in his chest explode into excruciating pain.

Damn his own arrogance! Foolishly he had chanced his life and the lives of his men. Stupidly he had tempted fate, knowing that, if caught, the dangerous Cedric would react. Because of it, an innocent man fell. All for what—a kiss? As exhilarating as the sensuous interlude had been, it was not worth the horror that had followed. It was not worth Devin's life, what little there was left. Nor was it worth Chandra's censure. That, he knew, was still to come. He dreaded the moment when her pent-up fury unleashed itself on him. When it did, he would not attempt to escape it.

Sighing, he glanced over as the knight came up beside him. "We need to make camp. The light grows too dim," said Sir John. Seeing Aleck's nod, he rode back to tell the men.

Slowing his stallion, Aleck dropped back among the troop. Soon the group pulled to a halt by an outcropping of rocks that jutted from the moor. The place provided shelter from the cold night winds that blew over the barren landscape. Reining in his steed, Aleck slipped from the saddle and placed his hands around Chandra's waist. She fell toward him like a limp doll. When her feet met the ground, Aleck steadied her.

"You're frozen," he said, his hands on her arms. Pulling her plaid free of her belt, he wrapped its length over the top of her head, draping it around her shoulders. His fingers worked quickly, massaging her arms, trying to get the blood flowing. "There will be a fire soon. You can warm yourself by it."

Flimsy as a rag, her body joggled under the pressure of his ministering hands. They ran along her back, her shoulders, then her arms again. The heat flowed through her, and as the numbness left, the pain returned. Devin, she thought, seeing his face anew. First there was disbelief, then sorrow, and lastly resignation. Slowly her head lifted. Blank eyes stared up at the man who had murdered her cousin. "Take your hands from me," she said, her voice low.

Aleck's hands stopped their movement; he gazed down at her, holding her shoulders. The coldness in Chandra's eyes froze his soul.

Abruptly her fury broke free. *"Murderer!"* she screamed as the flat of her palm struck his face; Aleck didn't flinch. Her other hand rose, striking him twice as hard. Still he remained unmoving. "I hate you!" she cried, then her small fists pummeled his head, his shoulders, his chest, until her anger was spent. "I hate you," she repeated, tears streaming down her face. Overwhelmed by her heartache, Chandra ran to the cover of the rocks, where she sobbed out her grief.

The entire camp had fallen silent, all within its bounds warily witnessing the incident. Even now, only the muffled sounds of Chandra's crying could be heard. As Aleck watched her from afar, he yet felt the sting of her hands. Her anger was merited, and he hadn't tried to deflect the blows. Releasing his long-held breath, he realized that he felt oddly drained.

Sir John hesitantly came to his side. "Should someone go after her?"

"No," he said, keeping a vigil on Chandra. "Let her be."

The knight, Aleck knew, was still unaware of why they had fled Lochlaigh Castle in such a rush. The two had had no time to talk, and Aleck waited for the question that was sure to come.

"The girl—she said—" Sir John cleared his throat uneasily. "What exactly happened that made us run for our lives?"

"I killed her cousin."

Chapter
7

Through the breaks in the trees, the towers of Montbourne Castle loomed in the distance. Having crossed the border between Scotland and England nearly an hour ago, Aleck was relieved to see the familiar edifice. Darkness would soon settle around them, and he much preferred the warmth of his bed to another sleepless night spent on the damp ground. He was thankful to be almost home.

At a steady canter, the huge steed narrowed the distance that separated Aleck from his destination. Turning from the road, he led the procession of men and horses across the well-known terrain, his ward sitting in front of him, fingers gripping the pommel of the saddle. Her rigid young body held itself away from him, as it had since the troop had quit their second camp at dawn. These last two days she'd kept herself isolated from everyone, refusing to speak, refusing to eat, and Aleck was concerned.

He gazed down at her erect head, noting how her long, lustrous hair was tumbled and tangled. The heavy feeling renewed itself in his chest. She hated him, and he could not blame her. He deserved her scorn. Not only had he killed her beloved Devin, but he'd abducted her from her home. The question was: What was he to do with her now? Sighing, he urged his mount into a gallop.

Chandra heard the drone of his breath, then clutched the pommel as the stallion hit a faster stride. She felt Aleck move, then his arm banded her waist. Immediately she tried to pull free.

Dragged hard against him, her shoulders met the solid wall of his chest. "Keep still, Chandra," he ordered above her head. "We've but a mile to go. Try to relax." In defiance, she stiffened further; Aleck sighed again. Stubborn and doltish, he thought. She'd remained inflexible the day long, and she'd surely suffer for it tomorrow. Sore she would be, and all because she abhorred his touch. "Your misery will soon end, little one. Take heart, it won't be long before you are free."

Although Aleck meant something else entirely, Chandra construed his words differently. Eagerly she viewed the huge fortress sitting atop the next hill, relief washing through her. In a short while she'd be riding back toward the border—if he would lend her a horse. If not, she'd walk. It mattered not, just as long as she was headed home.

Aleck felt how she'd relaxed against him; his tight hold on her eased. *Free* was all he'd had to say, and the strain seemed to have flowed from her like a narrow river sweeping into the open sea. Then the thought occurred that she'd misunderstood him. Deciding he'd wait until they were safely inside the castle before he explained what the word *free* really meant, he kept his eyes on the trail, dreading her reaction.

A shout sounded high on the battlement, echoing through the lush green valley below, and as the troop rode the final uphill stretch, the gates to Montbourne Castle were thrown wide. Passing under the portcullis, his ward nestled between his thighs and held securely in his arms, Aleck viewed the many within his household who'd come to greet him, his chief steward at the fore.

"You've returned early, milord," Marlowe said, curiously eyeing Chandra. "'Tis good to have you home."

"Aye, Marlowe. 'Tis good to be home." Aleck looked round behind him. Sir John and the hundred-plus men soon filled the lower bailey. "Make ready some food, Marlowe. The king's men are famished. Afterward prepare the hall so that our guests can bed down. They've had a hard two days' travel and will be staying the night." The chief steward cleared his throat and shifted his head slightly toward Chandra. "The Lady Lochlaigh will be staying indefinitely," Aleck added. "Prepare the room next to mine." Chandra's head whipped around. The light of accusation shone in her eyes. "By free, little one, I meant this." His arms swung away from her, and he dismounted. "Until I decide what to do with you, you will have to remain here," he said, looking up at her. Then he smiled. "Welcome to England and to Montbourne Castle."

Fire erupted in Chandra's breast as hot fury scorched through her veins. "I'd rather be in hell," she said, glaring at him. Before Aleck could react, she grabbed the reins. Her small foot struck out, hitting him square in the jaw; Aleck stumbled back. Urging the steed about, Chandra spurred the beast toward the open gates.

Aleck lunged at the fleeing horse and caught hold. His fingers bit into the leather saddle as he tried to hang on. "Damn you, halt!" he shouted at Chandra, at the stallion, but neither one paid him any heed.

Stunned, James's soldiers watched the abrupt clash. All were frozen in place. Wanting to shake loose Aleck's hold, Chandra guided her mount directly at one of the men, intending to crash into his horse. Attempting to pull himself astride the charging beast, Aleck hovered midway between the saddle and the ground, looking much like a bumbling sot after a long night's worth of drink. Unaware of his appearance or what awaited him, he glanced forward. The impending collision was mere seconds away. Cursing, he released his grip and fell flat into the dirt.

Relief washed through Chandra the instant he let go, and again she aimed for the gate. A cry went up behind her. At Sir John's quick orders, the ranks closed; a line of men on horseback blocked her exit. Reining around, she searched frantically for another way of escape. Her heels struck the steed's flanks, and the two headed for the outer stairs. The stallion passed the steps, and she leapt from his back onto the stones, then ran them, climbing to the battlement.

By now Aleck had found his feet. Halfway across the yard when she'd bounded to the steps, he was already after her. His booted strides echoed off the stones behind her, and raw fear drove Chandra to the top. She reached the wall walk and scurried along it, dodging several guards who'd stood watch. Partway around the battlement, she saw a half dozen men coming toward her from the opposite side. Sir John and the others had taken a second set of stairs and were attempting to cut her off.

Hysteria bubbled inside her, for Aleck and the guards were quick on her heels. Skidding to a halt, she pressed her back against the stone merlon, then eased toward the crenel. From the corner of her eye, she could see the shadowy countryside below. She glanced left, then right at her pursuers as they converged on her from both sides. Her small dirk lay hidden in her boot, awaiting the right moment to be revealed. This, Chandra decided, eyeing Aleck as he loped toward her, was the time.

Seeing she was trapped, Aleck slowed his urgent strides slowed to a walk. He waved his hand, and the other men stopped where they were. Sir John stood several yards beyond Chandra, his men close behind him. "It's over, little one," Aleck said, deliberately moving toward her. Spying the open space behind her, he feared she might cast herself over the wall. "Come," he prompted, "let's go into the hall where food and wine await us. Afterward, a hot bath will be prepared. It will ease your aches from this long day's ride. A good night's sleep in a warm, soft bed, and you'll feel much better." He eased nearer. "On the morrow, Sir John and his men will ride south to report to James. He will carry a letter from me explaining what has happened. Until our king responds, you'll stay here at Montbourne as my guest." His hand reached out, and his long fingers gently took hold of her arm. "Come, sweet, do not fret. No one will harm you. This I promise."

As he spoke, Chandra studied him carefully. A bruise was forming along his jaw where she'd kicked him, bits of straw clung to his hair, and dirt streaked his cheek and chest. In the dim light, his sky blue eyes shone with sincerity; his thumb lightly stroked her arm. Then mentally she saw Devin's face as she last remembered it.

"Come, sweet," Aleck repeated, urging her away from the crenel.

Devin, she thought, pretending to accede to Aleck's gentle command. Slowly she stepped forward, her head lowered; then, lightning fast, her hand went for the dirk.

Belatedly, Aleck saw the thing whip from her boot. *She's small, but she's quick.* Sir John's words rolled through his head as he viewed the blade a mere breath from his heart.

"You murdered my cousin, Sassenach. As payment, you too will die."

Rage, anguish, and fear all culminated in her wide gaze. Her hand quaked from the untamed emotions spinning through her. Aleck was certain she couldn't kill anyone, not even the man who'd slain her cousin. "If it will ease your pain to avenge Devin, thrust your blade into my heart. But know this. I did not intend to harm your cousin. I meant only to defend myself against your uncle. You saw for yourself how Devin leapt between us.

I had no warning. He did it to protect you, Chandra. Had you stayed out of the fray as I commanded, your cousin would still be alive and you would yet be in Scotland. I am not the only one to bear the burden of guilt. But I shall take the blame." He moved toward her, making certain the blade's tip touched the leather covering his chest. "Go on. Seek your revenge."

I am not the only one to bear the burden of guilt. . . . His words twirled through her mind until she was dizzy from their force. It was true. If she hadn't tricked her guardian—not once, not twice, but thrice!—his temper wouldn't have erupted, and he'd never have sought to punish her as he had. Likewise, if she hadn't disobeyed him by rushing forth, intent on casting herself between the two men, hoping to stop the fight, Devin wouldn't in turn have bounded forward. He'd done so because he felt that he had to protect her.

Aware that Devin's death was as much her fault as her guardian's, she still tried to deny it. Placing the blame on Aleck helped ease her conscience, and were she to rid herself of the man who'd killed her cousin, all her hurt would surely go away. Wouldn't it? Her hand shook as she pressed the dirk into the leather just above his heart; its tip sliced through the sleek hide. He didn't move. As she searched Aleck's face, his eyes remained steady with hers; her courage wavered. Then it fled. The dirk fell from her hand. Turning, she thrust herself at the crenel.

Death, sweet death, take this pain from my heart! The lament tumbled through her head just as she attempted to throw herself over the edge, but Aleck captured her before she even met the stones framing the opening.

"No!" she screamed, struggling against the powerful arms surrounding her. "Let me go . . . let me die!"

Aleck pressed her against him. "Never," he insisted, then gathered her more closely to him.

Unable to free herself, her struggles at last ceased. A great sob jerked from the depths of Chandra's soul; her sorrow seemed to consume her. Her head spun crazily, and a welcome blackness swallowed her.

Quickly Aleck hoisted her into his arms, then carried her down the stairs and across the courtyard. James's men watched in silence, a wide path having formed through their ranks. "Make ready her room," the earl said to his steward.

"'Tis ready, sir," Marlowe responded; on thin legs, he rushed toward the doors of the great hall and threw them open.

Aleck passed through the expanse, his unconscious burden cradled against his chest. Firm strides carried him to the upper level and the apartments, his steward scurrying along in front of him. Just as Aleck reached the door of the room adjacent to his own, another door opened farther down the corridor, and a scantily clad woman walked from inside the chamber.

Damn! He'd forgotten all about Felicia, then felt certain an ugly confrontation was in the offing. "Open the door," he commanded Marlowe, "and keep her out."

Marlowe looked in the direction of his master's nod; he gulped. "I'll try, milord, but it won't be easy."

"Do your best," Aleck snapped as he entered the room, then kicked the panel shut in his steward's face. As he carried Chandra toward the wide bed centered against one wall, a moan slipped through her lips; his eyes dropped to her mouth. That enticing bit of flesh had been the cause of his downfall. Yet knowing that made little difference. Even now it beckoned to him. Forcing his attention away from Chandra's face, he settled his ward gently on the feather mattress. Then, noting her flushed cheeks, he touched her brow. She felt feverish. The backs of his fingers trailed along her soft cheek in a light caress. "Rest, little one," he whispered, his gaze caressing her face once more. Then he strode back to the door and threw it open. "Marlowe—" he began, then saw Felicia standing beside his steward. By the look on her face, she was perturbed; her eyes had an unpleasant glint in them. Ignoring her, he continued, "Please have Mistress Marlowe report to me at once. The Lady Lochlaigh is not well." His steward scurried down the hall, deserting Aleck and the disagreeable Felicia.

"Not even a hello, Aleck?" she asked.

She appeared calm, but Aleck knew a volcano churned inside her, ready to erupt. "'Tis good to see you, Felicia," he lied, strongly wishing she were anyplace but in his home. With all that had happened in the past few days, he didn't wish to be thrown into another broil. Instead of swords, however, the weapons used would be their tongues, and Felicia's was certain to slash him to ribbons. "As you can see, I am otherwise engaged," he said, trying to forestall her. "We will talk later."

The moment he'd seen her with his steward, Aleck had taken a stance in the doorway, his hard body blocking all possibility of entry. His arm extended across the opening, his palm braced against the stones framing the door, and to Felicia it appeared as though he were protecting something of great value. Through the unobstructed space beneath his outstretched arm, she caught sight of the young woman who lay on the bed. Sweet and lovely, the girl was not the big-boned, toothless hag that Aleck's imagination had conjured. Slowly Felicia looked back to her lover.

Viewing him closely, she thought he was different. Physically he was the same—virile, handsome, sexually appealing—but beyond the familiar exterior, he was a changed man. He seemed far less arrogant and far less absorbed in himself. Worry showed on his face, and Felicia felt certain the Lady Lochlaigh was the cause of his concern. "Truly, darling, you are most occupied," she said, her eyes again skipping toward the bed. "That much I can see. When you are through playing nursemaid, you may find me in my room." She paused. "Or better still, in yours."

Belatedly, Aleck remembered their parting words—that she was to await him in his bed, nude and ready. He firmly wished they had never been said. "When I have finished seeing to my ward, I shall come to your room, Felicia. Then we will talk." From the corner of his eye, he saw movement along the corridor. Short and round, a white cap covering her graying hair, his steward's wife—Winnie, as she was called—hurried toward his room in her usual rolling gait.

"My Felix said you wanted to see me, Master Aleck," she said.

Her familiar address did not offend the earl, for she'd referred to him as "Master Aleck" since he was a toddler. "Aye, Winnie. The Lady Lochlaigh seems to have taken a fever. I need you to attend her." His arm fell to his side, allowing Winnie passage. After she'd entered, his hand returned to the stones. "I shall pay a call on you later," he said to Felicia.

"As you wish," she said stiffly, then turned and headed toward her room.

Aleck watched the provocative sway of her hips as they undulated beneath her shift and flimsy wrapper. "Felicia," he called, annoyed by the artful maneuver, for he knew she attempted to seduce him. She pivoted his way. "Make certain you are fully clothed. Although my visit will be brief, a lady never receives a gentleman unless properly dressed."

Felicia spun on her heel and marched the few remaining steps to her room. The door banged shut, the noise resounding through the upper corridor. Shaking his head, Aleck wondered why he'd ever taken up with volatile Lady Emory in the first place. She'd acted in a fairly restrained manner, but he knew by the set of her jaw and the calculating look in her eyes as they'd focused upon his ward that his former mistress—a decision he'd made on seeing Felicia again—had already devised several ways to fell Chandra. Incredibly, she didn't even know the girl. Yet Felicia was territorial—viciously so. He'd not let Chandra suffer the woman's maliciousness, not after all she'd borne already.

Another thing bothered Aleck, and had done so since the moment it had happened. He was certain, through cunning, she'd planned to trap him into marriage by becoming pregnant. It was not done because she loved him, desiring him alone, for Aleck was aware that Felicia loved only herself. No, it was done because she coveted his money and his title, which, Felicia knew, would afford his wife a great deal of power. Foolishly, he'd almost been caught in her deceitful web, insidious spider that she was. Knowing she wasn't to be trusted ever again, Aleck was determined to end the affair. He intended to tell her shortly, but he suspected she already knew.

Turning away from the door, he saw Winnie fussing over Chandra. "She's terribly flushed, Master Aleck," she said as he came to her side. "But the fever is not too high." She patted the girl's cheeks. "Wake up, child, and give old Winnie a look-see." Chandra's eyelids fluttered open. Briefly she stared at the woman, then her eyes fell closed. "Her mind's a ways off," Winnie commented, "and apparently she's happy that it is. What happened to the poor thing to make her so?"

Under Winnie's stern frown, Aleck related many of the events of the past two days, but not all. Conveniently he kept his vain, self-proscribed attack on Chandra to himself. But he knew that Winnie was not fooled.

"Aye, as you say," she stated, inspecting him closely. Then she turned her gaze on the flame-haired girl who looked like a waif. "Poor lost soul, she's suffered a terrible shock. She's exhausted—mentally, physically, and emotionally—no thanks to you. Let's hope a long sleep is all she needs. Take yourself out of here so I can undress her and give her a quick wash. If you behave, you can return when I'm done."

"Whatever you say, Mistress Marlowe." He bestowed

on her a dazzling smile. As usual, she was unmoved by his appealing manner; Winnie was wise to him. "First I must speak to the Lady Emory, then you may find me in my room. Alone," he added, spying her censuring look. Aleck took himself to the door. "Give her the best of care, Winnie, as only you can do." She seemed not to hear him, for like a mother hen, she was already clucking and cooing at the bedraggled little chick given into her keeping. The door closed behind him.

Aleck approached Felicia's room. When she answered his light knock, he was surprised to see her appropriately dressed. For some reason, perhaps because he knew her temperament well, he had expected defiance. But there appeared to be none as she politely invited him into her room.

"What needs to be said, Felicia, will take only a moment. It can be done here in the hall just as easily. On the morrow, the king's men will be returning to London. You'll be accompanying them."

Felicia studied him closely. "When you left here, you seemed quite eager to return to my arms. Something must have happened for you to want to be rid of me so quickly. An explanation would be welcome."

"Things are not the same as they were, Felicia. At least, not for me. What we had together was an enjoyable interlude. You know, as do I, that sooner or later it was bound to end. We sought pleasure in each other, and neither of us was disappointed. But now, it is over. I hope we might part as friends."

Through shuttered eyes, Felicia studied him for a long moment. All her plans lay shattered. She should have insisted on going with him. But then, she wondered if doing so would have made a difference. "The girl—do you fancy yourself in love with her?" Her throaty laughter filled Aleck's ears. "If so, darling, pray she is nothing like Elinor. You're too passionate a man to suffer yet another frigid bride." Boldly her hand met his chest; her palm edged downward over the smooth leather to his waist, then lower. "Too passionate by far."

Aleck caught the intrusive hand. "And too wise to fall for your artifices, Felicia. We both know why you are so eager to share my bed. When it is time for me to produce an heir, the babe's mother will be of high morals and will possess a more tender nature than yours, *darling.*" He tossed the word at her with vigor, for he'd always despised its use. Simultaneously, he threw her hand away from him. "As for the Lady Lochlaigh, I am responsible for her care, nothing more. I suggest you attend to your packing. Dawn is not that far off." He stepped back from her door. "Farewell, Felicia. If it gives you any ease, I'm certain you will not be alone for long."

The door slammed forcefully in his face, and on a low laugh, Aleck headed toward his own room. Ordering up a hot bath, he paced the floor until Marlowe and several other servants arrived. After giving his master a quick shave, the steward left with the Earl of Montbourne's soiled clothing held in front of him.

On a sigh, Aleck finally settled into the steaming tub where he relaxed his body, but not his mind. For a long while, he pondered what to do about his ward. When the water had cooled, he dried off, dressed and fell upon his bed to gaze at its broad canopy. His arm flung above his head, he absentmindedly traced the depressions in the headboard outlining the Montbourne crest. Should he send her home or keep her here? And James—what would be his reaction? Aleck was certain he'd be given permanent residence in the Tower. What a boggle it all was. Admittedly he'd blundered, and there seemed no viable way to right it. Fool, he called himself, knowing all too well where to place the blame.

A knock sounded on his door, breaking into his thoughts. "Come." Winnie's head peeked around the door. "I'm alone," he reassured her, and she entered the room.

"She's sleeping peacefully," the woman told him. "I managed to get some broth down her, but only a bit. By tomorrow, I'm certain she'll be far better."

Aleck saw that she studied him. Although freshly bathed, he still felt fatigued. Apparently Winnie noticed such.

"You'd best be getting yourself something to eat and some rest 'fore you end up sick. The food you ordered is being set on the tables now."

Aleck rose from the bed. Shoving his feet into his shoes, he looked over his shoulder at the woman. "Have a tray sent up to the Lady Lochlaigh's room. I'll be in there."

"Aye, I'll do that." She turned to leave.

"Oh, and Winnie, the Lady Emory will be departing with Sir John at dawn. Send a servant girl to help with her packing. When the knight has finished his meal, tell him I wish to speak with him. Again—"

"You'll be in the Lady Lochlaigh's room," she finished for him. "She's a pretty little thing—fresh and innocent. A sight better than the tarnished harpy that's been traipsing the halls around here of late." Before Aleck could respond, the door thumped to.

Winnie and Felicia must have had words while he was gone, he decided, which was not surprising, for both women were headstrong. It was just another reason that Felicia should be on her way.

Aleck crossed the room to the connecting door leading into Chandra's chamber, an apartment meant for the next Countess of Montbourne. The last woman to occupy the room had been Aleck's mother, for his own bride had refused to do so. Elinor had insisted on a bedchamber far from his own and had kept herself within its four walls until the day she'd died. As he thought about it, he was amazed that he'd ordered the room readied for his ward.

Slipping quietly through the door, Aleck looked at the

small creature lying in the center of the huge bed. Her long hair, brushed and shining like polished copper, spread over the white linen pillow cover. Her face and hands, washed and glowing a soft pink, peeked from the voluminous gown that hid her body. He could only assume the nightdress belonged to Winnie. One hand was laxly tossed upward, lying not far from her head, the other rested on her stomach where the blankets met her waist. She resembled a small child lost in slumber and having not a care in the world.

He crept toward the chair nearest the bed and sat down. Agony filled his heart as he gazed at his ward, for when she awakened so would her sorrow. "Ah, sweet, if I could change it I would," he whispered. Then he rested his head against the chair's back. In silence he watched her. How long he stayed thus, he didn't know, but finally a light rap sounded on the door. Answering it, he saw Winnie, his dinner in hand. Averse to disturbing his ward as he ate, he instructed that his meal be taken to his room. Winnie would stay with Chandra until he'd finished.

Because he'd eaten little over the past two days, Aleck thought he'd be ravenous, but he did no more than pick at his food. Shoving the tray to one side of the large writing desk where he sat, he gathered quill, ink, and parchment from the drawer. It was time he composed a letter to James. What the hell would he tell his sovereign? That he'd botched his assigned task? There was no doubt he had. A cynical laugh erupted from his lips as the letter was quickly written in his mind.

Dearest Majesty:
 In the space of fewer than three weeks, I have assaulted the Lady Lochlaigh, killed her cousin, abducted the girl, and used her as a shield while your trusted soldiers and I fled the Highlands, the clan Morgan pursuing us until we had the good

*fortune to run into the hundred men you sent north
to give us further strength. I might add they arrived
not a minute too soon. We are now at Montbourne
Castle. On the more positive side, I did manage to
save my ward's life. After her attempt to skewer me
with her dirk had failed, she tried to cast herself off
the battlement, but I prevented such, holding her
until she at last fainted from the horror she had
suffered over the past two days. Of course, it goes
without saying that the Lady Lochlaigh is now
paralyzed with grief and has taken a fever. Should
she survive, I am certain she will be requesting a new
guardian. Given the circumstances, I cannot fault
her. Perhaps, in your benevolent wisdom, you have
some suggestions on how I might undo the muddle I
have made of things. I eagerly await your response.*
    Your obedient servant, Montbourne.

That should fairly well cover it, Aleck thought, not yet
having put pen to paper. When he did, his message was
brief.

Sire:
    *The Lady Lochlaigh and I are now at
Montbourne Castle. Sir John will supply the details
of our journey and the happenings that precipitated
our leaving Scotland.*
    Your obedient servant, Montbourne.

Coward, he accused himself. A fist met the wood panel
that secured his room. "Come."

Sir John entered the chamber. "You asked to see me?"

"I did." Dribbling candle wax on the folded parchment, Aleck pressed his signet ring into the seal. "When
you leave on the morrow, Sir John, the Lady Emory will
be accompanying you to London. This," he said, handing the letter to the knight, "goes to our sovereign.

Should James have any questions, which I'm certain he will, please explain the events that foreran our sudden departure."

The knight turned the letter over in his hand. "The girl—what do you plan to do with her?"

"Not surprisingly, she has taken ill. She will stay here until she has recovered. At that time, I shall decide what to do with her. Unless, of course, our king makes the decision for me. He may appoint someone else as her overlord—something I wish he had done from the start. Things might have ended differently if he had."

"If I am to supply the details, shouldn't I know exactly how the young man died?"

Aleck hesitated, but then he relented and explained how he and Cedric were about to face off, how Chandra had tried to stop the impending fight, and how Devin, fearing his cousin would be injured, had cast himself between the two men.

"Why was the Highlander so eager to draw your blood? Is there something else I should know—that James should know?"

"'Tis not important why it happened," Aleck said. "Her cousin is dead, and slain by my own hand. 'Twas a mischance, an accident, but the Lady Lochlaigh believes otherwise. I cannot blame her. Her hatred of me is understandable."

"It may not give you much ease, but know that the lad caused his own death. Had he kept from between you both, he would still be alive."

"Aye . . . maybe." Aleck's fingers raked through his hair. "In truth, Sir John, my temper caused the man's death. Nothing you say will excuse it." He noticed the knight's questioning stare. "I am weary of thinking about it. Tell James I shall be at Montbourne until I hear from him. I wish our parting were under more favorable conditions. You have served me and our sovereign well. I hope we meet again."

Sir John extended his hand; Aleck took it. "I hope, sir, that all ends well for you," the knight said. "Perhaps we'll soon see each other at court."

"I doubt I shall find myself at court anytime soon. Not unless James orders me to London. No, I am happy here at Montbourne and this is where I plan to stay." Their hands unclasped, and the two bade each other farewell. Just as the knight reached the door, Aleck called: "Take care, Sir John, that the Lady Emory does not make your journey an unpleasant one. She is in ill humor, and knowing her as I do, I'm certain she'll attempt to make everyone suffer because of it."

"Thank you for the warning. I'll keep far from her, as will the others."

The knight left, and Aleck returned to Chandra's room. Winnie sat in the chair he'd vacated earlier. "I'll sit with her," he whispered.

"You could do with some rest yourself," she said, slowly rising from the chair. "But if you insist on staying with her, I'll not argue with you. Call me if you need me."

Aleck watched the woman as she left the room, then folded himself into the chair. Endlessly he gazed at Chandra. Except for her whispered breath and his own, silence cloaked the room. Forcing his mind to remain vacant of thought, he stayed in that one position for hours. Just before sunrise, his eyelids drooped; Aleck dozed.

Chandra stirred. In the last remnants of her dreams, Lochlaigh Castle sat on a distant hill; a hawk soared above its towers. After several sweeps, the great bird flew away. Then all went black.

Slowly she awakened. Her eyes opened, and a frown crept across her brow as she stared at her surroundings. Confusion gripped her, for she could not fathom where she was or how she'd gotten there. A soft snore met her ears, and she turned her head to locate its source. There in the chair a dozen feet from her sat her guardian. Memories welled, then flooded through her, especially those of the previous night. Why, she wondered, had he saved her?

A searing anguish filled her anew. With all her being, she'd wanted to avenge Devin's death—an eye for an eye. By slaying his murderer, she'd hoped to lessen her guilt, her pain. But her courage had failed her. Faced with her unbearable heartache, her own cowardice, she'd tried to throw herself from the battlement, ending her accursed existence, but her guardian had prevented her from finding the relief she sought. Because he had, she was again made to suffer from her grief, the weight of it hanging like a heavy stone in her chest. Was that why he guarded her now? So that she would not attempt another plunge to the ground, this time from the window, ending her misery? Undoubtedly he thought it was a fitting punishment for her disobedience. He was cruel to make her suffer so.

Then again, perhaps he simply feared she might attempt another escape. In spite of the pain she carried, Chandra vowed she'd never act as foolishly as she had the night before. Life was far too precious. Devin would have loathed knowing that she'd tried to end her own. But escape Montbourne? That was a genuine possibility. Given the opportunity, she'd do precisely that—flee!

Aleck's head bobbed, and he started awake. Drawing a long breath, he looked at his ward and noted that she still slept. His muscles felt cramped. Needing to stretch, he rose from the chair and quietly crossed to the window. A dusky pink glow striped the horizon, announcing the dawn. Shortly, the hazy red globe peeked above the distant hills. Aleck briefly viewed nature's wondrous spectacle. Then the sound of men's voices drew his attention to the yard below.

Saddled horses were being led from inside the stables and gathered from the pens. The reins for each were handed off, one by one, and Sir John and his men mounted their steeds. One of them helped Felicia climb astride her own horse as her trunks were placed in a cart. Within a few short minutes, the whole rode through the gates and away from the castle, heading south toward London. Aleck felt relieved to see them go, especially his former mistress. On a sigh, he rolled his head along his shoulders, releasing the tension that had settled in his neck. Now all he had to worry about was James's reaction. That, and his ward, of course.

From the bed, Chandra peered at him through lowered lashes. Apparently he'd spent the entire night in the chair. She hoped he suffered for it, too. He drew another long breath, then expelled it. His hand rose to massage the nape of his neck, and he turned toward her; Chandra pretended to sleep.

The door leading into the corridor creaked open, and a plump woman stepped into the room with Chandra's clothes draped over one arm. Her possessions appeared clean, she marked, the tunic repaired. The newcomer stopped at the bed's foot and placed the folded articles on a low chest, the Morgan plaid atop them. After a brief glance at Chandra, she ambled on toward the window. Whispered words were exchanged between the woman and Aleck, then on a nod, he moved toward another door and disappeared through it, the panel closing behind him.

"You can stop pretending and open your eyes, deary," the woman said in a normal tone of voice. "Master Aleck has gone to get some rest. He insisted on staying with you the night through, but old Winnie will keep you company now." Chandra remained unresponsive. "Oh, tosh, girl," Winnie admonished, "having raised six children of my own and then overseeing Master Aleck's upbringing, do you think I don't know when someone's feigning sleep? My brood used the trick hoping to avoid the first tasks of the day, especially during the winter. It didn't work. Of course, for those who insisted on ignoring me—the rascals wanted to dally under the covers the day long—I always had a quick solution."

Through the tiny slits of her lashes, Chandra watched Winnie cross to the pitcher on the washstand, pick it up, and again come toward the bed. Realizing her intent, Chandra popped to a sitting position. "You wouldn't dare . . . would you?"

A smile split Winnie's face as the pitcher quickly changed directions. "'Tis something you'll never know, but at least I'm now aware that you are not altogether slow of wit." Water splashed into the basin atop the washstand, then Winnie dipped a cloth into the cool liquid and wrung it out. "Here, wipe the sleep from your eyes."

The cloth dropped from the woman's fingers; Chandra caught it. "I am far from being slow-witted," she insisted, eyeing the woman.

"That, milady, is something which remains to be seen."

Chapter

8

Three days later, as Chandra paced in her room, which by her own choosing had become her prison, she still puzzled over Winnie's words.

"Slow of wit, indeed," she said to the four walls. Under normal circumstances, such an action might be considered a bit irregular, but sequestered as she was, she longed to hear a human voice, even if it was her own.

Admittedly, the lack of contact with those at Montbourne had been her own doing, for despite her guardian's repeated requests that she join him at meals or walk with him inside the castle compound, she'd refused all such invitations. Other than seeing a servant or two each day when her meals were delivered to her door or while her bath was prepared, she had to create her own diversions, which were few. The days were long and tedious for a woman accustomed to being quite active, and she quickly grew weary of her self-imposed seclusion.

"Slow of wit, indeed," she repeated, then wondered if she actually might be.

Chandra stopped in front of the window and looked out over the grounds. She wanted to be gone from here, but there seemed to be no plausible way of escape. The walls were too high, the guards too numerous. No one could possibly get in or out of the castle unless they were meant to. Knowing as much, she conceded she had but one recourse. Somehow she had to persuade her guardian to set her free. To do that, she needed to speak with him.

Chandra dreaded the prospect of again meeting him face to face, for she feared her abhorrence of him would spew forth, if not from her lips, then by way of her eyes, ruining her chance at freedom. Yet no other option existed. Somehow she had to gain control of her emotions; then, with her words and actions carefully orchestrated, she'd plead her case. If good fortune shone upon her, she'd soon be on her way home to Scotland, to the Highlands, to Morgan lands and the people she loved and longed to see. She imagined they worried about her and impatiently awaited her return. All except Devin, she thought, her sorrow welling anew. Damn him! she cursed Aleck silently, wishing she'd done him in when she'd had the chance. Damn him to hell!

Refusing to give way to tears, Chandra fought them back. This was her last hope, she knew. She must face him. Quickly she gauged the angle of the sun. It was nearly time for dinner, which was served at eleven. Dashing to the basin, she splashed clear water onto her face. After she'd patted it dry, she took up a hand mirror, then lightly pinched her cheeks, for she'd grown pale from lack of sunlight and fresh air.

A brush, procured earlier by Winnie from the wealth of supplies stored at Montbourne, swiftly stroked through her unbound hair. She straightened her clothing and smoothed the Morgan plaid beneath her belt, then rushed to the door. Twisting the latch, she was startled to find the thing locked. She wondered, had it always been so? A tiny frown marred her brow, and after a moment's deliberation, she decided it had. She'd not known it, though, because until now she'd never attempted to venture from her room.

A long breath flowed from between Chandra's lips, marking her exasperation. Unknowingly she'd been kept prisoner in this vast, finely appointed chamber. Incarcerated in such luxurious surroundings, she could hardly complain. Yet it vexed her that her rebellious action, her self-imposed seclusion, was not fully self-imposed at all. Had the door been locked because he'd anticipated she'd make another break for freedom, or had he feared a second attempt on his life, her next one, in all likelihood, fatal? Since the secured entry prevented her from accomplishing either, she doubted he'd lost much sleep over what she might or might not have done.

Eyeing the door across the way—the one she'd seen Aleck slip through—she moved toward it. Amazingly, when she tried the handle, the latch gave way. The heavy wood panel swung open, and she stared into a small room. A long, narrow table stood against the wall to her right. Dazzling multicolored lights speckled the entire area as the sun beat against a large stained-glass window set in the opposite wall, a lone chair positioned in front of it. A strip of finely woven carpet ran the floor, leading from her door to another. Chandra followed the soft woolen path, then released the second door's latch.

On quiet hinges, the door opened to reveal an even larger chamber than her own. Chandra peered around the door's edge, her teeth tracking nervously along her lower lip. Dared she enter? Knowing it was someone else's apartment, she hesitated and viewed the area anew. The furnishings, consisting of chests, tables, chairs, several hanging cupboards, and a huge canopied bed, were of the finest wood, all highly polished. As in her own room, tapestries covered the gray stone walls, adding warmth, while thick carpets dotted the floor.

"'Tis grand," she said to herself on a mere whisper. Once again, she regarded the large bed.

Centered on the headboard was a crest. The ornate embellishment sported two hawks, arrows clutched in their powerful feet, and the word *Montbourne* carved into a ribbon of wood that scrolled beneath the whole. *His* room, she realized, attempting to quietly back away, but movement caught her eye, and the man in her thoughts came into view. Holding her breath, Chandra prayed she'd not be spotted.

Aleck stopped beside the bed, unaware that Chandra stood only yards away, watching him. In two quick moves his shirt came up over his head, to reveal a striking emerald-encrusted medallion. The shirt fell to the mattress, and he crossed to the basin. Water splashed onto his face and arms, droplets flecking his chest. With a piece of clean toweling in hand, he turned around and began patting his skin dry.

The cloth moved from his face down over his chest, its breadth richly sprinkled with curly black hair that darted down his flat, hard belly and disappeared into his tight-fitting breeches, and Chandra could not help but admire his superior masculine build. The towel grazed up his arms, one at a time, over corded muscles, their strength apparent. His long fingers tossed the toweling aside, and Chandra remembered that those arms and those fingers had wielded the sword that killed Devin. Exceptional her guardian might be, but he was also a murderer.

A clean shirt slipped down over Aleck's head and he began tucking the silk into the waist of his breeches. That's when he noticed that the connecting door stood ajar. "Spying on me, little one?" he asked, the last of the loose material pushed from sight. Not surprisingly, she refused to answer. "I know you're there, Chandra. Quit acting like a child and come hither."

Slowly she made her way into view. "I hadn't realized

this was your room. The other door was locked, so I tried the second. It led me here."

"I know where it leads," he said, studying her. "I thought you preferred your own company. Have you grown weary of being alone?"

She gazed at him long and hard, unsure whether to lunge at him, her nails aimed at his arresting blue eyes, or fall at his feet, begging him to release her so she could go home. "Whether I had grown weary of being alone or not makes little difference. I simply discovered that I had no way out of my room except through here," she said, remaining calm. "The question is why?"

Aleck chuckled. "I think you already know the answer."

"Indulge me," she said, looking straight at him. "Why was my outer door locked and not this one?"

"In order to escape, you would have had to slip past me," he answered, not in the least bit willing to relate that he'd forgotten to lock it that morning. Each night he went quietly into her room to check on her. After a short stay, he made his way back to his own room. But hours later, he always found himself awake. "To do so would be almost impossible."

Chandra's fingers trailed over the top of a chair's back. She walked nearer to him. "You risk much, milord, especially when it might not be escape that I desire." She saw his arched brow. "I might still wish to gain my revenge. While you lie abed, slumbering peacefully, you could be awakened by a quick, sharp pain. But only briefly, for you'd soon sleep forever."

"Not likely." He moved to the bed's end. "You no longer have a weapon, and you'll not find one anywhere within reach." He casually leaned his shoulder against the carved bedpost. "A word of warning, little one. Should you ever come near my bed at night, you will fast discover it is you who suffers a quick, sharp pain, but it will be followed by hours of pleasure. There will be no sleep, only continuous ecstasy until the dawn breaks. Possibly even longer."

Blinking, Chandra wondered if he'd implied what she thought. Before she could shoot an adequate response his way, one that dripped sarcasm, he shoved away from the post and came toward her. Quickly she backed up a step.

His low laughter rumbled forth. "'Tis not night, Chandra, and you are not overly near my bed. At the moment, you have nothing to fear." He moved past her to the open window. "Come. I want to show you something."

Cautiously she made her way to the large window set inside an alcove. She stopped several feet short of him, ready to flee.

"Those trees," he said, pointing across to the opposite hillside. "Do you see the stones beyond them?"

Chandra stepped closer. "Aye," she said, glimpsing the rising walls. "I see them."

"That is Montbourne Hall." Pride echoed in his voice. "When it is finished, the castle will be closed and that will be my new residence. I just came from there, but if you like, I'll take you to see it after our meal. It will afford you the opportunity to enjoy the sunshine and fresh air. This time, will you honor my invitation?"

To ride free, Chandra thought, trying to mask her excitement. With luck, as they headed from the castle over to the next hill, she could escape him. The border, she knew, was less than an hour's ride away. Oh, Scotland. How she longed to see her homeland again. "Your invitation is accepted," she said, her tone serene. "It will dispel the monotony of the day."

Although she appeared reserved, even somewhat bored by the prospect of seeing his new home, Aleck noticed a breathless quality to her voice. It hinted at excitement and possibly anticipation. He surveyed her expressive eyes, then offered her a pleasant smile.

"Would milady also like to dine in the hall below? If so, I believe our meal awaits us."

Chandra nodded her assent; then, at the wave of his hand, she preceded him to the door that led from his room into the hallway. As they traveled the corridor, she studied the upper level, searching out any extra sets of steps that might descend to either the kitchens or another passageway below. There were two such stairwells, and Chandra took mental note of their locations, just in case she failed in her impending escape.

She quickly followed her guardian down the main staircase. Viewing the great hall for the first time, Chandra found she was thoroughly impressed. Damask-covered tables were set with silver plates and goblets. Tapestries lined the walls while fresh herbal grasses covered the floor. The place was impeccably clean and in excellent repair. "Why do you want to abandon the castle?" she asked, following him to the table. "Especially when it still has many years of use?"

"Since your country and mine are now at peace, and it is to be hoped that they shall remain so, the place has outlived its day. Times are changing. As you will soon see, my new home demonstrates that they are."

"What if Scotland and England decide to take up arms against each other again—what will you do then?"

"The castle will still be standing. It will afford us the protection that it always has."

Aleck helped Chandra into her seat at the head table, then settled into the chair next to hers. Eyeing him, she asked, "Has Montbourne suffered much over the years? I mean—has it seen many battles?"

"There have been several." He reserved the fact that they'd been exceedingly bloody. "But naught has happened in recent years."

"Did Montbourne always see victory?"

"All but once," he said. "More than a century ago,

your countrymen managed to gain entry to the castle. One slew my forebear and abducted his wife and infant son. The place lay unattended for more than two decades."

"What happened to the boy and his mother?"

"The young widow became her abductor's new bride."

"And the boy?"

"When he gained his maturity, he came south and reclaimed his birthright."

Chandra's gaze slowly moved toward the doors at the opposite end of the hall. "I suppose even after all those years, Montbourne still beckoned to him."

"I suppose it did. It was his home."

Trenchers of food were placed on the table, and Aleck watched as she served herself. She longed for her home, he knew. But in good conscience, he couldn't just set her free. Danger lurked over every hill and behind each tree. No woman could survive such a long journey on her own. Why he hadn't released her only a short way from the Morgan stronghold, Aleck couldn't say. But something had compelled him to keep her with him. Something he was unable to fathom. Something he readily denied. Yet he realized that at the first opportunity, she'd try to escape him. That he could not let her do.

He blamed himself for her sorrow. Were it possible, he would offer to escort her, but to do so meant great risk, not simply to his life, but also to her own. Cedric's wrath was bound to descend upon him, and Chandra was certain to be caught in the fray. How very convenient it would be for the man, Aleck thought. With his niece dead, accidentally entrapped between the two, much like Devin, the Highlander could claim the title of chief, an ambition he'd long held. No, he'd not chance such a happening, and he'd not ask anyone else to hazard such a journey either. Besides, it was now up to their king to decide what was to be done with the Lady Lochlaigh. He could do naught but await word from James.

Aleck served himself. The two ate in silence, lost in their own thoughts. When the meal was over, he rose from his chair and assisted Chandra from hers. "If milady is ready, we shall journey over to the next hill."

"I am more than ready," she said, her anticipation growing.

"Yes," Aleck responded, noting the determination in her eyes, "I'm certain you are."

Chandra stared after him as he walked toward the doors leading from the hall. He was suspicious of her, she decided, trailing along behind him. Somehow she had to ease his doubts so he'd lower his guard. Then, and only then, would she be able to make her escape.

Stepping from the dim hall into the bright sunlight, she closed her eyes and basked in its warmth. Fresh air filled her lungs, invigorating her. Opening her eyes, she saw a lad break from her guardian's presence to dash off toward the stables. As she slowly walked to Aleck's side, she ordered her jittery nerves to relax, lest he become even more suspicious. "'Tis a bonny day," she remarked, her manner casual.

"Aye, it is," Aleck agreed, looking down at her. Already foreseeing her course of action, he decided to play along with her. "'Tis even more bonny outside these walls." A heart-stopping smile spread over his lips. "But never as lovely as you," he finished as his finger traced the line of her cheek.

His sky blue eyes mesmerized her, and for a moment, Chandra felt lost. The sound of hooves snapped her from her trance. Her gaze tore itself from his, and she saw the boy returning from the stables. Reins gripped tightly in his hand, the lad led Aleck's stallion toward them. Passing the leads over to his master, the boy scurried off toward what Chandra assumed was the door to the kitchen area. A frown crept across her forehead as she turned back to Aleck. He was already in the saddle.

"Am I expected to walk?" she asked.

"Not at all, milady." He extended his hand, palm upward, to her. "You shall be riding with me."

Surely he was jesting. But his hand remained fixed. Chandra studied his face. "And if I refuse?"

"Then we will simply have to postpone our outing." His hand motioned for her own. "What say you, little one? Do we stay? Or do we go?"

One horse, she thought. Slim as it might be, there was still a chance she could escape. Knowing she had no other choice, she slipped her fingers over his slightly calloused palm. His warm hand closed over hers, and he urged her closer to the stallion's side, then leaned down, his arm surrounding her waist. With little effort, he lifted her from the ground to settle her in front of him on the saddle.

Dear God, grant me the occasion to flee him. The entreaty tumbled through her mind as her guardian, his arm firmly around her waist, spurred the large beast toward the gate. Out onto open land, the stallion was given full rein. It galloped across the lush green terrain, then up the hillside into the trees. At its master's command, it slowed to a walk. All the while, Chandra remained very still, and Aleck wondered if she'd given up hope of escaping him. Soon they stopped beside the large stone building that was under construction.

"Down with you," Aleck said, starting to swing Chandra from the saddle. Her hands grabbed his forearm, shoving it from her waist; her head whirled around, and she stared at him. Aleck chuckled. "I am not fool enough to allow you to stay astride while I dismount. Not this time, milady. One such error was enough."

Before she could protest, Chandra landed on her feet. Silently she cursed her luck, then she cursed him. Afterward she cursed herself. She knew she should never have counted on his making the same mistake twice. She'd have to find another way to gain her freedom. As he slid from the saddle, Chandra noticed that the underside of his jaw retained a slight discoloration. She hoped the bruise pained him still. Glancing around, she saw no workers about. "Where is everyone?" she inquired.

"In the village, I imagine, with family and friends." She seemed surprised. "Today is Sunday. I don't ask anyone to work on this particular day."

Somehow she'd lost track of the days. "Oh, I didn't realize it was the Lord's day." She looked up at the building in front of her, then glimpsed the sky. There was yet hope. With no one to stop her but him, she might have a better chance to escape. "Shall we go inside?"

"In a bit." He led the stallion toward the trees and tethered it to a low-lying branch, giving it enough lead to graze, then returned to Chandra's side. "Now, we shall enter."

Gaining what Chandra thought would eventually be the front doors, she was swept through the wide opening, under some archways, and on into the center of Montbourne Hall. Through another set of arches she spied a staircase of dark, rich wood, banded by a pierced-panel balustrade. It angled up an outer wall, leading to the floors above. Ornately sculpted plaster decorated the tall ceiling while the walls were crowned with carved moldings. The embellished pattern of plaster and molding, she soon discovered, continued throughout the huge house. Light flowed through the bank of windows that graced each outside room. His hand holding hers, Aleck pulled her through the entire downstairs, explaining the use of each area and what it would hold in the way of furnishings. Bright and airy, the place was none other than magnificent. By the time they'd come full circle, Chandra was breathless from their trip.

"Let's see the upper level, shall we?"

Aleck drew her up the stairs. From room to room he took her, his long strides measuring one to her two. Many times he cautioned her about the obstacles that stood along the way, for he was concerned that she might injure herself. Exiting yet another room, Chandra finally pulled free of him.

"Stop!" she cried. "You're making me dizzy."

A playful grin crossed his face. "Sorry, but in my enthusiasm, I sometimes forget myself. Come, there's one more place I want you to see, then we'll leave."

He motioned her ahead and Chandra drew a steadying breath, then preceded him along the corridor. She couldn't help but smile to herself, for he seemed very much like a small boy on his first adventure. In fact, she hadn't thought it possible, but she was actually enjoying herself. That was, until she stepped into the next room along their circuit.

Through the large windows, she spied the castle across the way. At first glance, it reminded her of home. For a short time, her sorrows had vanished, only to return. And she could not help wondering how she had so easily forgotten. *He* was responsible for the pain she felt, for the anguish in her heart. How could she possibly feel the smallest amount of pleasure with him? After all, she despised him, didn't she?

"This will be my room," Aleck said, his shoulder meeting the doorframe. Crossing his arms over his chest, he watched as his ward looked around her.

"'Tis grand," she said, heading slowly toward the window. Below her, she saw the horse. She had to get away. Strangely, she knew that if she didn't, she'd soon be lost. She glimpsed another door, much like the one that led from her room to his at the castle. Slowly, she strolled toward it. "I suppose this is meant for your countess?" she inquired, viewing the room beyond. "'Tis grand also."

"The room is meant for the woman I marry, but when I take my vows again, I will insist she sleeps with me."

Chandra's head swung in his direction. "You were married?"

"Aye, I was. But only briefly."

She frowned. "W-what happened to your bride?" she asked, wanting for some unexplained reason to know.

"My wife died a few months after we were wedded."

No emotion showed in his voice, and Chandra wondered why. "You sound as though you don't miss her."

"In truth, I don't." He noted her stunned look. "The marriage had been arranged. I neither knew nor loved the fair Elinor. Perhaps in time I could have learned to care for her, but it was not to be."

"Had she been ill?"

"No." He drew a long breath and expelled it. "She died of fright."

Chandra blinked. "Fright?"

"Aye." His ward appeared more than a little confused. Aleck couldn't rightly blame her. "To put it bluntly, she was frigid. She feared having me in her bed—having to perform her wifely duties. Elinor came to me a virgin and left me a virgin—not that I didn't try to woo her. Each time I entered her room, she became emotionally distraught. I can only assume her panic is what killed her."

Chandra could not imagine any woman rejecting him. Not unless he had murdered his late wife's cousin, just as he had hers. "I hope your next bride will be more understanding of your needs," she said, peeking back into the other chamber. Her guardian was across the room from her, the farthest he'd been all day. If only . . .

"But whether she stays in your room or the extra one you've prepared," Chandra said, casually venturing through the door, "I'm certain she'll be most appreciative of your efforts to make her comfortable. The view is grand from here," she called, moving deeper into the room. "The grass and trees are so very green."

Aleck heard her walking about the adjoining room. On her last words, he smiled. "It's what's known as an English green. I believe you know the term already." He started to straighten from the doorframe, intending to follow her, when from the corner of his eye he saw a flash of red streaking down the hallway toward the stairs. Cursing vividly, he whirled; then, swift of foot, he chased his fleeing ward. Having strolled easily through one door, she'd dashed out the other. The vixen, he thought, gritting his teeth. She'd tricked him again. "Damn it, woman. Stop!"

His quick strides were fast approaching her. Panicking, Chandra hiked her skirt and ran for her life, brushing past a beam that supported a scaffold of sorts. The thing teetered, and she scurried from beneath the swaying platform, with canvas-covered containers of paint and plaster sitting atop the wood, just as it began to collapse.

Not far behind her, Aleck cursed anew. There was no time to stop, so he vaulted over the tangled mess that had come crashing to the floor. His feet landed on the other side of it, one plunging into a spinning bucket full of paint. Cursing again, he hopped around on one foot until he finally kicked the thing free. Spying his ward at the top of the steps, he took off after her. Blue fire blazed in his eyes.

Chandra heard the loud crash, but she dared not look back. However, when she reached the stairs, she glimpsed her guardian, a bucket flying free of his foot, a trail of paint sailing after it. Like a raging bull, his nostrils flaring, he charged her way. Mother of God, she thought, he meant to kill her. On a shriek, she scurried down the stairs and out the wide opening, then on toward the trees.

As Aleck's feet hit the first level of his new residence— the one his ward had obviously meant to ruin—he didn't remember touching even one of the steps. In fact, he could almost swear he'd surpassed all sixty of them in one giant leap. Had he looked back, he'd have noted a bright white footprint on every sixth tread, but his eyes remained fixed on his ward. Out the door he sped; then, a dozen yards from her, he saw she'd finally gained the stallion's back. "You'll not escape," he yelled as she urged the horse through the trees. "Give it up, Chandra." He chased after her through the wood. "You can't get away." She refused to listen, and while she weaved through the growth, Aleck cut straight down the hill. She kept just ahead of him, and he knew he had to act now, before she broke from the trees, before she urged the stallion into a gallop. "Chandra, stop!"

She heard the warning in his voice, but chose to ignore it. Home, she thought, exiting the wood. She pointed the large steed north, excitement filling her breast. As her heels struck the beast's flanks, attempting to spur it from a trot into a gallop, a shrill whistle filled the air. The stallion skidded to a halt; Chandra did not. Flying forward, she nearly somersaulted over the horse's head. But for grabbing its neck, she would have. With a thud, she landed on her bottom. Tears stung her eyes, then clouded them completely. Through the haze, she saw her guardian loping toward her.

"I warned you," Aleck said, slowing to a walk.

He'd won. She remained his prisoner. "No!" Chandra screamed. Anger and fear pushing her, she sprang to her feet. At a full run, she continued north. Her tears blinding her, she tripped, but caught herself. *Ladybird, ladybird, flee . . .* "No!" she cried again, somehow knowing he was after her. "You'll not keep me here." Footsteps thundered in her ears. Were they hers or his? "I want to go home. I have to—I must. Please, let me go home."

Aleck trailed just behind her, ready to catch her should she fall, Chandra's sobs tearing at his heart. His anger had fled. Through compassion-filled eyes, he watched her. She'd bounded to her feet, and he'd thought the chase was again on, but she'd only gone a few yards when she stumbled. Righting herself, she appeared dazed, wandering aimlessly. Confused by her actions, her words, he soon realized that her spirit was nearly broken. She could take no more, and Aleck cursed himself for having caused her so much misery.

"Please," she implored again, then Chandra's knees buckled.

Aleck caught her. "Hush, little one," he crooned, turning her toward him. He held her fast in his arms. "Everything will be all right."

Her face nestled against his chest, Chandra sobbed out her despair, her tears soaking through his shirt. A gentle hand stroked her hair as soothing words were whispered in her ear. She could not say what the tender utterances were, but nonetheless they eased her. She felt safe, cared for, and comforted in the arms surrounding her. For a moment, she truly believed she was home. Soon she quieted, and her strength slowly renewed itself. Her senses returned, and she realized who held her. Drawing a ragged breath, she pulled away from him. Embarrassment riffled through her, but somehow she managed to hold his gaze. "I cannot stay here," she said, her misty eyes beseeching him to understand.

"I know," Aleck responded, his voice deep and husky. "It won't be long, little one, and you'll be on your way back to the Highlands."

"When?"

"Soon. I need to make arrangements for an escort. You'll not leave until I am assured your journey will be safe and that you'll be protected."

"Tomorrow?" she asked, the glow of excitement rising on her cheeks.

Knowing that she wanted so desperately to leave him, Aleck felt strangely unsettled. Was he truly that much of a fiend? "Possibly, but I cannot promise," he said in answer to her question. "It may be the day after, or even the one after that. Just bear with me, and by week's end you'll be on your way."

Chandra felt like spinning around in circles, shouting

her joy to the heavens. However, she managed to restrain herself. "Thank you," she said simply.

His heart heavy, Aleck viewed her for a long moment. "Chandra, I know you fault me for causing Devin's death," he said, and noticed the light fade from her eyes. "In some ways I fault myself as well. I never meant for it to happen. It was not intentional. Were I able to change it, I would. Know I speak the truth."

Did he? Chandra wondered, searching his face. His expression was open and unwavering. She had no chance to discern the truth, for a shout rose in the distance. Both she and Aleck turned to see Marlowe coming toward them. The old gelding that he rode lumbered up to them. "This just came, sir," the steward said, handing Aleck a letter.

Turning it over in his hand, Aleck viewed the seal. A knot formed in his stomach as he ripped through it. Unfolding the missive, he read it twice; then, on a heavy sigh, he handed it to Chandra. "It seems our plans have changed," he said, and watched as she read the letter herself.

Stunned by the words that met her eyes, Chandra frowned up at him. "This cannot be. I don't understand."

"It is simple. Our king has ordered us to London."

Chapter
9

Dressed in their finest, the courtiers were gathered in the Presence Room at the royal residence for an evening banquet. Patiently the colorful array waited for their sovereign and his queen to make their entries. A celebration was at hand, but no one seemed to know why. Some said it stemmed from another of Anne's whims; the woman always enjoyed a good round of pleasure—all at the treasury's expense.

Feeling exceptionally nervous, Chandra turned her attention from the lingering crowd, who preened and strutted much like a covey of peafowl, and looked at the man beside her. Swathed in black, save for the gold, jewelled embroidery embellishing his clothing, her guardian was resplendent in a satin doublet, trunk hose, and leather shoes, a cape draping across his broad shoulders. He was possibly the most handsome male there. A leopard, she decided, again perusing him from his ebony hair to the tips of his polished shoes, that was what he resembled.

Like the regal cat itself, he appeared composed, self-assured, and Chandra wondered how he could possibly remain so calm in the midst of all this pomp. Just the thought of meeting their king struck fear into her. Did Aleck not realize that their sovereign held supreme power? In his own eyes, James was second only to God. Recognizing such, Chandra had a strange feeling that judgment would soon be passed on them both; hence her trepidation.

"Relax, little one," Aleck said, offering her a reassuring smile. "Our sovereign is quite amicable." Beautiful, he thought, thirstily drinking in the sight of her for at least the hundredth time. And for the hundredth time, he fought to keep his desire in check. "You have no reason to fear him. If anyone is subject to his wrath, 'twill be me."

"'Tis easy for you to say," she snapped, fiddling with the lace collar rising from her shoulders and spreading behind her head.

A collet monte was what Winnie—who, at Aleck's request, had come with them to act as both chaperon and lady's maid—had called the decoration while attaching it to the gown. Chandra called it a nuisance—constantly snagging her upswept hair, the shiny mass perfectly coiffed and adorned with a white feather—as she did the rest of the clothing she wore, especially the French farthingale hidden beneath her skirt.

The thing resembled a wheeled cage and was every bit as cumbersome. Once it had been draped with the colorfully embroidered white satin gown—which she suspected had belonged to the late Countess of Montbourne, but had been quickly altered brief hours ago to accommodate the Lady Lochlaigh's measurements—Chandra had fallen into the giggles. She looked as though she'd plunged through the center of a round, cloth-covered table and, unable to free herself, now sported the thing as she traveled about the palace.

More embarrassingly, her neckline sank far too low, exposing the top halves of her youthful breasts, which were painfully compressed against her chest. She was tempted to pull her bodice higher, but wisely resisted the urge. Her stocking-clad feet ached unbearably from the stiff shoes she wore, and she thought several times to kick the torturous things free.

Fashion, the scourge of womanhood, she berated silently, sullenly, wishing she'd donned her own clothing instead. But, eyeing the other women in the room, all dressed as ridiculously as she, Chandra knew she'd have felt very much out of place. Besides, at the moment, she desperately wanted to blend with the rest, else her king would readily single her out. As would they all, she decided of those at court. In Highland dress she'd be the object of ridicule and laughter, the whole barely deigning to acknowledge that she also was a peer.

"Very easy for you to say, indeed," she stated, cooling herself with her white lace fan, knowing it was impossible for her to relax.

"Easy, you think?" Aleck asked, his eyebrow arching. While Chandra had been considering her comfort in dress, her comment referring to such, Aleck was pondering a physical comfort of a different sort. Belated as his regret might be, the last thing he desired was to incur the king's anger. Howbeit, because of all that had happened, the strong possibility existed that the executioner's axe would meet his neck. "Not so, milady. I don't relish sitting in the Tower with the likes of Raleigh and the others, invariably waiting."

She frowned. *If anyone is subject to his wrath, 'twill be me.* "Is that where he'll send you—to the Tower?" she asked, her mind just digesting all that he'd said.

"If not to my death."

Chandra blinked. It was one thing for her to desire his end, but for their king to do so was another matter altogether. Especially when it was James who'd caused the entire debacle. Had he not meddled in Chandra's and Aleck's lives, none of what had followed would have transpired. Chandra now faulted James for all that had come to pass. "I hope the Tower alone is your punishment, should he decide to chasten you."

"Thank you," Aleck said, a touch of drollness in his voice. "And I wish the same to you, milady."

"Me?" she asked incredulously, missing the fact that he teased her. "Is my life also at risk?"

"'Tis a possibility," he replied, glancing at his fingernails, continuing the jest. "One never knows with James."

"I thought you said he was quite amicable."

"He is, usually. But lately he's been beset by a succession of disobedient subjects. I doubt he'll abide any more. A word of warning—whatever he says, whatever he requests, keep in agreement with him. 'Tis the only way to ward off disaster."

Since arriving here yesterday, Chandra had heard snatches of talk about the latest uproar to encompass the court. James's cousin, Arabella Stuart, heir to the throne after James and his progeny, had defied her sovereign's edict that she not marry without his permission, secretly wedding William Seymour, who was twelve years Arabella's junior. Chandra imagined that at five-and-thirty the woman had grown weary of waiting and, having fallen in love, decided she'd wait no more. They were discovered, however, and James, livid over the challenge to his authority, had banished the aging Arabella to Lambeth and young Seymour to the Tower.

The deed, to Chandra's estimation, was done probably more out of fear than anger, for William also held claim to the throne, a definite threat to James. Ever resourceful, the two lovers, with the aid of friends, had managed to escape their prisons. Disguised as a lad, Arabella had fled to the Thames estuary where she'd boarded ship. William, dressed as a carter, had ambled out the Tower gates under the guards' noses. Having missed his rendezvous with Arabella, he also set sail for France. But sadly, the pair were not reunited. William had found his freedom, while poor Arabella was ultimately recaptured. She now sat in the Tower, her heart undoubtedly broken.

Should she say or do the least little thing that James thought unacceptable, would she and Arabella find themselves close neighbors? Chandra wondered. Fearing so, she quickly decided she'd not pose even a shred of opposition to her sovereign, no matter what he required. "I'll hold your warning fast. 'Tis Scotland I wish to see, not the Tower."

"And I, the north of England. Besides, the place leaks," he said of the old Norman fortress and its many additions. "The sort of exercise I most enjoy does not include running about a musty old room, bucket in hand, catching the rain as it pours through the cracks in the ceiling."

Throaty laughter erupted next to Aleck. Both he and Chandra turned toward its source. "From my own experience, I can attest it does not," Felicia said, moving a step nearer the couple. Cognizant of the man and his mannerisms, she noticed he'd grown tense, guarded, but she was not deterred. "'Tis well known that what you *most* enjoy is usually done indoors, dearest Montbourne, but I've yet to see you do it with a bucket. An intriguing notion, is it not? Perhaps you'll someday devise a use for the thing. You are, after all, exceedingly creative and extremely adept."

Aleck turned slightly. The move placed him between his ward and his former mistress. "Lady Emory," he greeted, his voice cool.

She suspected Aleck hadn't recognized the significance of his action, but its underlying meaning was not lost on Felicia. His sudden protective stance, alongside the formality of his address, shouted tomes. Jealousy rippled through her, but she masked the emotion with an appealing smile, one she knew attracted masculine attention. "Lord Montbourne," she responded with a stately nod, then moved around Aleck. "This must be your inexperienced young ward, the Lady Laylock."

"Lochlaigh," Chandra corrected, noticing how the woman's indifferent gaze traversed her from head to foot, stopping briefly at Chandra's exposed bosom. The Lady Emory seemed to have found her lacking.

"Yes, forgive me. Scottish names are so very difficult to remember," Felicia stated dismissively. Her feather fan brushed the tip of her chin. "This is your first time at court, I presume. Should you stay long, you shall become more accustomed to the events here. In fact, I'm certain you'll quickly become one of us. In the meantime, there is much to see, learn, and do." Her fan quickly hid the side of her face. "When you are ready, and if you are daring enough to slip from under your guardian's ever watchful eye," she said in a loud aside, "there are several attractive men whom I'm certain you'd relish meeting." Over the fan's feathers, she glimpsed Aleck as she named names. "And, of course, there is Lord Whitfield."

Aleck's jaw clenched and his eyes narrowed, for the man she'd mentioned was a renowned rake. Aleck knew him well. Too well, in fact.

Pleased that she'd been able to cause him some anxiety, Felicia smiled to herself. "Let me know when you feel adventurous. We'll explore together," she said, the fan falling from her face. "I do hope your stay is highly educational as well as enjoyable." With a wave, she swept into the gay multitude, seeking out yet another member of the court.

Puzzled by the episode, Chandra stared after the woman until at last she was swallowed by the crowd. A question on her lips, she turned to her guardian. His eyes were shuttered by his long lashes, but she could see that he, too, watched after the beautiful Lady Emory. Instantly, Chandra's confusion cleared. They were lovers—or at least, they had been. Wishing she could deny it, but knowing she could not, Chandra felt strangely grieved by the knowledge. She pushed the unnerving sensation aside; then she reviewed the woman's actions, more so than her words. The break between the couple had been recent. They had quarreled, it was apparent. Then, in her mind, the query surfaced: Had she, Chandra, been the source of their rift?

Aleck's attention turned toward the young woman beside him, whereupon he saw that she studied him intently. He could only imagine what thoughts tumbled through her head. Despite her naiveté, her woman's sense had alerted her to the truth. He'd not attempt to deny it, but he was determined to keep his ward away from the vindictive Felicia. The woman seemed want to destroy Chandra's innocence; already had the man chosen for her ruin. The debaucher would die first, Aleck vowed, as would anyone who dared touch her. Of course, Felicia's cloaked threat might be false, meant simply to mock him. The entire conversation might have been staged as retaliation for his having abruptly ended their liaison, but Aleck could not risk the threat coming true. Intent on keeping his ward from harm, he said, "You shall stay far from the Lady Emory while we are here. Do not seek to trick me, either. For should I see you with her, or hear that you have been together, you will suffer for your disobedience. Is that clear?"

Chandra disliked his tone and opened her mouth to tell him so. But before she could speak, a trumpet sounded, heralding James's arrival in the Presence Room. Following the lead of the other women close by, Chandra sank into a deep if rather awkward curtsy, while beside her, Aleck posed an elegant bow. She promised herself that she'd practice the act of respect further, then peered through her lashes toward the throne. Having come from behind a curtain, her king crossed the area, his gait a strange sort of hobble. Unkempt he appeared, and Chandra wondered if it was true that he bathed not at all, changing his clothes only on special occasions, as Winnie said.

"Rise, my children. Rise," he called after he was seated, waving everyone upward.

"Children?" Chandra whispered to Aleck.

"Aye. He thinks he is father to us all, whether we be Scottish or English."

"Since he is king, I suppose he can think whatever he likes. Who would dare dispute him?"

"No one, if he is wise."

Blond and tall, a young man stepped up to the throne. When he'd bowed before the king, his hand was quickly captured by James's and pressed to the king's cheek. A frown creased Chandra's brow. "Who is he?" she inquired, watching the affectionate display.

"'Tis Robert Carr."

"And the young woman?" she asked, noticing the beauty who came forward to stand at Carr's side when he stepped away from his king.

"She is Frances, Countess of Essex."

As Chandra watched, the couple smiled into each other's eyes. "They appear to be quite smitten—no, very much in love," she commented. "Are they betrothed?"

"No."

"Are they to be?"

A heavy sigh flowed through Aleck's lips. "I doubt it. But one cannot fully say." He saw Chandra's questioning look. "The countess is already married to the Earl of Essex. Unless Essex dies or the marriage is somehow miraculously annulled, there seems to be little chance of the two lovers marrying. Besides, for the moment, Carr is James's favorite."

"Favorite?" she asked in complete innocence.

Aleck paused, assessing Chandra. "There is much you will discover while at court," he said at last, "most of it startling to one who has had little experience in the ways of the world. I caution you to watch and to listen, but also to keep your tongue tight between your teeth, lest you give offense. What might seem unnatural to you or to me is quite normal for another. It is not for us to understand, only to accept."

"So?" she asked, not understanding him in the least.

"So, when I or anyone else uses the word *favorite* at court, it means far more than what you may imagine. Carr and our king are involved, Chandra. They also are lovers."

"Oh," she said, her mouth having worked several times before the word finally slipped out. "I shall be most careful to keep secret what you've shared." She frowned. Carr and the married countess were paramours, as were Carr and their king. But what of Anne? "Does his queen know?" she asked, still confused by it all.

Aleck's low laughter rumbled forth. "It is no secret, little one. Anne knows, as does everyone else. Simply protect yourself and do not speak of it openly. It is the wisest course to take."

Chandra thought they were all to one degree or another immoral, her guardian included. "I shall heed your words," she said, certain it was risky not to.

"It would be prudent if you did so all the time, especially while we are here. In fact, I bid that you do."

He yet held rightful claim as her guardian, but Chandra still bristled whenever he issued her an order. Despite her indignation, she smiled sweetly. "Since I do not plan to be at court long, doing so should not present too great a problem. Actually, I welcome your advice, for as you say, I have very limited experience in these matters. You English, however, seem quite comfortable with everything that goes on. I imagine I'll learn a lot by watching not simply you, but also your peers. From what I've heard and seen heretofore, I'd say all of you are masters of decadence," she said, already forgetting to keep her thoughts quieted.

Studying Chandra, Aleck thought about her words. As to the latter, her impressions were fair, and so long as she voiced them only to him, there should be no problem. As to the former, he could not help but wonder if she hoped to learn significantly more than what he thought necessary. She baited him, he knew. Yet to what limits was she willing to go? And from which of his peers would she seek her knowledge? None, he decided, vowing she'd stay forever innocent. "Provided you merely watch and remain uninvolved, there will be no difficulty, Chandra. At least, not between us. However, if you cross the boundary, that is when you and I will have at it."

Her jaw set, Chandra stared at him. An ultimatum, was it? "Much as we did when you first crossed unbidden onto Morgan lands, I suppose?"

"Far more heated and much more devastating, I fear. Being older and certainly more clever, I am not prone to playing childish pranks. You are now in my territory. Here I play a man's game. Disregard my commands, little one, and you'll fast discover what the contest is really all about."

"I presume the Lady Emory is one such casualty of your manly play?"

"When she entered the game, she knew the rules. Be assured, the woman is no novice. Hence she is able to protect herself well. You, my sweet innocent, cannot."

"I may lack sophistication in some areas, milord, but know I am very astute in others. I am not a fool."

"Then do not test me. Whatever it is that you plan to do, know that in me you have met your match."

Chandra had not *planned* to do anything. Still, her guardian had become quite agitated at the idea, though she knew not why. Once she discovered what it was that disturbed him, she intended to use the information to unhinge him further. He could consider it payment in kind for all the misery he'd caused her. "You might think you can best me," she said, "but don't venture too strongly that it is so. Besides, we are no longer at Montbourne. This is James's territory, and it is now his game we must play."

"Aye," Aleck agreed, "but until our sovereign pronounces otherwise, I am your guardian. Therefore, for now, the game is still mine, Chandra, and so are the rules."

"Then I shall seek to change those rules."

"How?"

"I'll speak to James."

"When he is ready, he will summon us."

"And when might we expect such?" she asked.

"It could be tonight, tomorrow, a week hence, even a month. With James, one never knows. He is aware we are here. When he is ready, he will give summons."

"A month?" she nearly cried, and saw his nod. "Why, then, am I standing here, pressed into your late wife's clothing, ridiculous as it looks, when I could be elsewhere, truly enjoying myself at that?"

"Because," he said, his gaze raking over her, "our king may just decide to call us forth tonight. For the clothing, Chandra, it is not Elinor's. Upon our arrival, our queen inquired if you needed anything. I informed her that you were without suitable clothing to appear at court. She is the one who sent the attire to you, evidently hoping to make you feel comfortable so that you might enjoy your stay."

Chandra felt duly chastened. She had made an assumption based on very few facts. All she had known was that Winnie had presented her with the gowns and other accessories, then made the necessary alterations after Chandra tried each one on. Naturally she'd thought the clothing had been brought with them from Montbourne. Who else but Elinor would have had such finery? But obviously her assumption had been wrong. Even if she'd been correct, her spiteful comment had been uncalled for. "I spoke out of turn. It was rude of me to do so. I apologize."

"'Tis Anne of Denmark who should hear your apology, not I." Aleck looked toward the area where James sat. "It seems, little one, the opportunity to excuse yourself has just presented itself."

Chandra turned toward the dais even as the queen's arrival was heralded. As with James, deep curtsies and elegant bows marked the gathering's show of reverence for Anne. When Chandra lifted herself from her curtsy, she felt Aleck's hand grip her arm. "What are you doing?" she demanded as he started propelling her toward the dais.

"You wanted to offer your regrets, didn't you? This is your chance."

Her heels dug into the floor. "She knows nothing of my error. 'Tis you whom I offended. 'Tis from you I ask forgiveness."

Aleck pulled up. "Then you do not wish to meet our queen?"

"Not yet."

"And James?"

"I am not ready to face him either."

"Then we'll wait until we are summoned," he said, his hold relaxing. "Until then, I ask that you grant me your trust. My experience, Chandra, far outweighs yours. If I issue orders, it is done simply to protect you. So do not pose me any problems. Please?"

A trumpet sounded again, and Chandra was saved the need to reply. "What's happening?" she asked, watching as James, Anne, and those in their close company stepped forward.

"We are about to begin the banquet. After we've eaten, we are to be entertained by one of the queen's masques."

After the royal entourage had seated themselves, the rest were ordered to take their places. Approaching her own chair, Aleck beside her, Chandra attempted to descend gracefully onto it, but the farthingale prevented any such move. Each time she lowered herself, her skirt popped up. So did Chandra, for she feared the thing would fly completely over her head. Hearing Aleck's deep rumbling laughter, she turned a cold eye on him. "What, milord, causes your mirth?"

Spying the frigidness in her eyes, he sobered. "Not a thing," he fibbed, trying to bite back his grin. "If milady will allow me to help her, we can both join in the feast." At Chandra's nod, he lifted her skirt from behind; his ward nearly fell into her seat. "'Tis tricky, but you'll soon achieve mastery of it."

"I do not plan to be here that long."

"Such news is certain to break my heart," a masculine voice interjected; Aleck looked up to see the newcomer seat himself at Chandra's left. "I had hoped that milady would stay for a while—until we all flee London, that is. Along with summer comes the plague," he said, his dark head leaning toward her, a smile on his lips. "Or at least the fear of it."

Aleck's gaze narrowed on the man. "Lord Whitfield," he said coolly. "I thought you'd taken a tumble from your horse and broken your neck."

Leaning back in his chair, Viscount Whitfield inspected Alexander Hawke closely. Having gauged the man and the situation correctly, he broke into a wide smile; suppressed merriment danced in his green eyes. The two men were possibly the most sought-after bachelors at court, but the viscount wanted to claim that distinction solely as his own. To his delight, it looked as though the competition was about to be felled. A small nudge might expedite the matter. It was worth a try.

"Thought, Montbourne? Or hoped?" the viscount asked, intent on raising the earl's hackles. "'Twas only a minor spill. A bruise or two, that's all. You'll just have to keep hoping." He gave Chandra a conspiratorial wink.

"The man is forever trying to chase me away from the young beauties who have gained his interest, but, alas, without much success. I suppose that is why he has yet to remarry." Boldly he regarded her face, the curve of her graceful neck, then Chandra's bosom. "I doubt he lets me win you over as easily as he did the others, though. You truly are a beauty. One of the rarest I've seen. And innocent, too, I'll wager."

His jaw clamped, Aleck eyed the viscount as though he'd just spotted vermin. Were he able to do so, he'd squash the pest between his thumb and forefinger, flick him away into the rushes, then grind his heel into him, making certain the little nuisance bothered no one again. "And as her guardian, I tell you: So she shall remain," Aleck warned on what could only be termed a growl. "Haven't you another place to sit, Whitfield?"

"The chair was vacant," he said with a shrug. "Now it's not."

"I suppose it was the Lady Emory who pointed you in this direction?"

"I haven't laid eyes on her today, so it would have been impossible for her to do so."

Aleck backed toward his own chair, situated to his ward's right, his cold stare remaining on the man. Whitfield was Aleck's junior by two years, but by experience they were equally met. Aleck didn't trust him in the least. He knew him too well. Vowing to keep an eye on the viscount for as long as he and Chandra were at court, he swung his sword outward and made ready to seat himself.

"Here! Watch what you're doing," a man's voice objected strenuously.

Aleck bounded from the man's lap back onto his feet. "My pardon," he said, spinning around. "My pardon again, but you're sitting in my chair."

The fellow harrumphed. "There are other seats available, sir. This one is taken."

Aleck's hand tightened around his sword's hilt. "Agreed, sir. And if you refuse to vacate it so that its rightful occupant may reclaim it," he said, leaning close to the man's ear, "you'll find that you shall have no reason to sit ever again. Unless, of course, you are buried ensconced in a chair. Now, away with you."

The man quickly came to his feet. With several hasty apologies, he sped off toward another chair.

His mood fast deteriorating, Aleck claimed the seat before someone else could attach himself to it. Glimpsing Chandra, he saw she was engaged in light conversation with Whitfield. As her laughter readily bubbled forth, its usually musical sound began to grate on Aleck's nerves, especially when it was followed by Whitfield's deep chuckle. So the meal continued, her attention on the man at her left.

From the corner of her eye, Chandra saw a capon fall upon Aleck's plate. Using his knife, he attacked the thing with a vengeance. How delightful, she thought; he was clearly perturbed. Witnessing the exchange between the two men, she'd quickly comprehended that they were not exactly on the best of terms. She'd taken the viscount's lead, needling Aleck however and whenever she could. By the end of their meal, he'd grown most surly. Had Chandra been wiser, she'd have known her capricious behavior would not go unpunished.

The trumpet sounded again. "Come," Aleck said, rising from his chair. "Let's find a place in the gallery so we might watch the masque from above."

Chandra rose to her feet, then looked at the viscount. "Lord Whitfield, would you care to join us?"

"I believe he has other plans," Aleck said, before the viscount could respond.

Above Chandra's head, the men's gazes clashed. "Actually," the viscount said finally, "I had planned to view the masque with some old acquaintances of mine. However, I don't see why we cannot all group together in the gallery."

"Wonderful," Chandra chimed in, a smile lighting her face. "We shall meet you above."

Lord Whitfield was not in the least deterred by the forbidding look Aleck Hawke cast his way. "Keep eight places for us. We shall see you soon." With a slight bow, he disappeared into the crowd.

Immediately, Chandra felt herself being pulled along. She saw they were headed toward the outer doors. "Where are we going?"

"To your apartment."

"Why?"

"It is time for you to retire for the evening."

"But we have not seen the masque."

"Nor will we," he said, his determined strides carrying them closer to the exit.

Chandra twisted free of his hold. "Why are you behaving in such a callous manner? I've never seen a masque, and I'd very much like to. It is not late, so tell me what is wrong with doing so?"

"I do not like the company that you keep," he said, reaching for her arm again; she managed to evade his hand. "If need be, Chandra, I'll throw you over my shoulder and carry you from here. Do you withdraw as would a lady, or do you go like a sack of flour?"

"Why don't you approve of Lord Whitfield?" she asked, backing away from Aleck; slowly he stalked her. "He seems friendly enough and most kind."

"That is the problem, little one. He is known to be *too* friendly at times, especially with innocent young ladies. You have no idea what he is capable of. Nor will you discover such—not as long as I'm your protector."

"You attack the man's character, but I'm certain he is no more of a rogue than you are. How do I know I'm safe with you?"

"You don't." Seeing her surprised stare, Aleck chuckled. "Come. I shall hand you over to Winnie's care. There you will be quite safe." As he reached for her again, his name was called from behind him. Turning, he spied Sir John heading toward him. When Aleck looked back, he saw his ward making her way toward the stairs leading up to the gallery; Whitfield loped toward her. "Damnation!" He closed his eyes and gritted his teeth, then took off after her.

"Trouble?" Sir John asked, having caught up to the earl.

"Where she's concerned, when is there not?"

"Unfortunately, there promises to be more."

Aleck glanced at the knight. "James?"

"Aye," Sir John responded as the two reached the stairs. In the crush, their progress slowed. "He was not too pleased when told what had transpired. Though I have no idea what he intends, it does not look good for you, Montbourne. I thought you should know."

The two men climbed the stairs. "By the way I was summoned here in such haste, I had expected as much, Sir John," Aleck said, his gaze tracking Chandra and Whitfield as they made their way across the gallery. "I appreciate your warning."

"I've heard talk that he intends to speak with you tonight after the masque."

"As always, I'll be at his disposal."

Reaching the gallery, the two men parted, Sir John wishing Aleck well. Having lost sight of his ward as the crowd flowed toward the seats, he quickly made his way to the area where he'd last seen her. He scanned the group, looking for the flame-red hair that was exclusively Chandra's, and caught sight of her at the fore of the gallery. Centered among at least a half dozen young swains, Whitfield beside her, she sat close to the rail. Excitement painted her cheeks and laughter danced in her eyes. With a muttered oath, Aleck elbowed his way toward his errant ward. There was no way to extract her from the group without making a scene, so he intended to keep watch over her—closely.

"Excuse me," he grumbled, brushing past an elderly duchess. Unknown to Aleck, she teetered on the stairs, promising to tumble down them, until the hapless woman's husband caught hold of her arm. No actual damage was done, but a discordant rumble went through the crowd nearby; all eyes turned to Aleck. Unaware of the censuring looks cast his way, the Earl of Montbourne fell into his seat, three rows back from his ward. From there he eyed her and her hopeful suitors, Whitfield in particular.

"Don't look," the viscount said, leaning close to Chandra's ear, "but your guardian sits just above us. He seems most attentive to all that is happening around you. Dare we expect trouble?"

"I cannot say for certain," she responded, turning her face fully toward the viscount, whereupon she spied Aleck from the corner of her eye. "However, Lord Whitfield—"

"Jason," the viscount corrected with a smile.

"Jason," she repeated, smiling also. "His mood is quite glum. Since he takes his position most seriously, perhaps we should remain on our best behavior and forego any controversy. I don't wish to raise the ire of our king."

"Surely you are jesting, aren't you?" Jason asked, a wicked gleam in his eye.

Chandra studied him. "Why is it that I feel you'd rather enjoy seeing Montbourne make a complete fool of himself?"

"Because I would," he responded. "He deserves no less."

"I cannot agree."

"Then you hold some feeling for him, correct?"

"Other than contempt, no," she said with certainty.

"Then, sweet Chandra, you are lying to yourself." Noting her frown, followed by her look of protest, Jason chuckled. "I believe the masque is about to begin," he said, pointing to the floor below. "You'll enjoy it, I'm certain."

Above the couple, Aleck viewed them at length. Their heads together, they conversed with ease, gazes and smiles meant solely for each other. How cozy, he thought invidiously. He refused to acknowledge the emotion that ripped through his body; jealousy was foreign to Aleck Hawke. Yet his jaw clenched tighter as the two remained under his cold glare.

"They are quite a striking pair," Felicia said from behind him. "Don't you agree, darling? I had hoped to introduce them, but it appears Lord Whitfield found her on his own."

"You are lucky he did, Felicia," Aleck said over his shoulder, his eyes still on his ward. "For had you been the one to intervene, you would have regretted it. As it is, should anything happen, only Whitfield will feel the force of my anger. Leave it at such."

Shocked by the force of his statement, Felicia settled back in her chair. Finally it dawned on her: Aleck was actually in love with the girl! Could it be? she wondered, hoping somehow it wasn't. Unable to disallow what she knew to be true, Felicia stared at the back of Aleck's head. His lustrous black hair shone under the torchlight. Her fingers tingled, wanting to thread through the familiar locks, and Felicia lamented over what might have been had Aleck not ventured to Scotland.

Just as the masque started, a rather plump young woman positioned herself next to Aleck, leaned toward him, and tapped his arm with her fan. "It is good to see you again, Lord Montbourne," she said with a giggle. "I thought you had escaped to the countryside for the summer."

Aleck recognized the girl as Lady Alison Fick; her

father and mother, the Earl and the Countess of Radferd, sat directly behind her. Engrossed in his ward, he'd not seen the three converge on him. What else? he wondered, a curse rebounding through his mind several times over. Behind him sat his former mistress; before him, his aberrant ward. Now, beside him was the chit who constantly chased after him, hoping someday to make a match. It would not have annoyed him so, but her parents were as eager as she. Women! At the moment, he readily condemned them all.

Certain that things could get no worse, Aleck fast discovered he was mistaken. The masque progressed, and Chandra's light laughter floated up to his ears, followed by Whitfield's deep, seductive chuckles. The pair's merriment was soon drowned out by the Lady Alison's snorting guffaws as she rolled against him. Would this night ever end? he wondered, groaning in silence.

Finally, to Aleck's great relief, the entertainment came to a close. He rose, intending to intercept Chandra before she escaped him again, but found his way blocked by the nubile Lady Alison, nuisance that she was. "Excuse me," he said, trying to make his way around her, but to no avail.

"Why, Lord Montbourne," she said, giggling, for he'd inadvertently clasped the thickness of her waist trying to maneuver around her, "I hadn't realized I appealed to you."

Aleck stared at her, confused. "What?"

"Your caress." Flirtatiously she tickled his hand with her feather fan. "I had no idea you cared."

"God's wounds, woman," he growled, shoving her back into her chair, "stay forever out of my way."

Blinking furiously to control her tears, Alison watched forlornly as he loped up the stairs and out of sight. "Do not fret, Lady Alison," Felicia said from behind her, bending close to the younger woman's ear. "He rejected me also." She sighed dramatically. "But I do at least have the memory of sharing his bed. Something you do not." Her fan tapped the girl's shoulder, and with a nod at Alison's startled parents, Felicia strolled toward the stairs.

Gaining the landing above the gallery, Aleck searched in all directions, then cursed openly. The profanity drew several stares, but Aleck cared not. While he and the Lady Alison had grappled near their seats, Chandra had made her way up the steps and again disappeared. Certain she was still with Whitfield, he pushed his way through the throng toward the steps. Halfway down, Aleck spied his ward and Whitfield at the doors leading from the Presence Room. Caught in the press, he could do naught but wait until his feet hit the level flooring. When they did, he was after the couple.

Under a darkening June sky, Chandra and Lord Whitfield strolled the palace gardens alongside at least two dozen other couples, conversing about nothing in particular. Then they came to a large oak. "Probably planted by some Norman prince," Jason commented as he and Chandra left the path to walk under the huge sweeping branches.

"Do you think so?" she asked, knowing the tree was ancient. "Five hundred years is a very long time. I doubt it was planted by a Norman."

"Well, perhaps by a descendant, several hundred years later." He rested his hands at his waist and, with legs spread, gazed up at the tree. "'Tis three hundred if it's a day."

"Possibly."

"Possibly? Look at its trunk. Its width would make a half dozen or more of you."

Chandra walked to its base. Turning, she attempted to press her back against the rough bark, but found she couldn't. "'Tis hard to tell by this silly-looking gown I wear, but I think it's more like eight."

By the time Chandra looked away from the tree, Jason was directly in front of her. His hand captured her chin and he looked into her eyes. "He's a fool if he lets you escape."

"Who?"

"Montbourne."

Chandra's gaze fell away from the viscount's. "There is too much that stands between us, and all because of our king."

"Would you care to tell me?"

"No. 'Tis best left unsaid." She looked up again. "Besides, I'll soon be returning to Scotland and to my home. Montbourne does not like the Highlands. He is an Englishman to the end."

"A pity," Jason whispered, a tender smile claiming his lips. "You would have been good for him. Still, if it is not to be, I wish you well and Godspeed, wherever your journey may take you."

Chandra's lashes fluttered closed as Jason leaned toward her. Just as his lips touched her cheek, she felt them being jerked away. Her eyes flew open to see her guardian standing over the viscount, who now sat in the grass.

"Damnation, cousin," Jason said, pulling himself to his feet and brushing off his backside. "You don't have to be so testy about it all."

"Cousin?" Chandra questioned, moving forward.

"Aye," Jason said, "though he doesn't like to admit it. His father and mine were brothers. We share the same surname. That is about all."

"Would you care to tell me?" she asked.

"By your own words: 'Tis best left unsaid." Jason Hawke looked to Aleck. "For now, at least. Since I'm no longer welcome, I shall take my leave. Lady Lochlaigh."

He sketched a bow. "Aleck," he said with a nod. "Good night to you both."

As Chandra watched the viscount saunter up the path, a hand caught hold of her arm, and she was thrust up the lane behind him. Looking up at her guardian, she noted a small tic jumped along his jaw. His attention straight ahead, he remained reticent, forbidding. Like a hunter in the sky, circling in silence, ready to attack. She wished he'd speak.

Not until they reached the upper levels of the wing where their apartments were situated did Chandra find the courage to utter a word herself. "Naught happened in the gardens. I don't see why you're so upset." He didn't answer. Spying the door to her room just ahead, she breathed a sigh of relief. "Where are you taking me?" she demanded as they traveled past it. Her heels dug into the floor. "Let loose of me."

Aleck ignored her. In a dozen more strides, they stood outside his room. Opening the door, he shoved his ward inside, then slammed the panel shut. A lone candle burned in its holder on a table beside the bed. His gaze trained on her, he watched as Chandra backed away from him. "I told you I play a man's game, and it is done by my rules. You disregarded those rules, Chandra, so it's time to discover what the contest is all about."

"I don't know what you mean," she insisted, keeping far from him, but she was fast running out of space. "You speak in riddles."

"Do I?" His sword came free of his waist. He tossed it at the bed and it slid across the covers, landing on the floor with a clatter. "I think not, little one. You are eager to experience all that happens at James's court, good and bad alike. Who better to teach you than I?"

Chandra gulped as his cape fell across a chair and he began to work the fastenings at the top of his doublet. If he meant to frighten her, he was succeeding. "Stay away from me or I'll scream."

Intent on scaring the wits out of her, Aleck continued to stalk her. She had no idea what intrigues were played out in these halls, what dangers lurked behind each door. Were she to be drawn into even one such cabal, innocent as she might be, it could spell her death. "Scream away. No one will think much of it—they'll assume I've made another conquest, my exceptional skills at lovemaking having driven the chit nearly insane. Laughter is all you'll get, Chandra, not help. Believe me when I say it's true." It was a lie, but she had no way of knowing that. "A tutor you want, a tutor you shall have. The best there is in all of England. Rid yourself of your clothes and make ready for your first lesson."

Chandra stared at him. She'd wanted to worry him, annoy him, give back what had been his due, but she'd never expected this. "I promise never to disobey you again," she blurted, backing close to the wall.

"I've heard those words too many times before," he said. Aleck freed himself of his doublet and tossed it at the chair. It missed its mark, but neither of them noticed. "No, little one, I fear you've played your game once too often. Now we'll play mine."

Chandra stumbled back against the wall. The farthingale popped up; she fought it down, only to hear Aleck's chuckle.

"Here, let's rid you of that thing," he said, pulling the tails of his silk shirt from the waist of his trunk hose.

"'Tis fine where it is," she insisted, holding on to the thing through her dress.

"I thought you despised it. Called it ridiculous, I believe."

"Did I?"

"Yes, you did." Before Chandra could protest, her hands were pushed aside, her skirt was raised, the tapes were released, and the farthingale collapsed at her feet. Long fingers spanned her waist, lifting her a few inches into the air. With a rake of Aleck's heel, the thing spun like a top across the floor. "Now your gown," he said, setting her on her feet again.

Chandra squeezed herself against the wall. "No," she cried, tears stinging her eyes. "Please, don't do this."

She attempted to break free, but Aleck's hands hit the wall, trapping her. "Why?" he asked, leaning into her.

His hard body pinned her to the wall, his hips pressing intimately against her own; Chandra suddenly felt dizzy. Something quivered in the pit of her stomach while tremors raced up and down her spine. She was hot and cold all at once. Was it fear? Or something else entirely? She found she couldn't hold his gaze. Nor could she speak.

"Why?" he asked again, his breath fanning her face. She remained mute. "Is it this you want?" His lips traced her cheek to her jaw, then along the side of her neck. "Or is it this?"

The tip of his tongue flicked upward again; a small moan bled through her lips, and Chandra's head jerked aside. "No," she insisted, her heart pounding in her ears. She felt as though she couldn't breathe. "Don't."

"Why?" he questioned once more, his lips playing at the corner of her mouth, his hips moving suggestively. She whimpered, and he knew she felt his arousal. "Tell me."

"B-because I am not ready for this," she said, her voice a mere whisper.

Aleck would have disputed those words. Given a few short minutes, she'd be more than ready. Even now, he knew he could have her, and easily. Were he a lesser man, he'd take advantage of that knowledge. But her innocence prevented it—that, and the fact that he cared about her. Maybe too much, he thought, trying desperately to quell the hard ache that throbbed low inside him. "No, you're not," he said, then realized his words were naught but a groan. He pulled away from her. "You may not be ready, but you seem to want to tempt fate. Not every man will free you as I will, Chandra. Your innocence and beauty are alluring. You know you have the power to arouse a male. You have felt that for yourself." Two streaks of red painted her cheeks, but Aleck ignored her embarrassment. "A virgin is a rarity at court. Whether you know it or not, you are already being singled out."

"If you speak of your cousin, you are wrong. Jason would not harm me."

"Jason would have you as quickly as you could lift your skirts." Chandra's eyes widened. He'd shocked her. Good. "But he is not the only rake vying for the honor. Persist in this game, arranged simply because you wish to defy me, and you'll lose." Mutiny danced in her eyes; Aleck's gaze bored into her. "Take heed. If anyone has the pleasure of lying between those shapely legs of yours, first and foremost, it shall be me. Look upon it as payment for what I've been made to suffer." She seemed stunned, then appalled; Aleck chuckled. "Believe me, little one, you'll experience as much enjoyment in our union as I will. Ecstasy is what we'll share."

At the same time that Chandra's mouth flew open to refute his words, so did the door. A half dozen feet shuffled into the room. "Ah, Montbourne, there you are."

Aleck spun round, his gaze affirming what his ears had already borne out. *Damnation!* Of all times, why had James picked this one? Not wanting to expose Chandra's identity, he remained firmly fixed between his ward and the door. "Your Majesty," he said, his head bowing slightly.

"Not interrupting anything, am I?" James queried, his head tilting. "You, there, step forward and greet your king."

Chandra had nearly dissolved into the wall when she'd heard who had entered. There was no way around it. She had to obey James's command, she knew. On shaky legs, she inched sideways, until the king could see her.

Studying the girl, he glanced at Montbourne, then back to the beauty who hugged the wall. "'Tis the lovely Lady Lochlaigh."

Chandra made an inept attempt at a belated curtsy. "Sire."

"No need for that, child," he said, waving her upward. Then he looked to Aleck. "What I have found here makes my decision far easier," he said in his Scottish burr. "I was, at first, most upset by all that had happened. 'Twas an embarrassment, to say the least. I do not fault you entirely, Montbourne, for from what Sir John told me, I understand you were continually provoked.

"And you, Lady Lochlaigh," he said, his attention shifting to her, "I am grieved by your loss. But I feel your cousin's death could have been avoided had you quelled your Scot's stubbornness. 'Tis hard to do, I know—I'm cursed with the same affliction myself. However, as your guardian, Montbourne had full control over you. You should not have baited him as you did.

"Likewise, Montbourne," he said, his eyes pinpointing Aleck again, "you should not have lost your temper. Since you are English—restraint supposedly being an inherent part of you—you have no excuse. To steal her away from her home. Tsk, tsk. 'Twas a fool thing to do." He moved a few steps closer to the pair, their eyes duly downcast. "At first I was troubled how this might work out, but seeing you thus, I no longer have any qualms. Happily, the embarrassment will be undone, the Lady Lochlaigh's reputation saved.

"Look upon me now," he ordered, and Chandra's and Aleck's gazes beheld him. "Congratulations, my children," he said, a smile trailing across his face. "In just a few days, you shall be wedded."

Chapter
10

Hearing James's words, Chandra nearly collapsed. At the same time, she saw Aleck stiffen. Madness, she thought, wanting to scream her objection. Yet she could not. Their king had spoken, and his edict must be followed. To defy him meant disaster. Arabella had outfaced him, and because of it, the woman now sat in the Tower.

Dazed, Chandra listened as James set forth the arrangements. A private betrothal ceremony was to take place in the morning. By week's end, the couple would be married. A small wedding would be preferable, considering the circumstances. Yet a celebration was in order. Naturally, the funds for such were to come out of Montbourne's purse, not the king's. James, however, offered the use of the Chapel Royal and the banqueting hall, as well as the bishop who'd officiate at the wedding. "Inside of a year, I'll expect an heir from your joining. It will assure the continuation of both your lines, combining two houses into one, and linking both countries as well. I know, Montbourne, that you oppose a united

Britain, as do many of your English brethren. Look upon this marriage as a beginning to that new union. Mark my words: Someday it will actually come about."

With a bow and a curtsy, Aleck and Chandra bade their king farewell. The moment he and his attendants had left the room, the door closing behind them, Chandra attacked Aleck. "This is ludicrous!" she cried. "You must do something. We *cannot* marry."

Slowly he turned to face her. "What is it you want me to do?" he asked, wondering if she truly thought him that abominable. "Our king has spoken. We cannot defy his command. Not unless we wish to suffer his wrath."

Chandra could hardly believe her ears. How could he just give in so easily? "Then you do not intend to seek a private audience and request that he reconsider?"

"What would be the point? You heard him. He had already intended to see that we were wed. Finding us thus simply affirmed his decision. Obviously he believes we are . . . uh . . . exceptionally fond of each other."

"Fond of each other?" Her words were an incredulous shriek. His ears still ringing, Aleck cast her a dark frown, but Chandra missed it. "He must be blind," she ranted. "How can he possibly think such a thing?"

"The notion probably came to him because of the way he found us. We are not exactly attired in the normal fashion in which one receives visitors."

She noted Aleck's extremely informal mode of dress. Her own raiment was less than conventional. Though nothing had happened, it certainly appeared that it had—or at least that it would. On the floor near the door lay her farthingale. James had nearly stepped on it when he entered the room. What else was the man to believe?

Another thought struck. She pictured her gown and undergarments lying atop the farthingale, the remainder of Aleck's clothing carelessly strewn in the same general area. Imagining the scene further, and how things could very well have progressed, she suddenly felt all hot and quavery. Delay his arrival, and their king probably would have caught them in her guardian's bed. Biting back a groan, Chandra was now grateful that James had burst into the room when he had.

"'Tis all your fault," she accused angrily, trying to fight back the heated flush traveling up her body. "You are the one who has caused this mess. Think of a way to free us from it."

Aleck knew he was at fault for much of what had transpired, but he was unwilling to take all of the responsibility. "As I recall, our king said we were equally to blame for all that has happened. Finding us half dressed had nothing to do with his decision." She appeared not to believe him. "He could have caught us in bed naked and joined in, for that matter. I tell you, his mind was already set. There is no way out of it, Chandra. So I suggest you accept the fact. In just a few days we will be married."

"'Tis not fair," she insisted. "How can he expect us to marry? We cannot even abide each other. Doesn't he know we are enemies?"

"Enemies?"

"You are English and I a Scot. 'Tis like oil and water—impossible to mix."

"Are you certain of that?" he asked.

"Aye, I am. We will never come together."

"Oh, but I think we will." She questioned him with her eyes. "James has ordered us to produce an heir, and he expects to see evidence of such before our first wedding anniversary. There is only one way for us to make a babe, Chandra. We'll definitely come together."

Chandra trembled at the thought. If she allowed him mastery over her, she'd lose herself altogether. She was fast becoming powerless against the force of his masculinity. Whenever he was near, whenever he touched her, whenever his lips foraged hers, whether the kiss was born of anger or desire, she felt herself succumbing. Soon she'd surrender completely. The knowledge frightened her. Somehow she had to resist him and the feelings he evoked or she'd be doomed. She'd no longer be an entity unto herself. There would only be him, she being his slave. Masking her fears with indignation, she glared at him. "I'd sooner die than lie with you," she stated, then turned on her heel and headed for the door.

Like a spear, Chandra's words pierced Aleck's male vanity. Elinor had uttered nearly the same phrase. *I'd rather die . . .* And she had. Vowing he'd not be made to remain celibate in his second marriage as he had his first, Aleck strode after her. Just as the door opened, his hand met the wood. The panel slammed shut; Chandra spun round and faced him.

"Do not doubt that we shall become man and wife, Chandra—in *every* way. An heir we have been ordered to produce and an heir we shall have. Be assured: However long it takes for my seed to find its mark, that is the length of time you will share my bed. Until we are certain you have conceived, expect it to be nightly. Either you can willingly participate and gain pleasure from our union, or you can lie with your face hidden in the pillows, pretending to have swooned. Whichever you decide, your body is mine to do with as I please. Should you find you abhor my touch—though I doubt you will—pray that our firstborn is a boy, for in my line only males are allowed to inherit. Remember, for as long as it takes, you will *lie* with me."

A brood mare—was that how he perceived her? Or was it as a whore? To him, she was merely female, a receptacle for his seed, an object on which he could slake his desire and gain his pleasure. Were all men this unfeeling? "After I've fulfilled my duty and have presented you with an heir, what then?"

"When that time comes, if you have no fondness for me, you may return to Scotland and Lochlaigh Castle."

She appeared relieved. Again his vanity felt the sting. "But if you go, Chandra, our son will remain with me." Whether it was pure arrogance or simply that he needed to trust that it would be so, he was unable to say, but he was certain that by then, things would be far different. She'd not leave him. And she'd never desert her child. "You have several days to make your decision. Come to me willingly, and I promise to give you pleasure. React as my first wife did by attempting to push me away, and you will discover my patience has been exhausted. One way or the other, you will be mine." His gaze softened, as did his words. "Do not fight me on this, little one. We have no choice but to wed. Let us make the best of it. Especially since our fate is already met."

Chandra searched his face. He seemed sincere, almost apologetic. His threats, she realized, were generated by what he'd suffered during his first marriage. His vanity would not allow him to abide such a rejection again. Chandra fought down a blush, for she imagined him to be a gentle and caring lover, a man who bestowed pleasure as well as seized it. Otherwise he'd find no joy in the act himself. But too much had gone between them, too much stood in their way. To accept him freely as her husband was to betray her very existence. Her clan would never forgive her. "I will think about what you have said. But do not expect me to hold feeling for you. Because of Devin, I'm not certain I ever could."

At length, Aleck studied her face. Expelling his breath, which unknowingly had been suspended in his chest, he bent and retrieved the farthingale, then looped it over her arm. He opened the door and urged her into the hall. "Rid yourself of your guilt and your anger, Chandra, and you may discover that you already do."

She gazed at the panel long after it had closed in her face, his words tumbling through her head. Was it possible that she actually did hold some affection for the man, the emotion masked by her guilt and anger, as he'd said? Blether, she decided. He hoped to manipulate her mind, convince her that a genuine attachment actually existed, all to make her more receptive to sharing his bed. A useless move, she thought; no such feeling dwelled inside her. Or so she wanted to believe.

She turned and, gathering a handful of skirt, walked toward her own room. Curious stares came her way from several servants in the hallway, but she was unaware of their presence or of the comical sight she presented. She opened the door and stepped inside.

The moment Winnie saw her, she gasped. "Child, you're so pale," she said, waddling toward Chandra from the hanging cupboard where she'd been placing a newly altered gown. "Are you ill?" Then she spied the farthingale. "What's happened? You haven't been accosted, have you? Master Aleck should be made aware of this!"

"Master Aleck knows all there is to know. He's the one who has done this." The farthingale sailed through the air. It ricocheted off the carved bedpost and fell to the floor. "And he's the one who is the cause of all my misery."

Winnie's eyes widened, then sparked with unexpected fire. "The rascal didn't defile you, did he?" Chandra shook her head, and she breathed a bit easier. In a motherly fashion, she placed her arm around the girl's shoulders. "Just the same, I suppose the knave hoped to take unfair advantage. Here, child," she said, leading Chandra toward the bed, "let's sit, and you can tell old Winnie all about it."

Winnie's girth settled onto the mattress beside her, and Chandra spilled out her version of the evening's events. Not having had anyone to confide in, especially an older woman, for a very long time, she held nothing back. Lady Emory, Lord Whitfield, Aleck's bold overtures, the king's interruption, all tumbled from her lips. "He has ordered us to be married," Chandra moaned, her head resting against Winnie's ample bosom. "The deed will be done by week's end."

"Does the thought of having Master Aleck as your husband really upset you so?" she asked gently. Chandra pulled from Winnie's arms to gaze at her. "I have known him since birth," the older woman said. "He has many faults, his temper being the worst of them, but he has many virtues as well. He is kind to a fault and is most caring of those less fortunate than himself. Since you say neither of you has a choice—James has sealed your fates, hasn't he?—perhaps it is time you searched out the man who has remained hidden from you. You may discover he is very much to your liking."

A frown crept across Chandra's brow. "Are you saying I should just accept what is to come? That I should yield to the king's wishes and those of my soon-to-be-husband?"

"What are their wishes?"

"I've been ordered to produce an heir or at least become pregnant before a full year turns after saying our nuptials."

"And you oppose this?"

"Should I not?"

"As a woman and a wife, not to mention a subject of the Crown, what other option do you have?"

Chandra scrutinized Winnie. "None," she admitted finally.

"Precisely," Winnie replied. "The outcome remains the same. You and Master Aleck are to be married. Out of marriage comes children. It is a fact of life."

"But I don't love him," Chandra insisted.

"Do you believe it is a prerequisite before having knowledge of each other?" Winnie asked bluntly, and Chandra blushed. "If that were so, my dear, half of all marriages would never be consummated. Possibly more. I do not speak simply of the nobility. To be certain, with them marriages are made to combine wealth and power.

Love has nothing to do with the couple's joining. Still, people of lesser circumstances are wedded without the benefit of love.

"When my Felix and I were first married, we had known each other only a few short weeks. I was the eldest of six girls. Times were not the best in my family. Food was scarce, my mother was ill. So when Felix offered for my hand, my father insisted that I marry. I did so simply to ease the burden that the others carried. It wasn't until I was expecting our third child that I realized I had grown to like Felix Marlowe. By the time I'd given birth to my sixth and last, I was quite fond of the man. Were anything to happen to him now, I don't know if I'd survive without him, simply because I love him so. To say you do not love Master Aleck now does not mean you will not love him in the future."

"Your story is much like a fairy tale," Chandra said, "but your husband did not murder your cousin. There was hope for you both. For us, there is none."

"You use the word *murder* most freely. Did Master Aleck stalk your cousin and slay him in the shadows?" Winnie waited, but Chandra didn't respond. "If so, then yes, I would call it murder. However, if, as I was told, Master Aleck sought to defend himself against another and the young man vaulted unexpectedly into the middle of the fray, Master Aleck's blade striking him inadvertently, I would say your cousin's death was a mischance, unintentional and without design or malice. Master Aleck suffers because of what happened. This I know. Were he able to change it, he would. Yet you seem unwilling to forgive him. Why is that?"

Chandra said nothing. Unable to hold Winnie's gaze, she looked away.

"Maybe it is not my affair," Winnie said, rising from the bed, "but in my opinion, you are avoiding the truth. You conveniently hide behind your cousin's death as you would a shield. I think it is time you looked inside and discovered why you are compelled to do so."

Long after Winnie had helped Chandra out of her dress and retired to the small adjoining room, Chandra ruminated over what the woman had said. The truth? She *had* avoided it, but no longer could. She faced it fully, and Chandra felt even more torn than before. Caught between loyalty and what someday might very well be called love, if it were given time to blossom, she found herself at an impasse.

She was a Scot, chief of her clan. Strength, allegiance, duty were expected of her. She could give no less. As The Morgan of Morgan, she had to think of her kinsmen first, herself last. So much was expected of her, so much lay on her shoulders. To be a woman, one imbued with the normal hopes, dreams, and desires of her gender, figured not at all. Especially if, as a woman, the man she wanted was English. To admit candidly that she cared for Alexander Hawke meant she would be ostracized. Because she wished to remain head of her clan, she'd kept her feelings secret—even from herself—and had done so from the moment his arresting blue eyes had first looked into her own. That was why she'd hidden behind Devin's death, why she used it as a shield, why she would continue to do so. How else could she keep the man she desired at bay? He was, after all, forbidden to her.

Now that she was being forced to marry him—the Sassenach who'd invaded their lands, killed one of their own, and abducted their chief—would her clan see her as a traitor? Or would they recognize that she'd been powerless and excuse her for what she could not control? Their king had ordered them wedded, had he not? Chandra counted on her clan's understanding; but to have it, she must remain constant and true. To them, the Sassenach was an enemy; therefore, he was hers also. If only it could be otherwise. But, alas, it could not.

Knowing she had little choice but to forever deny what she felt, for her loyalty belonged first to her clan, she tucked the truth away again, disavowing she'd ever discovered it at all. Yes, they would wed. Yes, they would come together as man and wife. And yes, she would give him an heir. But she could never give him her heart. At least, not openly.

On a heavy sigh, Chandra slipped beneath the covers of her bed. Sleep came quickly, and she was carried north to the place of her birth where she felt safe, protected. From the hill opposite Castle Lochlaigh, she viewed her home. There, above the fortress, circled the winged hunter. Patient and silent, the great soaring bird searched for its vulnerable prey. Not even in her dreams could she escape the legend. He was always with her, as he always would be, that masterful hawk forever in control of her destiny.

Chandra's cold fingers rested on Aleck's forearm as he led her from the chapel. The ceremony completed, the service having been read from the Book of Common Prayer, the wedding procession wound its way to the banqueting hall and the feast that awaited them. Certain her legs would give way, Chandra found herself leaning against her new husband. Embarrassed by her sudden lack of vigor, she sought to stand alone, but her knees wobbled uncontrollably. Without his support, she was unable to take another step. She wondered if this would be the way of their marriage: she forever relying on his strength to get her through the days to come.

Having depended upon herself for so long, she balked at such a notion. No man would hold rule over her, she vowed silently. Then she was mindful that when she'd pledged her troth to Alexander Hawke, she'd waived her freedom of choice. He was her husband, and by that position alone he retained supremacy over her. She had to obey him in all things. A distressed groan slipped through her lips, for Chandra just fully understood what she'd relinquished. Why had she consented to this marriage? Being confined to the Tower would probably have been less restrictive. There she'd at least have kept some dominion over herself, her cell functioning as her own tiny kingdom for all the years of her imprisonment.

"Wishing you'd chosen another course?" Aleck asked, leaning close to her ear. He drank in the sight of her. Clothed in a blue satin gown richly embroidered with silver thread; her long hair flowing to her waist, which, on her wedding day, marked her virginity; she was nothing less than stunning. However, a thick ribbon of black crepe was wound around each slender arm, detracting from her otherwise flawless appearance. Viewing the ugly wrappings, Aleck became annoyed. "Is it Devin's loss or the loss of your freedom that you mourn?" She didn't respond to either question. Aleck studied her carefully. "Were I to venture a guess, I'd say it was the latter. Besides wearing black, mutiny shines in your eyes. 'Tis obvious you are making some sort of statement."

Chandra shot him a hard look. "Well, you are wrong," she lied, although her show of mourning was indeed her way of being rebellious.

Aleck's eyebrow arched. "Do I also err when I submit that you now wish you'd chosen confinement in the Tower instead of marriage to me?"

"No, you don't err. I'll not deny the Tower carries greater appeal. Had I a clearer head, I would have told James that."

They had passed through the intricate mazes of galleries and courtyards to stand at the entry to the hall where the feast was set. Aleck smiled down on her. "But, alas, our sovereign never heard those words, and now it is too late. Tsk, tsk. You are married and naught can change it," Aleck teased; then he chuckled and winked. "You'll soon change your mind as to which you prefer, little one." Her hand came away from where it rested atop his arm, his own fingers lifting it, then his lips brushed a kiss on her knuckles. "Especially since we have not yet shared a bed."

At the touch of his lips, fire shot up Chandra's arm. With his words, her breath caught in her chest. Then, as his arresting eyes met hers, glinting in the most tantalizing manner over her hand held a mere whisper from his sensuous mouth, giddiness overtook her. Unable to hold his gaze and still retain her sanity, Chandra quickly looked away. Pulling her hand from his grasp, she entered the hall, her legs less steady than before. The sensation unnerved her. It was as though she'd sipped too much wine, though she hadn't taken a drop. Intoxicated—that was how Alexander Hawke made her feel. Moaning softly, she wished he didn't have that effect on her. How could she conceivably fight against his overpowering masculinity when finally they were alone? An impossibility, she decided. And it was so unfair.

They were enemies, held nothing in common—yet they were now husband and wife. After the wedding feast, which had been prepared for what she assumed were an intimate few, he would take her to his bed. She couldn't deny being drawn to him. His attraction was overwhelming. No woman appeared able to resist him. Although she tried to mask it behind a motherly sternness, even Winnie wasn't immune to his captivating ways. Yet Chandra worried whether she could give herself to him without being continually attacked by feelings of remorse.

All during the ceremony she'd thought of her clan. *Betrayer! Whore! Slut!* Those were the words she'd heard, and had nearly repeated one of them while uttering her vows. Thank goodness she'd caught herself prior to its having slipped through her lips, saving herself much embarrassment. She dreaded what awaited her once the feast ended and they retired to his room. She'd promised herself that she would remain true to her clan—but in the end, who would actually hold her heart? Her family? Or, as Devin had titled him, her lord of legend? Her legs wobbling uncontrollably, she felt forlornly certain it would somehow be the latter. *Betrayer!*

A strong hand settled at her waist, and its owner guided her to the head table. "Thank you," she whispered, slipping into her chair.

"My pleasure," Aleck replied, seating himself.

Chandra's gaze turned to him. Arrayed splendidly in black and silver, her new husband was, as always, most handsome. She wondered why he appeared so relaxed. Never had he objected to being forced to wed. It was as though he welcomed the loss of his freedom—if, indeed, he'd lost it at all. The Lady Emory, she'd noted, had approached him on more than one occasion over these last several days. What words had passed between them, Chandra couldn't say, for she'd always been too far away to hear. For some reason, it vexed her that his former mistress—if she was his *former* mistress, as Winnie had assured Chandra—would take such blatant liberties in the public eye. At Lord Montbourne's betrothal ceremony, too! Watching him still, Chandra considered what role she was meant to play in their marriage. Besides that of breeder, was she expected to serve in any way at all?

While Chandra studied him, Aleck in turn surveyed her. "By your frown, I'd say something troubles you. Dare I ask what it is?"

The sound of his voice snapped Chandra from her trance. "Nothing troubles me," she said, and her attention fell to her hands, clasped in her lap.

"Look at me, Chandra," Aleck said. When she continued to view her hands, he captured her face, gentle fingers nudging it toward him until she looked up. "Do not hold your feelings from me. If something gives you worry, tell me."

Briefly she searched his eyes. Wondrous, she thought.

And compelling. Feeling as though she were sinking into those mystical blue orbs, she blinked. "I was merely thinking that you've managed to take all this—the betrothal, our wedding—quite well. I was just wondering why?"

Aleck bit back a grin. "Do you wish me to throw a tantrum? If so, I'll attempt it, here and now."

Stunned, Chandra watched as he started to rise from his chair, drawing a deep breath as though he thought to shout down the rafters. Immediately her hand caught his arm. "Sit," she commanded in a harsh whisper, then glanced around her. "'Tis not the place to make a spectacle of yourself. Nor of me."

A chuckle escaped him as he fell back into his seat. "Already you sound like a wife. You give orders well."

"Only when necessary," she responded, then looked out over the hall. The "intimate few" that Aleck had said were invited had grown to nearly two hundred guests. "Are all these your friends?" she asked, noting there were not enough places set at the tables for the crowd.

"The original list was one-quarter this size. 'Tis known that these things have a way of getting out of hand. In our case, I suppose everyone is eager to see the woman who downed the great Aleck Hawke, the man who insisted he'd not remarry."

Chandra studied him intently. "If, as you say, you were so set against remarrying, why did you not object to our being forced to wed? I don't understand you."

"Sweet wife, you are far more appealing than the Tower. Let it rest at that."

His wife's next words died in her throat as several people rushed toward the dais, offering their congratulations. For the moment, Aleck was saved further explanation. He watched Chandra converse with an elderly countess whose name had slipped Aleck's mind, and wondered what he'd tell her. The fact was, he'd offered no objection to James's command simply because he didn't disfavor having the Lady Lochlaigh as his wife. How would she understand such a justification when he barely understood it himself? Whether it was to appease his own guilt, or from an overwhelming need to protect her, or something else entirely, he couldn't say. But he wanted her. It was possible that he desired her because she posed a challenge, for he knew she didn't want him. Whatever it was, she was now his. So she would remain.

More and more of the guests, invited or not, came forward. As the bride and groom accepted their greetings and well-wishes, Chandra felt a bit out of place. The women who were close to Aleck's age or younger inspected Chandra carefully, apparently searching out all her flaws. Their words were friendly, but she suspected that after the lot of them had departed, they would all gather elsewhere to discuss what, in their estimation, the new Countess of Montbourne lacked. Only a few of the female well-wishers were genuine in offering their congratulations, but Chandra noted that these women were generally elderly and had by now lost all interest in the male gender, their own husbands included.

While several young women flirted shamelessly with Aleck, possibly trying to see if his bride was the jealous sort, Chandra stared out at the sea of faces. A sadness encompassed her, for she knew none of these people. Never had she thought she'd share what should be the most memorable day of her life with strangers. Then again, she'd never thought she would be forced to marry Aleck Hawke. Fate, she concluded, didn't always cooperate with one's own wishes.

As her gaze swept the hall, Chandra spotted a familiar face. Lord Whitfield lazed against a column at the room's rear, his attention apparently trained on the head table. She wondered about Aleck's response when he learned his cousin was in attendance. Then the Lady Emory came into view. Stopping beside Jason, she spoke to him briefly. He seemed to shrug, then pushed away from the column. Offering her his arm, Jason guided the woman forward, and Chandra grasped that they were coming toward Aleck and herself.

"The bastard is certainly bold."

Hearing Aleck's words, Chandra's head swung round. "I could say the same for your mistress. Or was she part of your original guest list?"

"*Former* mistress," Aleck pronounced, his eyes still on the pair. "The Lady Emory no longer holds my affections. And, no, she's as much an interloper as my cousin."

The Lady Emory no longer holds my affections. But he must have loved her once, Chandra thought, watching the woman as she gracefully made her way toward the table. The Lady Emory was undeniably stunning. Knowing the two had shared the most intimate relationship possible, Chandra couldn't help feeling somewhat inferior; she lacked her rival's sophistication and experience, as well as the Lady Emory's great beauty. Because of her less remarkable features, along with her naiveté, Chandra felt certain the rather roguish Lord Montbourne would be very disappointed in his new bride. Then she wondered who had actually ended the affair. Her husband? Or the Lady Emory?

"Cousin," Jason greeted Aleck, drawing Chandra's attention. He and Felicia stood in front of the table. "You look rather glum for a man who has just captured the loveliest maiden in the land. Or is it my presence that puts such a sour look on your face?" He bounded up onto the dais and perched a hip on the table's edge. "Not to worry. I'll soon retreat, as will the charming Felicia. We just wanted to wish you our best."

"Best? I cannot imagine there being such a thing with you, Whitfield," Aleck said, his tone unfriendly. "Nevertheless, offer your congratulations, then remove your backside from the damask. You're wrinkling it."

Undaunted, Jason smiled. "Tsk, tsk, cousin. I do hope

your mood lightens, lest you frighten your bride." He turned to Chandra. "Your hand, milady," he commanded. Palm up, he wiggled his fingers; Chandra's hand came away from her lap and settled into Jason's. With a wink and a smile, he lifted it to his lips. As his kiss fell on the backs of her fingers, he saw his cousin stiffen. "I have a gift for milady," he said, pulling back. He turned Chandra's palm upward. From his free hand dangled a gold chain adorned with a pendant dotted with emeralds, a smaller replica of the one Aleck wore. He dropped it into her hand, pressing her fingers around it. "'Twas our grandmother's," he said, "made especially for her and given to her on her wedding day. It matches the family heirloom handed down from generation to generation. I believe the original hangs around your husband's rather stiff neck. Now the more delicate version is yours. Along with my gift, I offer this wish: May your lives together be forever happy."

Jason leapt from the dais, and Felicia stepped forward. "If happiness eludes you," she said, her attention centered on Aleck, "you know where to find me."

It was Chandra's turn to stiffen. The woman was certainly brazen. Because of what she and Aleck had shared, apparently the Lady Emory felt no compunction over speaking most frankly to her former lover, his new bride's sensibilities be damned. The couple strolled off toward the rear of the hall, and Chandra heard Aleck's soft curse. Whom it condemned, she couldn't say, but she doubted it was the Lady Emory. Ignoring him, she opened her hand. "'Tis beautiful," she said, inspecting the pendant. "Was it really your grandmother's?"

"Aye, the pendant was hers."

"I would have thought he'd give it to his own bride," she said, fingering the emeralds.

"Normally one would think that. But it is hard to predict what Jason will do. His giving it to you does not surprise me."

"Why are the two of you so unfriendly toward one another. Did you argue?"

"'Tis a family matter, Chandra. Someday I will explain why we are at odds, but today I'd rather not be reminded of our troubles. Do not press me on it."

"As you wish," she said, gazing again at the pendant. "Would you object if I wore it?"

"'Tis yours. You can do with it as you like."

Aleck's tone was exceedingly cool, but Chandra nonetheless slipped the chain over her head. Other than holding it all through the banquet, she had no place to put it. The pendant settled at the cleft of her breasts, which were again pressed painfully against her chest. She'd be glad to be free of her borrowed gown, another of Anne's castoffs, Chandra thought—then swiftly changed her mind. For when she was at last unclothed, she'd be in the bridal chamber, Aleck alongside her. Chandra's nerves quivered. She dreaded the moment when she'd truly give herself to him. *Slut!* The word rang through her head, assaulting her, for again she'd thought of her clan. No longer certain where her allegiance lay, Chandra felt her spirits sink. Why, she wondered, foundering in her misery, had this happened to her?

A trumpet heralded James's arrival, drawing Chandra's attention. After he'd settled into his place, and the courtiers had offered their reverence, Chandra and Aleck included, the merrymaking commenced. First was the feast. A line of servants marched from the rear kitchens, each carrying a large tray of succulently roasted meats upon his shoulder. Soon the fare lined the tables. Rich sauces, a variety of fruits and vegetables, cheeses and breads followed. Wine flowed freely all through the meal, and for some time thereafter. If Aleck worried there wouldn't be enough to feed all those in attendance, he needn't have. Everyone ate to repletion and then some.

Next, a bridal masque was performed, followed by musicians and jugglers. Absorbed in the variety of amusements, which seemed to comport themselves all throughout the huge room, Chandra momentarily forgot her cares.

Aleck noted the high color in her cheeks; a bright sparkle lit her eyes. He knew she'd eaten little and imbibed too much, and he wondered if she was actually drunk. Her cup came away from the table once more, its silver rim aimed at her lips. "Enough, sweet," he said, catching her wrist before she could take another sip of wine. Spying her frown, Aleck chuckled. "Climbing into your cups won't save you from what awaits you. Come. Our guests seem eager for us to begin the dancing."

Wresting the cup from her fingers and placing it on the table, Aleck took her hand and urged her from her chair, whereupon he led her out into the dawdling crowd and released her. At his signal, music filled the hall. Quickly the guests gathered round, waiting for the bride and groom to lead them into the first steps of the la volta.

"Milady," he said, bowing; then he offered his hand. "I would be pleased if you were to do me the honor."

"I cannot," she said, shaking her head. "I know none of your dances."

"Then you shall learn."

Chandra had no time to object, Aleck having guided her into the center of the floor. As she tried to follow his steps, the guests joined them. All danced expertly—all except Chandra. Somehow she managed the several turns, though not gracefully. Then she felt the press of Aleck's left thigh; his left hand met her midriff and she was hefted into the air. Chandra landed on her feet, but her leap could be considered nothing more than inelegant.

"You did well," Aleck commended with a smile.

"By whose standards?" she countered, and heard his

deep laughter reverberate in her ears. "'Tis not funny," she scolded, again trying to follow his lead. "Laugh at me again, and I shall leave you standing here alone."

Merriment twinkled in his eyes as he bit back a grin. "I shall be most attentive to remaining somber." He turned her again. "La volta was our late queen's favorite dance. Then, as now, 'twas often performed at court."

"'Tis probably what finally killed her," Chandra returned, knowing the leap was just ahead. When it came she executed her second jump with more grace than her first, but she still felt awkward and ungainly. Her gown and farthingale didn't help matters either. It was a mystery to her why these women allowed themselves to be trussed up in such cumbersome raiment. Comfort, it seemed, easily gave way to style. At least, with the courtiers it did. While Chandra remained at court, she too would be constrained by their practice of dress. Eager to be away from all this pomp and to again wear her tunic and simple wool skirt, she asked, "How soon might we leave here?"

Aleck studied her. "I'm surprised you're so anxious to desert our guests. But if that is what you truly wish, our bedchamber is ready and waiting."

A fiery blush touched Chandra's cheeks. "'Tis not what I was asking."

"But it is my response," he said, smiling down at her. "Tonight, sweet, we go no farther than our room."

The two had stopped dancing. Chandra stared up at her husband, wishing she could say his words held no appeal, but she couldn't. Perhaps it was the wine, or possibly the festive mood of the crowd surrounding them, or maybe it was simply Aleck himself, but as he gazed down at her, an excited feeling trembled through her. It left her nearly breathless.

"What is it, Chandra?" Aleck asked, for she seemed to have fallen into a trance.

Chandra blinked, but just as she was about to respond,

a group of men dashed from seemingly nowhere. With much jostling, they surrounded Chandra, separating her from Aleck. He watched as his wife was swept away by the merry bunch to the opposite end of the hall. One man bowed and presented his hand, and Aleck assumed he'd requested that Chandra join him in the dance. She looked Aleck's way, then appeared to agree, for the two fell in with those courtiers who hopped and twirled around the floor.

"She's deserted you already, I see," Felicia said from behind him. Aleck turned to her, and Felicia offered him a provocative smile. "Since you've lost your partner, perhaps you are eager to seek another."

"My preference, Felicia, is simply to watch. So, if you'll excuse me, I shall take my leave."

With a nod, Aleck left Felicia to her own companionship; then, finding a quiet spot, he attended the movement of his young bride, ready to intervene should the revelers who'd stolen her from his side become unruly. The music concluded, and the dancers milled, awaiting another tune. A cup was shoved into Chandra's hands, and she quaffed the sweet liquid. Aleck shoved his shoulder away from the column where it rested, intending to take charge of the situation before she became fully inebriated. But the musicians struck up another measure, its sprightly melody announcing the couranto.

Aleck relaxed when the cup in Chandra's hands was set aside. His shoulder planted against the column again, he watched as the young man who hoped to be her partner explained the dance's introduction. Three men led the ladies they'd chosen to one end of the room, then retreated. Upon their return, each asked his fair maid to join him. As expected, she presented her back to him, refusing. Going down on his knees, the man begged for her hand. Of course, after much cajoling, the woman relented, accepting his invitation. The couple then proceeded to the floor.

Aleck's bride seemed eager to try this new dance. After the young man had shown Chandra the light springy steps, Chandra learning them quickly, he led her to the spot where in a few moments he intended to retrieve her. He retreated. High color marked her cheeks. She appeared to be enjoying herself, so Aleck decided not to play the interloper. There would be time enough to regain his bride so that they might share another dance. Right now, he'd allow her her own recreation. His would definitely come later.

Suddenly Aleck stiffened, his gaze centering on the newcomer who'd settled on one knee, pleading for Chandra's hand. The bastard, Aleck thought, eyeing his cousin closely. When Chandra had finished playing the coy damsel, finally relenting and accepting Jason's invitation to dance, Aleck came away from the column. While the pair moved onto the floor, joining the other couples, he strode to another corner of the hall, where he waited.

Chandra followed Jason's lead, wondering if her husband watched them. When she'd been swept from his side, she had been most relieved. Caught under his mesmerizing gaze, his fabulous blue eyes holding her spellbound, she couldn't fathom what was happening to her. Her emotions had spun out of control. All her senses were attuned to him, and whatever he desired, she would give willingly.

The feeling confused and frightened her, for she'd always governed her senses completely. No one had ever had the power to sway her, until now. His command of her had stunned her, and Chandra was thankful for the interruption. She could only imagine what might have happened if she'd not been spirited away to the opposite end of the room. There she'd thrown herself into the merrymaking, trying to calm her nerves; but now, with Aleck's cousin as her partner, she feared she'd gone too far.

"I see you wear my gift," Jason said, his hand holding hers. They faced each other as they performed the quick hopping steps of the couranto. "I'd have thought my cousin would order you to keep it from sight."

"He said it was mine to do with as I pleased," she said, then studied him closely. "Why are you so hostile to each other? You are, I presume, his only family."

"Aye, I am."

"Well?"

"'Tis best if your husband tells you what keeps us at odds." He spied her disappointed look. "An exchange, then," he said. "My story for yours." She seemed puzzled. "In the garden, you said too much stood between my cousin and you. I assume whatever it is has to do with why you've draped yourself in mourning. True?"

"'Tis true."

"Then it is my story for yours or none at all."

"Agreed," Chandra said, then allowed herself to be led to a quiet corner.

Making certain they stood in full view, for he was sure his cousin watched them, Jason relayed his and Aleck's story. "Our fathers were twins, though not identical, Aleck's father being firstborn. All through life, they were most competitive, as were Aleck and I in our youth. None of us got along. It was always one set of Hawkes against the other. I never did fully understand why.

"When Aleck and I were still quite young—he eight, I six—our grandfather died. All at Montbourne was given to Aleck's father. Then, upon our grandmother's death, six summers later, an old nurse came forth, stating it wasn't Aleck's father who came into the world first, but mine. Only a few months prior to that event, we had moved to the old castle, my father having squandered all his funds. He was most eager to follow through on those words, for he had always wanted the title and the lands that belonged to the heir. Of course, there was also the money. He petitioned our queen, presenting his lone witness, but Elizabeth denied his request, for the old nurse was obviously senile. The rejection didn't sit well, but we remained at Montbourne. My uncle was our only source of income.

"My father always enjoyed his ale and wine, but he began to drink. Quite heavily, in fact. One brutal winter's night several years later, he managed to draw Aleck's father into a fight. Swords were their weapons. My uncle suffered a fatal wound." Jason paused briefly and looked at his hands. "'Tis said Aleck's father had defeated my own fairly, leaving him with no more than a nick on his arm. When my uncle turned his back, my father charged. The sword went straight through the man. Realizing what he'd done, my father fled the castle, out into the night. He was found the next day, frozen to death."

"Are you saying Aleck blames you for his father's death?"

Jason shrugged. "Sins of the father, I guess. But I didn't make it easy for him, either. My father was flawed, but I still loved him. I also had lost a parent and hurt equally as much as Aleck. But all the attention was centered on him, the new Earl of Montbourne. The situation came to a head, and we, too, quarreled. My mother and I left the old castle. It was best that we did, for I gained my independence, and though not as wealthy as your husband, I can now provide nicely for myself. I hold my own title, too."

"And your mother?"

"She lives quietly on my estate near Nottingham." Jason cocked his head. "Now you know my story. 'Tis time I learned yours."

Chandra quietly explained all that had happened between Aleck and herself, leaving hardly anything untold. "That is why I wear mourning, Jason. Very much as with you and Aleck, it is a loved one's death that keeps us apart. I don't know if I could ever forgive him. Devin should never have died."

Gentle eyes looked upon her. "Though it might not seem so, my cousin is a man of great caring, Chandra. Never would he harm a living soul—not unless it is to protect someone who is most precious to him. Then, and only then, would he be willing to kill. What happened to your Devin was an accident. Believe me when I say Aleck suffers for what has happened. I know him. It is the truth."

"Winnie said nearly the same thing."

"Then 'tis time you believe what is told you. See him not as an Englishman, not as the man who accidentally slew your cousin, but for the man he is. Rid yourself of your hatred and resentment, for happiness awaits you. Open your heart, Chandra, and let it in."

He placed a kiss on her cheek, and Chandra watched as he took himself off into the crowd. When she could see Jason no more, she turned her attention to the room at large, searching out Aleck's whereabouts. Not seeing her husband, she moved around the hall's perimeter. Still no Aleck. Spying the Lady Emory, she knew he wasn't with her, and breathed a sigh of relief. She edged into a corner, then on tiptoes again scanned the crowd. A hand took hold of her arm. Turning, she stared at her husband.

Aleck's emotionless gaze ran over her from head to foot. "Your girlish amusements are ended, sweet wife. 'Tis time you see to your husband's."

Chapter

11

The door to Aleck's room closed with a thump. The sound exploded in Chandra's ears; she jumped. The time had come—but she wasn't prepared for this. If lightning bolts could slice through thick stones and mortar, she prayed one would find her straightaway.

From across the room, Aleck viewed his new wife. Soft candlelight kissed her pale skin. Wide-eyed and staring, she appeared close to fainting. It wouldn't surprise him in the least if she did. Certain he knew her thoughts, he chuckled. "Our maker won't intervene, Chandra. It was in His name that we took our vows. I am your husband and you are my wife. As it is written, we shall become one."

Chandra's gaze fell to his feet. What he'd said was true. Tonight, clemency would shun her. "I know I'm expected to submit, but—"

"'Tis not your submission I want," Aleck interrupted. "'Tis my desire for you to partake."

"But you said—"

"I know what I said. 'Twas male vanity speaking. I'll

not force you, Chandra, 'tis not my way. You must come to me freely. The choice has to be yours."

Sincerity met her when she looked at him again. "How can I come to you when so much stands between us?" she asked. Feeling nearly overpowered by his wondrous eyes, she turned her back to him. "Too much has happened."

Keeping by the door, Aleck surveyed her bowed head. When he'd seen her with Jason, jealousy had ripped through him. Anger driving him, his first response had been to tear the two apart. He'd waited though, ready to strike. When she was alone, he'd pounced, practically dragging her here, where he'd planned to make her succumb to his mastery. But as the door closed, he'd thought of another place, another time. Then, as now, his temper had driven him to react, and it had nearly spelled his death.

Knowing he couldn't harm Chandra—at least, never again—he'd relented in his quest to have her at all cost. The choice, as he told her, remained hers. But he couldn't help but ask, "Are you certain we cannot bridge those things that keep us apart?" She didn't respond. "'Tis more than Devin's death, isn't it?"

"Yes—no." Air filled her lungs until they nearly burst; she expelled her breath on a sigh. "I cannot say."

Quietly Aleck crossed the space between them. His hands fell upon her shoulders; he eased her around. "Look at me," he said, his finger urging her chin upward. Her eyes met his. "'Tis your clansmen, isn't it? You think they'll label you a traitor, don't you?"

"Yes," she admitted, unable to lie to him. "'Tis my greatest fear that they'll say I betrayed them and brand me a turncoat, among other things."

Anger slashed through Aleck as he imagined those "other things." "They cannot castigate you for something you could not control. James ordered us married. One cannot refuse one's sovereign without suffering some sort of penalty. Surely they'll understand that you had no choice."

"I did have a choice," she insisted. "I could have chosen the Tower. Or even death."

He searched her face for what Chandra thought was an eternity. "I suppose you could have," he said, maddened to think she'd choose either. "But you didn't. Why?"

"I don't know," she hedged, trying to look away, but he wouldn't allow it.

"The truth, little one. Why didn't you refuse me as your husband?"

A thousand lies crossed her mind, but she could speak none of them. She felt herself crumbling inside. Her words came out in a rush. "As head of my clan, I should have, but as a woman—"

Chandra swallowed the rest, knowing she'd said far too much. He now retained control over her, and she'd given it to him. He knew she felt attraction for him. She saw it in his eyes, their questioning look having grown perceptive, then confident. Why had she allowed him such knowledge? Doomed, she thought, positive she'd succumb to his masculine appeal.

Aleck watched the play of emotions over her face. She hadn't meant to expose her feelings that way, especially to him. A tiny groan escaped her throat, and she attempted to face away, but again he wouldn't allow it. His arms surrounded her, holding her fast. "There is no reason to feel embarrassed, sweet. As a man, I want you with all my being. We are married. Nothing can change it. You're my wife, Chandra. For this one night, allow yourself to feel what it is like to become a woman—fully, completely. I'll not disappoint you," he whispered, his warm, sweet breath fanning her face. "I promise."

His words rushed through her like a river of fire. Each inch of her flamed with want. Were she a man desiring a woman, enemy or not, she could slake her lust— violently, if she wished—and no one in her clan would question her right to do so. But as a woman, she was expected to keep herself pure, reject that which her family deemed a menace. Even if it meant taking her own life, she must not submit. How unfair it was that they judged her differently, simply because of her gender, Chandra thought. She heard her name, and looked up at the man whom she purportedly should renounce.

"Allow yourself to be fulfilled, sweet," Aleck urged, his lips a gentle breath from her own. "Take what you want. Forget everything else. For once, give in to your own needs and experience the enchantment that awaits you this night. The choice is yours."

Mesmerized by his words, Chandra stared into his alluring eyes. They entreated her to surrender to her own desires, to surrender to him. From the moment she first saw him, she'd been intrigued by this man. To deny that she felt something for him would be a lie. Forever conscious of their needs, their wishes, she'd given so much to those whom she led. Just this once, why couldn't she seize what she wanted? Weary of fighting against that which she craved most, her inhibitions fled. On a small whimper, her hands rose; her fingers threaded through his thick, ebony hair. "Kiss me," she implored, not knowing she did.

A groan trembled in Aleck's throat, then his impatient mouth covered hers. Hot and moist, his lips worked their magic, teasing, playing, devouring the sweet temptation offered him. Like honey, he thought, fighting the need to take her fast and hard. From the day he'd nearly ridden over her, he'd wanted to lie with her, had done so many times in his dreams. Virginal, he reminded himself, knowing he had to be gentle with her. She'd made her choice. Elation filled him. But he wondered if regret would later claim her.

The fire in his loins flamed with a potency that nearly consumed him, and his concern was tossed aside. He wanted her. She was willing. That was all that really mattered. Tomorrow could bring what it might. His eager tongue traced her lower lip, then his teeth nibbled gently on its fullness. "Open to me," he prompted on a husky whisper. "Let me taste you fully."

Hearing the urgency in his voice, Chandra complied. As his tongue slid between her lips, exploring freely, all feeling rushed deep into her belly. The force of it frightened her, for she ached. She clung to him, heat radiating through her, spiraling upward from her core, and thought she was melting. Certain she'd dissolve into a liquid mass at his feet, she felt his tongue withdraw. His foraging mouth left hers; Chandra moaned at its loss.

Momentarily he traced the delicate folds of her ear; his teeth teased the lobe. "I want to feel your skin—feel its silken touch against mine," he whispered, his lips playing behind her ear. "Let me unveil you, Chandra. Allow my eyes to behold your beauty."

His hands already worked at the fastenings of her gown. She tendered no protest, and each layer of clothing fell away until she was revealed fully. The chain and pendant fell from his fingers, and as his thick lashes shuttered his ardent gaze, he drank in the sight of her.

Long, flame-red hair lay like a fiery mantle around her shoulders, plunging to her waist; ivory skin, no longer pale, held a rosy blush. Her breasts, full and high, their tempting nipples taut, begged to be possessed by his hands and mouth alike. His eyes skimmed her small waist to settle on the soft russet curls nestled at the juncture of her satiny thighs. The secrets hidden there beckoned to him, and he felt himself harden painfully. Perfection, Aleck thought, then his hands worked at his own clothing, nearly tearing it from his body.

Naked, they stood facing each other. Accustomed to viewing a man's nudity, for the males in her clan weren't much given to modesty, Chandra felt no embarrassment whatsoever. Powerful and strong, proud and tall, the man in front of her was far more exceptional than any she'd ever seen. A sculptor's hand could not have fashioned such perfection—not to Chandra's eyes. Unexpectedly, she leaned toward him. Her lips touched his broad chest beside the emerald-encrusted medallion resting there. "Make love to me," she whispered, her breath fanning the crisp black hair, her lips moving upward alongside the thick gold chain. "Make me forget everything—everything except you."

Her words pierced Aleck like a flaming spear. If he'd thought himself aroused before, he found he was mistaken. Pulsing with fire, his blood flowed through him like molten lava; his whole body burned with the intensity of his longing as his loins throbbed unbearably. Worldly as he was, never had he wanted a woman this much. Despite her request, he hesitated. "Is this what you truly desire?" he asked.

Chandra looked into his questioning eyes, which had darkened to indigo. In their marvelous depths, yearning conjoined with doubt. "Yes . . . truly," she whispered, and knew in her heart that it was so.

Her words had barely left her lips when Aleck lifted her into his sinewy arms. "Then so be it," he said, carrying her to the bed. The cool sheets met Chandra's back. Whipping the medallion over his head, Aleck tossed it aside. It clattered against the stone floor; then, all at once, he was beside her. His large hand settled at her waist while he leaned over her. "You'll forget everything, little one," he said, his voice husky. "Everything except me."

Chandra's lashes fluttered closed just as his mouth captured hers. Again it worked its sweet magic. When his tongue traced her lips, she opened to him willingly. Impatiently she drew the moist sliver inside, where it played in abandon with her own. Aching to touch him, feel the smoothness of his skin, she lifted her arms, and anxious fingers glided over his sleek shoulders, smoothing and caressing the rippling brawn. They stole toward the nape of his powerful neck, then threaded through the thick, black tresses crowning his head. They curled in his locks, and she pulled him closer, feeling he held himself too far away. Chandra moaned as Aleck's lips pressed forcefully against hers. His mouth foraged briefly, then deserted hers altogether.

Aleck gazed at the redness of Chandra's mouth, then into her inquiring eyes, which had flown open the instant he'd pulled away. He hungered for her, wanted to devour every bit of flesh she offered him. Yet in his urgent need, he feared bruising her, hurting her. The time would come when the heat of their passion dictated the force of their joining. Wild and free their next union might be, but their first must be achieved with care. "We need not rush," he said, his hand coming away from her waist, his thumb lightly brushing her lips in order to soothe them. "Go easy, sweet. Allow yourself to feel each new emotion fully before experiencing another." His fingers trailed over her cheek to her temple, then into her silken hair. He spread the lustrous strands over the pillow. "I want to make love to you, Chandra, but I want the pleasure to be solely yours. Will you trust me to give you the joy you crave?"

Trust me . . . Those words settled inside her, and as Chandra searched his face, she wondered if that were possible. His open gaze remained steady on her. All at once she realized that, except for Jason, he'd always been honest with her. She was the one who'd broken whatever trust lay between them. She was the one who'd been dishonest. He promised her pleasure, but what about him? "Don't you desire the same for yourself?"

"My pleasure will come through you. By giving, I, too, will receive," he said. "Will you trust me?" Seeing her nod, his own excitement grew. No woman had ever agreed to award him such power over her body as had Chandra. He'd not abuse it. Far from it. "Then, little one, you must do everything I say." Again she nodded.

"Place your hands beneath the pillow, then close your eyes and let your mind float free. Don't think. Just allow yourself to feel." Her hands found the place he'd named, and Chandra searched his face again. His look promised fulfillment. Slowly her eyes closed; her breath flowed from her lungs, and she relaxed fully. "Just feel, Chandra," he whispered, his lips brushing hers. "Feel the pleasure I give you."

Lashes sealed against the outside world, Chandra felt the touch of his lips on hers, then they lightly trailed across her cheek to her ear. Teeth nibbled softly on the small lobe. A moment later, his open mouth, moist and warm, traced her throat. Instinctively her head sank deeper into the pillow as her neck arched, giving his lips more freedom to play. His tongue laved her throat, stopping at her pulse. Momentarily it teased the spot, then his lips sucked gently. Chills ran down her spine, gooseflesh rose on her arms, and she shivered from head to toe.

Aleck drew back to gaze at her; Chandra's eyelids fluttered. "Don't look, sweet. Feel the sensations. Hold each one to yourself and enjoy it." Her eyelids settled and she relaxed again. "That's it, love. Become one with the moment." His attention had moved to her breasts, and he surveyed the taut nipples. Wanting to taste them, he eased his hand over her waist. Slowly his fingers glided upward to capture one breast's fullness; his palm grazed over its crest, and her flesh dimpled. He leaned toward the tempting peak and whispered, "Experience the pleasure."

The words skimmed over her breast, then his hot tongue flicked against her nipple. His teeth tugged gently just before his mouth covered the crown. As he suckled, lightning shot through Chandra, bolting up, then down. She jerked at its force; her fingers curled into the underside of the pillow. Distantly she heard Aleck's chuckle as his mouth lifted. The energy that had raced through her settled deep in her stomach. It pulsated, ready to renew itself, and when his lips captured the second peak, it charged through her again; her breath rushed into her lungs.

Hearing the air hiss between her teeth, Aleck smiled to himself. Then his lips left her breast to brush along her satiny skin until he reached her navel. His tongue played lightly in the tiny recess, then moved to the outer edge of her hip. Down one leg and up the other, his kisses rained freely; Chandra moaned softly. When at last his mouth came full circle, Aleck aimed it at her center. His lips brushed her curls, and Chandra's whole body nearly propelled itself from the bed. "D-don't," she cried as her hands flew from beneath the pillow to cover herself.

Aleck's heavy-lidded gaze met hers. "Does it give you pain?"

"N-no," she said, her voice unsteady.

"Then close your eyes, sweet, and enjoy the sensation."

Her vision blurred by desire, she looked at him. After a moment her lashes slowly closed; her hands fell to her sides. He urged her legs apart, and Chandra opened to him. Settling between her outstretched thighs, Aleck devoured her with his eyes. Swallowing a groan, he leaned toward her. Chandra felt the brush of his lips, then the soft flick of his tongue. As it traced her silken folds, probing tenderly, a tempest of longing swept through her; her fingers curled into the bedclothes as she attempted to hold on. Buffeted by the winds of passion, she felt she was about to sail into oblivion, never to return. Frightened, she blurted, "Stop . . . please! I can endure no more."

Aleck settled back, his heels meeting his sinewy haunches, and saw that her eyelids were squeezed together tightly. She dared not look at him. Her emotions spun wildly inside her, he knew. Fearing their force, afraid she'd be forever lost, she refused to allow her desire to fly free. "'Tis only just begun," he breathed huskily, determined that she experience the ultimate of all sensations. Then as he knelt between her legs, his fingers claimed her. Expertly he coaxed her with the rhythm of his hand until she was again wet and wanting. Impatient to taste her anew, his lips found her, his tongue probed, and when her hips writhed against him, he left her to move above her. Again they were face to face. "Look at me, Chandra." Her eyes came open. "'Tis time for my pleasure as well. Guide me, sweet," he said, taking her hand. Her cool fingers found him. At her touch, he throbbed intolerably; droplets seeped from the slick crown. He fought for control, his head falling back. A growl escaped his throat, then air filled his lungs as he steadied himself. "Show me the way," he implored on a rasp, and he was unerringly led to the haven he sought. He eased into her, meeting her maidenhead. "Kiss me, Chandra."

Their lips met eagerly. When he felt certain his teasing mouth held her spellbound, he thrust upward, then slid into her fully. When she was accustomed to him, he moved, slowly, gently. At her prompting, the rhythm soon increased. She seemed eager for release, and Aleck lost himself in her. Her pleasure was his. Only by giving could he receive. His hand slipped beneath her enticing little bottom, drawing her closer. The cadence of his lovemaking changed as his hips gyrated against her. A small cry filled his ears, and as he gazed down at her, ecstasy painted her beautiful face. Holding still, he felt the remnants of her joy. Tiny spasms caressed his manhood, and he could no longer contain his own desire. Once, twice, he drove into her, and with a guttural cry, he spilled his seed deep inside her.

Their heartbeats slowed as breathing soon eased; Chandra lay dazed. A sweet warmth filled her. Never had she experienced such bliss. And Alexander Hawke was its source. Her beloved lord of legend. Her enemy once, he was now her husband and lover. She was damned if she'd ever abandon him. She'd be his for as long as he desired her, as long as he wanted her by his side. Her clan would simply have to accept that, for she'd never leave him. These new feelings wrapped themselves snugly around her, and Chandra wondered if this might be love.

His heart overflowing with joy, his body still covering hers, Aleck looked down into Chandra's glowing face. Ecstasy didn't begin to describe what he had felt, still felt. He was amazed by the experience, at a loss for words. Tempted to taste her lips again and relay his pleasure to her, his head descended.

At the same moment, the door securing their privacy burst open; loud laughter echoed through the room. With a cry, Chandra snatched at the sheet as Aleck rolled away from her. Hidden beneath the cover, they both stared at the many frolickers who'd joined together for the bundling party, including their king. Nearly all were drunk.

"We're too late," James said on a heavy lisp. "The deed has already been done."

Their sovereign stumbled toward the bed, and Aleck sat up with a jerk. "Aye, it has," he stated, placing his body between his trembling wife and their uninvited guests. "Fortunately for us, you missed the event. Since no sport exists, kindly take your leave."

"Pah!" his king replied. "You need not be so unfriendly. We only came to wish you well." Seeing double, James noted how both Lord Montbournes glared at him. Not desiring in the least to do battle with two Aleck Hawkes, the king wisely beat a retreat. "Children, children," he said, turning to his flock, "we are not welcome here, so let us depart."

With much grumbling, the group turned, then weaved

its way out the door. Only two remained, and Chandra felt highly uncomfortable. While the Lady Emory coldly appraised Chandra, Jason perused his cousin, his manner nonchalant.

"Do you wish to follow the others, Whitfield?" Aleck asked after a moment. "Or need I rise and toss you out on your ear?"

"Not necessary, cousin. The Lady Emory and I were just leaving. Come, Felicia. The marriage has been consummated, and from what I can see, our newlyweds are quite stricken with each other. Let us give them some privacy to continue what they were doing."

Felicia's frigid stare shot briefly to Aleck, then she spun on her heel and marched through the door. With a wave, Jason sauntered after her, the panel closing behind him.

Aleck leapt from the bed, a vivid curse rolling from his lips as he shoved a sturdy chair against the door. The sheet held fast to her body, Chandra sat up. "Do you expect them to return?"

"I expect most anything to occur as long as we remain at court." Retrieving the medallion and slipping the chain over his head, he strode to a chest and pulled out some clean clothing. "Rise, sweet," he said as he started to dress. "After I've awakened Winnie, she will help you dress."

Feeling somewhat shy, she continued to hide behind the sheet. "What do you plan to do?"

"We leave immediately for Montbourne," he said, his eyes glinting. "There we can do whatever we like, for as long as we like, and no one will dare disturb us. We have much to share, Chandra. All of it more pleasurable than what has already passed between us."

Remembering the enjoyment of their union, Chandra felt a hot blush flow over her. How could anything possibly exceed the ecstasy that had already been theirs?

Aleck thought she seemed not to believe him. "We've only touched the edge of rapture, sweet. Tomorrow, at Montbourne, we'll seek its core."

Chandra stood by the doors leading into the great hall at Montbourne. The glow of love shone in her eyes as she watched her husband traverse the expanse between the stables and herself. They had just returned from their daily outing, and he'd handed over the stallion to the boy who awaited them. The one horse was all they ever used, for they preferred to ride together. What a ride it had been, Chandra thought, recalling their amazing interlude. One wouldn't think such a thing possible. Not on a stallion's back. But considering the man and his insatiable lust, she'd learned to expect the unexpected with Aleck. Admiring his handsome features, which were bathed in warm sunlight, she knew she'd never tire of this man. Her contentment lay in him. The past month seemed like a dream—a dream from which she never wanted to awaken.

"Well, milady," Aleck said, "did you enjoy this day's ride?"

"Aye, I did," she said, a smile teasing her lips. "Milord is a fine horseman. I am impressed by your skill."

A knowing look danced in his blue eyes. "My choice of a mount has a lot to do with my dexterity. Bestride the best, I tend to give it my all. I've not fallen short yet—have I, love." His last three words were a statement, not a question. Chandra's profuse blush made him chuckle. "Come, my little filly. Let us see if my prowess is greater indoors than it is out."

"Don't you ever tire of . . . of—you know," she whispered, for they were now inside the hall, and she feared her voice would echo through the vast room.

"Making love?" he asked boldly, his words bouncing off the walls. The servants' heads turned their way, and Chandra nearly melted through a crack. "Not to you, I don't," he said with a wink. "Not when you give me such excruciatingly sweet pleasure."

They reached the stairs just as Winnie came from the back hall, her arms laden with mended clothing. "Since you're headed upstairs, you can take these with you." She eyed both Aleck and Chandra sternly. "Tear another stitch while in the throes of passion, and you'll be repairing your own clothing from now on. I have too much else to do."

The large bundle was heaped into Aleck's arms. "We'll be most careful while disrobing, Mistress Marlowe. In fact, to save you any more work, we'll remain undressed the day through."

"'Tis your home. You can run naked through it, if you like. Just don't tear another thread."

Her mouth agape, Chandra had listened to the exchange. After Winnie waddled off, she blinked and stared at her husband.

"Do not let her candidness startle you, sweet. She practically raised me. Unpolished she might be, but she's one of the finest women I know." He shifted the bundle in his arms. "Come. Let's find our chamber. We have other clothes to see to, and they must be handled with great care."

Chandra wanted to speak to Winnie, but she had to do so alone. Today was the one-month anniversary of their wedding, and she hoped to spend the evening alone with her husband, their meal served in their room. "I'll be up in a moment," she said, waving him on. "I need to talk to the servants. I won't be long."

His lazy gaze fixed itself on her. "Promise?"

"Promise."

Chandra proceeded toward the back hall, and Aleck ascended the stairs. Halfway up, he met the descending Felix Marlowe. "Two letters arrived while you were out, sir," his steward announced. "I placed them on the table in your chamber."

"Thank you, Marlowe." Aleck shifted the bundle again. "As soon as you are able, search out the finest wine I own. I shall need it for tonight."

The man bobbed his head. "Right away, sir."

His steward rushed on down the stairs while Aleck climbed them. Inside his room, he laid the clothing aside, then sought out the letters. The first, he discovered, was from Felicia. Giving it a cursory read, he tossed it aside. The second was from Sir John. Unlike Felicia's, the contents of Sir John's held his attention. One paragraph particularly caught his eye.

> . . . 'Tis more than rumor, I fear. James is livid over the clan Morgan's unprovoked attacks on its neighbors. Those who are loyal to the Crown suffer greatly, while others who still question such authority are incited to join the cause. Our king amasses an army of nearly five hundred to ride north. The casualties promise to be heavy—for those at Lochlaigh, at least. For your wife's sake, I thought you should be made aware of this.

Damn the luck! If Chandra learned what was happening at Lochlaigh, she'd strike out for the Highlands. Somehow he had to keep her ignorant of these events— past, present, and future. Or else his and Chandra's tranquillity would be destroyed. Yet, for her sake, he felt he should try to intervene. Cedric was the instigator of this insurrection. The others, no doubt, followed the man blindly. To slaughter the whole would be a travesty of justice. He must persuade James to temper his anger at the clan Morgan. Tomorrow he intended to ride to London.

Soft footsteps fell in the hallway, edging ever closer to his room. Slamming Sir John's letter inside the pages of a book that lay atop the table, Aleck wiped the harsh look from his face. The sound of his wife's steps hinted she was mere feet away from the door. Pretending boredom, he gazed at the fingernails on one hand—and caught sight of Felicia's letter, which somehow had fallen to the floor. Snatching it up, he searched about for a place to hide it. A low chest stood open only a yard away. Tossing the letter inside, he slammed the lid with his foot. A second later, Chandra entered the room. "What took you so long?" he questioned, his voice a near squeak.

Her brow furrowing, she stared at her husband. He strode toward her, an odd sort of smile claiming his face. "It's been no more than five minutes since I left you," she defended, keeping near the door.

"More like ten," he countered. "Even a second is too long to be away from you." The door slammed, and Aleck swept Chandra up into his arms. He carried her toward their bed. "I missed you, sweet. Your absence has left me feeling empty. Renew the joy in me. 'Tis the only way I'll be whole again."

Chandra lay sideways on the bed and watched her husband strip from his shirt. In his haste, the linen ripped. She'd mend it willingly, a hundred times over, for as long as he came to her, and then some. The leather breeches slid down his sinewy legs. Save for the medallion, he stood naked. The emeralds winked at her, and her hand itched to touch the spot where the heavy gold circle rested against his chest. Her gaze tripped lower, and she marveled at his stamina. For the fourth time today, he was fully aroused, hard and ready. Pulling her own clothes free, tossing them on the floor, she lay back and opened her arms, then her legs. "Come to me," she whispered, beckoning him.

Aleck's knee indented the feather mattress as his weight settled on the bed. "You're a bonny lass, Chandra. A woman who knows my own heart." His knuckles grazed the tuft of red curls, then two long fingers slipped inside her, creating a rhythmic play. His thumb teased the bud, rotating it gently. She arched against his hand, moaning softly; Aleck chuckled. "You want me, don't you?"

"Aye," she breathed.

"Show me where."

Her hand captured his engorged member; she urged him toward her. "Here," she said, its moist crown meeting her secret place, the place only he had known.

She was hot and wet; Aleck eased into her until he lost himself completely. "Make me whole, Chandra. Renew my joy."

To Aleck's delight, he found rejuvenation again, and again, and again, Chandra being his sole pleasure. As dawn broke, he kissed her forehead, then slipped quietly from their room, Sir John's letter tucked in his belt. When Chandra awakened several hours later, she discovered he had gone.

Chapter

12

Late in the afternoon, Chandra entered the empty bedchamber, Aleck's repaired shirt in her hand. She glanced at their bed, and loneliness filled her. He'd been gone since dawn, and already she missed him terribly. Why hadn't he awakened her so they might have said a proper farewell? Slipping his note from her pocket, she read it again.

> *The sun's rays streak across the horizon as I write this, love. A messenger arrived from London. A matter of great importance commands my immediate attention, so I must ride south and see to it. As I gaze at your beautiful face, I hesitate to leave. But knowing that you will be awaiting me makes the thought of my homecoming so much sweeter. I hope to return by week's end.*
>
> *Forever, Aleck.*

On a sigh, Chandra tucked his note into her pocket and moved to the chest where Aleck stored his shirts. She opened it and found it full. Searching about the room for another place to stow the article, she caught sight of the chest nearest the table. As she crossed toward it, Chandra's head suddenly swam. Too much wine, she decided—she remembered how during their celebration of their one-month anniversary Aleck had poured the sweet liquid in a thin line down her nude torso. A rush of excitement quivered through her, settling in the pit of her stomach, for she still felt the magic of his tongue as he'd licked the wine from her skin. Week's end, she thought. That was far too long for him to be gone.

Kneeling by the chest, she folded Aleck's shirt, then lifted the lid. A piece of parchment caught her eye. She spread open the letter and noted the date; then, as she read the entreating phrases, her gaze hardened. A matter of great importance, he'd said. Well, Felicia Emory held minuscule importance to Chandra. If he'd ridden all the way to London to see his former mistress—if, indeed, the word *former* applied!—simply because she'd begged him to do so, upon his return there would be war.

Angrily Chandra crammed Aleck's clean shirt into the chest. Tossing the letter atop it, she rose and slammed the lid. *"Darling,"* she mimicked the Lady Emory's endearment, then kicked the chest. Limping off toward a chair, she fell into it, slipped off her deerskin boot, and massaged her toe.

The blackguard! Wasn't one woman enough? Given his sexual prowess, she doubted he could remain faithful to any of her gender. She envisioned it now: a deep rut extending from Montbourne to London, as he continually traveled between wife and mistress. He'd spend more time on the road than off. Soon the incessant journeying would wear him thin, not to mention what it would do to his horse. If those were his plans, Chandra thought to put a quick stop to them. She'd not stand for such antics. Either he stayed loyal to her or their marriage was finished. Orders or not, she'd return to Lochlaigh, her king and her husband be damned!

A little more than two days after leaving Montbourne, Aleck strode along the corridor at the king's royal residence. On his arrival two hours before, he'd requested an immediate audience with James. He'd bathed, shaved, then donned clean clothes; now he made his way to the king's privy chamber, where the two were to meet. Tired from his long journey, stopping only to feed, water, and rest his stallion—himself also—he prayed his wits were sharp enough to convince James to withdraw from the stand he'd taken on the clan Morgan. For Chandra's sake, he had to succeed.

Rounding a corner, Aleck nearly collided with the Lady Emory. His hands fell from her arms where they had spontaneously gripped her in order to steady her. "My apologies, Felicia," he said, frowning down at her.

"Aleck, you are here. I hadn't expected you to arrive so quickly after receiving my letter." She noticed his inexpressive look. "You did receive it, didn't you?"

"I did, Felicia, but your request that I return to court is not why I am here."

Her eyes flashed with anger. "Why, then, are you here?"

"'Tis a matter of urgency. Right now, I am on my way to see the king. I have no time to discuss it—nor do I intend to. Excuse me, but I must depart. James awaits me."

Staring after her former lover, Felicia studied his retreating form for several moments. Her mind set, she took herself off to her apartment to make preparations.

At nearly the same time several hundred miles north at Montbourne, Chandra sat in the huge bedchamber that she and Aleck shared. His note rested in her hand, for she'd just read it again. Her initial anger had soon turned to melancholy. Surely he hadn't left their bed to find his way to Felicia Emory's. Or so Chandra prayed, for her heart was breaking. Indecisiveness claimed her; then her anger flared again. "Damn him!" she snarled, bounding to her feet. Swinging toward the open door, she saw Winnie standing under its arch.

"You seem vexed," the woman stated. "Has something upset you?"

"No," Chandra snapped. "I'm bored. 'Tis all."

"As you say," Winnie responded, examining Chandra's face a bit longer. "A visitor has arrived at Montbourne. Since Master Aleck is gone, my Felix hesitates to allow him in. But he refuses to leave and says he'll scale the wall if need be. Perhaps, as the lady of the manor, you should inform Felix what you think he should do."

Confusion marked Chandra's brow. "Who is this visitor?"

"Master Jason. He has not been here since he was little more than a boy. That he has come now worries me. Maybe something has happened to Master Aleck. If so—"

Chandra brushed past Winnie and ran along the corridor, then down the steps. Once outside she rushed through the yard on toward the outer gates. "Raise the portcullis," she shouted to the guards. They hesitated. "Raise it, I say!"

The heavy wooden grille groaned as its spiked ends lifted from the earth to expose the deep holes created by centuries of constant battering. The outer gate swung open, and Jason urged his horse into the yard. "Well, fair lady, I take it your husband is not at home," he said, leaning an arm on the saddle's pommel. "Else I'd probably still be sitting outside."

"Then nothing's happened to him?" she asked, staring up at Aleck's cousin.

"Not to my knowledge. But if it has, let me be the first to offer my condolences and to ask for the young widow's hand," he said with a smile and a wink.

Chandra sent him a censuring look. "Jason, you truly are a devil."

"Aye, as well as a blackguard, a rogue, and a knave. I've been called all of the above—plus a few other, uh, *endearments*, which shall remain unspoken by me." He glanced around the yard. "Where is your husband, anyway?"

"He's gone to London on a matter of importance. A messenger arrived. Aleck left two days ago at dawn."

Jason marked the dubious tone of her voice. "Have no fear. He'll soon return."

"Why have you come?" she asked, not wanting to think of the Lady Emory, nor of the possibility that her husband might soon be with the woman, if he wasn't already. "Winnie said you've not been here since you'd left years ago."

"For a visit, of course." It was a lie, for he'd heard rumors about the clan Morgan and the army that James had amassed. Straightaway, after stopping briefly at his estate near Nottingham, he'd headed here to inform Aleck of the king's plan. Apparently, Aleck had already gotten word of it, but he doubted that Chandra had any knowledge of the goings-on in London. Or in Scotland, for that matter. But she seemed most annoyed, and Jason believed it had something to do with her husband's departure. He couldn't help wondering if the two had quarreled. "Must I sit atop this horse the rest of the day, or are you going to invite me inside? I could do with a bit of food and a cup of wine—if milady so offers."

Chandra apologized for her bad manners. After Jason's horse had been stabled, the two entered the hall. Ordering some food and wine for her guest, she joined him at the table while he ate.

"The place seems smaller than I remembered," he

said, examining the old hall. "It's been a long time since I've seen Montbourne. When I'm through, you can take me on a tour."

"I'd enjoy that," she said. "Since I've not seen all of it myself, we could explore it together."

"Allow me to guess which room it is that you have the most knowledge of." He chuckled at Chandra's sudden blush. "When I finally marry, my own bride will be kept as ignorant as you, Chandra. Years and years will pass before she's familiar with her home. 'Tis a family trait, I suppose."

"'Tis something you shouldn't discuss so freely," she said, still embarrassed. "But since you have, when I meet the young woman, I shall warn her what she faces."

Jason laughed. "You would, wouldn't you?"

"Aye, readily."

"Aleck was wise to bring you here—although you are both missed at court."

By whom? she wondered. Certainly not by anyone she knew. "I did not like it there. Everyone's manners were lacking."

"Including mine," he said. "I'm sorry about the bundling party. James always thinks it a lark to burst in on a young couple, hoping to catch them nude, wanting to jostle and annoy them. As an Englishman, I'd normally blame such bad practices on his Scottish upbringing, but you are of the same heritage, but not of the same ilk. Our king, I fear, simply has a bawdy sense of humor."

"Why did you join them, Jason?"

"To annoy Aleck, of course."

"And the Lady Emory?"

Jason surveyed Chandra. "She's unhappy that Aleck has withdrawn his affections. She'll get over it soon enough." His new cousin seemed not to believe him. "Were I you, I'd not worry myself over the Lady Emory. She is part of his past. You are his present and future. Believe it, Chandra, for it is true."

Her gaze fell to her hands. "Had I not found her letter—the one his note said commanded his immediate attention; the one that he'd claimed was a matter of great importance—I might agree with you. As it is, I cannot."

"You think she is the reason he's gone to London?" He saw her nod. "You are wrong—so very wrong."

"How can you say I'm wrong, especially when I saw her letter myself?"

"Because 'tis known that James—"

Chandra waited. "Go on. 'Tis known that James what?"

Jason could have bitten off his tongue. "'Tis not important," he lied.

"I say it is." The moment the words had slipped from Jason's mouth, an ominous dread had filled her soul. "It has to do with the clan Morgan, doesn't it?" He remained silent. "Tell me, Jason. What has happened? What is James planning?"

Jason sighed heavily. "Aleck will attend to it, Chandra. I can say no more. It is not my place to tell you." Noting the stubborn set of her jaw, he studied her intently, then rose from his seat. "I have a strong feeling he was afraid you might react irrationally. Because of my error, I will have to remain here until my cousin returns to make certain you don't."

Chandra stared after him as he strode to the door. "Jason!" she shouted, but he ignored her call. It didn't take much intelligence to guess that he intended to make certain the gates were secured against her leaving. Anger bubbled inside her. Its source wasn't simply Jason, but Aleck. Especially Aleck! Though relieved to know it was not Felicia, but James that Aleck sought out, she was still livid. He'd tried to keep her oblivious to the fact that her clan faced trouble. She was its leader. What right did he have to usurp her authority in matters that affected her people's welfare? None! Jason didn't need to say more than he had. Instinctively, she'd known that danger threatened her family. He could bar the gates if he liked. Nothing would keep her from her clan. Even if she had to dig beneath Montbourne's thick walls to gain her freedom, this night would find The Morgan of Morgan on her way home to the Highlands, and to Lochlaigh.

Well after midnight, Aleck finally found his bed. He'd spent the afternoon and evening with James discussing the clan Morgan. Adamant at first, the king had refused to back down from his command: The Morgans were to be eradicated. By their sixth cup of wine, James had wavered a bit. By their twelfth cup, each having been filled to the brim, his sovereign had changed his mind about destroying the clan. But Cedric Morgan's fate was sealed. The man was to be brought to London and imprisoned in the Tower, where he'd live out the rest of his natural life. On that, James refused to relent.

Chandra might not like her king's edict, but in the face of losing all her family, sacrificing her uncle might not be so difficult to accept, especially since the man would keep his life. Pray God that the clan didn't rally around Cedric, protecting him at the cost of their own lives. And pray God that Chandra learned nothing of this until it was over.

The king had agreed to detain his army, holding it in the south of England. Once James and his advisers had devised a plan to trick the rebellious Cedric into being captured, a plan that he promised Aleck would eliminate bloodshed, James would effect the strategy. Possibly within the week. Relieved that his wife's family no longer lay under the threat of the Crown, Aleck was now anxious to return to Montbourne.

Chandra. Her name rolled through his head, and a deep longing rose inside him. Amazement filled him, for it had been less than three days since they had parted, yet he yearned for her as though it had been a whole year. By week's end, he promised himself, she would again be in his arms.

Bone-weary and slightly tipsy, Aleck could no longer hold his eyes open. Tomorrow he'd set out for Montbourne. He yawned, then within moments, he slept.

Close to two in the morning, Chandra crept along the backstairs at Montbourne toward the kitchens and the cache of food she'd hidden close to the rear door earlier in the evening. Her soft deerskin boots padded down the final three steps, and she stopped to listen. Not hearing a sound, she dashed toward the outside exit, snatching up the leather bag as she came upon it, the low flame in the huge stone fireplace lighting her way.

Three guards walked the high wall, halting on occasion to view the yard, then look out over the black countryside. No moon shone this night, which was to Chandra's advantage. Keeping to the shadows of the sparsely lit courtyard, she worked her way toward the stables. Inside, she found no one about, and she quietly slipped along the line of stalls to the one she'd selected in advance. A mare stood inside, and at Chandra's approach, the frisky beast snorted. "Hush, lassie fair," Chandra cajoled in a whisper. "We'll be on our way in a minute."

Chandra quickly packed the mare's hooves with straw, covering them with squares of leather that she pulled from the bag she carried, binding each hoof above the fetlock with a narrow length of rope. Her task finished, she bridled the mare and led her from the stall. Time was priceless, and she might regret it later, but she forwent the use of a saddle. As she left the stables, the mare trailing silently behind her, the bag looped over her shoulder by its sturdy leather strings, she grabbed what appeared to be an axe handle, its head having broken free. Just in case, she thought, hoping she'd not have to use it.

Again she kept to the shadows, moving stealthily toward a little-used gate. Gaining her destination, she dropped the mare's reins and set the axe handle against an old barrel. Several others blocked the aged doors. With silent grunts, she edged them aside, creating a path and enough room for the door to swing open. Then she lifted the heavy wooden bar. A hollow thump met her ears as the thing fell to the ground. Praying no one had heard it, she eased the door open, then rushed toward the mare.

"You almost made it," Jason said; Chandra's heart leapt into her throat. He stepped from the darkness, stopping in front of her. "Aleck wouldn't have appreciated your running off into the night. Had you succeeded, he'd be mad as hell at me. God's wounds!" he exploded, then laughed. "On second thought, he would have killed me." A shout sounded from the wall, and Jason ordered the guard back to his post, assuring them all that everything was under control. While Jason's attention was averted, Chandra sidled toward the barrel. "Come, cousin," he said, turning her way, motioning her toward him. "I've had little sleep these past few nights." He bent to reach for the mare's reins. "Let's—"

The axe handle hit Jason between neck and shoulder; he fell face first to the ground with a hard thud. Fearing she had indeed killed him, Chandra stooped beside him. He still breathed, but he was out like a snuffed candle. "I'm so sorry, Jason," she whispered, her hand smoothing over his cheek. "But it could not be helped." Pressing her fingers to her lips, she then placed them on his forehead. "Farewell, cousin. I hope Aleck goes easy on you."

Rising, she searched the wall to note that the guards faced away from her. Retrieving the bag, which had fallen from her shoulder, she led the mare out through the open gate. Together they descended the hill. Quietly, furtively, they walked across the dark and barren terrain, but once they reached the cover of the trees, she leapt into action. The leather coverings were pulled from the hooves, the straw brushed away. In a trice, she was astride the mare's back, and they were heading north. She didn't look back—not until she reached the border.

"Sweet Scotland," she said almost breathlessly; at last she'd crossed the boundary! Reining the mare in and around, she viewed England's shadowy landscape. Tears stung her eyes as she envisioned all she had left behind. Aleck. Her lord of legend. Her husband. A sob rising to her throat, she imagined his face as he rose above her, his compelling gaze holding her spellbound. As she turned the mare north once more, her heart aching intolerably, she wondered if she would ever behold his handsome visage again.

Aleck spun upward from his dreams of Chandra. A soft, warm body lay next to him; a slender hand moved low on his belly. He felt himself harden. "Ah, sweet," he said in a groggy haze, rolling toward the woman beside him. "Is it really you?"

"Yes, darling. I'm here."

Darling?

The word clanged through Aleck's head; the fog lifted from his brain. He bounded from the bed to stare at the dim figure reposing on the mattress. His eyes confirmed what his ears had told him. "Bitch," he grated, snatching his breeches from the floor and shoving his legs into them. Striking a spark with a tinderbox, he lit the candle. The flame illumined Felicia's nude body. "Get from my bed and dress yourself," he commanded, his anger barely held in check. "Then leave my room."

Not in the least bit fazed, Felicia remained where she lay. "I hadn't meant to startle you, Aleck. I simply wanted to ease your tension and give you pleasure. Come join me. You know I have the power to satisfy your needs. My body is yours, Aleck. Let's enjoy a lusty romp for old time's sake, hmmm?"

"God's wounds, woman! You must be insane to think I'd ever lie with you again. 'Tis over, Felicia. It has been since the day I met Chandra."

Felicia's gaze sharpened. "So, the little Scottish bumpkin has stolen your heart, has she?" Her throaty laughter erupted. "I cannot imagine, as backward as she is, that she could ever satisfy a man such as you."

"Naive she might be, but she is eager to learn, Felicia. And I am eager to teach her. She gives me pleasure beyond anything I've ever experienced. No other woman can make such a claim, not even you."

Feeling as though she'd been dunked in the North Sea, Felicia sobered. "You truly are in love with her, aren't you?"

"Aye, I am," he said without hesitation, just now realizing it was true. His heart swelled with the knowledge. "Because of that love, I have sworn to remain faithful to her until the day I die. I would never risk losing her—never. Take yourself from my room, and should ever we meet, do not approach me again. Is that clear?"

"Yes, very," the subdued woman responded. She rose and donned her wrapper, then quietly made her way to the door. "Aleck," she said, once she'd opened the panel; he turned her way. "I hope your bride knows how fortunate she is."

Aleck stared at the door for a long while after it had closed. God! Had he responded blindly to Felicia's nudity, his dazed state allowing him to believe it was Chandra, he would have broken his vows. Madness, he thought, wanting to be away from here and back in his wife's arms. Glimpsing the window, he saw it was nearly dawn. He dressed quickly, stashing his meager belongings in a leather satchel. Shortly his boots struck the stones along the corridor as he headed toward the stables. *Home,* he thought as he rode north. Home to his wife. Home to his lover. Home to his flame-haired Scottish lass. *Chandra.*

Jason coughed and sputtered as he tried to draw air into his lungs. Doused with a bucket of water, he'd jerked awake. Rising to his feet, his hand easing the pain in his neck, he stood face to face with Winnie.

"Where is the countess?" she asked, glaring at him.

He blinked, then looked around him to see the open gate. A curse rolled from his lips. "I'm doomed," he blurted.

"Aye, you are," Winnie agreed. "I thought you were watching her."

"I was—caught her, too. But she was too quick." Stars still twinkled in his head each time he moved. As he retrieved the axe handle, he winced at the pain. "This must have been her weapon." He tossed it aside. "Have a boy saddle my horse. I'll go after her."

"Too late for that," Winnie said. "By now, she's a long ways off."

"Then I'll go to London to tell Aleck—if he hasn't already started back."

"Someone else will ride south," she said, hands on her hips. "You'll stay here so you can take your lumps when Master Aleck arrives. Into the hall with you."

Jason half expected Winnie to grab hold of his ear and march him toward the door. Although it hadn't been till later years that he and his parents resided at Montbourne year-round, he remembered how the woman had reprimanded him during his visits when he was quite young. A devil, he was. He'd not deny it. But her twists and pinches were mild compared to what he'd suffer on Aleck's return. *Damnation!* Why hadn't he stayed in London?

For the next two days, Jason paced his room. When the

shout went up that Lord Montbourne was approaching the castle, he closed his eyes, gritted his teeth, then headed toward the hall's main entrance, where he waited. Jason noted that Aleck's gaze snagged him straightaway. His cousin slid from the saddle, his booted feet hitting the ground with a thud. In a few hard steps, Aleck was upon him.

"What the hell are you doing here?" Aleck asked.

"A fine way to greet a guest," Jason countered, dreading the moment of revelation.

Aleck stared at his cousin for a long moment. The look wasn't friendly. "Where's Chandra?" he questioned, striding into the hall.

Jason swallowed his urge to gulp. "As a matter of fact, that is why I am here."

Aleck stopped in mid-stride and spun round. His cold eyes froze his cousin to the spot where he stood. "What do you mean?"

Drawing a deep breath, Jason set himself to explaining. "I came to Montbourne some four days past to apprise you of the rumors at court concerning the clan Morgan, but you had gone. I was informed you'd left on matters of importance, so I assumed you had already heard."

"And?" Aleck asked, dread rippling up through him.

"And in conversation with Chandra, I let slip that James—"

"You did what?" Aleck fairly shouted, grabbing hold of Jason's shirt, jerking him toward him. "Don't tell me she knows about this, cousin, or I'll—"

"I caught myself before anything was actually said," he broke in, wrestling free of Aleck's grip. In no way did Jason desire to brawl with his cousin. They were fairly evenly matched, but in good conscience, he refused to strike an injured man. For when Aleck learned Chandra was gone, his heart was certain to be torn in two. Besides,

Jason blamed himself. "Intelligent as she is, Aleck, she managed to guess the truth. I set guards at every gate—"

"Chandra!"

Aleck's voice boomed through the hall as he ran toward the stairs. Jason loped after him. He caught Aleck's arm just as he started to bound up the steps. "She's gone, Aleck. She escaped us two days ago. Winnie told me that other than some provisions, she took only the clothes she wore when she first arrived here, her plaid included. She's returned to Scotland, Aleck. She's returned to Lochlaigh and her clan." Blue ice, Jason thought as he looked into his cousin's eyes. Then his hand was shaken from Aleck's arm. "What is it you plan to do?" the younger Hawke asked, following his cousin to the kitchens.

Without preamble, Aleck snatched a large square of cloth from a servant girl's hands. His action startled her, and she scurried from the room. "Since your stupidity has placed my wife in grave danger," he said, tossing a loaf of bread, a brick of cheese, dried fruits, and some nuts into the middle of the cloth, now spread across a small table, "I have no choice but to go after her."

Jason watched as Aleck wrapped the cloth around the provender, then tied its ends together. As Aleck started to lift the makeshift sack, Jason again caught his arm. "I'd think that since it is you who killed her cousin and abducted her in the first place, it is you who are in the most danger, not Chandra."

Aleck hoisted his cache. "Her uncle wants her dead, Jason, for then he'll become chief. He is unaware of what James is arranging for him, so he will plan and plot until the deed is done. Pray God she still lives, cousin. For if she is dead, when I return, you, too, will die."

Jason chased after Aleck as he left the kitchens. "You're foolish to go alone," he said. "Wait until we can assemble some stout men to ride with you."

"There is no time for that. Be assured, I am able to take care of myself. Chandra is not."

"There is no possible way that you could fend off the entire clan," Jason countered. "Think about it, Aleck. You're one man, alone."

"And she is one small woman, alone."

They had neared the doors leading into the courtyard. In his exasperation, Jason snarled, "Damn it, Aleck. Is it your wish that I inherit all this? If so, I'll take it—gladly."

The words sliced through Aleck like a knife. He'd lost a loved one because of the father; he'd not lose another because of the son. "You son-of-a—" His fist met Jason's jaw before the last word was uttered. Striding over his unconscious cousin, Aleck quit the hall.

By the time Jason managed to drag himself from the floor, Aleck was gone. The younger Hawke feared it would be the last time he ever saw his cousin alive. His words had been uttered in anger, for Aleck had refused to take heed. Obviously, he'd hit a raw nerve.

Staggering toward the stables, pain still shooting through his head, Jason ordered his horse saddled. As he rode south toward London, he decided that he would not soon return to Montbourne. Unfriendly lot, he dubbed them, his jaw and neck causing him extreme misery. After he'd seen his mission to fruition, he intended to break all contact with the Montbournes. For now, though, he planned to apprise James of the situation. The king's army would not remain inactive for long. Of that Jason was certain.

Under a moonless sky, several hours before dawn, Aleck urged his steed onward, keeping to the shadows of the trees. Heavy clouds rolled above the moors; rain appeared to be in the offing. With maybe a mile, no more than two, until he at last spotted the walls of Lochlaigh Castle, he wondered how he might gain entry. Perhaps

Jason's cautioning advice held more validity than Aleck had first thought. Alone, he could do little. Yet with an army thundering behind him, he lost the element of surprise. But the force of one might not be enough. Damn! His hasty ride to the Highlands had been ill-conceived, but little could be done to change that now. Somehow he had to discover his wife's whereabouts. Pray she still lived, he thought. Chandra, sweet Chandra. He could not bear it if she were forever lost to him.

Aleck heard a rustling in the treetop directly above him. The wind, he decided—then wished he'd thought twice as an eerie cry sounded and a nude figure dropped from the branches. Cedric. The name shot through his mind, recognition taking hold. The stallion shied and reared; Aleck tumbled to the ground. Rolling over, he leapt to his feet and reached for his sword. Too late; the swinging mace flew at his head, the spiked end grazing his temple. His legs buckled and blood streamed from his wound. Desperately Aleck fought to retain consciousness. *Chandra!* Her name seemed to whistle through the trees just as the blackness won out.

Not far from where Aleck had been felled, a set of inquisitive eyes watched through the darkness. The Morgan warrior dragged the limp form to the edge of a deep ravine. Shoving his quarry over the rim, the man whooped loudly; then wrapping his plaid around his body, he ran off into the night.

The onlooker stepped from behind the tree that shielded him. Loping to the cleft in the ground, he peered over its rim. The big man lay on his back at the bottom. With care, the watcher climbed down the steep-sided chasm. Reaching the horseman, he knelt and pressed his ear to the man's chest. He was amazed to discover that the man still lived.

In quick order, he bandaged the man's wound with a length of linen ripped from the horseman's shirt, its tail pulled free of the buckskin breeches. Then he drew the man's sword from its scabbard and set to chopping down a number of young saplings. Afterward he fashioned a litter, tying the poles together with strips of leather cut from the horseman's jerkin. Next, he rolled the injured man onto the conveyance, then scrambled up the steep walls once more.

Finding the skittish stallion not far from where it had bolted, he led the horse along the edge of the ravine. Finally, they reached the point where the sharp sides eased to a gentle slope. The stallion snorted as it was routed back along the floor of the narrow chasm; a quick hand covered its nose and stroked gently. The horse quieted.

Half an hour later, the litter secured to the saddle, the tousle-haired lad emerged from the narrow gap. On into the night, he silently guided the stallion along the paths he knew so well, the injured horseman in tow. Just as the rain began to pelt the earth, the trio reached the broken-down bothy hidden deep in the wood. He could not speak, but Owen called the deserted croft his home.

Chapter

13

Pink fingers of light stretched upward from the horizon, marking the dawn. The early morning rains had ended, the clouds dissipating. Fresh and clean, the air was filled with the scent of heather, the first of its flowers opening on the moors. The day promised to be exceptional, but Chandra seemed not to notice the beauty of the Highlands. Standing high on the battlement at Lochlaigh Castle, she looked south, toward England. Never had she thought she'd miss the lush greens of its landscape, but she did. It was the man she missed most, not his homeland.

Worry knitted her brow as she reexamined the past few days. She'd hoped her return to Lochlaigh would be joyous, but it was not. On her arrival, she'd found her clansmen locked in turmoil, all squabbling among themselves. Some welcomed her, elation showing on their faces; others had simply glared their discontent. Of the latter, Cedric seemed the most hostile, his disposition the surliest of the lot.

Each day was a struggle as she tried to keep her wits sharp and her temper in check. Having demanded that the raids on their neighbors be stopped, she kept a tenuous hold on those who were still eager for blood. How long they would obey her commands, she kenned not. This wasn't the clan she knew, the clan she loved and honored. A malignancy had grown within its core, and her uncle had fostered its eruption. But to ostracize Cedric meant stirring even more unrest, something she could ill afford. Her only hope was that their fear of James was far greater than their hatred of him.

"Remember the clan Gregor," she had told them shortly after she'd gained a full understanding of why their king was so angry, "for if you persist in this aggression, if you continue to disobey James, the name Morgan will be no more." Hearing those words, the majority had apparently grown thoughtful. The raiding and pillaging had ceased. So far, the self-imposed truce held. If it would only last!

A foot scuffed against the stones behind her, and she turned. "You seem overly intrigued with the southern view," Cedric said. "Does your heart now belong to England?"

"No," she snapped. "I survey Morgan lands. Naught else."

"You've changed, Niece," he said, studying her closely. "You hold a faraway look in your eyes. You long for something—or someone. 'Tis the Sassenach, I'll wager."

When she'd returned, Chandra had withheld any mention of her marriage, stating only that she'd managed to escape—which was true. While her clan had applauded her cunning, elated that she'd outsmarted her captor, Cedric had remained suspicious. He continued with his baiting questions, his niggling probes, apparently hoping to discover far more. Wisely, she kept her secret close, for if the truth of her marriage came out, she'd immediately be ousted as chief. Chandra knew that all too well. "Wager what you wish, Uncle. I am the same person who left here," she lied. "I am The Morgan of

Morgan—*your* chieftain. 'Tis best that you remember it." She strode past Cedric, away from the crenel, for she trusted him not. A small shove, and she'd be lying at the base of the castle. "Has something of importance brought you here? If not, I go to Devin's grave."

"'Tis not wise for you to venture alone onto the moor, Chandra. 'Tis dangerous for you."

"Dangerous? How so, Uncle? I am, after all, on Morgan lands. By right, no harm should come to me. Unless, Uncle, someone plots against me. Tell me, should I fear one of my clan? Does he intend to use his blade and cut me down by stealth?" Eyes expressionless, Cedric remained silent. "Since you have no answer, I must assume I'll be safe. If you need me, you know where I'll be."

By the time Chandra reached Devin's grave, the sun had crept higher, its rays warming the air streaming across the moor. Kneeling, she gazed at the barren spot, small tufts of moss and grass just starting to sprout from the broken soil. The first time Chandra had come here, she'd sobbed out her grief; the second, she'd sat silently. But this day, recollections filled her.

Devin's laughing eyes; his gentle smile; his bounding about the glade, only to tumble over the side of the ravine; their race down the hill; his protective arm about her shoulders as the arrogant Sassenach appraised her—it all came to mind. His sitting opposite her while making their list; his attack of violent coughing; Aleck's intervention, whereupon he'd carried Devin to his bed—all this she remembered.

As she and Devin stood outside her antechamber, his soft kiss had fallen on her palm. *He has the power to change the course of your destiny . . . your future is in his hands. Don't be afraid of this winged hunter. For all his fierceness, he might actually be a dove.* Her cousin's words spun through her head; it was as though she were hearing them for the very first time. She couldn't help but wonder if Devin had already foreseen his fate. Had he been saying his final farewell, letting her know he approved of the Englishman, encouraging her to accept what was preordained? *I hope, Chandra, that your lord of legend will be forever kind to you.*

A sword flashed in her memory. "'Tis easier this way," he'd said just before he fell to the floor, his life ebbing from him. Looking back on it, she had to agree. His end had been swift, not one racked with pain as he gasped for each breath while he wasted slowly away. She'd blamed Aleck for Devin's death, yet by the mercy of her husband's blade, her cousin did not suffer, and for that Chandra was most thankful. Yet the way in which Devin had died would always stand between Aleck and herself. Her clan would never accept it.

Do not let them dictate the course of your heart. 'Tis love that gives you life, Chandra. You have found it. Do not let it go.

Devin's voice boomed in her ears uttering words she'd never heard him say; she nearly fainted at its force. Impossible, she thought, drawing a swift breath. Then she felt a presence behind her. She whipped around on her knees. The moor lay deserted. A chill ran through her; she rose to her feet. Scanning the trees a distance away, she saw movement. Owen.

He motioned to her. The action surprised Chandra, for when spotted, he normally dashed through the wood, disappearing from sight. She moved toward him, then stepped under the sheltering limbs. He appeared pale, distraught.

"Owen," she addressed him by the name she'd bestowed on him. "'Tis good to see you." She wondered if he might be weak from hunger, for until now she hadn't thought about him. After her abduction, he might have gone with little food, her clan not seeing to his needs. "Are you hungry?" She didn't wait for a nod. "I shall go to the castle and bring you some food." Owen caught her arm as she started to turn away. Standing eye to eye with him, for they were nearly the same height, she saw the negative shake of his head. "What is it, then? Has something happened that worries you?"

He nodded, then pulled at her hand. Chandra assumed he wanted her to follow him.

"You wish me to go with you, right?"

Again he nodded.

"Is it far?"

His head bobbed.

"I'm curious, but I must return to the castle. I have been gone far too long already." It was inadvisable for her to allow Cedric much time alone with her clan. Even now, the dissenters among them might have grown by half. "Mayhap we could meet later."

Owen's head nearly shook from his shoulders. Then he lifted what appeared to be a gold chain from his neck and whipped it over his head; an emerald-encrusted medallion jumped from inside his frayed saffron shirt.

Chandra nearly fell to the ground when she saw it. Immediately she snatched it from his hand. It was indeed Aleck's. "Where did you get this?"

Owen pointed through the trees. Then, seizing her hand, he urged her to follow.

"Has he been injured?" she asked, already knowing he had been before seeing Owen's nod. There was no other way that someone could have wrested the medallion from him, unless— *Dear God, no! He is not dead!*

Chandra didn't hesitate. The heavy gold chain slipped over her head, and the medallion fell beneath her tunic to lie well below her breasts. Pulling her skirt up between her legs, she tucked the hem into her waistband. The blood pounded in her ears as she raced along the paths, tracing Owen's fleet steps, her heart crying her husband's name: *Aleck!*

At long last, they came to the little cottage. Nearly hiding it from view, a tangle of briers scaled the stone walls, stretching to the tattered thatched roof. The shoddy place appeared close to collapsing. Chandra was amazed to see it, for she knew nothing of its existence. Her quick footsteps carried her over the threshold of the open door; she skidded to a halt. Eyes adjusting from sunlight to shadow, she saw Aleck lying on the makeshift cot, a bloodstained piece of linen binding his head. His normally bronzed complexion seemed exceptionally pale; she felt her heart stop.

"Aleck?" she whispered, dropping to her knees beside him. He breathed steadily, and Chandra offered up a prayer of thanksgiving. Then her trembling fingers lightly touched his brow. Carefully unwrapping the bandage, she inspected the deep gash that streaked from mid-temple back into his hair. "How did this happen?" she asked, looking at Owen.

The boy stood back. His hands formed a large circle, then his fingers gripped together and he raised his arms above his head, rotating them in a wide arc. Suddenly they stopped; his fingers sprang apart. His hand slapped the side of his head.

Chandra stared at him. "A mace—are you saying he was hit by a mace?"

Owen nodded.

She looked at Aleck. Incredibly, he'd survived the blow. A miracle, she thought, then turned her attention back to Owen. "Did you see who did it?"

He grabbed hold of her plaid and pointed to it.

"A Morgan," she said; again Owen nodded. "Are you familiar with him?"

A scowl marked his face, and Owen strutted about the floor, beating his chest. He stopped, and swung his fists through the air.

Chandra gritted her teeth. A pompous warrior. "'Twas Cedric," she said, and Owen nodded vigorously. "Did he see you?"

At the shake of Owen's head, Chandra felt greatly

relieved. Then, by way of Owen's miming, she learned how Aleck had been shoved into a ravine and how the lad had fashioned a litter to carry her husband out. Aleck's stallion, she was told, had been hidden close by. As the story unfolded, Chandra felt her anger grow to insurmountable proportions. Her uncle would pay for his transgressions. This she promised.

"Has he awakened?" she asked about Aleck, her attention again falling on her husband. Once more she surveyed the ugly wound; her heart ached and she prayed he would live. A hand touched her arm. Looking up, she watched the slow shake of Owen's head. Then his shoulders lifted, as though he were asking what he should do. "I must go back to the castle and fetch some medicinals and fresh bandages. Stay here with him. I'll return shortly."

Chandra leaned toward Aleck. After placing a gentle kiss on his parted lips and receiving no response, she rose and walked out into the sunlight; Owen followed. Glancing around her, she found she was hopelessly lost. "Which way is the castle?"

Owen pointed in its general direction, and as Chandra looked up the hillside, her shoulders slumped, for the brae was naught but a mesh of briers and brambles, the same as the cottage. Noting her discouraged expression, Owen tugged at her hand. Again, he wanted her to follow him.

"But someone must stay with Aleck."

Owen put his palms together, then tilted his head, resting his cheek on his hands.

"He sleeps, you say." The lad nodded. "That he does, Owen. But I pray it is not forever." Deciding she had no choice, she waved Owen on ahead of her. Moving away from the cottage, she looked back at the door. "I won't be long, my love. Do not leave me, please."

Inside of a quarter hour, Chandra stood in the wood just below the place where she had always left Owen his food. He motioned that he'd remain there and await her return, so he could lead her again to the cottage.

"If I am not back in a reasonable length of time, go without me. Tend to my husband as best you can. I'll be along whenever it is safe. No one must find him, Owen. His life is at grave risk. I am relying on you. Guard him well." It was a large task for one who was not trained as a warrior, but Chandra felt that Owen possessed the ability to outwit nearly anyone who trespassed on his realm. "Thank you, Owen. I am forever indebted to you. I shall not forget this."

She slipped from the wood into the open, Owen keeping watch on her. To anyone else who saw her, The Morgan of Morgan seemed not to have a care in the world as she strolled up the hillside toward the castle. But when she reached the fortress's wide base, she scurried along its ancient wall toward the north tower. Coming to a mound of boulders surrounded by dense shrubbery, she disappeared from sight. Owen frowned; then, squatting against the foot of a tree, he waited.

Having ascended the staircase that spiraled up through the thick wall of the north tower and into its cellars, Chandra doused the torch she carried and emerged from the secret door hidden behind a row of shelving. Except for the area where she now stood, the place was little used. Above her, old furnishings littered the second and third floors; in the substrata below lay a rat-infested dungeon, its trapdoor centered in the dusty ground-level wooden floor.

She closed the portal, crocks rattling on the horizontal boards, and she remembered how as children she and Devin had found the concealed entry. Chasing around the stores of grain, they had hit the shelving with such force that the latch sprang free. Eagerly they had explored the winding steps, discovering the outer doorway. A pact was made, and they had vowed never to tell anyone of their discovery. Over the years the passage was used frequently as the two sneaked from the fortress to play in the wood.

She doubted that anyone else remembered its existence. At least, she hoped not, for it was her only link to the outside world whereby she could move in and out of the castle unseen. Her feet scraped along the rustic floorboards; then she held her breath and eased open the tower's outer door. No one appeared to be in the immediate vicinity, so she quickly slipped out. Ambling across the inner ward, she passed into the kitchens.

The women were busy preparing the late morning meal. Greeting them with nods and smiles, Chandra wended her way around the group and into the pantry. Procuring a canvas sack from a hook, she filled it with a length of clean linen, thread and needle, ointment, a mixture of herbs, a block of cheese, a skin of goat's milk filled from a dipper, an assortment of fresh fruits, two loaves of brown bread, and bannocks wrapped in a napkin, which she stashed on top. Hoping to make it out to the wood again unobserved, then on to the cottage, she was disappointed. When she exited the pantry, she saw that Cedric awaited her.

"What is inside that sack, Niece?" he asked, eyeing her closely.

Chandra viewed the man, anger and loathing roiling inside her. Quickly she willed the sentiments to be still, lest she erupt with the force of her malice. "'Tis food for Owen," she said, allowing him to look in the bag's top. "While on the moor, I saw the lad. He appears frail. Apparently, while I was gone, no one thought to feed him."

His hand fishing inside the napkin, her uncle pulled out a bannock, then bit into it. "With his poaching and thieving, he is naught but a nuisance," he said, his mouth spitting bits of oatcake. "You should chase him away from here and be done with him."

"He takes no more than a hare or two on occasion for his own needs. 'Tis not enough to cause concern. Besides, he bothers no one. As long as I am chief, he shall be allowed to remain. Do not challenge me on this, for I have spoken."

Chandra brushed past her uncle and headed for the door. Cedric strode after her. "Where do you go?" he asked, trailing her closely.

"To the spot near the wood. 'Tis where I always leave Owen his food."

"I'll go with you."

"'Tis not necessary."

"But it is, Niece. Outside these walls is no place for you to be alone."

Chandra turned on him. "I will go alone, Uncle. Owen is most timid. He trusts only me. You will stay behind, so that he doesn't become frightened. Find something to keep your attention. I will not be long."

Chandra marched from the inner ward to a postern gate. Ordering the guard to open it, she walked through, then traversed the hillside. As she made her way to the wood, she felt certain that Cedric scrutinized her from the battlement. Torn between seeing to Aleck's care and the definite possibility that he'd be found were she to take to the woods with Owen, she knew she had little choice but to wait.

"Owen," she called softly at the edge of the trees, then spied him crouching against a trunk. "Keep yourself hidden. After I withdraw, come fetch this bag. I am being watched, so at present I cannot return with you. When the castle sleeps, I'll find my way to the cottage. Do not allow anyone to see which direction you go when you leave here." She saw Owen's nod, confirming that he understood. "I am depending on you. You are the only one I can trust."

Placing the bag on the ground, Chandra turned and headed back the way she'd come. When she was halfway between the wood and the fortress, Owen jumped from the trees, snatched the bag, and took off in the opposite direction to the cottage. Chandra furtively looked up at the battlement, spotting Cedric standing at one of the crenels. Hatred for the man teemed through her. Pray she would be able to keep it in check, at least until Aleck was safe.

While climbing the hill, Chandra sighed heavily. His reasons known only to himself, Aleck had come for her, but foolishly he'd done so alone. After the initial shock she'd suffered on seeing him, the thought that he'd made a dash for the Highlands surprised and elated her. But now she wondered at his purpose. Had it been concern for her welfare that had caused him to be so reckless? Was it possible that he held affection for her, hence his irresponsible action? Or did he merely seek to return her to England in order to fulfill James's command that they produce an heir?

Chandra was uncertain, but the possibility existed that a new life formed within her body. Normally quite healthy, she now suffered from bouts of light-headedness and nausea. Her monthly flow was late by two weeks. The signs confirmed that she carried his child, but she was undecided whether or not to tell Aleck, should he live. Made aware that he was to be a father, he'd try to force her away from Lochlaigh, she knew, ordering her to Montbourne where undoubtedly he thought the child should be born—in his beloved England. It would be an order she refused.

Although torn, Chandra felt the weight of the responsibility she carried. She might wish otherwise, but she was her father's daughter. She would do naught but face her obligations squarely. Her clan abounded with unrest. As its leader, she had to somehow suppress the impending revolt, dissolve the factions, and bring peace and unity to Lochlaigh again. In order to carry out such a task, she had to remain here. Until it was done, Aleck could not learn of her suspected pregnancy. It was a secret she must keep unto herself.

She pictured Aleck lying on the cot in the dreary little cottage, his face pale, his head caked with blood, and her heart compressed. Worry over his condition escalated inside her. Pray that he survived, she thought, wanting to be able eventually to share her secret with him, wanting to be held in his arms again. The revelation had taken a long time in coming, but she now knew, fully, completely, that she loved him—loved more than her own life!—her handsome lord of legend. Duty decreed that she remain loyal to her clan, but if even one of them sought to harm her husband, she would quickly fell him. Already Cedric's existence held little worth. He would pay for his offense, and soon.

She entered the gate, vowing to protect Aleck. Tenaciously—even unto her last breath—she would keep him safe. Tonight, when everyone was abed, she'd escape the castle and hasten to his side, staying with him until dawn. He must live, she thought. He must! For without him, her life would be meaningless.

From the battlement, Cedric watched his niece walk toward the doors of the great hall. In his estimation, she seemed changed. The look in her eyes and the expression on her face had told him when she'd returned from England that she was no longer a girl. She possessed a woman's quality, one that attracted a man's attention. Ever astute, he'd concluded she'd lain with the bastard who'd abducted her, the one who now rested at the bottom of the ravine. Soon she would join her lover— but before she did, Cedric thought he might enjoy the Sassenach's leavings.

Disavowing that she was any longer his kinswoman, he intended to torment and misuse her. After marking her with his own seed, he'd cut her throat and toss her atop the bloated remnants of the man she obviously loved.

Traitor that she was, she deserved no less—the English bitch! And then Cedric would be the clan's new leader— The Morgan of Morgan.

Well after everyone was abed, Chandra crept from her quarters, down the stairs, and out into the inner ward. She was thankful that no moon shone tonight. Gaining the north tower unseen, she opened the old door and edged her way through the dark cellars. She gingerly felt along the shelves, her fingers avoiding the slice of splinters. Finding the right one, she pushed against it; the panel opened, and she slipped through onto the stairs. Without benefit of light, she slowly wound her way down the narrow stones. Then she was out the lower door, past the boulders and shrubs, down the hill and across the clearing, into the wood.

At first she was confident she knew the way, but as she wended deeper into the wood, she grew less assured. Sticks snapped beneath her feet, while low-lying branches snagged her hair and struck her face. The night creatures fell quiet at her noisy approach. Soon the woodland became a black den of stillness. Much like the grave, she thought, the pounding of her heart the only sound she heard.

After ten minutes, Chandra realized she was hopelessly lost. In the moonless dark, she could see no farther than a few feet. Keep calm, she told herself, feeling the first dregs of hysteria churning upward from the depths of her stomach. If they reached her throat, she knew she would scream. Taking a deep breath, she remembered the small burn that she and Owen had crossed. A fallen tree bridged the stream. Were she to find it, she'd be only a few hundred yards from the cottage.

Trapped in the eerie silence, Chandra's ears had grown quite sensitive. Like stiff taffeta, fallen leaves rustled on the forest floor; a twig popped, sounding like a gun's report. Something was close behind her. A wild boar?

Then she thought of Cedric. Dear God. Anything but him.

She ordered her feet to run, but they were frozen to the path. A hand fell upon her shoulder, and Chandra nearly leapt from her skin. With a soft cry, she spun around. "Owen," she breathed on a relieved sigh, "you nearly frightened me to death."

In the dim light, his teeth flashed white. It was the first smile she'd ever seen from him. Then he took her hand and led her through the wood. This time, Chandra paid close attention to the landmarks they passed. A jutting boulder, a gnarled pine, the gentle burn with the fallen log—all would lead her to the cottage. At dawn, she would again have Owen show her the way, marking each step she took. For Aleck's sake, she couldn't afford to become lost again.

They stood at the cottage door. "How is he?" she asked, needing to know before she entered. Seeing Owen's firm nod, her heart quieted and her nerves calmed; slowly she stole through the opening. A small candle burned atop a stool set close to the cot. His head turned away from her, Aleck appeared as though he'd not moved since she'd last seen him. "Has he awakened at all?" she asked Owen.

He shook his head, and his dark auburn tresses, wild and tangled, bobbed about his head; his deep blue eyes looked downward, staring at his bare feet. Chandra's hand touched his arm, and he looked up.

"You have done well, Owen. Had it not been for you, my husband would now be dead." Chandra's brow wrinkled. "You saw him with me that day above the loch. That is why you came to me, isn't it?"

Owen nodded.

"He will be pleased that you remembered," she said. A peat fire burned low in the old fireplace, and Chandra glimpsed a kettle of water resting near it. She asked, "Has the water been boiled?" He affirmed that it had been.

"Then bring it nigh, so I may cleanse his wound. Afterward I shall stitch it up."

Approaching the cot, Chandra noticed that the linen had been torn into strips, which were sitting atop a rickety table next to the ointment, herbs, and thread and needle. Everything appeared ready for the task that awaited her. Removing her plaid, she tossed it on the foot of the cot, then leaned over to see Aleck's face.

Lips parted, his soft breath whispered lightly in her ears. Long, black lashes lay against his lower lids. He slept still. "Love, I must attend your wound. There might be some pain, but I shall take care not to hurt you too much." Lifting his head, she unwrapped the fresh bandage that Owen had applied. To her surprise, the deep gash had already been cleaned. Glancing at Owen, who stood behind her with the kettle, she smiled her appreciation. "I see you attended him well, Owen. Again, I thank you."

With his free hand, Owen imitated the movement of sewing. Then he shrugged.

"Usually, but not always, women are better at sewing than men. Do not belittle yourself because you were not able to finish the task."

After washing her hands with a crude bar of soap, which she'd given Owen long ago but doubted he used very often, she rinsed them with a dipper of cooled water from the kettle. She cleansed the wound again, then using her knife, its blade held over the candle's flame then allowed to cool, she shaved a strip of hair from around the gash. Cleansing it yet again, she estimated the wound to be about three inches long. With needle and linen thread in hand, the former again held over the candle's flame, she took a deep breath and set herself to sewing.

With each tiny stitch she made, hoping to prevent a hideous scar, Chandra swore the needle pierced her own skin. Her teeth bit into her lower lip and she constantly winced. To Owen, she appeared to be suffering acute pain. When the final stitch was cut and knotted, there being more than forty in all, Chandra breathed a sigh of relief. The needle set aside, her hands began to shake, her nerves finally giving way to the pressure she'd faced. Commanding them to behave, she applied the ointment and wrapped Aleck's head with a fresh bandage. Finally she straightened and stretched, then kneaded the small of her back, trying to ease the ache that had settled there.

"You did well, love."

Chandra froze; her heart seemed to stop. "Aleck?" she queried disbelievingly, her eyes riveted on him. He appeared to be still asleep.

His eyelashes fluttered, then his lids opened. Slowly he turned his head. "Aye. 'Tis me," he said, his voice weak and hoarse. A faint smile crossed his lips.

"Oh, Aleck," Chandra cried, falling to her knees. Her arms went around him as her cheek settled on his chest. "Thank God you've awakened."

Feeling as if it were made of lead, his hand lifted from the bed and met her silky hair. "Aye. It's been a long sleep."

She felt his fingers awkwardly stroke her unbound tresses and thought of his first words. *You did well, love.* Hadn't she uttered nearly the same phrase to Owen, but without the endearment? A frown marring her brow, she pulled back and stared at him. "Just how long ago did you awaken?"

"Time eludes me, but you had not yet stepped through the door."

"But you didn't say anything. You didn't even move while I—while . . ."

Though his vision was clouded, even doubled at times, Aleck noted she'd grown quite pale. "While you stitched me up?" At her nod, he chuckled, then wished he hadn't. His head felt as though it might explode. "Would you have done such an expert job had you known all along that I was awake?"

Her gaze fell away from his. "You let me believe you felt nothing just to make it easier on me."

"And myself," he said, then discerned her confusion. "'Twas my male vanity that kept me so still. By your skilled hand, the scar should be minimal. Were the thing to have ended up looking quite ugly, my wife might have left me again."

Tears stung Chandra's eyes as she thought about the problems she had created for him. Were it not for her, he'd not be lying here now. "Forgive me for causing you so much trouble," she said, her trembling hand caressing his cheek. "You should not have come, Aleck. Especially alone."

"'Twas impetuous, I know. But when Jason informed me that you'd escaped him, I could think of nothing but your safety. With no preparation, I came here, straightaway."

"Poor Jason—I feared I had hit him too hard." Seeing her husband's raised brow, she elaborated: "He caught me just as I was about to slip through the gate. I had no choice but to set the axe handle to his neck. 'Twas a harsh blow I gave him. He is all right, isn't he?"

"Other than a sore jaw to go along with his pained neck, he is probably fine."

Light laughter bubbled from her throat. "He undoubtedly hates us both."

"I'm certain he will stay far from us in the future—which is fine with me."

"Do not blame him for what his father did."

"He told you?"

"Aye—at our wedding feast. He suffers, just like you, for he, too, lost his father. He was little more than a boy, Aleck. What happened between his father and yours was not his fault. Whatever has happened between you and Jason since, try to mend your differences. He is, after all, your cousin."

"I will think on it, but right now, it is your uncle who

concerns me. He is dangerous, Chandra. The bastard waylaid me not far from Lochlaigh. Tomorrow, we must leave here. Should we stay, I fear what might happen to you." He glanced around him. "How did I get here, anyway."

"'Twas Owen." She turned around, but the lad had disappeared. Looking back to Aleck, she noted his frown. "He is the one you thought was a poacher that day at the loch."

"Aye. I heard you say that he saved my life and that he'd come for you. But I remember nothing after Cedric dropped from the tree."

"Owen saw it all. He dragged you from the bottom of the ravine where Cedric had thrown you, and brought you here."

Aleck had wondered why he ached all over. Now he knew. Then he saw his medallion appear as she pulled it from inside her tunic.

"He came to me with this," she said.

She started to remove the chain from her neck, but Aleck stopped her. "For now, keep it with you." He watched as the gold circle slipped back inside her tunic, then said of the cottage: "'Tis not the best of accommodations, is it?"

"No, but 'tis unfortunately where Owen prefers to live. Good befalls us, though, for Cedric knows nothing of this place. Not even I knew it existed."

"'Tis a hovel, for certain," he said, looking around him. "But this night, it is our haven." At his movement, his head throbbed unbearably and the room seemed to spin. Damn! he thought, closing his eyes. He quickly opened them again, for he felt he'd twirl straight off the cot. He had to get control of his senses, fight off his dizziness and blurred vision, for on the morrow they must leave. He focused on Chandra's face. "The lad should come with us," he said, "for if Cedric discovers the boy's part in rescuing me, he'll be hunted down like a rabid dog. Tomorrow we go back to England."

Chandra knew he could not travel—not for several more days. Not wanting to worry him, she changed the subject. "Why didn't you tell me you were going to London to see James? What made you hide the fact that my clan was in trouble? 'Twas unfair of you to keep it from me. I am its chief."

"I had hoped to keep from happening exactly what has happened." He saw the question in her eyes. "The moment you learned your clan was in danger, you bolted, Chandra. Had I told you, instead of Jason, it would have been me who nursed a sore neck. I know you. You are far more impetuous than I. My hope was to seek an audience with James and convince him not to react so strongly against all the Morgans. It was Cedric who incited them into their acts of aggression, he who provoked them into attacking their neighbors. It should be he who atones for the wrongdoing, not the entire clan. That is what I told our king."

"And?"

"James agreed. His army is held in London. At present, your clan is safe. Cedric, however, will soon meet his fate." If he does not meet his end first, Aleck thought. Were he ever to face Chandra's uncle again, he'd kill the bastard! "If James's plan comes to fruition, your uncle will live out his days in the Tower. Our king might seem foolish, but he is, in fact, most sly. Vindictive, too. Diplomacy was needed to change his mind—you realize James had planned to destroy the Morgans, don't you?"

"I suspected such once I discovered what had been happening here at Lochlaigh. I have reminded them of the clan Gregor. For now, the raids have ceased." She studied Aleck. "Did you not trust me to speak on my own behalf?"

"With so much at stake, emotions could play no part

in negotiating with James, love. You were too close to the situation. In a moment of passion, desiring to protect those whom you love so dearly, you might have lost your temper or spoken out of turn. It would have boded ill for your family. That is why I did not tell you—why I went alone."

Aleck was probably right to keep her from London. Her Scot's temper might have clashed with the most notorious Scot of them all. Then she thought of Felicia Emory. She felt certain the lone reason for his trip south was to see James, but she had to be sure. "Was that the only reason you went to London—because of my clan?"

Aleck surveyed her. "No other reason existed. Why do you ask?"

Chandra drew a deep breath; her attention fell to her hands. "I found Lady Emory's letter. The date atop was just a few days previous to your departure. Since your note did not state why you had left—only that a matter of great importance needed your immediate attention—I, uh, I assumed—"

"You assumed I had gone to London to be with her," he finished. "Chandra, look at me." She did. "It was Sir John's letter that hastened me to London, not Felicia's. I will not deny that she was once my mistress. Over the years, I have had several. But on the day I met you, any desire I might have had for Felicia—or any other woman, for that matter—met a sudden death. From the first moment I saw you, you have held my attention. 'Tis you whom I've desired, and you alone." He sighed heavily. "I must tell you, while I was in London, Felicia did approach me. I turned her away. It is unlikely that she will ever trouble either of us again. Believe me when I say there is no one but you."

Studying his wondrous eyes carefully, Chandra considered whether what she saw in them could possibly be true. "Aleck—why did you come for me?"

A short laugh erupted from him; his head suffered for it. "Sweet," he said, the pain finally subsiding, "if you do not know the answer to that question by now, you will probably never know it at all."

"Do not mock me," she fairly snapped, desperate to know. "You risked your life. Why?"

His fingers touched the curve of her cheek, then one fell to her lips. "Because, Chandra, I have fallen in love with you. Kiss me, and I shall prove it."

Her soft cry of joy filled Aleck's ears, then their lips met. Hungrily they tasted each other. It had been little more than a week since they had last kissed, their lovemaking wild and sweet, but to both Chandra and Aleck their time apart seemed like an eternity. Tongues played momentarily, teasing and tempting. Aleck ached from wanting her, his beloved Chandra. His mouth tore away from hers. "Ah, sweet. I've missed you so. Come lie next to me so that I may hold you."

Chandra's gaze skittered to the cottage window. Through the briers she could see that the sky had lightened. There was no time for them to make love. Not now. "I cannot," she said, pulling away from him. She stood and noted Aleck seemed confused. "I must go back to the castle. Should Cedric miss me, you will no longer be safe."

"You cannot go. 'Tis you he now wants dead. I'll not allow you to leave." Grabbing hold of Chandra's wrist, he came up from the cot. Pain exploded through his head; nausea nearly leveled him. Hands gripping his temples, he fell back onto the bed; a loud groan bled through his lips. "Mother of God, be merciful," he whispered. Slowly the pounding in his head eased.

Chandra dropped herbs into a clean cup of fresh water and gave the elixir a quick stir. She eased Aleck's head upward. "Drink this, my love. It will lessen your pain."

As commanded, Aleck gulped down the sharp-tasting

concoction. He sighed as his head again met the cot. Gazing up at his wife, he saw double of her. "Chandra, please, don't go from here."

"I must, my love. The dawn approaches. For your sake, I cannot stay."

Gentle fingers caressed his forehead; then she turned away. Aleck watched her go, fear for her safety swelling inside him. "Chandra! God's wounds, woman, don't make me climb from my bed and come after you." She kept walking. He tried to lift himself from the cot, only to discover he couldn't move. What the hell had she given him? he wondered. "Chandra!"

Reaching the door, she looked back at Aleck. "I'll return tonight when it's safe. Sleep well, my love. And Aleck—I love you, too."

The words twirled through his already spinning head to settle in his heart. *Chandra, don't go!* The words screamed through his mind, but they refused to pass through his lips. Fighting against the blackness that had suddenly surrounded him, Aleck felt his eyelids close. He slept.

Having discreetly left the couple alone, Owen rose from his crouch outside the cottage door. "'Tis time we leave," Chandra said to him, throwing her plaid, which she'd snatched from the end of the cot, over her head. "He sleeps, Owen. When he awakens, should he try to rise from his bed and come to the castle, pour some more herbs down his throat. Whatever it takes, he is not to leave here. Understand?" Owen nodded firmly.

The pair wended their way through the wood. Chandra made note of each landmark and promised herself she would not forget the way to the cottage ever again. "I shall return when the castle sleeps," she said as they came to the edge of the clearing. "Remember, Owen, keep him still."

He nodded, then watched as she streaked out across

open terrain, the first light of dawn upon her. When she reached the boulders and disappeared, Owen turned back through the wood, where along the way, he gathered some special roots.

While Owen had watched Chandra advance across the clearing, so had Cedric. High above on the battlement, his eyes firmly upon her, he chased around the wall walk, peering over the crenels, trying to keep tabs on her progress. Then she disappeared. Confusion knitted his brow as he slowly returned to his post. He began to wonder if he'd seen her at all. Then below him, he caught sight of her as she dashed across the inner ward and into the great hall.

Where she'd come from, he couldn't say. But one thing was certain: She'd been out in the wood. The question was, why? Cedric could fathom no reason—unless . . .

Running down the stairs, he took himself to the stables. He saddled his horse, then mounted and quickly passed through the gates, out across the moors. Soon standing at the ravine's edge, he looked into its belly. "So, the bastard lives, does he?"

Cedric now knew why his niece had gone into the wood. Undoubtedly, she'd go to his side when night was again upon them. He'd wait and follow. Once and for all, the Sassenach would meet his end. But which of the two should he slay first?

Deciding he'd have more sport by making the English bastard suffer further, torturing his lover before his very eyes, Cedric made his choice.

Chapter

14

Well past midnight, Chandra fled the castle into the wood. Not missing a step, she hurried along the path to the cottage, her arms laden with a large fur robe. If her plan came to fruition, which she prayed it would, this night would be a night of love.

The cottage lay just ahead, and she slowed her step. Hearing her approach, Owen glanced out the open portal toward her. She motioned for him to come hither, and spoke to him briefly. Then she watched as he strolled away from his home, taking an opposite heading from the one she'd just traveled. Once he'd disappeared, she walked to the door.

Surprise filled her when she saw Aleck, candlelight illumining him. Bare-chested, he sat on the cot, his back against the wall. He appeared to be dozing. The herbs, she thought, then saw his eyes open.

"Chandra?" he breathed her name reverently.

"Aye."

"Thank God. I feared you'd never come." His brow furrowed as she moved toward him. "What do you hold in your arms?"

"'Tis our bed," she said, viewing him closely. "I intend to spread it on the floor."

Aleck's gaze darkened. "The lad—is it safe?"

"He has gone into the wood," she said, the large robe blanketing the dirt floor, fur side upward. "He will not return until I signal."

Eagerly Aleck watched as she began to disrobe. "Then you feel adventuresome, do you?"

"Aye—I have missed you."

He watched as her plaid fell to the floor and her tunic came over her head to reveal his medallion. The heavy gold chain roped over her shift where it covered her high, full breasts. Seeing its position, Aleck groaned softly.

"Your head—are you able to make love?"

"Does a bird fly?" he asked, scooting to the edge of the cot. He stood and eased his buckskin breeches down his legs.

"Aye, a bird flies," she said, thinking of the legend, "but never away from you."

His eyebrow arched; then, as he kicked the breeches away from his feet, he chuckled. Naked, he stood proudly before her. "You mean because my name is Hawke."

He knew nothing about the legend or what Devin had named him. Someday she would tell him, but now she just wanted him near her. "Aye, because your name is Hawke." Her skirt fell to the floor, then her shift lifted over her head. The glory of her body was revealed to him. "You've recovered your stamina, milord," she said, noting his arousal. "How is that possible?"

"I never lost it where you're concerned. You need only walk into the room."

She smiled. "I mean that you're up and about."

He grinned. "Precisely."

Her palm slapped against the middle of his chest just as he reached for her, staving him off. "Be serious, will you?"

"I am." Noting her censuring look, he sighed. "If you

mean I act nearly myself, it was Owen's doing. He fed me some foul-tasting mash that he cooked up from some sort of root. It rid me of my headache and renewed most of my vigor." He withheld the fact that he ofttimes saw double. As he viewed his wife, he was thankful this wasn't one of those moments. "Satisfied?"

"I will be soon," she said, her stiffened arm relaxing. Her fingers glided up his hair-roughened chest, winding around the nape of his neck. "But then you'll have to satisfy me again."

"Gladly," he said, his mouth descending toward hers. "Any hour of any day—all you need do is ask."

Their lips met, and their bodies slowly sank to the fur. Whether at Montbourne or Lochlaigh, his homecoming promised to be sweet. This time, Aleck was certain, would be the sweetest of all.

Chandra took the lead in their lovemaking, her lips softly tracing over his body. Her hand found him, stroking him in the fashion that pleased him. Then as her lips and tongue touched him, Aleck drew a ragged breath. His eyes snapped shut, and he swallowed hard. "Woman, you drive me insane," he grated, reaching for her. He lifted her hips so that she was astride him, and impaled her. "Now, Chandra, satisfy me, and I'll satisfy you."

"Gladly," she whispered, leaning over him. The medallion scraped against his hard belly as the tips of her breasts teased his chest. She inched higher, her long hair trailing along his arms. "Any hour of any day—all you need do is ask." Then her mouth searched out his.

Starved for each other as they were, the release they mutually sought was theirs in just a short time. They lay in the afterglow of their love, face to face, each marveling at the other. "I love you, Chandra. Do not ever run from me again. Promise me, this time you'll stay."

"I'll stay," she said, her finger touching his lower lip.

Until dawn, she thought, then wondered how she could possibly leave him. With his strength returning, escape seemed impossible. If only she could stay.

"Good," he said; then, catching her wrist, he kissed her hand. "Come here." He looped her arm around his neck. "Give me your lips, love." Their eager mouths met in an ardent show of affection. After a bit, Aleck pulled away. "I hate to admit this, but our lovemaking seems to have drained me. I've grown sleepy."

"Then we shall close our eyes. Rest, my love, so that you get stronger." She pulled the medallion over her head, then drew the chain over his, settling it around his neck. "I give this back to you. 'Tis where it belongs. Sleep, and so shall I."

Gazing at each other, their eyelids soon fell shut. Long minutes later, Chandra's reopened. Aleck slept, she knew. Surveying his handsome face in the dim candlelight, she felt her heart expand. She loved him so, yet soon she must leave him. Would he understand?

For several hours, she lay there studying him; at last, shortly before dawn, she slipped from the fur and quietly dressed herself. Just as she belted her plaid, Owen burst through the door. Her hand jumped to her mouth, a finger pressing to her lips. "Ssh." The sound was no more than a whisper. Then, noting that Owen seemed quite distressed, she tiptoed around the fur where Aleck still slept and followed the boy outside. "What is wrong?"

Owen pointed toward the path that led to the castle. He strutted, beat his chest, then swung his arms in the air.

"Cedric?" She saw his nod. "Is he in the wood?" Owen nodded again. "Mother of God, no."

Owen touched her arm and motioned toward Aleck, Chandra, and himself. Then he pointed up the hillside in the opposite direction of the path.

"You want us to go with you?" Another nod. "He is

still too weak to travel, Owen. Cedric will catch him. Dear God, I cannot bear to think what would happen then." Her fingers rubbed against her forehead. "I will head Cedric off. Snuff the candle and keep Aleck quiet. Otherwise, both of you might die."

Chandra started toward the path, but Owen grabbed her arm. His head shook vigorously.

"I must go." She saw his negative response to her words; then he tried to pull her toward the cottage door. "Set me free." He refused, and Chandra gritted her teeth. Her fist balling, she swung her arm in an arc; Owen landed in the dirt on his behind. "I'm sorry, Owen, but it couldn't be helped." With that, she lifted her skirt and scurried off toward the path.

Cedric fumed as he waited by the gnarled pine. Damnation! Would the dawn never come?

He'd spent half the night in the wood already, losing Chandra just after she'd entered it. His surveillance of her had been a disaster from the start. First he'd trailed her into the north tower, but she'd somehow vanished. Where she'd gone after she'd slipped through its outer door, he had no idea—a secret passage, perhaps?—but he intended to find out—later.

By the time he'd reached the postern gate, several of his loyal followers at his heels, she was already halfway across the field. Silently they'd given chase, but once into the woods and a ways down the path, Cedric and his men found themselves disoriented. His niece was nowhere to be seen. Striking off in several directions, he and his men always found themselves back at the same tree. When the dawn came, however, he meant to start his search. His niece and her lover were somewhere in this wood, and he aimed to find them.

The sound of splashing water caught his attention. Far below, he saw a shadowy figure moving toward him.

"She comes," he whispered, motioning for his men to hide. Soon, he'd have the Sassenach as well.

Just as Chandra foolishly dashed into the wood, Owen scrambled to his feet. Again he burst through the cottage door. This time he'd not be put off.

Aleck felt a rough hand shaking him. His eyes flew open. Chandra, he discovered, was no longer beside him. Turning his head, he saw Owen standing above him. The lad seemed frantic.

"What is it? Where's Chandra?"

Owen pointed to the door.

"She's gone?" Aleck saw his nod. "Damn her. She can never be trusted." He snatched his breeches from the floor. Shoving his legs into them, he stood. His head spun, and he listed to the right. Owen caught him. Trying to fight off the vertigo, Aleck noted there were two of the same lad holding on to him. The twins slowly came together. Finally there was one. Thinking he was all right, Aleck pulled away from Owen; without knowing how, he found himself on one knee. His hand clasped his forehead as his elbow rested on his raised thigh. Aleck breathed deeply until the dizziness subsided. "How long ago did she leave?" he asked, at last coming to his feet.

Owen lifted his hand for Aleck to see, the thumb and forefinger a hair'sbreadth apart.

His eyes upon Owen, Aleck shoved his feet into his boots. "Just a bit ago, you say? Then we should have no trouble catching her."

Aleck headed for the door, but Owen skittered in front of him, blocking his path and shaking his head forcefully. Aleck stared at the boy, for Owen had set himself to beating his chest, then he swung his fists through the air. Not understanding him, Aleck frowned. Then the lad's arms circled above his head, his fingers flying free, as though he'd released some object. Afterward he slapped his palm against the side of his head. Immediately Aleck was filled with awareness.

"Cedric—are you saying he's in the wood?" At Owen's nod, both fear and rage gripped the Earl of Montbourne. His fear was for Chandra; his rage at Owen. "Damnation! Why did you let her go?" Owen rubbed his jaw, then shrugged. Belatedly Aleck spied the bluish mark. "You are not the only one who has felt her sting. When she is determined to have her way, she'll go to any lengths to get it. I know this from experience." He grabbed hold of his sword where it rested against the wall by the door. "Let's go find her."

Chandra jumped as Cedric stepped into the path in front of her. "Uncle, you startled me," she gasped, her hand flying to her chest above her heart. She glimpsed the half dozen men who'd stepped from the shelter of the trees. "What are you doing in the wood?"

"'Tis a question that I should be asking, Niece. And don't tell me you were simply out for a stroll. I know he lives."

Blinking, Chandra asked, "Who lives?"

Cedric's eyes glittered. Latching onto her arm, he jerked her against him. "Do not be coy. The Sassenach— where is he?"

"In England, I suppose."

"Bitch! Do you think I am a fool? I know that you hide him. Now, where is your lover?"

"Think you are a fool? By your actions, I *know* you are a fool. Loose me, or as your chief, I shall banish you from the clan. Get from this wood and back to the castle. 'Tis almost dawn. There are chores to be done."

A short laugh erupted from Cedric's throat. "Aye, there are chores to be done—pleasant ones at that. Since you will not be chief for long, I see no need to obey you. Likewise, since you will not lead me to the English bastard, 'tis certain he'll come to me, for you'll be the bait."

His hand tightening around her arm, he spun Chandra around and propelled her down the path in front of him; his men followed. "You are insane, Uncle. The others will not stand for this," she said of her clansmen.

"Insane?" he asked, a wide smile flashing across his face. "Not insane, Chandra. To be chief has been my hope since I was old enough to understand the power that the position affords. Your father stood in my way once. Now 'tis you. But that will be rectified shortly. First, we'll find your lover."

Cedric's words spun inside Chandra's head. She thought of the agony her father had suffered before his death, and everything fell into place. Her heels dug into the ground just as they reached the stream. "You bastard —'twas you who killed him! You poisoned him, didn't you?"

"A misfortune, indeed—but also a necessity. I have different plans for you, but be assured, your death will be no less painful. You've betrayed our clan by becoming that bastard Englishman's whore. For that you shall pay."

"I am not his whore!"

"Aren't you? I can smell his sweat on you now. You've lain with him, and recently. Savor the pleasure of that moment, Chandra, for it will have been your last."

Catching hold of her unbound hair, he twisted her fiery tresses around his hand, then shoved her into the stream. She stumbled, her feet sloshing noisily in the water. Cedric jerked her hair, keeping her upright. Tears stung her eyes as pain needled her scalp, but Chandra was determined not to cry. As she blundered up the bank, in the distance, she spied the dim light in the cottage. Holding her breath, she prayed Cedric wouldn't see it. Suddenly the tiny beacon went out.

Mother of God, do not let Cedric find him. Aleck! Keep safe, my love.

As Aleck ducked through the door, sword in hand, Owen snuffed the candle, then grabbed the small leather pouch hidden by the fireplace. Dashing through the door, he nearly collided with the Englishman.

Holding his head, fighting off the dizziness that had claimed him again, Aleck uttered a soft curse. He was useless to Chandra. In his condition, how the hell could he possibly help her?

Aleck felt the touch of Owen's hand on his arm, then saw the boy was pointing at the wood. Dawn was breaking, and as Aleck gazed into the trees, he spied the shadowy figures as they moved toward the cottage. One, he knew, was Chandra.

His sword slipped from its scabbard. As he made to take a stance, Owen's hand met his forearm. The lad's head shook vigorously; he poked at Aleck's chest, and one finger bounded into the air. Then the boy pointed to the wood; seven fingers leapt toward the sky. The lad was right, Aleck thought. In the shape he was in, he couldn't possibly face that many men. Damn the luck! Why did his strength have to fail him now? Owen's hands shoved against him, and Aleck knew he had no choice but to seek shelter among the trees.

Just as the pair were swallowed by the dense wood on the opposite side of the cottage, the tiny group entered the clearing. Crouched behind a thick tree, watching, Aleck noted that Cedric was in the fore. He held Chandra prisoner by her hair.

"Which way now, bitch?" the man asked, then a shout erupted from one of his companions. Cedric spied the structure no more than a dozen yards in front of him. He pushed Chandra toward it. "So, we are at his lair, are we?" Chandra tried to struggle free of him; her foot kicked his shin. Cedric jerked her hair hard, the claymore's blade swinging to her neck. "Be still or I'll slit your throat."

Seeing the brutality, hearing her soft cry, Aleck instinctively tensed, ready to bound into the clearing. But as his thighs started to stretch, he felt Owen's hand on his shoulder, pressing him down.

"Sassenach!" Cedric's voice boomed into the air. "Come hither or your whore dies."

Again Aleck moved; again Owen held him down. Then all at once, eerily, a cry went up from the hill high above the wood. Cedric and his men looked at one another, startled. The yell signaled that invaders approached; it had pealed from the castle walls.

"What mischief this?" Cedric demanded, knowing that Lochlaigh was under siege, or soon would be.

"'Tis probably James's army," Chandra replied. "For your disobedience, you now face the king's wrath. All of you will suffer."

Cedric cursed. "Set your arrows to the place. Burn the bastard alive."

"No!" Chandra cried as Cedric began dragging her from the small clearing. Arrowheads primed, flints were struck, then bows drawn. Streaks of light arced through the air, striking the thatched roof. "No!" she shouted again as the flames began devouring the dried grass and reeds. Cedric's arm clamped around her waist. Lifting her, he forded the stream. Halfway up the path, she smelled the acrid smoke, saw the billowing plumes as bright orange flames leapt toward the sky. While Cedric pushed her onward toward the castle, Chandra's hand covered her belly. *Dear God, do not have let him been in there.* Their child needed his father.

On the other side of the clearing, Owen was prodding Aleck up the hillside through the wood. Several times he staggered and clutched at a tree, then, at Owen's prompting, continued. Pray God that Chandra was right, he thought, fighting his vertigo. The second most welcome thing he could see on leaving the thickness of the trees would be the five hundred soldiers who were presumed to be in London. The first would be Chandra safe and sound and Cedric dead.

The sun topped the horizon just as Aleck and Owen reached the edge of the wood. Stumbling from the trees, Aleck focused on the hillside by the castle, searching for his wife. Chandra and her uncle were nearly at the gate. Suddenly he heard the loud snort of a horse almost in his ear. Spinning around, Aleck felt his head twirl. He fell backward, landing hard on his rump.

"Rather reckless of you, cousin," Jason said as he fought to calm his horse. "I could have run you down."

Aleck bit back a curse, then with Owen's help came to his feet. Looking toward Lochlaigh, he saw that Chandra had disappeared. He swore vehemently. Eyeing Jason, then Sir John beside him, he released his breath. "Where are the rest?" Aleck asked, not caring how James's men had gotten there, just so they had.

"About two miles back," Sir John replied. "We saw the smoke and came on ahead."

"My wife has been taken prisoner by her uncle. They are now in the castle. I fear you may be too late."

While the men spoke, Owen dashed into the wood. Shortly he returned with Aleck's stallion, saddled and ready. "What happened to your head?" Sir John asked, eyeing the bandage.

Aleck tore the linen from his head and threw it to the ground. "Chandra's uncle waylaid me about a mile from here," he said, reaching for his horse's reins and missing.

"Are you certain you are up to this, Montbourne?" the knight queried, inspecting the neatly stitched gash that disappeared into the thickness of the man's hair.

"I'd not question him too much, were I you," Jason commented. "'Tis dangerous to one's health."

Surveying the bright purple and yellow bruise on the

viscount's jaw, the knight chuckled. "Whitfield, you probably deserved it.

"Aye, he did," Aleck interjected. Sheathing his sword, he managed to mount his horse, then extended his hand to Owen and lifted the lad up behind him. Owen, who had gone without sleep for nearly two days, rested his cheek against Aleck's bare back. In a few seconds, he dozed.

"Who is the lad, anyway?" Sir John asked.

"He saved my life, twice," Aleck said, glancing at Owen over his shoulder. "Hand me that length of rope." The knight took it from his saddle and passed it to Aleck. With Sir John's help, he wrapped it around Owen and himself, tying the boy firmly to him so he'd not tumble from the horse. "I'd hate to lose him now." The smoke grew thicker around them. "The whole wood burns," Aleck said. "Let's go meet the others."

At a canter, they struck off toward the oncoming army. Owen bobbed awake. When away from the smoke and approaching fire, the horses were slowed to a walk; Owen dozed again.

"How do you suggest we approach this situation?" the knight asked Aleck.

"What number came with you?"

"Nearly five hundred. Our ride was fast and hard. The troops are weary. They've had little sleep."

"Then we should sit at the front gate and try to talk them out of their foolishness. Cedric doesn't have full control of the Morgans, I'm certain. If they see the force that stands against them, they might come to their senses. Surely they'll know they cannot win."

"Or, simply because we are English," Sir John said, "they will choose to fight us to the last man."

"What about Chandra?" Jason harped.

Aleck turned to him. "While James's men keep the Morgans' attention, I'll try to find a way inside. Thanks to you, she is in grave danger." He looked to the knight. "Cedric's intent is to kill her, but on seeing the force against him, he might decide to keep her alive and use her as a pawn with which to negotiate. Let's move James's army to the castle as quickly as we can. To delay could spell disaster."

As they rode ahead, Owen blinking awake again, Aleck learned that at about the same time he'd reached the gates at Montbourne, the messenger sent from his home had reached London, the two having taken different routes. While the man was frantically searching for Aleck, he'd run into Sir John. The knight had gone straight to James with the information about Chandra's flight and the fact that he thought Aleck would give immediate chase. Their king did not hesitate. His army was on the move within a few short hours. The ride had been arduous, to say the least; they'd picked up Jason midway between London and Montbourne.

"I couldn't allow you to die in Scotland, cousin," Jason said with a shrug. "All Hawkes meet their ends in England. Why break tradition?"

Aleck eyed him closely. "Then pray, cousin, that I get Chandra away from her uncle alive, else you might be the first to be buried here."

Though James's soldiers were bone-weary from their travels, they were nonetheless eager to fight. In a quarter of an hour, Lochlaigh stood under siege.

When Cedric's party reached the castle gates, Chandra was immediately led to the north tower and roughly shoved through its door into the cellars. "Open the trapdoor," Cedric ordered two of his men. As the ancient access creaked upward, a sickening stench rising with it from the belly of the dungeon, he turned to Chandra. "Your new abode awaits you, Niece."

Pushed toward the yawning hole, Chandra felt her heart stop. "No good will come to you by this," she said, her feet digging into the floorboards. "James's men will destroy you."

"They have no way in—or they won't once we've found your hidden passage and barred it. Let them lay siege to Lochlaigh. Months will pass before they have starved us. By then, winter will be upon us. Weary of waiting, they'll probably go home to their warm beds and their plump wives." He turned to his men. "Throw her in."

Two of her errant clansmen grabbed her arms. Struggling against their holds, Chandra tried to keep from the opening. "No!" she cried, feeling herself being lifted. Her feet dangled above the gaping trapdoor—and then, she was dropped through it.

Stagnant water splashed onto her skirt as she landed, luckily, on her feet. The smell was nauseating. She gagged, then fought to keep the bile from her throat. As she stared up at the opening, its distance three times her own height, the door fell shut.

First there was naught but blackness, but as her eyes adjusted, she saw a faint light coming from an arrow loop set in the twelve-foot-thick stone wall. The sound of tiny feet, nails scratching, met her ears. Rats! she thought, hearing a squeak. Her skin crawled.

"Find that passageway," she heard Cedric's voice above her. "When you do, secure it."

Standing perfectly still, she listened to the scuffing sound of footsteps as they tracked the floorboards. Her heart sank when at last she heard an excited shout. What she imagined were sacks of grain fell onto the floor against the shelving. Thump, thump, thump went the constant noise above her. It stopped, then all was quiet. Tears stung her eyes as she realized she had no chance of rescue. She'd rot here in this foul-smelling hole, the rats devouring her flesh. It mattered not, she decided. Not if Aleck no longer lived. She thought of the tender life budding inside her. Her hand covered her stomach.

Please be alive, my love. For our child's sake, get me from this place.

A furry creature scampered over her foot. Chandra's heart seemed to jump to her throat; she dashed through the sludge toward the arrow loop. Its slanted opening, where it met the room, was wide enough for a man's body to fit inside, narrowing as it inched toward the outside wall. She jumped and her fingertips caught onto the ledge; feet scrabbling up the stones, she pulled herself onto the shelf. Three rats were quickly flung into the muck below. Arms wrapped around her raised knees, she sat quietly.

Chandra thought she'd be fairly safe now, with the light flowing through the loop, down the shaft toward her. But when night fell, she would no longer be able to see. She shuddered as she pictured the voracious pack of vermin scrambling up the wall to swarm over her. At the thought, she became sick. Hanging her head over the ledge, she retched violently. Finally, she straightened and wiped her face with the tail of her plaid. "Oh, Aleck," she whispered, looking at the heavens, "if you live, find me, love. This, I fear, I cannot bear."

Out in the yard, Cedric stood on the steps leading to the wall walk. The clan had gathered round to hear his words. "Our chief has betrayed us. She has lain with the Sassenach—the one who killed our Devin. Willingly she became the Englishman's whore! The smoke and fire you see is the destruction of their lair. I caught them there together. The bastard is undoubtedly burned to a crisp. Now James's army approaches to lay siege. The king wishes to destroy Lochlaigh, to destroy the Morgans. As Highlanders, it is time we stand and fight! What say you? Do we die as warriors, or do we surrender like cowards? The choice is yours!"

Several in the group looked at each other, uncertain that what Cedric had said about their chief was true,

Angus among them. Others whooped loudly, ready to fight. Then a shout sounded above them. All the Morgan men, followers and dissenters both, raced up the stairs to the battlements, Cedric at the fore. Reaching the crenels, they peered over the wall to see the nearly five hundred who stood in a line that circled the base of the hill. It appeared to many that Cedric had spoken true.

A loud cry swelled through the whole, the eerie sound sending chills down each Englishman's spine. When the Highland yell had ended, for a moment all was still. Then an unearthly screech answered from high above the castle; the hackles stood on each Morgan's neck. Hundreds of eyes quickly searched the sky. There above Lochlaigh, a hawk circled steadily.

"'Tis a bad omen," someone whispered.

Chapter

15

Aleck cursed loudly as he paced behind a large outcrop of rock that stood well below the castle. Since the moment he'd stumbled from the wood at dawn, he'd kept himself hidden, not wanting Cedric to know he was alive. In the interim, Sir John periodically brought word back to him about the negotiations—if one could call them such. Presently, they were at a stalemate, as they had been all day. Now, as the sun sank behind the distant hills, Aleck was vexed that they were no closer to getting Chandra from the castle than when all the bellicose posturing had started. The whole day had been wasted with the two sides blustering at each other; Aleck had grown weary of waiting.

"Look, inform Lord Penrose to tell the bastard who now insists he's chief that James wants the Lady Lochlaigh. If he releases her into Lord Penrose's care, the army will retreat."

"But James wants Cedric, not Chandra."

A violent epithet hissed through Aleck's lips. "I know what James wants. 'Tis Chandra who is in danger. Get her out of there, and Penrose can do as he will. He can level the place if he wishes. I want my wife."

Sir John arched one eyebrow. "I'll speak to Penrose," he said of the commander who'd led the force from London to Lochlaigh. "But he is one who goes strictly by the book."

"Then lend me your dag, and I shall shoot him dead."

"Not a good idea, Montbourne," the knight said, his hand covering the wheel-lock pistol's breech protectively. "I'll speak to him now."

Sir John rode away, and Aleck's backside hit hard against a flat rock as he sat down. "God's wounds!" he exploded. "If there were only some way to get in there, I'd rescue her myself." He felt a hand poking at his shoulder. "What is it?" he snapped, turning on Owen. The boy pointed to the castle. "Not now. I have to figure a way to get inside." He was poked again. Frantically Owen gestured to the fortress. The lad appeared to be miming the opening of a door. Owen glanced from side to side, then stealthily crept through the imaginary portal. "Are you saying you know a secret way to get in?" Owen nodded. "Damnation! Why didn't you tell me this before?"

Owen shrugged, and Aleck remembered that when he'd mentioned it earlier, the lad was dozing against his back. "Show me where this entry is."

Picking up a stick, Owen drew a circle in the dirt, then pointed to the castle. "Lochlaigh," Aleck said; the boy nodded. A line was formed to the side of the castle, and Owen pointed to the woods. "Aye, the forest—or what's left of it."

Owen formed dots in the dirt, looking like a path from the wood to the northern tip of the castle. He patted the rock next to where Aleck sat, then with his arms made a large arcing circle. Afterward he again opened the imaginary door. Aleck stared at Owen. Then it dawned on him.

"The entrance is behind some large rocks below the north tower?" Owen nodded. "Did you see Chandra go in that way?" Owen affirmed that he had. A smile claimed Aleck's lips, and he ruffled the boy's hair. "Good lad!"

This action brought a frown from Owen, and Aleck apologized for having been too personal. "When it is dark, you may show me the way," he said. The boy pointed to Aleck's wound. The lad's head gyrated, his eyes crossing. "'Tis better, Owen. The light-headedness has left me, thanks to your roots, unappetizing as they are. My vision, though, is still doubled at times." Owen shrugged. "'Tis impossible to cure everything, Owen. You've worked a miracle already." He patted the boy's shoulder. "I'll be fine."

Aleck drew his sword from its scabbard, then looked thoughtfully at the boy again. "Here," he said, pulling something from the top of his boot. "'Tis Chandra's dirk." He'd placed it there after retrieving it from one of the leather pouches hanging on his saddle. Since the time he'd disarmed her of it, he'd kept it close to him. With its edge, he cut a piece from the rope Sir John had given him earlier, then fashioned a belt around Owen's waist. "Where we're going, you'll need your own protection." He tucked the dirk into the makeshift belt; then they waited. Finally, when the sky had darkened sufficiently, Aleck said, "'Tis time, Owen. Let us find Chandra."

Having just finished with a ten-minute tirade, which had fallen upon the one calling himself Penrose, Cedric now stood on the wall walk listening to his clansmen argue among themselves. Ever since the hawk had made its appearance above Lochlaigh, tensions had been taut. Not only did he have to contend with the arrogant English outside, Cedric was besieged by the squabbling, superstitious lot inside. After he'd refused to release the

Lady Lochlaigh, telling the swelled-headed Penrose to take his bony hide from Scotland without her, he'd turned to see several of his clansmen staring at him.

"Why did ye tell him that?" one asked. "Give her to him, if that's what he wants."

"The bitch stays here," Cedric snarled, pushing the man aside.

"Do not call her that," another interjected, glaring at Chandra's uncle.

"Why?" his companion asked. "Ye heard Cedric. She has lain with the Sassenach—the one who killed Devin."

"'Tis Cedric's word only that it's so. Who is to say he speaks true?"

"Silence!" Cedric thundered, weary of the bickering. "Light some more torches. 'Tis grown far too dark to see."

Halfway down the stairs, for he intended to visit his niece, torment her if possible, he heard the voices rise again above him. Looking over his shoulder at the pair he'd just reprimanded, he saw they were engaged in a scuffle; a fist flew, hitting one in the jaw. Others, who'd drawn nigh to watch, started shouting and snapping. Before Cedric reached the wall walk again, two dozen men were employed in a brawl.

"Ye took our chief into the north tower," Angus said, stepping into Cedric's path as his foot struck the second-to-last thread. "What did ye do with her?"

"Get out of my way," Cedric ordered.

"Not until ye tell us what ye've done with her."

"Cedric is chief now," one of his henchmen said, shoving Angus from the head of the stairs. "Whatever happens to her, she deserves it."

Stumbling, Angus teetered on the edge of the wall walk, nearly falling over its side. A supporter of Chandra's caught his flailing hand and gave a hard tug; Angus's feet landed squarely on the stones. Breathing a sigh of relief, he glared up at the taller man who'd pushed him; then his fist met the man's nose. Another dozen quickly leapt into the fray.

Seeing the madness encompassing him, fights breaking out all over the Morgan stronghold, Cedric conceded that he was fast losing control. "Enough!" he shouted, marching from spot to spot along the battlement, but no one listened. After ten full minutes of trying to quell the rebellious lot, he cursed vigorously. Turning, he strode toward the stairs. He had an appointment to keep. He'd been thinking about it all day. It was a warrior's prerogative to rape and pillage. The time had come to claim that right and slake his needs, his niece suffering in the process. The bitch, he decided, was now his.

At the overspread of darkness, Aleck and Owen swiftly made their way across the field and into the wood. The stench of smoke was still heavy in their nostrils as they tracked their way to the closest spot affording them a quick jaunt to the north tower. They waited.

Lord Penrose was preparing to approach the castle. Torchbearers ran beside him and two dozen soldiers guarded his rear as he traveled up the hillside. Stopping a suitable distance from the castle wall, Penrose called out his terms.

At the commander's first movement, Aleck and Owen dashed toward the boulders. Breathless, and apparently unseen, they slipped behind the shielding rocks. Just as Cedric's voice bellowed out over the battlement, cursing Penrose, Aleck entered the hidden door. He groped against the wall, searching for a torch of his own. He was in luck. Taking it from its holder, he struck his sword against the stones. Sparks met the torch's head, igniting it. "Get inside, and close the door."

Owen hopped through the opening. The panel shut, and the two climbed the narrow staircase as it wound upward. Finally, they came to a small landing and another door.

"Hold this," Aleck said, passing the torch to Owen. Then he set his sword aside and shoved against the door. It wouldn't budge. Checking the frame for a secret latch, he saw none. Again he pushed. Nothing. Then his back settled against the panel. Using the strength in his thighs, he shoved full-force. His powerful muscles bunched, then stretched; a groan of exertion vibrated in his throat. Crocks rattled on the other side; the door moved an inch, but no more. "Something blocks it," Aleck said, spinning around to glare at it. So close, yet so far. Anger exploded through him. "Damn!" His fist rammed the door. "Damn!"

Owen's eyes widened and he fell back a step. As he did so, his back hit a protruding stone. Behind him, a hidden door opened, and he tumbled through it, landing on his seat.

Aleck's head jerked to the side. Seeing the new entry, he grabbed his sword. "You bring good fortune, Owen," he said, smiling. He pulled the boy to his feet and took the torch. Another set of steps lay inside the door, spiraling upward. "Come. Let's see where these lead."

Using his sword, Aleck cut through the thick cobwebs strung from wall to wall. The passageway, he decided as he ascended it, had not been used for close to a century. Winding upward, he at last saw the landing. "Hold the torch close so I may see." He passed it to Owen, then crouched to examine the new entryway, which was far smaller than the first. His fingers ran around the edges. Pulling them away, he gazed at the black marks on his hand. "Soot. 'Tis probably an old fireplace. Since you found the last one, tell me, Owen: Where is the trigger?"

Owen switched the torch to his other hand, then reached for the lever, which was in plain sight. He pulled it, and the catch sprang free. With a whoosh, the small door swung toward Aleck, nearly knocking him back down the steps. Arching an eyebrow, Aleck stared at the lad. Owen simply shrugged.

Having crawled through the new opening, into the fireplace, then on into the room, the two looked around them, the torch illumining the area. Old furnishings were stacked here and there, cobwebs threading from one piece to another. Dust lay thick on everything. Spying the doorway, Aleck nodded toward it; then he and Owen crept across the floorboards. Once through the opening, they carefully wended their way down the tower stairs into the cellars, careful to be quiet though no one seemed to be about. As he walked lightly across the floor, Aleck saw the sacks of grain stacked against the shelves. "That is why we could not get in. Which way now, Owen?"

Below the two, balled up on her ledge, Chandra heard the soft tread of feet, then Aleck's voice. Was she dreaming? "Aleck," she cried with all the force in her lungs.

Her yell sounded as though it had risen from the bowels of the earth. Aleck spun on his heel. Torchlight streamed over the floor. "There," he said, pointing to the trapdoor. "Chandra?"

"Hurry, Aleck!" she cried, hearing his feet tread the boards above her.

The trapdoor lifted and the torch was shoved through the opening. Aleck's gaze first lit upon Chandra, curled in a knot on the window ledge. Then he spied the floor; it was dense with rats. "Don't move," he ordered, then withdrawing the torch, he searched the room. A thick hemp rope lay in one corner. "Get it," he said, jerking his head at the coil, and Owen rushed to fetch it.

Aleck passed the torch to the boy, then set to knotting the rope several times over, a foot back from its end. Then he lay on his belly, the medallion dangling from his neck as he lowered the rope through the opening until it hung halfway down. As Owen held the torch inside the pit, Aleck viewed his wife. Huge blue eyes stared from her pale face; she shook uncontrollably. He'd kill Cedric when he again saw him, Aleck swore.

"Sweet, I'm going to swing the rope to you. Don't reach for it. Let it come to you. When I give the word, I want you to stand as best you can and swing out over the floor. Whatever you do, don't let go. Do you understand what I've told you?"

"A-aye."

"Easy does it, then."

The rope swung toward her; Chandra grabbed for it. She missed and nearly tumbled to the floor, but caught herself.

Aleck swallowed the explosive curse that had leapt to his tongue, for fear he'd frighten her further. Steadying his own nerves by drawing a deep breath, he looked at her closely. "Chandra, listen to me. Let the rope come to you," he said, enunciating each word carefully. "Do not—I repeat—do not reach for it. Are you ready?"

She nodded, and Aleck began to swing the rope again. Like a pendulum, it swayed back and forth, back and forth, until at last it fell into her lap; Chandra snatched it up and held on to it.

"That's my girl," he said gently. "Now, carefully rise to your feet."

Scooting around, Chandra got her feet under her, then rose to a half crouch. "'Tis all the further I can stand," she said, her back hitting the top of the opening.

"'Tis enough," Aleck told her. "When I tell you, I want you to swing out above the floor. Can you do that?"

"Aye. 'Tis like when Devin and I were children. We swung out over the stream and dropped into it."

Aleck smiled at her. "I did the same, sweet. But this time don't let go. Whatever you do—*don't let go*. Remember, wait for my command."

"I'll wait."

"Good," he said, easing from his belly to his rump.

The rope's knotted end slanting down between his legs, Chandra holding it, he sat sideways at the top of the opening and braced his booted feet against the frame opposite him. Quickly he looped the other end of the rope around his waist, tying it off. "Are you ready?" he asked, gripping the hemp where it ran between his thighs.

"Aye, but 'tis dark down here," she said, for Owen had withdrawn the torch as Aleck positioned himself.

"You'll be up here quick enough." He grasped the rope tightly and locked his arms. "Swing, Chandra."

Aleck felt the rope jerk as her full weight hit it, then it swayed, touching one thigh, then the other. Muscles bulged, veins popping up along his arms as he held fast to it. When the rope settled, he began pulling it up, hand over hand. Finally Chandra's reaching fingers brushed his leg. Looping the rope around one wrist, he grabbed hold of her forearm and pulled her up through the space between his legs. Her other hand latched onto his leg. The rope fell away as his arm clamped around her waist. Dragging her up over his lap, he set her on the floor.

Chandra scrambled away from the hole, and the rope was unwound from Aleck's waist. His legs came up out of the pit's opening; he rolled onto his knees. Chandra was on hers, facing him. In the torchlight, blue eyes studied blue. "Come here," Aleck growled, his hand reaching for her. In a breath, they were in each other's arms. Their lips met in a hard, ravenous kiss. Too soon, it was over as Aleck pulled away. "I thought I had lost you," he said, his gaze devouring her face.

"And I you. The cottage—the fire. How—"

"'Twas Owen. He awakened me. Come," he said, rising to his feet, drawing Chandra with him. "There's no time to explain. We must leave here." Taking her hand, he bent and retrieved his sword from the floor. When he straightened, his eyes betrayed him. Blinking twice, his vision cleared. "Let's go."

The trio were a dozen steps away from the dungeon's

gaping mouth when the outer door flew open and Cedric came through it. For a second, everyone froze. "So the bastard lives yet!" Cedric grated, his claymore scraping from its scabbard, and he kicked the door shut behind him. "But not for long."

Hatred gleamed in Aleck's eyes as he stared at Chandra's uncle. "Take her from here," he said to Owen, passing her hand into the boy's.

Owen tugged Chandra toward the stairs. Her attention on her uncle, she blindly followed. Noting the direction they took, Cedric raced across the floor, blocking their escape. "No, Niece. I'm not through with you. When your lover is dead, I'll enjoy the spoils of my victory. It has been a while since I've ridden between a woman's legs. The experience should be sweet."

Aleck was instantly at Chandra's side. Rage tore through him at Cedric's words. "You incestuous bastard! Attempt to touch my wife, and the instrument you think to use will be cleaved from your body." He saw the surprise on Cedric's face. "Aye, Cedric, she is my wife, and only I shall touch her. Your plans are a bit premature, I'd say, especially since it is you who will breathe his last. Come." His sword clasped tightly in one hand, he motioned Cedric forward with the other. "Stand ready to die."

"'Tis you, Sassenach, who will meet his end."

Cedric launched himself at Aleck, and the earl leapt in front of Chandra and Owen. "Get back," he ordered over his shoulder.

The blades clashed just as the two reached the wall, away from the fight. Owen held the torch high, lending light to the battle. Chandra watched through frightened eyes. Give him strength, she prayed for Aleck, knowing he was not fully recovered.

Steel sliced and clanged loudly amid the echoing stones. The force of the blows struck sparks. The contest was one of power and skill as Aleck and Cedric danced around in a circle. Each blow was met and deflected, neither taking the advantage. Then as Aleck spun round, his sword catching the downward thrust of the claymore, he felt his head swim. When again he faced Cedric, the man had gained a twin.

Cursing under his breath, Aleck struggled to clear his vision. Cedric's blade swung, and Aleck failed to meet it with his own. Swiftly the claymore plunged, aiming at Aleck's heart. Miraculously, its tip hit the medallion, then glanced off to sting Aleck's shoulder. Blood streamed from the wound. He heard Chandra's gasp.

Cedric's laugh echoed through the room. "You grow slow, Sassenach. Soon your whore will be mine."

The words struck fury into Aleck. His sword swung wildly, forcefully. Instantly, Cedric was on the retreat. The blade sliced low, cutting through his belted plaid, nicking his thigh; Cedric's breath hissed through his lips. Then Aleck's sword brushed his chest, slashing diagonally. The wounds were superficial, unlikely to rob him of his strength, yet Cedric found he couldn't gain the upper hand. Rage drove the Englishman, he knew, but the superhuman force guiding his powerful blows was yet undefined. Then Cedric realized: It was death that came at him.

Aleck's unleashed fury drove Cedric ever closer to the wall where Chandra and Owen stood watching. His vision finally clearing, he shouted: "Move away from there!"

The two made a dash from the spot, but, blocked by sacks of grain, they were forced to pivot and head the other way.

Aleck's blade continued to beat at Cedric's, backing him nearer the wall. It descended in a whistling arc but missed, hitting the floor, Cedric having jumped from beneath it. Spinning, he latched onto Chandra's hair, its length trailing out behind her as she scurried for safety, Owen several feet ahead of her. A cry erupted from her as he jerked hard; her back met his chest. Using her as a shield, Cedric pressed the edge of the claymore to her throat. "The sword, Sassenach. Drop it or she dies."

No sooner had the words left Cedric's mouth than the outer door crashed to the wall. Angus and about three dozen of his clansmen flowed through the opening, Cedric's six cohorts with them. Streaming into a half-circle, they blocked both door and stairs.

Spying the hard look in his kinsmen's eyes, Cedric edged along the wall, around the sacks of grain, and backed out toward the center of the room. "Keep away," he warned as the group moved closer, "or your chief dies."

"Ye might have killed one, but never two," Angus said, now standing close to Aleck. The squat man with the bowlegs noted Cedric's fast look. "Aye, Cedric. The truth is out. We know ye poisoned Colan. Yer loyal followers didn't like the look of death when it faced them. Seems they were willing to tell all. Release our chief, and we'll go easy on ye. Harm her, and the whole clan will tear ye limb from limb. 'Tis a gruesome death, to be certain."

While Angus spoke, Owen passed the torch to the man nearest him. Crouching low, he worked his way behind the group, disappearing among the sacks of grain.

"Since 'tis obvious I'll suffer either way, the bitch goes with me—unless, of course, you have it in your minds to allow me to leave Lochlaigh." He backed up several steps as the men pressed closer. "Stay back or else." The blade indented Chandra's skin. "Make up your minds, and quick."

From the corner of his eye, Aleck saw Owen's head bobbing among the sacks. The boy was nearly at the back of the room. "When Chandra is freed, do you really think you'll not be hunted down and torn apart?" he asked, taking two steps forward. Cedric retreated the same number. "Penrose is here because James has ordered that you be taken back to London. You'll be allowed to live out your natural days in the Tower. Give yourself over to the English, Cedric. 'Tis the only way to assure that you live."

"In a prison? 'Tis a different death in itself. No, I'll take my chances out on the moors. And she goes with me."

"Cedric, she's your niece—she's family," Aleck said, inching closer. "You know how important family is in the Highlands. Don't break that trust any further than you have."

A short laugh erupted from Cedric, and Aleck moved again. He now stood less than a dozen feet away from the two. "Aye, she's family," Cedric said. "She's also Colan's daughter. Had he listened to me, none of this would have happened. But no. My bastard half brother had to swear fealty to James. 'Twas his own fault that he died. He suffered for his transgressions. The agony was grand to see. He was no Highlander—he was a traitor. Just the same as his daughter."

All the while Cedric spoke, Aleck's gaze was locked with Chandra's. *Steady, love. Steady.* His mind repeated the phrase over and over. Then behind the pair, Owen sprang up from the sacks, Chandra's dirk in hand. The trapdoor yawned only half a yard from Cedric's feet. Dear God, let it work, Aleck thought, looking to Owen.

The man blinked, noting how close Aleck had gotten. "Get back or the bitch dies."

At Aleck's quick nod, the dirk sailed through the air, end over end. The blade sliced into the center of Cedric's back. His eyes widened. His hand flexed and blood trickled from the cut on Chandra's neck. Then Cedric gasped his last as his eyes rolled up into his head; the claymore fell from his hand. He toppled backward, his momentum carrying Chandra with him; Aleck's body was already in motion. Snatching her arm, he pulled her against him. A sickening thud met their ears as Cedric's head hit the edge of the trapdoor; he disappeared through the hole.

As Angus and his men rushed forward, surrounding Chandra and Aleck, a squealing noise ascended from the dungeon. The torch was thrust over the opening, pouring light into the cavity. Rats swarmed over Cedric's body, gnawing at his flesh. Chandra shuddered. "Take me out of here, please." Immediately Aleck led her from the room, out into the night air.

"Yer clansmen, it appears, have come to pay their respects," Angus snarled down the hole, then his foot kicked the trapdoor shut. "Come, lad." He motioned to Owen, who'd bounded out from among the sacks. "Ye did a grand job, ye did. Proud of ye, we are."

With much thumping of his back and tugging of his shoulders, Owen also was led from the room. Out in the inner ward a short, but joyous celebration took place. Finding their chief in the yard, the Sassenach's lips on hers, the clansmen encircled the pair and shouted their approval.

"'Tis not the place for this," Chandra whispered up at Aleck, having pulled back.

"Why, sweet? They seem to be enjoying it."

"Ah-hmm." Chandra and Aleck turned to see Angus. "Not that I mean to be insultin' or the like, but what do ye want us to do with the English rabble outside?" he asked.

Aleck looked to Chandra. She said, "Show the commander and a small detachment of his troops inside. He'll need to confirm that Cedric is dead, so he can report the fact to James."

Shortly Penrose rode through the gate. He was accompanied by two dozen men, including Sir John and Jason. "Well, cousin, I see you saved the day," Jason said, peering down at Aleck.

"Actually, the hero is Owen, here." Aleck's arm went

around the boy's shoulders. "He's the one who felled Cedric. I think we'll take him back to Montbourne with us. He's brought us nothing but good luck."

Owen swung from under Aleck's arm. "No!" he shouted. "This is my home."

The whole compound fell silent as everyone stared at the boy. Then Chandra stepped forward. "You can speak! Why haven't you done so before, Owen?"

"My name is not Owen—'tis Royce. I am the son of Colan Morgan. Lochlaigh is my home."

Her brow furrowing, Chandra gazed at the lad. The hair color, the forehead, the eyes, the chin—why hadn't she seen it before? "Come, Ow—Royce. Let us go inside."

Aleck's and Chandra's wounds, amounting to no more than a cut and a nick, were cleaned; then at her direction, a small group gathered in the antechamber of Chandra's room. On one side stood Aleck, Jason, and Sir John; on the other were Chandra, Angus, and several more of her clansmen, elders all.

Leaned against the table, Chandra said, "Tell us your story."

Under the scrutiny of so many eyes, Royce had grown nervous. He opened his mouth and let out a squeak, then quickly cleared his throat. "'Twas nearly thirteen years ago that I was born. My mother lived in a bothy along Lochlaigh's northern border. The Morgan of Morgan had been out riding his boundaries when his horse bolted. Grouse had flown up in its face. He was thrown and injured badly. My mother knew herbs and roots, and on her rounds to collect some, she found him. Somehow she got him into her hut. For nearly a month, she cared for him."

Chandra looked to Angus. "I remember the time," he said. "The Morgan was gone 'bout a month. 'Twas not long after yer mother died, as I recall."

"Go on," Chandra said to Royce.

He shrugged. "Well, I came along about nine months later."

"Did my fa—our father know about you?"

"He did. He came often, bringing us food. Many times he spent the night. But he'd never take us to the castle. Said it would cause too many difficulties."

By "difficulties" Chandra assumed her father had been referring to her, as well as the fact that Royce, as he was now known, was the bastard child of The Morgan of Morgan. Then Chandra asked, "Were your mother and our father ever married?"

Royce's head sank. "Not that I'm aware of."

"And your mother, where is she?"

"She died shortly after our father did. That's why I came here to live in the wood."

"I asked you at least twice to come stay at the castle with the rest of us, did I not?" He nodded. "Why didn't you—especially since you are my brother?"

"Because I did not belong."

"Is that what our father told you?"

"In so many words," Royce said.

"If that is true, then it was wrong of him to make you feel unwelcome." Chandra couldn't imagine her father doing such a thing. Yet he was a proud man, and he was most protective of her. "Why have you refused to speak all this time?"

"'Twas because of what I had said."

"Which was?"

Royce drew a ragged breath. "One day our father came to the hut. 'Twas after his return from prison. I asked to go to the castle, but he refused, as always. I became angry. I shouted that I hated him—that I wished he were dead. Two weeks later, he was."

"And you blamed yourself for his death because of what you'd said."

He nodded. "I swore never to speak again."

Chandra's heart went out to him. "'Twas Cedric who killed our father, Royce. You had nothing to do with it."

"I know that now."

"Is that why you now speak?"

"I speak because this is my home. I will not leave it. I have avenged our father's death, using your dirk. I am a Morgan. This is where I belong."

As Chandra viewed him, pride shone in her eyes. "Aye, you are a Morgan. And, truly, this is where you belong, for you are my brother. By right of tanistry, you should be The Morgan of Morgan."

"Ye are the chief. Yer father named ye," Angus said. "The lad, here, is just that—a lad."

"Do you not see Colan Morgan's face in his face?" she asked. She saw their nods. "Has he not displayed the courage and the strength that are required to be chief?"

"Aye, he has," Angus agreed, as did the other men of the clan. "But he is too young."

"He is," Chandra acceded, "but he will not be too young for very long. It is at this time, as your chief, that I shall name my successor. 'Tis Royce Morgan, son of Colan Morgan. When he reaches the maturity that I deem acceptable, I shall step down from my position as your chief, and Royce will become The Morgan of Morgan. So, my brethren, I suggest you teach him all he needs to know and do it quickly. I have a husband. His home is in England. I shall not stay here at Lochlaigh forever." She noted how Aleck's eyebrow rose; obviously he'd thought they would leave that night. "Your task is at hand. Do not tarry. My brother awaits your instruction."

Before her, Royce fell to one knee. He kissed the knuckles of her right hand. "I thank you, milady," he said, blue eyes gazing up at her.

Chandra urged him up from the floor. "A hug would do, Royce. After all, you are my brother."

Awkwardly he threw his arms around her; a quick

squeeze, and he withdrew. He then fished in the small leather pouch that he'd snatched from the hearth, its string now hanging round his neck. "'Tis the ring our father gave me. I guess it really belongs to you."

Remembering how it was said to have been lost, Chandra immediately recognized the token he offered. She took hold of it. "If he gave you this, Royce, he held you in great esteem. Give me your hand." When Royce obeyed, Chandra slipped the heavy gold ring onto his forefinger. Though it was a loose fit, the ring, she knew, would not be lost. "It has belonged to each Morgan chief for the last hundred years. Someday soon, you, too, shall claim that right." She looked to Angus. "Your first order of instruction is to teach this lad the importance of cleanliness. Take him and give him a bath."

"Gladly," Angus said. Before Royce knew what had happened, two sets of hands had clamped onto his arms, two more around his ankles. He was hefted into the air and carted out the door.

"'Twould be interesting to see what color he really is," Aleck said from the corner where he'd stood quietly. Then he moved to her side. Though he was saddened that Chandra would give up her title as The Morgan of Morgan, he was also relieved. "You have done all the Morgans proud, my love. They will never see another chief to match the likes of you."

"At least not until another woman holds the title," she said, smiling up at him. A mischievous twinkle sparked in her eyes. Forgetting that they were not alone, Aleck groaned. He started to reach for her.

Jason cleared his throat behind them. "Well, cousins, perhaps it is time we leave the two of you alone."

"Splendid idea," Sir John said. He thumped Jason's back, then caught the viscount before he hit his knees. After pleasantries were exchanged—Aleck thanking Sir John for his help, Chandra apologizing to Jason for waylaying him—the two men headed for the door.

"Jason," Aleck said in afterthought; his cousin turned. "Come visit us at Montbourne sometime in the near future, will you? We have some old wounds to heal. I ask that we begin as soon as possible."

Jason's gaze softened. "I shall do that, Aleck," he said, hoping their estrangement would soon be ended. He smiled. "But only if you promise to control your temper. My exceptional looks must be maintained. After all, *I* am now the most sought-after man at court."

When the door had closed, Chandra giggled. "He is right, you know."

"Right?" Aleck asked, staring down into her beautiful face. "About what?"

"He has claimed your position."

"What position?"

"Most sought-after man at court."

"He can have it. I have more interest in another position."

"Which is?"

"I'll show you."

Sweeping Chandra up into his arms, he strode through the connecting door leading into her bedchamber. He set her on her feet, then disrobed her. "I should bathe, Aleck. The dungeon—"

"No," he said, kicking boots and breeches across the floor. "You're fine just as you are. I want you, Chandra. God, how I want you. I need to know you are real."

They were on the bed, lips, arms, and legs entangled. Then Aleck was in her. Wildly, sweetly, their desire exploded through them, around them. Nothing yet had compared with this bliss. Never could a woman please him as did Chandra; never could a man be so tender as Aleck. Then, as their soft cries echoed off the walls, becoming music in each other's ears, they knew it was the melody of a forever love.

Much later, Aleck lay beside his wife. The uninjured side of his head was propped against one hand, the palm of his other smoothed low over Chandra's flat belly. "Do you really think so?" he asked almost reverently.

"Aye. The signs are there."

"Then tomorrow we go back to Montbourne. My son shall be born there."

Chandra slowly shook her head. "We stay at Lochlaigh."

"Why?"

"Because Royce needs me."

A disgruntled frown formed along Aleck's brow. "The lad is capable of taking care of himself. In fact, he's done just that for quite some time."

"Aye, but he is my brother. I would like to get to know him."

"You hope he will become as close to you as was Devin," he stated, knowing how much she missed her cousin. Maybe she thought Royce could fill the void.

"'Twould be nice."

Aleck's gaze dropped away for a moment. "About Devin . . . Chandra, I—"

Her finger fell over his lips. "'Twas an accident. He was so gravely ill, Aleck. He even said that it was better this way. He did not suffer. I could not have abided seeing him in agony. Maybe Devin felt that way, too. Perhaps that is why he did what he did."

"Aye, maybe so."

Thoughts of Devin left her. "So, we shall remain at Lochlaigh, then?"

Aleck studied her for a long moment. He hadn't had a chance to tell her, but while in London, negotiating with James over the clan Morgan, he'd declined the title of duke—which James insisted he'd hold for Aleck's son—so he had no immediate plans. Chandra was his reward, and because he loved her so, he could refuse her nothing. "If I agree to stay, what will you give me in return."

She rose. "This." Her lips met his. When the kiss ended, Aleck's head spun, but it wasn't from his injury.

"I suppose you should set yourself to teaching me all there is to know about the Morgans," he said, his finger trailing over her breasts. "Otherwise, because of my ignorance, I might offend. 'Tis a fact, sweet: This Hawke is in an alien nest."

Soft laughter bubbled from Chandra's throat. "Then lie back, my fairy-tale prince, I have a story to tell."

Aleck's head sank onto the pillow; he stared up at his wife. Eyes bright with promise, she straddled him.

Her finger traced the outline of the medallion. It had saved his life, and she was thankful. "'Tis the story of the hawk and the ladybird," she said, then, knowing he was ready, eased down on him.

Aleck drew breath shakily. "Sounds interesting," he rasped, his large hands claiming her hips.

"One of the refrains says: 'Ladybird, ladybird, fly, sweep to the heavens ever so high.'"

"Then soar, sweet, and take me with you."

Eager to please her beloved lord of legend, Chandra did as he asked.

AWARD-WINNING AUTHOR OF
<u>DEEPER THAN ROSES</u>

Charlene Cross

☐ MASQUE OF ENCHANTMENT ....67699-7/$3.95

☐ HEART SO INNOCENT ....67700-4/$4.50

☐ DEEPER THAN ROSES ....73824-0/$4.99

☐ LORD OF LEGEND ....73825-9/$5.50

JULIE GARWOOD

Julie Garwood's gloriously romantic, breathtakingly passionate novels have made her one of America's most beloved romance authors. *USA Today* says that it is her "timely subjects set against a timeless background that attract so many modern readers."

Now she brings us her most compelling novel yet, the story of an indomitable Saxon lady determined to fight for her freedom in a world ruled by men...a woman whose life would be transformed by the rare, unexpected gift of love.

SAVING GRACE

Pocket Books
Proudly Announces

ALMOST A WHISPER

Charlene Cross

**Coming from Pocket Books
Spring 1994**

**The following is a preview of
ALMOST A WHISPER . . .**

"I sympathize with you." John Kingsley's words sailed across his desk into Leah Balfour Dalton's ears. "I know it has been a most difficult time for you and your siblings—"

"*Difficult?*" Leah cried, waves of dissension rolling through her. She sprang to her feet; gloved hands hit the desk's cluttered surface. Nose to nose, she stared at her father's former solicitor. Her world was spinning out of control, and she couldn't seem to stop it. She was beyond sorrow, beyond grief. Anger had become her driving force. "My parents are dead—first my mother, then my father. Barely a fortnight had passed when the next blow was struck—cruelly, I might add. As though we held no worth at all, we were tossed from our home—much like slop from a bucket, sir—and cast on the mercy of others. Hope, Kate, Peter—you are aware that Peter has weak lungs and has been ill since birth, are you not? Then there's little Emily, who is barely five. All of them are in a foundling home not far from here. It is a dreary place, Mr. Kingsley, unfit for tender young hearts such as theirs, and unsuitable for Peter's condition. They are miserable, sir, and most depressed.

"Young Terence, on the other hand, being four-and-ten, and the oldest boy, managed to escape the orphanage, yet he suffers equally as much. Without explanation, he was torn from his studies, his tutor dismissed. You realize, don't you, that his marks were exceptional? Presently, in order to earn his keep, he is reduced to mucking out stalls and firing the bellows for a smithy named Jones in Leeds. As for myself, though well-educated, I have been unable to find a suitable position with a decent wage—one that would allow me to bring my family together again."

Beneath her gloves, Leah's once soft white hands were now badly chafed. To be close to the younger children, she had taken a job as a scullery maid at a local inn, earning less than twopence a week. Yet pride prevented her from relating her own acute situation and the abuse she continually endured as she was constantly harassed by her lecherous employer. Her youthful bottom bore a multitude of bruises, resulting from the innkeeper's insistent pinches, delivered whenever he was away from his wife's sight. As she gazed at the solicitor, his attitude seemingly one of apathy, she decided that she'd never allow this man to know just how low she'd truly sunk.

"Difficult, you say? That word doesn't begin to describe the horrors we have suffered—are still suffering, sir. Unless you plan to help us, you may keep your sympathy. The emotion alone does us little good."

John Kingsley peered at Leah over his wire-rimmed spectacles. "I am fully aware of your circumstances, Miss Dalton. I am also aware of what has happened to your family since your father's death. It is tragic, but unfortunately I am unable to offer you any assistance. And whether you desire it or not, you still have my sympathy."

Leah's mouth flew open, but he waved her off. "If you hadn't noticed when you first burst through the door, unannounced, I am otherwise occupied. I would appreciate it if you would take your leave so I might get on with my work. I have a letter to finish and a strong-willed niece to deal with before my departure. I hope to have these tasks completed inside of a quarter hour. Where is the chit?" he grumbled, viewing the wall clock. "She was to be here twenty minutes ago." His faded blue eyes returned to Leah. "As for seeking me out again, I should inform you that tonight I set sail for India in the queen's service. I shall be gone a very long time, Miss Dalton. Now, good day to you."

In truth, when she'd stormed his office, she hadn't marked how engrossed he'd been in his work. As she looked around her now, she saw the place stood in disarray. Folio cabinets lay open, files bulging from their shelves, Mr. Kingsley's assistant quickly putting them in order. A meager assortment of luggage was stacked in one corner of the room. Similarly the outer office held a multitude of trunks and hatboxes. She remembered how she'd nearly tripped over the trove when she'd first stepped from the sunlight into the dimness of the reception area. Undoubtedly the first collection belonged to his niece.

Her attention shifted back to the desk's top. By the solicitor's left hand lay a bankdraft, the amount indecipherable from where she stood. Pen poised over the letter he'd been framing when Leah had first launched herself into the room, he scrawled the words: *I remain your most obedient servant, John Kingsley, Esq.*

Feeling suddenly drained, she sank back into the chair. "I suppose it is utterly hopeless, then," she whispered across the way. "I cannot believe he would leave his own children without means of support. We were not overtly wealthy, but certainly we prospered more than most. Dear Lord! There is so much I don't understand."

Her dejected tone drew John Kingsley's attention. "Miss Dalton, your father hadn't intended on any of this happening. Your mother's sudden illness, his horrible accident as he rode breakneck from the south of England—" He swallowed the rest, Leah's gaze having shot to his face. "I apologize for my choice of words. Terence's death was indeed a tragedy. It is all a tragedy. I am extremely sorry for everything you've suffered."

Leah studied the man. So many unanswered questions, she thought, her suspicions escalating. "Why is it, Mr. Kingsley, on the few occasions we needed to hastily contact my father, our messages were always relayed to him through you? Likewise, sir, why have you refused to respond to my written queries, requesting to know where he is buried?" The man remained silent. "I am certain you know far more about my father than his family ever did," she remarked, "including my mother."

"Terence Dalton was a good man. I both knew and liked him. We were old friends."

Leah noted how he'd hedged her questions and dismissed her statement. "Yes, he was a good man, but he absented himself from his family far too much."

"His business was in London. For it to function effectively, he had to remain there."

"While his family remained in Leeds. Strange, don't you think, that he'd prefer to keep us all so far north?"

"It was my understanding, Miss Dalton, he wanted to

protect you from the rot and decadence that is London. It is not the ideal place to rear a family."

"Perhaps you are right, Mr. Kingsley. London may not be the ideal place to rear a family. But I am certain there are areas close by that are quite acceptable."

"Did your mother ever complain about these arrangements . . . about Terence spending so much time in London?"

"No, but—"

"If your mother didn't object, I'd say you have little reason to question your father's motives."

Elizabeth Dalton had been a gentle soul, unassuming, sweet, given to an easy smile. Leah resembled her physically: flaxen hair, tilted green eyes, and full pouting lips. But that was where the resemblance ended, for Leah was far more independent than her mother could ever have hoped to be. It was not fully by choice that Leah had become so self-sufficient. Given her father's long absences from Balfour and her mother's lack of disciplinary skills—the ever youthful Elizabeth seemed no more than a child herself—Leah had taken it on her own shoulders to be the stabilizing factor in her siblings' lives. That her mother hadn't objected to *these arrangements* didn't mean they were acceptable to the rest of the family, especially to Leah. She remained distrustful.

"Mr. Kingsley," she began just as he pulled a clean sheet of paper from inside his desk drawer.

"Miss Dalton," he countered, taking hold of his pen. "You say you cannot find suitable employment, correct?"

"Yes, that is correct."

"I assume it is because you lack a proper reference."

"That, and the fact that I don't have any experience."

"You helped rear your brothers and sisters, did you not."

"I did."

"And you helped them with their lessons, I suppose?"

"Yes."

"Excellent," he said, scrawling the salutation *To whom it may concern:* across the top of page. "There is a family I know just outside York who is in need of a governess. This letter of introduction should allow you the opportunity of securing an interview. I hope it will afford you that which you seek."

As his pen continued across the paper, Leah realized his sudden desire to assist her was nothing more than an evasive maneuver. He hadn't answered any of her questions. "What I seek, Mr. Kingsley, is the truth. Why was my father buried elsewhere than the churchyard at Leeds?"

The bell over the outer door jangled stridently; the solicitor's attention fired toward the sound, as did Leah's. A portly little man rushed into the room, a letter in hand. By the look of him, Leah thought he appeared distressed.

"Fields," the solicitor sharply admonished his coachman by name, "have the courtesy to enter without making such a commotion." He peered around the man. "Where is Miss Kingsley? The two of you were to be here some time ago."

"Sir, your niece—she's disappeared," the harried man responded. "The house staff searched everywhere. This letter is all we found."

A dark frown settled across Kingsley's forehead as he quickly scanned the contents of the note. "Damnation!" he erupted. "The ungrateful chit has eloped!"

Startled, Leah watched as he sprang from his chair, his gaze casting about the desk's surface. Shoving aside the unfinished letter of introduction meant for her, he grabbed hold of the paper he'd set his signature to, crumpled it, and tossed it down. The thing skittered across the desk, dropped to the floor, and settled at Leah's feet.

"She is much like her father," he snarled between his teeth. "A bad seed." The wall clock began striking the hour. "We're late," he said. "Farnsworthy, we must leave at once. Help Fields load your luggage in the coach."

"Yes, sir," his assistant replied, locking the last of the folio cabinets lining the rear wall. "What about Miss Kingsley's luggage, sir?" Farnsworthy asked. "The private conveyance is past due. When the driver arrives, there won't be anyone here to tell him your niece won't be needing passage to London."

The bankdraft was snatched from the desk and quickly locked away in the top drawer. "Damn the girl for the problems she's caused me," the solicitor ranted, the key disappearing into his pocket. "I should have had the sense to decline guardianship of her when I had the opportunity to do so. But no! Like a cork-brained fool, I took her in."

Red-faced, he strode from behind his desk. Leah realized

he intended to desert her. "Mr. Kingsley!" she cried, leaping from her seat. "The letter of intro—"

"I have no time to waste, Miss Dalton," he said, eyeing her from across the room. He walked into the waiting area; Leah sped after him. "If Mr. Farnsworthy and I are to make any progress, we must leave this instant. We have a ship to board in Hull at eight o'clock this very night. I shan't chance its sailing without us." Slipping his wallet from his pocket, he pulled several bank notes from inside. "Here, I shall employ you to take charge. When the hired coach shows up, you are to instruct its driver to load this gaggle of trunks and hatboxes, then have him disburse with them."

"But are they not your niece's?" Leah asked, confused.

"They are, Miss Dalton, but she is no longer in need of their contents. She has made her choice, and I have made mine. The coachman is to take her possessions to the nearest charitable institution where they are to be distributed to the poor." He placed the bank notes in her hand. "The man has already been paid his fee to London. Don't allow him to convince you otherwise. You may tip him for his trouble. The remainder of the money should help alleviate some of your financial difficulties. I trust, Miss Dalton, you will make certain what I've asked is thus executed."

The outside door opened, the bell clanging loudly, then the panel slammed to. Through the etched glass pane, Leah watched as Mr. Kingsley climbed into his coach—what she assumed was his own luggage lashed atop its roof—to seat himself next to his assistant. With a snap of the whip and shout from the driver, the vehicle rolled away.

Leah's fingers curled around the bank notes, her shoulders slumping. She briefly viewed the mound of luggage, then made her way back into the inner office. Again beside the chair, she stooped to retrieve the ball of paper that had skipped across the desk, landing at her feet. A feeling of hopelessness enveloped her as she sank into her seat. Her impromptu visit to Mr. Kingsley had produced none of the results she'd desired. The solicitor had been purposely evasive, not once responding fully to her questions.

Leah loved her father, but she resented him as well. Elizabeth Dalton's last breath had passed through her lips while calling for her beloved Terence. It was his failure to at his dying wife's side, when he was needed most, that angered Leah so. True, it was said, his own life had ended as he rode north to Leeds, his horse stumbling on a pitch-black road between London and Balfour, the tumble he'd taken breaking his neck. Yet, why had his family not been informed of his accident until over a week after its occurrence? And why did his resting place remain secreted from his children?

Too many mysteries, she thought, her attention centered on the line of folio cabinets against the far wall, each marked by a letter of the alphabet. Her gaze caught the *D*. Placing the money and crumpled paper on the desk, she rose from her chair and made her way to the cabinet where she jiggled the latch only to discover it was locked.

A letter opener lay on the desk, and Leah quickly retrieved it. The thin blade slid between the abutting doors, slipping the lock. Shuffling through the folders, she finally hit on the one she sought. Inside, she found a single sheet of paper, a solitary line written across it.

"Eighteen Hanover Square, London," Leah whispered, committing the inscription to memory.

The address was unfamiliar to her, the letters posted to her father from his family being directed to a point on St. James's Street. Another mystery in a string of many, she thought, for Terence Dalton's past appeared to be riddled with secrets. Leah was suddenly certain the missing pieces to his life lay in London at this address. It was there she'd find her answers.

She hadn't accepted Mr. Kingsley's statement, insisting that she and her siblings were impoverished. Not when a few short weeks ago, they had wanted for naught. To learn the truth Leah realized she had to somehow get to London, an impossibility, she knew.

Dejectedly, she placed the file back with the others, then sealed the cabinet doors. Seated again, she stared at the crumpled ball of paper resting atop the desk. Curious as to its contents, she seized the thing and smoothed it out over her lap. A tiny frown marred her brow as she scanned the letter.

. . . *If the young woman standing before you has properly introduced herself, you are already aware she is my* niece, Miss Anne Kingsley. I am in a fix, dearest Madeline, and must ask the greatest of favors from you. The girl is my ward. Her guardianship is a responsibility I took on to myself two months past. A mistake, I fear, for she has been a thorn in my side ever since. She is much like her father—headstrong and impudent. I am unable to take her with me to India, yet I fear leaving her alone, especially when she fancies herself in love with an Irish bounder who followed her to York from Ulster.

My late brother and I had been estranged for over a quarter century, therefore you heard me speak not at all about Giles or his family—mainly because there was nothing good to say about any of them. (I shall explain everything about Giles and myself upon my return.) As it is, considering my niece's lowly upbringing, she is in need of a firm, yet charitable individual to guide and watch over her. I could think of no one except you, dearest Madeline. Your patience is renowned, as is your ability to tame the most brutish of creatures who have managed to stumble into your path. I must warn you: The girl has a beastly temperament and lacks even the simplest of manners. I am certain you will be able to instill in her the proper social behavior. A touch of refinement will do the girl a world of good.

I know I am causing an imposition, Madeline, but I could think of no one else who would be willing to take her under wing. A bankdraft has been issued in your name for Anne's care. From the remainder, you may issue her a weekly allowance. . . .

Her curiosity piqued, Leah came to her feet and searched through the papers littering the desk's top. Finally she unearthed an envelope. Turning it over in her hand, she eyed the inscription: *The Right Honorable, The Countess of Huntsford; 7 Berkley Square; London.*

As Leah stared at the address, an idea formulated. She realized her intentions were risky; she could fail miserably, and at great cost. Before she lost her courage, she rounded the desk, retrieved the letter opener, and forced the drawer's lock. The bankdraft in her possession, she gasped upon seeing the amount. A king's ransom, she thought, knowing it would take her an eternity to earn even a pittance of the sum meant for Anne Kingsley's care.

Inside her soul, wickedness wrestled with virtue. She thought of Hope, Kate, Peter and little Emily, languishing away in that dismal orphanage, each robbed of the joys of childhood. And Terence, who was given to scholarly pursuits—he was now reduced to manual labor in order to survive. What choice did she have but to pursue the course she'd already decided upon?

The faint sound of wheels lumbering along the roadway snapped Leah from any indecisiveness she might have felt. Quickly she snatched her reticule from the chair and dashed into the reception area.

Thou shalt not steal.

. . . he that speaketh lies shall perish.

The Biblical passages boomed inside her head just as the bell jingled over the outer door; Leah drew a deep breath, attempting to steady herself.

"Missy," the coachman said, doffing his worn hat, "did someone here hire a coach to the south?"

"Mr. Kingsley did," she answered truthfully, the excerpt from Proverbs still ringing in her mind.

"Sorry I'm late, but one of the horses threw a shoe. These here things yours?" he asked, motioning toward the luggage.

"Everything is to be loaded."

As the man began shuffling cases, hatboxes, and trunks through the doorway, Leah again fought with her conscience.

Beware the loss of your immortal soul, the dogged voice needled within her, and her resolve wavered.

The last of the collection stowed in the boot and atop the coach roof, the man came inside. In the dim light, he eyed her closely; Leah swallowed hard, her guilt and trepidation nearly choking her.

"You look a might peaked, Missy. Are you sure you're up to traveling such a long way? The road ahead is difficult, if not downright hazardous."

Her siblings forlorn faces, as she last remembered seeing each of them, leapt to mind. Leah felt her determination renew itself. She'd readily walk through the fires of hell if it meant putting an end to their misery and suffering. "Hazardous—yes," she replied, sweeping through the opening out onto the step, knowing her course was set. "Since I have no other choice, this is the avenue I must take."

The door to Mr. Kingsley's office closed behind them. "Where to, Missy?" the driver asked, assisting Leah into the coach.

"Seven Berkley Square, London."

Berkley Square
London, England

"You are charitable to a fault, Madeline Sinclair," the ninth Earl of Huntsford said, then shook his head. Sighing, he ran his fingers through his thick auburn hair. In the other hand, he held John Kingsley's letter. "I suppose if a cat dropped one of her litter on our stoop, you'd snatch it up in a trice."

"Doubtlessly I would," the countess responded from the same settee she and Leah had sat upon earlier in the day. "Since I've been deemed the champion of the downtrodden, what else would you expect?"

"If you remember, *I* am the one who termed you such. And I would expect a bit more prudence from you, madam. You cannot forever be taking in every stray that lands on our doorstep."

"I'd hardly call the girl a stray. Heavens, Ian! She is John Kingsley's niece. What was I to do? Slam the door in her face?"

"From what I've gathered from Kingsley's letter, it might have been far wiser if you had. Apparently his niece has nearly run him ragged since he took guardianship of her. And this young man whom she fancies herself in love with—if he is truly that eager to wed and bed her, don't you think he'll find her? I cannot be forever poking about the gardens after dark watching for a ladder to swing against the house."

"She has agreed neither to communicate with nor to see him while she's in my care." The countess smiled pleasantly. "Besides, she's in the front bedroom, two doors from yours."

The earl rolled his eyes. "You are most thoughtful," he said, envisioning himself continuously leaping from his bed at the least little sound, to stare from his window at the street below, searching for the girl's swain. After several nights with no sleep, he'd gladly set the ladder to her sill himself. "I assume you will expect me to introduce her into London society by escorting her to the round of balls and social events scheduled these next few months. If so, I doubt Veronica will be too pleased with a third party tagging along."

"Veronica would survive," Madeline insisted. "But absolutely not. I had planned to escort her myself. Were she on your arm, none of the young gentlemen would dare approach her."

Ian Sinclair chuckled. "It is a match that you're after, isn't it?"

"Possibly. At the very least I hope to present her with a choice. She can make up her own mind who it is she loves."

"How old is she?" Ian asked, finding himself curious, for the letter never mentioned such.

"Eighteen, nineteen—no more than twenty, I'd say. She's far too young for you."

Blue eyes netted blue. "Did I say I was interested?"

"No, you didn't. But the girl needs someone closer to her own age. Definitely not a father-figure."

That stung; Ian came away from his position near the fireplace. "I wouldn't exactly describe myself as an old codger."

"Nor would I," Madeline said.

"I'm still in my prime."

"Agreed. But time *is* slipping by."

"When is it not?" he queried, then focused on the issue needling him. "Why do think the girl wouldn't be interested in a man my age?"

"I didn't say she wouldn't be. I simply mentioned that a man closer in years to her own might suit her needs better. I didn't mean to give insult, so calm yourself. Leah should be joining us shortly. I'd like very much for your first meeting with her to go well."

"Leah?" he asked. "I thought her name was Anne."

"Both are correct. Since her mother's name was also Anne, *our* Anne was called Leah to avoid confusion. She prefers the name she's most accustomed to, so we are to call her Leah."

Ian fought the urge to shake his head, thereby clearing the muddle from his brain. "Leah—Anne—whichever she desires, so be it," he said, then glanced at the mantel clock. Seven thirty. A brandy—that's what he needed to settle his nerves. For some unexplained reason, he felt the girl's presence was going to wreak havoc in their lives, especially his. "If you don't mind, I will retire to the study for a few minutes. I'll not be long."

"Don't imbibe too much, Ian," the countess said as he strode toward the doorway. "I wouldn't want Leah to get the wrong impression about us."

Coming up short, he turned around. "Had you not the most peculiar way of throwing disharmony into a man's life, I wouldn't presently be deserting you for the soothing effects of a brandy."

The countess sighed heavily. "Your father always said the same thing. But from the day we married until the day he died, he was never gone from my side for more than five minutes at a time. Oh, Ian, I do hope you will soon find that special someone so you, too, can experience a love very much like the one your father and I shared."

Ian's gaze softened on the woman who presently held his heart. "Not everyone is as fortunate as were you and father. It may be, Mother, that I shall never find that special someone with whom I can share a deep and abiding love. I might have to settle for companionship instead."

"Veronica?"

"Yes, Veronica. We are well-suited in temperament and share many of the same interests. I plan to ask for her hand at the end of next month."

"I caution you not to act in haste, Ian. Veronica is a delightful young woman, but I doubt you will be happy with her. Mark my words. Your special someone is out there, somewhere, waiting for you to come into her life."

A dark auburn eyebrow arched quizzically. "And how, pray tell, will I know she is the one?" he asked, doubting such a woman existed. At thirty-three, he'd yet to find her!

Madeline smiled up at him, confidence showing in her gaze. "You'll know, son, the moment you see her."

"Should I encounter the lady you speak of, Mother, I'll let you know. Right now, I want nothing more than to seek out that brandy."

Having descended the steps only a moment ago, bathed, coiffed, and dressed in the gown the countess had selected for her, Leah inspected the portrait she'd seen earlier that day. Her head tilted one way, then the other as she assessed the virile figure inside the gilt frame.

Thick and rich, dark auburn hair crowned his head. Her fingers itched to feel its texture, an impossibility, she knew.

Her attention affixed itself to the man's face, with its angles and planes, each perfectly positioned to form a striking effect. Exceptional, she thought, studying his shapely lips.

The eyes drew her.

Magically the artist's hand had captured the glint in his subject's deep blue gaze, and Leah wondered what could be the root of the man's mirth. Informally posed, his arm resting on a pedestal, his flowing white shirt open half way down his broad chest, he seemed to be boldly flouting propriety, and enjoying every minute of it.

Tight black breeches molded to his narrow hips and sinewy thighs. Impressive, she concluded, for not much had been left to the imagination. Or had it? Fire burned her cheeks as her gaze quickly skipped back to the man's face, and his laughing eyes. It was now *Leah* who had become the source of his merriment! Or so she believed. Mortified, she wanted to kick herself for her daring appraisal and the fantasy it evoked.

Demanding her fluttering heart behave, she stepped forward to read the name plate attached to the ornate frame. "Ian Sinclair," she mused aloud, "ninth Earl of Huntsford."

"At your service, Miss Kingsley."

Leah spun round, nearly colliding with the man who had unknowingly crept up behind her. *"You,"* she cried, glancing at the portrait, then back at him, her embarrassment flaming anew.

"Yes, we are one and the same," Ian said, a grin teasing his lips, for he'd noted her blush. What had she been thinking? "Since I am here in the flesh, you may inspect me more closely." He stepped around her and centered himself beneath the huge portrait. "Which do you say? Of the two, who is the more handsome? Me or my likeness?"

Look for
Almost A Whisper
Coming from Pocket Books
Spring 1994